LOVE IN THE LINER NOTES

PAGANS & POP STARS
BOOK ONE

KATTA KIS

For the sex educators, fighting the good fight.

For all the writers wading through rejection and keeping your
head above water in the query trenches.

For the co-architect of my real-life HEA, thank you for believing
in me, being there for me, and building me cost spreadsheets
with the total waaaay down at the bottom of the page. :]

CONTENT NOTE

This book has its light-hearted and silly moments (as well as
explicit and enthusiastically consensual sex) but it does deal with
some heavy stuff including: attempted sexual assault, accidental
death, bullying, and dealing with trauma.
If any of these are particularly troubling to you, please take care
of yourself if you choose to read *Love in the Liner Notes*.
Thank you.

JOIN MY NEWSLETTER

Keep up with me and my work by signing up for my newsletter! It's once a month with freebies like Cazzi's consent class syllabus, exclusive behind-the-scenes fun, and no spam. :]

RK AND ANGELA ALICE: FOUR YEARS STRONG
OMG has it really been four literal years since pop prince RK,
our fave baby bae fresh off of the BeatBoyz implosion, broke our
hearts (and spank banks) by getting with the infamous Angela
Alice? He might be washed up and she might be crazy, but rumor
is she's backing his comeback solo album and new record label
venture. Maybe strange bedfellows really can last.
*Cheers to the pop prince and the B***** Queen of metal! Keep*
proving us wrong in the hottest way possible.
—Celebrity Watcher Magazine

Rohan "RK" Kapoor couldn't remember how he had gone from discussing lyrics to fighting with his girlfriend, but then, he never could quite pinpoint the tipping point of these things. It was never just one fight, it was four years' worth of half-finished arguments wrapped in new complaints. He tried to breathe, to see clearly through his anger and hers. If he stayed calm, she might let it go and he'd get a chance to actually get out of this awful rental house to do some recording today.

"You're not listening to me! You don't think *maybe* with a

couple platinum albums under me I don't fucking know what I'm doing?" Angie snapped. Her anger breathed around them, crackling in her white-blonde hair, sparking in her pale gray eyes, gleaming in her sharp teeth. It was magnificent, honed to be frightening, to overwhelm.

Even though he towered over her, it hit its mark. He leaned away because it was the most controlled way to recoil.

"I am listening." He kept his voice measured. "But that doesn't mean I have to take every suggestion you give. Is it so bad that I want to write this album myself?"

He didn't bother bringing up the platinum albums he'd been on. She wouldn't care. She'd started this fight, offering criticisms he didn't ask for veiled as "help," because she thought she could win. If he yelled, she'd yell back and he'd destroy his voice for another day in the studio trying to keep up with her ridiculous lung capacity. His producer and ex-bandmate Rick was downstairs with some woman Rohan had never met but Rick swore was his best friend. No need to make a scene some stranger would hear and leak to the press.

"How about you take any of my suggestions?"

"I thought you were here for moral support!" It was only the first day of recording. They'd barely been in this rental house in this tiny somewhat picturesque NorCal town for twenty-four hours, how long had she been stewing about this? She'd promised her backing his comeback album and the label they were launching off of it had no strings attached, that she'd just be here in case he needed her, that she'd needed a vacation anyway—

"I thought you respected my opinion. What the hell happened to being partners?" Angie slapped her hand down on the dresser, making the whole thing shudder.

"This isn't about you! Or us!" Rohan snapped, his voice getting dangerously loud.

"What the fuck is it about then?" Her volume rose to match his.

"Me!" He hissed, trying to get her quiet again. "This is *my* comeback."

Angie crossed her arms and looked at him like he was spouting nonsense. "Are you calling me a narcissist?"

"Are you seriously making this about you?" He couldn't believe it, but he wasn't surprised. When was it not about her?

Angie, aka Angela Alice, the Bitch Queen of Metal, opened her mouth and let out a guttural roar that built into a screamo yell until she shrieked at him in high C like a goddamn banshee.

There was no way they were avoiding a scene now.

CAZZI MULDOON FELT like she was in a dream. After nearly two years, it was surreal to be sitting on a gingham couch next to her best friend Patrick, so close she could feel the heat from his arm next to her. He was *here*. In her town, within reach. On a work trip sure, but who fucking cared?

He smiled at her, his dark cheeks plumping the same way they always had, and tucked a slender loc behind his ear. The locs were longer, but the rest of him—from his lovely rangy body under dark gray clothes to his favorite kicks she'd bought him years ago—was exactly the same. Her stomach knotted, glittering and jittering. It had been nineteen months, two weeks, and three days since, since, since…

This wasn't a dream. He was here, he was real, and it was all she could do not to repeat what made him ghost her last time.

"This is surreal," he said, but he might have been talking about the sheer number of ceramic chickens on the mantle. And the walls. And the end table.

"Yeah," she said. Dammit. They didn't cover how to talk to your formerly estranged best friend, the current love of your life, in her Ph.D. program. Would it have killed them to include that? Surely it fell under the purview of sexual health and education.

"I'm glad you're here." She looked around the Airbnb. A large chicken with deeply traumatized eyes stared back at her from the coffee table. The painted gaze seemed to follow her. "It's um, a nice place."

"It's cheap and it's close to you." He looked sideways at her through his locs. She couldn't get over how long they were now. Their time apart seemed to be measured in hair. She'd cut hers and he'd grown his.

"Oh," she said, because apparently words were now hard. She'd talked just fine when they'd video-chatted and called and texted. Since he started talking to her again two weeks and one day ago, they hadn't been out of touch for more than a few hours. She smiled, hoping it showed him everything she couldn't say.

"Caz I—"

Thump! The sound of faint, angry voices filtered down through the ceiling.

"Is everything okay up there?" Cazzi frowned upwards. The worrier in her strained to hear what was going on.

Patrick shrugged. "They're always like that."

Cazzi frowned harder.

"They're... passionate."

"If there's anything that worries me, it's calling fighting 'passionate.'" She returned her gaze to him. "How passionate are we talking?"

"Caz, you're not going to save him. He's fine." He brushed his fingers against her cheek and she almost didn't note the pronouns he'd used. The voice she'd heard sounded female, but she didn't want to assume.

"Okay." She swayed towards him before she could stop herself. She pulled back, her face hot. "Sorry. I-I know after last time you probably still just wanna be friends. I can be friends. I—"

He kissed her.

Time went slow, sweet. His lips against hers, his warm, hard muscles under her hands. His palms, calluses against her cheeks. They pulled apart for air and she saw everything she ever wanted in his eyes. Nearly fifteen years of waiting had paid off, and he loved—

Someone screamed.

The problem with the body is that it remembers, no matter how much you try to forget. Cazzi ran, against all of her training, pounding up the stairs as the dreamy feeling dissolved and the scream became the echo of the one she'd never made.

———

THE DOOR BANGED OPEN, seconds, it seemed, after the shriek left Angie's mouth. Rohan and Angie stared, their fight holding its breath as they took in the woman who dared interrupt them.

Purple and brown hair streaked her white face, half-covering eyes that vibrated from Rohan to Angie, taking everything in. For a moment, they all stood, suspended. Then she shoved the hair from her face, straightened, and said in the most disturbingly normal tone, "Okay. I'm here to help."

"Um, what?" Rohan said.

Her face was placid now, politely bland with no teeth and reassuring eyes. "Why don't you tell me what you're fighting about?"

Angie cocked her head, turning the full force of her anger on the strange woman. "Who the fuck are you?"

The woman blinked, her expression faltering, her shoulders slumping just enough for Rohan to write her off. People rarely could handle Angie at her worst. He edged a step forward, ready to put himself on an intercept path between the two women's gazes. Whoever this nosy woman was, she didn't deserve to be on the receiving end of Angie's anger. It never ended well when people tried to diffuse their fights. It was better for everyone if Angie and him could just hash this out in peace.

The woman pressed her fingers to the center of her chest, then her left wrist. Her shoulders squared and she put on a not-quite smile that was too pleasant to be real. "You seem to be having a disagreement. Can you tell me about it?" She looked at Rohan. "You first, please."

Despite himself, he had to admit it was kinda impressive, the way she rallied. He wouldn't bet on her in a fight against Angie, but still.

"Do you know who we are?" He asked, genuinely wondering. If she was a pap... well if she was a pap, she wouldn't be standing there without a camera.

"You're friends of Patrick's." Though she spoke like she was reading a script, her expression warmed for an instant at his ex-bandmate's full name. "And you're having a problem with your relationship."

"Oh, really?" Angie narrowed her eyes, nostrils flaring as she sized up the other woman.

Rohan crossed his arms. What did this woman know? How dare she judge them? Couples fought and he couldn't remember a time when they hadn't. It was just how he and Angie communicated. Did he like it? No, but... well, he wasn't quite sure how that sentence should end.

She studied them, her pleasant expression staying in place but going brittle like a mask. "Tell me, does this feel good? Does your fighting feel productive?"

Rohan glanced at Angie. What kind of nonsense questions were these?

Angie caught his gaze and rolled her eyes. "What do you think?" Angie asked her, tone sharp. For a moment, they felt like a team again, them against the world—or in this case, this woman with her brittle blank mask.

The woman's smile widened, like a teacher rewarding a tentative student. "I think you've gotten to the point where it hurts more than it feels good. Maybe you could use a break?"

Rohan's breath caught, instinctive denial on his tongue but—*it hurts more than it feels good...* the words clicked in place, fitting the tightness in his chest, his jaw, his fists. When was the last time they'd relaxed together? He tried to remember. There were scraps of happiness here still, right? *It's just a rough patch, everyone has them.*

The woman watched him like she knew exactly what was going through his head. Like she knew he didn't quite believe what he told himself.

Angie recoiled. "Fuck off! You don't know anything." Her snarl was legendary, able to clear a room of reporters in a minute flat. It felt like dull knives on his skin, her anger too familiar to be sharp. It also felt like a lie, anger covering something—Fear? Pain? He studied Angie, trying to figure it out.

The woman faced Angie, expression not even flickering this time. "Please, explain it to me."

It's just a rough patch, Rohan tried the words again as he traced Angie's familiar features, her familiar rage. The old piercing scars around her eyebrows, the ink slashing up the line of her neck, the furrow of her brow as she focused, the angry clench of her fists... *Things will be good again after the album. We'll be on equal footing, we'll see each other more, we won't fight so much, the sex will be good again, I won't feel like I'm proving a point staying with her...Oh fuck. Fuck. Fuck, fuckity fuck.*

"I don't need to explain a damn thing to you," Angie turned and headed for the door. "Come on, Ro, let's get some fucking privacy."

The strange woman moved, sliding aside to let her go but Rohan didn't move. He knew when Angie bluffed. He saw it in the uneven set of her shoulders, the way she chewed off her lipstick.

He studied the other woman. "Is it that obvious?"

There was a faint flicker of emotion behind her eyes, maybe sympathy, maybe regret.

Rohan felt sick. The last time he'd felt this sick he'd been sitting alone in Angie's home studio—their studio, not that she was ever there—trying to reason this relationship better until he gave up, emotionless and nauseated. He'd almost left her then but she'd convinced him it would get better. It was just a rough patch.

That had been over a year ago.

Angie spun, looking at him. "What are you talking about?" An edge of panic crept into her voice.

But Rohan kept looking at the woman with her sad eyes. "Is it worth saving?"

Her face was a blank slate, no expression, no bias. "That's up to you and her."

Angie opened her mouth but Rick emerged from behind her. "Caz, let them work it out."

The woman—Caz—went soft, her whole body bending towards his friend like a flower to the sun. She smiled, really smiled. It transformed her. Suddenly, she was a real person instead of the automaton she pretended to be.

She was tallish for a woman, dressed in black except for her big purple Doc Martens. Tattoos peeked from under her long sleeves and her face seemed free of makeup. Not pretty, exactly, pretty didn't seem to be the point, but capable.

Rick's normally stoic face melted, his eyes crinkling and his lips turning slightly upwards.

Holy fuck, that's what love looks like. When had he last looked at Angie like that? When had she last looked at him like that? He remembered when they felt that good, many parties, many albums, many singles, many interviews ago.

He turned to Angie. "I can't do this anymore."

"What?" She gasped like he'd sucker-punched her. Her pain ached in his bones.

He almost backtracked, almost caved, but he watched the way Rick looked at Caz. It made Rohan feel tired, so damn tired.

When was the last week he and Angie went without a fight? Hell, when was the last day? "This, us."

"Because of *her*?" Angie's fists bunched at her sides and she leaned in towards Caz. If Caz was tallish for a woman, she was no match for Angie. Standing in just her socks, Angie towered easily. Her long, straight hair brushed Caz's shoulders. Even out of her dead-white make-up and ragged stage clothes, she radiated exactly the kind of destructive menace that made her hated by parents across America.

Caz looked up slowly, her gaze taking in Angie's tattoos, her bland expression snapping into place. Behind her, Rick took a step forward. Angie's whole body went taut.

"Because of us," Rohan said firmly, stepping between them. Keeping Angie from railing into someone—again. God, how many times had he done this over the years? "We're not working, Angie. You can't deny it."

"Watch me." She grabbed his collar and kissed him, hard.

Kissing Angie was always heady: sex, drugs, and rock and roll fused into one high. He let the feeling wash over him. He almost forgot what he was saying, why he wasn't mad, just defeated, just done.

"Deflection," said a voice, clear and cool. Caz. He opened his eyes and she watched him like she knew exactly how he felt. Rick tried to drag her back but she didn't move. Her gaze was a lifeline.

He broke the kiss and looked at Angie. There were tears in her eyes, her anger and sadness and panic waiting to drown him.

"I'm sorry." He walked out.

2

*"Hey pretty boy,
Have you met me?
Got blood on my hands
Ice in my veins
Come closer
Let me sink my teeth in*

*Hey scary girl,
Wickedest thing I ever seen
My darkest dream
My favorite sin
Come closer, sink your teeth in*

*They say we're strange bedfellows
Well,
Opposites attract
We're proof of that
Twisted into one crazy heart
They can't pull us apart"*

— "Strange Bedfellows" by Angela Alice and RK on *Bitch
Queen Cometh*

When the man named Ro walked out everything went to hell. The woman with the angelic face and Satanic tattoos lost her shit and threw anything she could get her hands on. Pillows, blankets, toothbrushes, a notebook, a necklace, a chicken-shaped clock. Not at Cazzi or Patrick but at the walls away from them. Then she sank into the middle of the floor and sobbed like her heart had been torn out. Cazzi swore the room got colder and darker.

"Can we talk?" Patrick asked, ignoring the woman on the floor.

"In a second," Cazzi ventured closer. The woman looked very distressed and vaguely familiar. "Hey, um…" She shot Patrick a look.

He sighed. "Angela."

Her eyebrows shot up, wait was this…Angela Alice? Patrick nodded. She took another look at the woman with her long white-blonde hair and flowy black dress. Well, that explained the tattoos. "Hey Angela, can I get you anything? Do you want to be alone? Should I call someone?"

The sobbing stopped and Angela Alice turned her gaze on Cazzi. This time she was ready for it, fingers already on her protective and calming sigils. This time Angela caught the gesture. "Clutch your cross all you want. You can't pray me away."

Cazzi tugged the neckline of her shirt down, exposing the protective pentacles tattooed between her breasts.

Angela studied them, her shoulders dropping a hair. "You're pagan. Wiccan?"

Cazzi shook her head. "An eclectic witch of sorts. You?" She recognized the other woman's tattoos from various Satanic traditions.

"It's not magic. It's just me," Angela glared, the moment lost. "You destroyed my relationship."

"Couldn't even if I wanted to. Can I help?"

"You fucking helped enough."

Cazzi softened her expression. "I know it hurts."

"Don't get condescending," Angela snarled. How had Cazzi not recognized that voice from the radio? That face from the magazines, the internet, the billboards? If this was Angela Alice, then the gorgeous South Asian guy who'd just dumped her must've been RK, from Patrick's old boy band, Beatboyz. So many famous people. Famous people meant press... she suppressed a grimace.

She was so deep in her thoughts she almost missed Angela's next words. "You think you're some kind of therapist?"

"Not quite," Cazzi replied. "Look, we'll be downstairs if you need anything." She backed towards the door. Why had she said she was staying? This woman didn't want her help.

"Like I'm staying here." Angela cast her gaze around the room. "They can make this damn album without me."

She stood up, holding herself like an avenging martyr. With her tear-streaked mascara and smudged lipstick, she looked tragic and triumphant, her rage nearly visible around her as she stalked out. Patrick and Cazzi watched her go, unable to help themselves.

Maybe it was diva charisma, but Cazzi didn't think so. If she was religiously inclined, she'd call it the work of the devil. But she wasn't and she'd met too many Satanists to write it off like that. No, there was something uniquely strange about Angela Alice. Cazzi would be quite happy if she never had the chance to find out what it was.

"Can we talk now?" Patrick asked, his voice low. God, she

loved it when he spoke from his chest, the last thing it made her want to do was talk.

She faced him. "You sure that's what you wanna do?"

He'd never looked at her like that, like he wanted to push her up against the wall and do everything she'd ever hoped he would. "No. But let's do this right."

She sighed. "If you insist." She could wait for more kissing but god, not much longer.

He brushed a hair off her cheek, his touch lingering but hesitant. "Was it okay? The kiss? I forgot to ask."

Her face went hot. "More than okay, but thank you for checking in. Now, what did you wanna talk about?"

He frowned. "A lot actually I—"

"Where are they?" A figure in black and silver barreled up the stairs. "Is she keeping him again? Because I swear, I'm going to—"

Patrick went stiff against her, and not in the way she'd like.

The speaker pulled up short, taking in the two of them and the empty room behind them. He or maybe she was slender, East Asian, and tall, dapper in a long black pea coat, silver leggings, impeccable makeup, and a cascade of black curls sweeping over their forehead from the unshaved side of their head. They were, in short, beautiful. And vaguely familiar.

Fucking hell, not another one. She had no idea who this person was but she would bet she should.

The latest pretty goth cocked their head. "Rick, where the hell is my talent?"

Patrick shrugged, his expression closed. "They broke up. For now."

"I don't care about *her.* Where is Rohan?"

"He took off." Patrick stepped back, no longer touching her.

"Look, we don't know where he is and we're in the middle of something here," Cazzi tried not to snap but she didn't try hard. She had the anxious feeling she was rapidly running out of time for something.

"Uh-huh. And who are you?"

Patrick's fingers found hers and squeezed before she could respond. "Caz. That's my business partner," he murmured, his touch falling away again.

Oops.

She reached out a hand. "Cazzi, Patrick's… um, friend." She hesitated then said, "She/her pronouns. Seriously, we're… it's important."

"I'm Benji Nakamura," Benji smiled distractedly, shaking her hand like they were on autopilot. "They/them. Tell me, Patrick's um…friend. Did you have something to do with this?"

"Why would she have anything to do with Angela and Rohan?" Patrick asked sharply.

Benji shot him a look but returned their gaze to Cazzi. "Because they would've never broken up by themselves. Is he into you?"

"Who?"

"Rohan, of course!" That must be what Ro was short for.

"We literally just met." She shrugged. Should she feel bad about possibly causing the break up? Doubt crept in. *This is why you don't run in like some know-it-all asshole.* "He broke up with her."

Patrick's shoulders were visibly tight. "Rohan isn't a fuckboy, Benji, come on."

"Yeah, yeah, he's all about that monogamy, I know." Benji grinned. "Fucking finally." They punched the air. Welp, maybe she shouldn't feel bad. "How permanent do you think it will be? How devastated is he?" They asked Patrick.

He shrugged.

"Wow." Cazzi glanced between the two of them. "You really didn't like his ex."

Patrick grimaced.

"Angelica can fuck right off as far as I'm concerned," Benji snarled. It was almost as impressive as Angela's… or maybe

Angelica's, all the names were getting confusing. They *were* the same person, right?

"You've never even met her," Patrick reminded them.

"I've seen what she's been doing to him." Benji stepped closer. "Better to cut the cancer out now, good riddance to bad love and all."

Cazzi flinched, caught off guard, remembering Patrick ghosting her. She glanced at him, had that been what he was thinking when he cut her off?

He caught her eye and looked away, breath hitching, expression closing down.

No! She wanted to shout, *Don't you fucking dare shut me out again.*

"Oh, I'm sorry," Benji said silkily, their voice demanding attention. "Is the fact that one of our financial backers just broke up with our talent and stormed out not holding your attention?"

Holy shit. If she wasn't on the brink of finally getting somewhere with Patrick, she'd be very tempted. As it was, her body wasn't that picky. She ignored it. But damn, *that voice*. Nobody accidentally had a voice like that.

Patrick groaned. "This is going to be a mess, isn't it?"

"You've got connections though," Cazzi said, rubbing his arm. "You'll figure it out."

Benji looked at her like she wasn't listening. "Of course we will. Who do you think I am?"

Oh hell, she grew up in LA, she knew that kind of question. Benji was some kind of famous. When had her life turned into an anime full of beautiful people? And where was the door? "Benji Nakamura?" She hazarded.

Benji groaned, cupping their hands over their eyes, careful not to smudge their makeup. "Whatever. Do either of you lovebirds know where our singer went?"

"You don't know?" Patrick asked. "I thought you'd have chipped us all by now."

Benji dropped their hands. "Don't give me ideas. He's not answering his phone and we have less than two weeks to get this damn album done and launch this fucking label. If you see him, tell him to get his ass to the studio." They turned to leave.

"Wait," Cazzi said, "Aren't you gonna give the poor guy time to recover from his breakup? Haven't they been together, like, a while?"

Benji sighed. "I'd like to, I really would. But this is his neck as much as mine." They headed back to the stairs. "Remind him of that when you find him."

Patrick exhaled hard and followed them. His shoulders were practically up by his ears.

"Where are you going?" Cazzi scrambled to follow. Patrick showing that much tension in his body language was worrying as fuck. She felt like she was missing something. Like she was losing him again. *No, no noooo*— she clamped down on the anxiety.

"It's my neck too," he replied. "Can you wait for me?" There was something strange in his expression, almost panicky, but he was gone before she could parse it.

"Why stop now?" Cazzi muttered to the empty stairway.

PATRICK "RICK" Jones left the house as quickly as he could walk without running, every muscle coiled tight. He felt like he was choking. He should be happy, Rohan's disappearance notwithstanding, his friend would show up again, he always did. But Patrick should be *happy*.

He'd kissed Cazzi. She'd kissed him back. It'd been good.

Hadn't it?

Better than last time, not that last time had been *bad*. Right up until he remembered why he shouldn't be kissing her. Then the buzzing in his brain had taken over and it had all gone to hell. But this time was different. They were both free, they both wanted to. Wanted to do more. No partners to hurt or lie to or just never tell and drift away from out of guilt.

More would be really nice. He'd wanted that for a while. For too long. Longer than he'd been single.

Shame sawed discordantly through whatever song was stuck in his head, disrupting it. Suddenly his brain was buzzing again, full of feedback, his pulse juddering out of time.

Go away, god, go away, go away. He fisted his locs, trying to focus on the texture under his fingers. He rubbed them together, listening to them making faint noises against his ears.

There were too many feelings, too many sounds, too many sensations. He couldn't focus.

He wanted to enjoy this. Why couldn't he enjoy this?

He looked around, trying to pay attention to his surroundings as he trudged up the hill of the backyard and out onto the street. He turned left, focusing on the map in his head. He knew this street, though he'd never seen it outside of Google Maps Street View and the pictures she'd sent him. A hodgepodge of houses in various styles and levels of upkeep. Manicured lawns and drought-friendly gardens next to dead yards populated with corn hole boards, bean bags, and red Solo cups. It was what he'd always imagined a college town would look like. At this time of the afternoon, it was deserted, the only other person on the street was a lanky professor type who biked by with his hands clasped behind him like he was about to launch into a lecture.

Cazzi's street. Her house was there, right in front of him. A little one-story cottage painted blue with hedges green from the winter rains and a chair for reading in. Though he couldn't see it from here, he knew the welcome mat said "Oh hi Mark. How's your sex life?" He'd bought it for her some apartments back.

His breath eased and he realized he'd been nearly panting. This was her space. He'd be safe here.

There was a gate but it wasn't locked. He opened it without

thinking, walking up to the chair set in the least visible part of the yard. Exactly where she'd want it.

He'd just sit here, catch his breath. Then go look for Rohan. It'd be fine. He'd done his research before he'd come. Clementine was a good enough place, Cazzi raved about it, diverse enough that he probably wouldn't get the cops called on him for Sitting While Black.

He pulled out his phone, staring at the picture of his cat on the lock screen. If he were home he'd be holding Scoot in his arms, his face buried in her tortoiseshell fur. Then he could listen to her purr (she always purred when he picked her up) and relax. But maybe if he just sat here and didn't think his brain would calm down.

If that made everything gray again, so be it. He couldn't stand to feel right now.

His phone vibrated, buzzing out the rhythm to "Baby Love" by the Supremes. Grandma was calling. He picked up immediately. "Hi, Nana."

"Patrick, I'm looking for the good catnip but I can't find it."

"For you or for Scoot?"

"Baby, you know that cat's got enough. I'm making my special tea. The contractors working on your studio keep tromping all over my kitchen and making a ruckus. It's working my last damn nerve."

Technically, it was his kitchen as his Nana had been living with him ever since her separation from his Grandpa, Patrick Sr. He pushed the memory of that aside. He could've bought her her own place but he liked having her in his house, it reassured him, knowing he'd be able to be there for her. "I brought the last of it with me in my tea blend but I ordered more and it should be arriving today or tomorrow."

She sighed, and he pressed his lips together, worried but knowing she wouldn't like it if he pestered her about it. "Damiana?" She asked.

"Got plenty of it," he said. "Want me to stop the work on the studio?"

"No, no," she said. "Flooding's a time-sensitive repair. It'll only be more expensive the longer you wait." She'd managed Grandpa Pat's very successful repair business for fifty years so she'd know. "Is Cazzi there?" She brightened. "Put that girl on, it's been too long."

His stomach tightened. He shouldn't have left Cazzi like that. Hell, he shouldn't be sitting here not doing the thing he left her to do. "She's not here right now but I swear I'll put her on later."

"You better." He could hear the smile in her voice.

"Yes, ma'am."

"Bye, baby. Make me proud."

"Bye Nana." He knew she meant the album but he couldn't help thinking about the first time he and Cazzi kissed and feeling like Nana wouldn't be proud at all.

———

ROHAN CIRCLED the town of Clementine in under two hours, wishing he'd brought his sunglasses. It was really fucking sunny for January and yet somehow ridiculously cold for California. NorCal was weird like that. As a lifelong Angeleno, he didn't understand anything approximating seasons. Sure, he'd toured all over the world and seen snow through bus windows and spring outside hotels but he'd never been terribly interested in spending time anywhere that got colder than sixty degrees. Fuck, it couldn't be warmer than like, forty. He'd jogged the better part of the way back to the rental. Angie was probably gone by now.

She didn't stick around when she lost an argument. There'd been fights that sent her into hiding for days, making Rohan frantic with worry. Now, as he opened the front door of the rental, he was glad of her disappearing act. He didn't know if his resolve would hold right now if she really tested it.

"Rohan?"

He froze. He didn't recognize the voice and he was in no condition to deal with paps.

"Is that you?"

He didn't answer.

"Patrick?" The voice rounded the corner and he saw Caz brandishing a large ceramic chicken. "Oh."

"Don't." He threw his hands in front of his face. "I'd die from the headlines alone."

She looked at the chicken like she hadn't seen it before. "What, like 'Man Bludgeoned with Disturbed Farm Animal'?"

He laughed even though it wasn't that funny. Then he kept laughing until he gasped for air and his stomach hurt.

"Oh hell." She put down the chicken.

"What the fuck?" He wheezed and then giggled when his gaze caught the chicken again.

"I'm guessing you didn't cry and need the release." She reached out, telegraphing her motions like an overly enthusiastic mime, and patted him tentatively on the back when he didn't pull away.

It just made him laugh all over again.

"Benji is looking for you."

That made him stop real quick. "Shit, I'm late for recording."

"That was my impression. Are you actually up for recording?"

"You really aren't in the industry, are you, Caz?"

She narrowed her eyes. "You're going to pull that 'the show must go on' crap aren't you?"

"Seeing as this album is mostly coming out of my pocket, yes."

She sighed. "I'll call Patrick. He's out looking for you."

Rohan shrugged and ran upstairs to gather his notebook and his talisman, the rough edges of the sigil scraping over his fingertips familiarly. He clenched his hand around it, letting it ground him before putting it on. The room was in typical post-Angie anger disarray and he tidied it up automatically. She'd thrown his stuff, of course. Hers was gone.

Why did I put up with this for so long? His talisman swung in front of him as he straightened up and he tucked it under his shirt out of habit. He didn't want that strange woman asking questions about it. The cold weight of the gold made him feel steadier and he realized he'd been gritting his teeth, his stomach knotted with rage. He exhaled hard, letting it go, for now. It'd be back.

When he returned, Caz was pacing.

"Patrick's not answering," she said without prompting.

Rohan called Benji. "Is Rick there?"

"Hello to you too, asshole," Benji replied. "Don't tell me he's missing too."

"He's not answering his phone, Caz is worried."

"Caz, huh?" There was a musing tone in Benji's voice Rohan didn't care for. "I'll try to call him. Take her with you. She and Rick have some staring into each other's eyes shit going on."

"You caught that too?"

"Don't make it sound like it was hard," Benji said. "Too bad, we'll have to find you another rebound."

"Wait what—" Rohan looked at Caz, and walked into the kitchen. "Rebound? Her? Me? What?" The chicken clock stared suspiciously at him. The damn kitchen had more chickens than cooking supplies.

He could almost hear Benji shrug. "People do weird shit after a big break up. She got you out of your shitty relationship when all your friends couldn't and you already call her by the nickname Rick used for her when I saw them. Whatever, just get here, okay?" They hung up, leaving Rohan staring at the phone, confused.

He walked out of the kitchen. "Is your name not Caz?"

She looked at him. "It's Cazzi."

"That's your full name?"

For some reason that seemed to annoy her. "Is Patrick there or not?"

He shook his head. "Benji thinks you should come along. He'll probably turn up at the studio eventually."

"No, he'll come back here. He asked me to wait."

"Shouldn't he be back by now? Or at least answering his phone?" His phone buzzed and he looked at Benji's text. "He's not answering Benji's calls either."

Cazzi's face lost what color it had. "You don't think something happened to him, do you?"

Rohan blinked. "I mean, probably not."

That didn't seem to reassure her. "I gotta go look for him. What if he drove? He hates driving. What if he got pulled over? I think the cops are okay here, but what if…?" She looked stricken.

"He's fine. Probably." But Rohan's stomach knotted up again, thinking about all the things that could go wrong in some random small town.

"Bad shit happens." Her eyes said she spoke from personal experience. "I gotta find him." She scrambled out the back door, fast but careless, almost slipping on the chicken throw rug in the hall.

"Fuck." Rohan ran after her. "Where are you going?" He caught up to her, grabbing her arm as she stumbled over the deck. "Hey, hey! Stop!"

She froze in his grip, every muscle under his grip locked tight. Her hair stuck to her face and her eyes were wild. "If you don't let me go I will hurt you. I don't want to hurt you."

"Look, can you calm down? I know that's a stupid thing to say but just listen a second."

"Let me go." Her words were stilted, her face expressionless. It was freaky to see that detachment when she was pretty much panting, her muscles quivering under the pressure of staying frozen, her hands in white-knuckled fists.

"I'm afraid you'll run away." She was straight up freaking him out, reminding him of Angie when she'd get too far into her memories. Angie refused to get help even though she knew she got erratic and destructive, leaving him to deal with her alone. It made him feel helpless, scared, useless. He could never seem to do the right thing when she got in that headspace.

"I can't promise anything." Cazzi sounded weirdly calm, her fingers pressed so hard against a tattoo on her left wrist they distorted the inked lines.

"Then I'm not letting go." He couldn't risk it, what if she hurt herself?

She sucker-punched him so hard he nearly threw up. He doubled over until he was sure he wasn't going to lose his lunch.

She was across the deck but still there when he straightened. "What the hell?"

"Trauma response," she said, matter-of-factly. "I warned you."

"Be clearer next time."

"Listen to women when they talk." She was still panting but somehow speaking normally.

That stung. "I do listen, thank you very much."

"Fine, then listen to me."

"Will you listen to *me*?"

She tipped her chin up. "I will do my best."

"Okay, look, we both want to find him. Let's combine forces. I'll drive, you try to figure out where he went."

She shook her head, too vigorously for her calm facade. "I'm not getting into a car with you. Not right now."

"Then how the hell are we going to find him?"

"He walked." She pointed at the car in the driveway. "There were two cars when I came. You know Patrick doesn't drive."

Rohan looked. Sure enough, Angie's black Tesla was gone. Only his car remained.

"Come on," Cazzi called. "I think I have an idea." She was already walking.

Rohan hurried to catch up.

3

WHERE ARE THEY NOW: BEATBOYZ
Who didn't have a Beatboyz poster on their wall, growing up? We sure did. (Let's face it, some of us still do.) For nearly a decade the LA boy band was a pop phenom, dominating the charts, performing to adoring fans around the world, and making some really memorable music videos ("Trouble" anyone? We're fanning ourselves just thinking about it). But what happened after Martin Meija infamously left the group five years ago? From dating Satanists to doing drag, you won't believe what hotties RK, Ricky Rick, Leo Starr, and Marty Mac are up to now.
—Celebrity Watcher Magazine

Adrenaline buzzed through her, making her hands shake. Cazzi tucked them into her pockets, just enough to keep them still but not so deep they would be a struggle to pull out. She tried to be grateful that she felt something instead of completely going numb, but it was a hard sell. What was clear was she really shouldn't have punched RK, even if he didn't happen to be a pop star.

She glanced back at him. He'd caught up with her easily, his long legs eating up the distance between them without anything so polite as effort. He didn't seem hurt, though his hand hovered over his middle, perhaps unconsciously. And of course, he was gorgeous: pretty like a Bollywood picture with warm brown skin, a face made for posters, and a tall, movie star body. No wonder Angela Alice wanted to keep him so bad. Cazzi wished he hadn't grabbed her arm.

"So where are we going?" RK asked, coming up next to her but keeping his distance.

She chewed her lip, debating her answer. "My house."

He pulled up short, "Um, why?"

"I think he's there."

"Again, the question: why?"

Because we always fly home to each other. "Just a feeling."

"You think he's looking for me in your living room?"

"I don't know why, I just know Patrick and he knows where I live."

"What's up with you two anyway?"

I wish I knew. "Can we just go? It's right around the corner and if I'm wrong we can go from there."

"Wait," RK frowned. "He picked the rental to be close to you? You're the reason I'm going to have nightmares about chickens for the rest of my life?"

"Yep, let's go." She bounced on her heels once before she stopped herself. Her muscles felt shaky and her anxiety screamed at her to *fucking go.*

"And you're not dating or secretly married or something?"

"It's complicated, okay?" She snapped, walking away without waiting to see if he'd follow. She didn't really care either way. She couldn't deal with some nosy fucker poking at her secrets right now.

"I've heard that one before," he muttered.

She picked up the pace, hoping she was right and Patrick was where she thought he was. Maybe his phone was dead. Or on silent. Or didn't have any service.

She forced air into her lungs. She knew intellectually what was going on with her body and how to handle it. Actually doing it was another matter.

Breathe. Focus on the present. Forgive yourself.

She pressed her fingers against the second-level calming sigil tattooed on her left wrist, picturing it in her mind. *It is my will to quell my trauma response and see the situation with clear eyes.* It cut the top off her panic, quieting the static in her head. She felt nearly calm. Her breath came easier.

They rounded the corner and she looked ahead to the front porch of her cottage, small but enclosed by a thick hedge, and with just enough space for a chair comfy enough to read in. She picked up her pace until she hit the angle where you could just see in and—-there he was, sitting there looking at his phone like there was nothing wrong. His clearly working phone.

Her lungs opened up and the sudden inrush of oxygen made her dizzy.

"See?" She told RK, pointing.

"Hmm." He replied, his eyes narrowing.

"What's that supposed to mean?"

"It means I'm having deep thoughts."

Jackass, she thought and sped up again to reach Patrick first.

"What are you doing here?" She asked, her annoyance and relief blunted by the sigil. Thank goodness for her coping mechanisms, she'd have even less chill right now if not for them.

He looked up, his eyes tracking behind her, reminding her RK was still there. "I didn't have a key," Patrick said like it was the most natural thing in the world.

Cazzi frowned, examining his face. It was stoic, his poker face nearly as good as her own. "Yeah, but *why* are you on my porch?" she asked, "I thought you were out looking for RK."

"Oh so you do know who I am," the pop star in question interjected.

"Dude, I called you by your name, like twenty minutes ago," she said.

"And you're welcome to use it, only the press and fans call me RK."

"Cool, thanks. Rohan, can you give us a moment?"

"I wish," Rohan said, coming around to stand in her line of sight. "But we really need to get to the studio."

"You shouldn't be working, you should be taking care of yourself. You know, processing your feelings over the relationship." Cazzi shot back, annoyance laced with concern. "Why don't you do that over there?" She gestured at an enclosed portion of the yard, as far away as the hedge allowed, which was barely out of earshot, but still.

Rohan sighed. "Whatever. I can give you guys like, five minutes." He went and stood facing the hedge, phone in hand.

Cazzi turned back to Patrick. "Okay, seriously, what's up? Did the kiss freak you out again?"

"*Seriously*, I'm fine." His voice was calm but his eyes were still guarded. He was putting distance between them and she didn't know why.

"You do know what FINE stands for, right?" She tried to make a joke but the words came out sharp.

He frowned. "You look stressed."

"Yes, well, you didn't answer your phone, so naturally I assumed you were dead," Cazzi said, deadpan. "Nothing stressful about that."

"Not at all." He matched her tone.

"Is your phone dead?" She crossed her arms, looking at the phone still in his hand.

"What?" He glanced down at it. Scoot, her kitty goddaughter was sprawled across his lock screen, all four paws in the air. The same picture was her phone's background.

"Or is there another reason why you didn't answer it?" She raised her eyebrows.

"Nana called."

"Oh." Cazzi blinked, thrown. "Is she alright?"

"She's fine, going a bit stir-crazy not being able to do her work with all the strangers in the house." Nana was an herbalist and conjure doctor, Cazzi couldn't blame her for not practicing with workers in the house.

"Fair," Cazzi muttered, relieved annoyance somewhat deflated.

He shrugged. "You're sure you're okay? You didn't get triggered by Rohan and Angie's fight did you?"

"Of course I did. Why do you think I rushed up there like a fucking dipshit? But that's not the point."

"It's not?"

"No, the point is that you're not answering my questions or my fucking phone calls."

Shock rippled under the mask of his poker face. Like he hadn't expected her to notice. Did he think she was that self-involved?

"Alright, five minutes is up." Rohan ambled back like things were just fine. But the tightness around his eyes and the hunch in his shoulders said otherwise.

She gazed narrowly at the pop star until he said, "What?"

"How long were you with Angela Alice?"

"Four years. Can we go now? You and Rick can talk when we're done."

"It's okay to not be okay, you know. To acknowledge your emotions."

"Is this supposed to be therapy? Because it's terrible."

She paused and recalibrated. He was right, she was being clumsy, patronizing even. She looked him in the eye and let sincerity leech into her expression. "I'm sorry. Professional hazard. I just like to make sure everyone's okay."

Rohan shrugged. "I'm fine."

"I know." She touched his sleeve slowly and briefly. "I'm really impressed. It takes a lot out of a person to break off a relationship. Especially one like that."

"Like what?" His eyes narrowed.

She caught Patrick's expression out of the corner of her eye. "Passionate." A thought struck her, a way to buy time and maybe undo some of the shitty impression she'd made with Patrick's friend. Maybe it would even help whatever freakout Patrick was pretending not to have. "Come in for a minute, will you? I made cookies, you can take some to Benji when you go to the studio."

Rohan looked suspicious but Patrick perked right up. "What kind?"

"Coconut chocolate chip." She grinned. They were his favorite.

A smile quirked his lips and fluttered in her stomach. "Alright," he said.

She looked at Rohan. He was watching them speculatively. "Okay, but we've gotta be fast or Benji'll have our heads."

Cazzi unlocked the door, glad she'd already cleaned up on the off chance she'd get Patrick to come home with her. And here he was, warm against her back. She just hadn't expected a third wheel.

The third wheel didn't look too happy about it either. She grabbed the cookie box, and popped the top, shoving it between the two men. Patrick grabbed one and took a bite, his eyes closing in pleasure that deepened those flutters in her stomach and reached lower. She jerked her eyes away.

Rohan stared at the cookies like he wasn't quite sure what to do with them. But by the way his gaze was unfocused, she didn't think it was her baking that bothered him.

"You don't have to have one if you don't want to," she said.

He blinked and took a cookie. "Sorry, just distracted." He caught the question in her gaze and looked away.

Patrick took another cookie, prompting Rohan to bite into his, a little self-consciously. His eyes widened and he took another bite. "Holy shit, these are good."

"Thanks." She smiled at him. "Take the box with you."

"You sure?" He asked but took the box.

She scoffed. "Dude, I made a second batch just for me. Don't worry about it." She snagged one from the box, just to see what he'd do.

He gasped and pulled the box back. "I thought you had your own!" He cried in mock horror.

Patrick rolled his eyes but smiled. Her shoulders relaxed at the sight. Maybe they were okay after all.

Cazzi laughed. "I'll give it back to you if you let me have another five minutes with Patrick before you whisk him off."

"Caz, we don't have the time," Patrick said apologetically. "Sorry. We've got eight songs to write and record in less than two weeks."

"Well, that'll be a good way to get your emotions about your break-up processed," she told Rohan brightly, trying not to feel like Patrick was avoiding, or worse, rejecting her.

"I'm not writing about her," Rohan said. "She'd love that too much."

"Taking the high road," Cazzi nodded. "Noble. I hope you're able to express that pain in other constructive ways though."

"I am not heartbroken," Rohan bit out.

"Why heartbroken? Why that word?"

"I don't know, because it accurately describes what I'm not?"

"That's okay," she said. "You don't have to be heartbroken. But it's equally okay if you are. I just want to make sure you allow yourself an outlet for whatever emotions you have."

"I don't need therapy, I just need to write songs. Helps me handle things just fine."

"I thought you weren't going to write about her," Patrick said.

"Jesus! You two are a menace."

"Just one?" Patrick asked, his eyes crinkling in a smile.

"Pat," Cazzi murmured, though she was fighting not to smile back. "Don't rile him. He's reactive right now."

"He is also right here." Rohan glared at them both. "And leaving. Rick, you coming?"

ROHAN STARED AT RICK. Cazzi, he didn't even want to look at right now. She may think she was some sort of mind reader but she didn't know a damn thing about what went through his head.

His jaw locked down, his stomach in knots. He couldn't tell what he was feeling, it felt like rage, hot and biting but it just made him want to collapse. To fall apart and maybe, embarrassingly, cry.

Rick sighed and nodded. "I'll talk to you later," he told the menace he called his friend.

Rohan caught her reaction out of the corner of his eye, a flicker of something complex and intriguing before she was blank-faced again, watching both of them carefully. "Thanks for the cookies," he forced himself to say.

"Come by if you want more," was all she said. But she looked at him like she could see everything as it twisted up inside of him. He was glad to get as far away from her as this tiny town would allow.

In the car to the studio, Rick was his usual silent self, breaking his quiet only to say, "She's right, you know."

"About?" Rohan forced the word through his teeth.

"Bottling that shit up."

Rohan resisted the urge to punch the steering wheel. Why couldn't they let up? Wasn't it enough that they were clearly, tauntingly in love? Wasn't it enough that Cazzi with her therapist mask tried to unravel his brain like tape out of a cassette? "Will she talk?"

"To the press? Never." Rick's vehemence was startling. Then he went silent.

"Why the hell did you disappear like that?" Rohan growled after a minute. *Why'd you leave me with her?*

"I didn't. Just taking a break." The look Rick shot him told Rohan the subject was closed. "Besides, this is about you. Not me."

Rohan stewed in silence for a few minutes. There were words pressing in under his skin, Hissing and whispering in his ears. "Oh hell," he snapped, "if I write a big sad song about Angie, will you two stop?"

Rick shrugged and turned back to the window.

Rohan took that as a yes. He stormed into the studio, said a curt hello to Benji, gave them the cookies, and slid into the booth. "Give me something angry," he told Rick. "Give me that one with the warped bass line you showed me."

The producer nodded, a smile ghosting around his lips. Rohan took a deep breath, put the headphones on, and let himself bathe in the darkly industrial beat for a few bars. The bass line twisted around him like a serpent, the beat plucking at his pulse.

He held his talisman in his hand, the gold heating until he could feel the sigils on either side of it imprinting on his palm. *I am my own person*, he reminded himself. When his heart beat in time, and his thoughts came in rhyme, he opened his mouth and let the pain out.

The words squeezed their way between his teeth as he remembered the last time he'd decided to leave, carving himself into the back of this fucking little disk of gold with a paper clip until he'd felt strong enough to admit maybe he wasn't okay.

> *"There's a room in your home*
> *Built of music and bone*
> *You cleaned out for my heart*
> *Then left me to rot*

> *"I covered myself in gold*
> *Trying to match your cold*
> *Bleeding music on the floor*
> *Better than waiting by the door*

He threw back his head and belted:
> *"Girl, I loved you like everything*
> *I thought we could weather anything*
> *But the only thing we couldn't do*
> *Was me and you.*

> *"I was yours*
> *I was yours*
> *I fought in every one of our wars*
> *I fought for you*
> *Leaving was all I could do*

"Ghost Girl, I loved you like everything…" he sang the chorus again.

> *"I was your shadow*
> *The possession after the possessive*
> *The curiosity, the accessory*
> *All you gave me were demons*
> *All I gave you was the dark side of my heart.*

> *That room in your home*
> *Built for the music in your bones*
> *Is empty again*
> *Ready for your pain*
> *I'll build my own*
> *Freed and alone"*

He repeated the chorus twice more and then signaled to Rick

to cut the track. Benji grinned from the chair next to the producer. "That was great," they told Rohan through his headphones. "We can definitely work with that."

"I'm not putting that on the album," Rohan said. "I'm taking the high road."

Benji rolled their eyes and bit into a cookie. "Why? You think *she's* gonna do that?"

"No, isn't that the point of the high road?"

Benji sighed. Patrick shrugged and began noodling on the M-Audio keyboard in front of him.

"Fine," Benji said, "What else you got?"

They worked on a couple of the songs he already had lyrics to but while they were good, they didn't cut to the bone the way the one he'd made up on the fly had. He couldn't help but wonder what Cazzi would make of the song if he ever showed it to her.

Not that he would. But he did ask for the demo when they were done. Rick sent it to his phone without comment.

After not enough dinner, Rohan lay in the bed he was supposed to share with Angie, staring at a blank note on his phone, trying to write something, anything that wasn't about her.

Fuck, he hadn't been this blocked ever. All he could think about was Angie's face when he'd dumped her. He was the asshole here, wasn't he? Dragging her upstate to dump her just because some random therapist lady wandered into their fight.

Wandered in and made me tell the truth...

He typed the words hurriedly then stared at them, trying to make verse, chorus, anything that didn't lead back to Angie. What was he doing? He couldn't write, he couldn't reinvent himself, it was too late, he was just sitting here lying to himself like an egomaniac—

He got up and walked out of the house, no direction in mind. His feet took him to the one person he knew in this town wouldn't prop him up just to get the album, the label off the ground.

CAZZI DECIDED to stop hoping for Patrick to show up and was getting ready for bed when there was a knock on the door. She froze, her rabbit brain cycling through a quick succession of horror stories before she realized it was probably him.

She checked the peephole anyway, frowning as she did. It wasn't Patrick. "Rohan?" She called through the door.

He looked up, "You said to come by if I wanted more cookies." He smiled into the peephole. It was an expression that was supposed to be charming but seemed forced. Even through the fisheye lens, she could tell he was tired and hurting. "Benji hogged the box."

She hesitated. She didn't really know him and it was late but he was Patrick's friend. He'd have warned her if Rohan was a problem. Plus it would make things awkward with Patrick if his friend/business partner hated her. She opened the door. "Come on in."

He looked at her PJ pants, sweatshirt, and slippers. "It's okay, I can come back tomorrow."

"You're fine," she said, ushering him inside. "I was just going to make tea, want some?"

"Yeah," the word came out hoarse and he cleared his throat with a rueful but real smile as he took his shoes off. "Sorry, did a lot of singing today."

She smiled back. "I'll put honey in it."

He thanked her and sat at the counter that jutted out from the cutout window in her kitchen. She handed him a variety pack of teas and left him to choose a bag, busying herself with the kettle. It was weirdly domestic. She hadn't made anyone tea since she moved out on her own three months ago. She hadn't realized she missed it.

"These really are good," Rohan said, taking a bite of cookie.

She hummed in agreement. She knew how good her cookies

were. They were excellent, but they weren't visit a near-stranger at 11:30 at night excellent. She had a guess as to why he was here but she wasn't going to repeat this afternoon's bumbling.

"Could I get the recipe?"

She looked at him in surprise. "Sure. Take your favorite chocolate chip oatmeal cookie recipe and swap coconut flakes for the oats."

"Huh." He examined the structure of the cookie like he was on a cooking show.

She suddenly remembered he'd won *Cooking with Celebs* four years ago after the band broke up. She'd watched it with Patrick who had been visiting her in grad school. They'd cheered him from her living room but not nearly as excitedly as Angela Alice and his ex-bandmate Leo Starr had in the stands. The show put them on a split-screen because they were cheering so hard from the audience. Cazzi spent the episode longing for the way Rohan mouthed *I love you* to Angela every chance he got, grinning with joy so strong it made her ache for the man who'd sat next to her as they watched it and had never said those words.

Back then, Angela had mouthed it back to him from the audience, beaming. The show acted like it was a huge deal, the host talking about her with wide eyes and bewildered glee. Cazzi hadn't known enough about Angela to get it. To her eyes, it had been a genuine display of support. She wondered what had gone wrong.

"Has Rick told you what's going on with him yet?" Rohan asked, knocking her out of the memory.

Deflection. "He's been busy."

"You're in love with him, huh?"

She exhaled hard. "Whoa there. I wasn't expecting the Spanish Inquisition."

He chuckled. "Don't like it when the tables are turned, do you?" He picked a turmeric-ginger blend, plunking the bag into his empty cup. "Anyway, nobody expects the Spanish Inquisition."

"Points for catching the reference." The water boiled and she poured it into their mugs. "I wasn't going to ask you anything, by the way, I figured you had enough of that earlier."

He frowned at the cookie in his hand. He'd only taken a small bite out of it. He didn't seem to be jonesing for another one but rather debating something.

Cazzi waited, leaning on the counter, watching him. Silence was one of her favorite tools when talking to a student.

He turned the cookie, examining it from an absurd number of angles. "I wrote a song," he said finally.

She blew on her tea and said nothing. His fingers were slender and long, the quintessential piano fingers. She watched the shadows from the weak kitchen light play over them.

"It was really good. I just can't use it."

"Oh?"

"It's about her. I tried it, what you said. I wrote about her and it was *angry*. I didn't know I was so angry." He looked up at her. "Aren't I supposed to be sad? Devastated or something? I'm the one who dumped her. I dumped Angie," he said, like the reality was just, finally dawning on him.

"Anger is a valid emotion. What made you so angry?"

"We were supposed to work. We were the poster children for opposites attracting, for I don't know, tolerance. Pop and metal coming together." He frowned.

Cazzi found herself leaning forward, she pulled back subtly, not wanting to distract him when he was finally opening up.

"We were supposed to work. It wasn't supposed to hurt." He paused. "Actually, that's a great line." He pulled out his phone and typed something in.

She thought about telling him to put it away but she wasn't on the clock and this wasn't a student she had to counsel. It was Sunday night and she didn't work for another eight hours. Or she wouldn't be working if she didn't have such a soft heart. She bit back a sigh.

He was humming to himself, typing away.

"Maybe you should get some sleep." She fake yawned to make her point, but it turned real halfway through. She should've been in bed hours ago. Not that she would've gotten much sleep between the whole Patrick thing and the meeting she had looming tomorrow.

He caught the gesture. "Sorry," he grinned and it was all charming again. She bristled at the fakeness. "You just really inspire me." He said it like it was an honor.

"I am not your muse," she said. "If you're here so you can use me to channel your angst you can leave right now."

"No, no." He was on his phone again. "I'm not writing about you, it's just," he looked up, "You make me… see things clearer. What I wrote today, the words that came out of me, were the most real thing I've written, probably ever. What I just wrote," he held up his phone, showing her the note app full of lyrics. "Same thing. You're like a truth serum and it kinda hurts like hell."

"Thanks?"

"No, sorry. It's a good thing, I swear." He met her gaze through his sweep of black bangs. "I really appreciate you. I… shit, I'm exhausted and wired and a little weird right now." He fiddled with the leather cord under his shirt. "Look, would you mind coming down to the studio tomorrow? You ask good questions and I can't write well when I'm not honest with myself."

Cazzi hesitated. This was getting intense fast and she wondered if this was a case of emotional rebounding.

"No pressure," he shrugged, getting up and wandering to her bookshelves, finding her small shelf of CDs almost immediately.

"Nice to see someone still buys CDs." He picked up her old copy of Linkin Park's *Minutes to Midnight*.

"I like reading the liner notes," she said. "It's kind of a shame how rare it is that artists put effort into them anymore."

"When I discovered liner notes as a kid, I read through every CD, tape, 8-track, and vinyl in my stepdad's collection." He put the CD back and ran his finger along the spines of the cases.

"That sounds like a project." Cazzi couldn't help picturing a small Rohan sitting in a pile of music, his head bent over a booklet. The image was too cute. She smiled.

He glanced at her and a brief smile touched his lips. "I made a mess but he didn't get mad, he pulled out his favorites and read them to me. Oh man," he laughed, picking up a copy of Beatboyz's *Trouble.* "We used to do so much extra shit for our liner notes. You know they let us trash the hotel room ourselves? The clothes were pre-ripped and pinned though."

Trouble was their third album when management decided it was time for the boys to grow up and be edgy. For some reason that looked like them looking bewildered in a destroyed hotel room. Rohan as the baby of the group appeared especially confused in the photo. Patrick had rolled his eyes so hard when he'd seen she bought the album.

"I was always terrified I'd leave someone out of my thank yous," he laughed, flipping through the liner notes. "I doubt anyone read them."

"I read them. I love thank yous and dedications. Patrick would always do the same one though."

Rohan grinned. "Yeah, we gave him so much shit for that."

"'For my family, you know who you are.'" Cazzi always checked every new Beatboyz album, just to see if this would be the one where that'd change. The one he'd finally acknowledge her. Maybe he thought he was protecting her. *Maybe he just thought I was family too.*

Then why had he kissed her?

"I'm sure Rick would be happy to see you." Rohan's voice broke through the memory.

She stilled. "You think you know my Achilles heel."

"Am I wrong?"

"What do you think?"

He looked at her seriously. "I think you two could be great together if that's what you want. I've never seen Rick look at someone like that and I've known him forever."

Her cheeks warmed. God, he really knew how to say the right thing didn't he? But he seemed sincere. It wasn't like Patrick hadn't realized how she felt about him. Maybe she didn't need to hide her crush anymore. "You're smooth."

"I'm pretty rusty actually. Will you please come by? Just to see? Pretty, pretty please?" He clasped his hands in front of her and looked up at her with big brown puppy dog eyes. It was fucking adorable.

"Now who's a menace?" She muttered.

His grin kicked up at the corner, turning crooked and a bit wicked. It made her breath catch despite herself. *Dangerous*. It was hard to remember he'd once been the baby of the Beatboyz, the adorable one who could break the internet with a well-placed "behind the scenes" video.

"Fine, but only if you stop looking like you're posing for a Beatboyz poster."

"I'll have you know my pictures were the best-selling of all the solo posters."

"And if I wanted one, I would've bought one."

"Did you buy Rick's?"

Cazzi gave him a dead-eyed stare. "I've known Patrick since we were knee-high and could barely talk."

"Really?" His eyebrows shot up. "How come we never met? I know his entire family."

She shrugged, trying to loosen her suddenly tight shoulders. She'd never asked to meet his bandmates and Patrick never offered. It'd been a good deal at the time.

Rohan yawned suddenly and it seemed to catch him by surprise. "Alright, you're right. I need sleep." He stood up, draining the last of his tea. "Thanks for the cookie." He took another bite—his second. "So the only thing you swapped out was the oats?"

She showed him to the door like he couldn't take the ten steps himself. The habit was so ingrained she forgot to question it. "I tend to bake with coconut oil too instead of butter."

"For the high smoke point?" He asked, putting his shoes back on.

She blinked, parsing out the term. She was a hobbyist at best when it came to baking. Patrick liked coconut and she'd gotten the love of it from him. "For the taste."

He turned just before she closed the door. "Please come," he said, dropping all humor and artifice. "Consider it an experiment."

She sighed. Patrick would be there, probably the whole day. And she was intrigued. She'd never really seen him at work, at least not this part of the process. "I'll stop by after work. Just tomorrow though and just for a few hours."

His smile was so small she nearly missed it and so warm it made her cheeks heat in response. "Thank you, Caz."

She hoped she wouldn't regret this.

4

———

THE CONDOM FAIRIES: PROVIDING GLOVES FOR YOUR LOVE
Clementine U has been sprinkled with pixie dust—and it looks
suspiciously like latex. The Student Health Services department
unleashed the
Condom Fairies: a small army of counselors and admin staff
armed with
rubbers for all. Stop on by their office in the Student Health
Building
or stop them in the street! The Condom Fairies have got you
covered.
—The Clementine Universibee

"Some high schooler stopped me at Nugget and asked me for one—right there in the bakery aisle!" Said Marcia, one of the senior counselors. She was white, with gray-streaked brown hair, and looked like she gave great hugs, not that Cazzi ever asked. One hand fluttered by the lanyard around her neck, the other held a cup of coffee with a Georgia O'Keefe flower on the side. "So of course, I gave her five." She laughed.

Most of the staff around the table laughed with her.

Cazzi hid a smile behind her own mug of tea that said *"I found out virginity was a social construct and all I got was this damn mug"* and made note of those who didn't laugh. What she saw didn't surprise her.

Staff meetings at the Clementine University Student Health Services department (which the kids just called S&S—sex and shrinks) were a Monday morning event that could easily tip from short and sweet to full-on trial by tirade. It all depended on how certain senior staff members were feeling.

Right now it was going alright but Cazzi's stomach was tight with nerves. Her name stared back at her from the meeting agenda next to a discussion of her proposed class. It wasn't until the bottom of the list but that just meant she'd be nervous the whole meeting.

"It looks like word is spreading about your project," said Yanni, their department head, an older Black woman with short natural hair and kind eyes. She looked at Cazzi and her friend and former roommate Eva with approval. "Well done on the social media push."

Eva, a plump Latina with a butch haircut and pink glasses, grinned. The expression lit and warmed her whole face. The Condom Fairies Program was her baby. That grin had been what first made Cazzi want to be friends with her back in undergrad. Now, a decade later, it was familiar but just as welcome.

So far so good. Cazzi's gaze slid over to Josie, the final member of the senior staff. The woman had been with the department longer than anyone else and looked like every year here had drained a little more color and happiness from her. Her mouth was a thin line, her arms crossed. She was somewhere between forty and sixty, white, and dressed in her usual cardigan with a pin of the University's mascot, Clemmy the Bee pinned over her left breast. She wore it like it was holy. As their sole admin support staff and the one who held the budget in her hands, she seemed to think it was her job to keep them in line. She opened her mouth and Cazzi braced herself.

"Why are we encouraging underage children who aren't even our students to have sex? It's immoral and a waste of department resources," she said, her voice high and querulous. All the remaining laughter died.

Yanni visibly suppressed a sigh. "Josie, we don't pass moral judgments on consensual non-harmful sex practices in this department."

"They're underage, they can't consent," Josie smiled triumphantly.

Eva caught Cazzi's eye. This was a new argument.

Yanni interlaced her fingers. It was a tell the entire department knew. Marcia cast her gaze upwards and the student workers sitting in on the meeting shifted nervously.

Yanni looked Josie in the eye and gave her a compassionate smile. "Will teenagers stop having sex if we stop giving them condoms?"

Josie's mouth pursed. She knew where this was going. "We don't have to encourage them."

"Encouraging them to be safe is better than keeping them in the dark and forcing them to take risks they don't need to."

Josie visibly switched gears. Her gaze slid and landed on Cazzi. "The Condom Pixies is one more unnecessary program draining department resources and now Cazzi wants to add another one!"

Adrenaline made her fingers go cold and her heart race but Cazzi straightened her spine and gave Josie her most professional bland expression. You couldn't give Josie anything to take issue with or she'd hold onto it forever.

Yanni's fingers tightened. "Cazzi's seminar is already on the agenda to discuss after we finish talking about Eva's program."

"It's a mistake," Josie sniffed. "You think the Academic Senate will allow it? Where's the academic value, the need? We're not their parents."

Cazzi kept her breath even as she said, "I believe my class *Sex and Consent: Exploring Modern Sexual Ethics* contains a lot of academic value, will have a high level of student interest, and is something this school desperately needs. Have you seen my numbers?" The statistics on what people in their students' age groups knew about sex and consent were awful. The statistics on assault, harassment, rape, and intimate partner violence made her sick. But they didn't surprise her.

Josie waved her words away. "The only numbers I care about are the budget projections. Not that it matters," she turned away, "You won't be able to mandate it, let alone get permission to teach it. You're not a professor and conservative parents will hate the course."

Cazzi carved a smile into her lips. "I like to think that this school cares enough about the welfare of its students to see reason." And not give in to regressive thinking.

Josie narrowed her eyes. Her one visible weakness was how much of her identity was tied up with this school. She'd worked here for her entire adult life and wore that like a badge of honor. Right now she was trying to parse Cazzi's words for any hint of disloyalty to the Clementine University.

Cazzi and Eva had spent way too much time psychoanalyzing her out of frustration after work. There wasn't much else you could do about someone like Josie, especially when she was in charge of the budget and was the only one who knew how all the computer systems worked.

Yanni sighed. "Cazzi, Josie has a point. I don't think this department has the clout to get your seminar on the schedule, let alone mandate it as you've proposed. But I think it's an important idea so let's brainstorm. Thoughts?"

Cazzi's stomach dropped. She slid a finger under her sleeve, tracing her first level calming sigil.

Marcia hummed thoughtfully. "What about a residency hall course?"

"That excludes students who commute from home or live off-campus," Cazzi said, thinking hard. "Could we do a deal with the Gender Studies department? Like, have them back us up?" She felt like she'd heard something about that happening before but she'd kept to S&S in her time here. Too many people at once were overwhelming, especially on top of a new job and a new town. Dammit, why wasn't she one of those extroverts who knew everyone within a month of moving somewhere?

"Are you suggesting having them sponsor the course?" Yanni looked thoughtful. "It could work. Though you might be able to sell it better with a co-teacher from the department."

"Not for a normal semester-long course," Josie said.

Marcia shot her a narrowed-eyed look. "What about an online course?"

Cazzi frowned. She'd never taught online and she worried it'd dull the empathy she wanted to emphasize in the class.

"What about Jan term?" Eva asked. "If they can teach classes about *Doctor Who* and Netflix I feel like they'd have a hard time throwing out a subject with solid real-world knowledge attached."

Jan Term was only a month long. Cazzi chewed her lip and then stopped herself. But it might be a good foot in the door.

"Good luck mandating a Jan Term class," Josie scoffed. "The whole term is optional."

"We'll cross the mandating bridge when we get to it," Yanni said, "Please keep a positive attitude, Josie. We're not here to shoot down out-of-the-box ideas."

Josie's lips went so thin they nearly disappeared. "I'm trying to keep things realistic. I haven't even brought up the paper-work it's going to take to get accounting to even approve her teaching as an adjunct while working full-time in another position."

"Another bridge we'll cross when we get there," Yanni said, her tone final. "Now, I think that gave Cazzi some good ideas to chew over," she looked at Cazzi who nodded. "So let's get back to the agenda and review our privacy policy for our new student workers here today. Everyone say hi to Matt and Linda."

The meeting went downhill from there. Josie changed targets again and Yanni did her best to rein her in but by Cazzi's estimate, the admin extended the meeting a good thirty minutes without saying anything constructive.

Afterward, Cazzi spent every free moment between student sessions wrestling with math and Microsoft Excel, two of her least favorite things. But dammit, the numbers didn't lie and she knew this class needed to be mandatory.

With barely twenty states requiring accurate sex education, most of the country was operating using a crapshoot of information gleaned from porn, rumors, the internet, and books. It made her sick with rage to think just having a better education could prevent so many sexual assaults, STIs, unwanted pregnancies, and abortions. And the shame. Oh, so much shame over sex, sexuality, and things done to people without their consent. Sex education could save people from so much of that. It had certainly saved her.

Tomorrow, thanks to about six calls and five voicemails to the department secretary, she had a meeting with the Gender Studies department. She hoped to hell they would sponsor her because her second choice was the Ethical and Philosophical Studies department (formerly the Philosophy department, formerly the Studies of Ethics and Philosophy department) and they could barely agree on what to call themselves let alone agree to take on a new sponsorship.

Between that and some of the issues she was helping her students work through during counseling hours, all she wanted to do was self-soothe by watching mindless TV with a carton of chocolate chocolate chip ice cream with chocolate swirls and some good weed.

Instead, she rode her bike to the studio, following directions from the address Patrick had texted her without comment. She tried not to read too much into his silence.

5

"*A thousand hands own me*
Two thousand watch me grow
I was never pure
No one thought this white stuff
was really snow

My name is in too many mouths
Heard too many people's doubts
They think they own me
For all I show
Nobody knows me

[chorus of voices]
Discontent rock star
Show us all your pretty scars
Feed us your pain
Without all the stains"
—"Temptation of the King" by User-Friendly Omega on *Suicide King*

Rohan threw the pen at the ceiling, hard enough that it stuck in the acoustic tiles, joining the other three. There were only so many times you could fuck with a track before you ruined it and they were getting pretty close with the four they'd come into the studio with.

"Ba-da-ba-daaa," he crooned to the ceiling, trying to find a topline melody that fit with the riff Rick was picking out on the keyboard. Maybe if he could find a melody he could find words that weren't about Angie.

"We need to work faster," Benji muttered, head in hands, elbows on the giant mixing board. Their computer rested on the laptop stand in front of them. It and Rick's computer did most of the work but no self-respecting studio lacked a mixing board—or a leather couch.

"Can't rush the process," Rick muttered from the keyboard, switching keys and trying an arpeggio. It sounded pretty but sparked nothing in Rohan.

"If you'd just let us—" Benji started.

"*No.*" Rohan snapped.

Benji groaned. Rick walked away. Probably for water or something.

Benji rolled their chair over. "We don't have the money to fuck around while you play Bob Dylan, Ro. We only have two weeks here. *Two weeks.* And we need eight more songs, mixed and ready to go."

"I know. Look, if we do a song a day and get it all mixed in six, we'll be fine," Rohan said breezily but his stomach clenched at the short timeframe.

"Then pull your head out of your ass and accept some damn help writing this album."

Rohan clenched his teeth. "I can do this."

"I'm not saying you can't. I'm saying you need help if you're gonna do this fast."

"I can do this!" Rohan snapped, standing up and pacing away.

"Should I come back later?" Cazzi paused in the doorway, Rick at her back, so close he was practically on top of her. Neither of them seemed to be uncomfortable with that.

Rohan exhaled hard and put on his good pop star smile. "No, no, I'm glad you're here."

She raised her eyebrows like she didn't believe him but put her tote bag down on the couch. She wore a nice coat and dressier black jeans, her Docs traded for professional ankle boots. Still no makeup but her hair was drawn back in a librarian-like bun, muting the purple streaks.

She looked a good five years older and much more intimidating, in a kinda hot uptight domme way until she sat down and gave him an encouraging smile. "Let's do this. Whatever this is."

"Why are you here?" Benji asked.

Rick perched on the arm next to her, crossed his arms, and glared at Benji.

"What?" Benji glared back. "It's a legit question."

"It is," Cazzi agreed, her voice smooth and even, same as her face. The therapy mask was back, both unnerving and somehow reassuring. She focused on Rohan. "Why am I here?"

Rohan swallowed, suddenly regretting his late-night epiphany. "I haven't come up with anything good all day."

"And how do you think I can help with that?"

"Um…"

She didn't move, her stillness both unnerving and comforting. Rohan's eyes ricocheted away from her, touching Rick's flat expression, almost like hers but less corporate, to Benji's bouncing foot crossed over one knee, to his own hands and the faint scar on his palm.

He remembered the gold sparkling on his skin, suspended in blood. He'd accidentally cut himself on the tip of the paperclip, rough from gouging his sigil into the gift Angie had given him. A gift he'd never quite liked but always wore because it made her happy.

He'd watched the blood well and drip in that studio she'd given him, where he'd write and write and she'd never listen. It had seemed oddly right to consecrate its rebirth in blood. The thought had felt as alien as the numb haze he'd been in. He'd wrapped his hand up and gone to spend the night at Benji's so he didn't have to be alone in that damn house that had never been his. He'd almost left her then.

"I can't stop thinking about her. Every time I try to write it comes out about her."

"So use it," Benji said, for about the tenth time that day.

"I told you I'm—"

"And I told you, fuck the high road. You know she's not gonna take it. Write your side and maybe we can beat her at her own game."

"Benji," Rick cut in. "Stop."

Benji glowered but stopped.

Cazzi cocked her head and looked at Rohan. "What are you hoping for out of the experience of making this album?"

"An album?" He shrugged.

She glanced at Benji and Rick then back at Rohan. Ugh, he couldn't read her at all. "Let's take a walk." All three musicians opened their mouths and she said, "Just five minutes. It doesn't seem like you're making much progress right now anyway." She smiled and stood up.

Rohan found himself standing too. Well, she wasn't wrong and he was curious. Maybe alone he could get behind her mask and see some of the real woman he'd caught glimpses of last night.

Benji sighed. "I'm gonna go to that Chipotle across the street, want anything?"

Rick stood and gave Cazzi an assessing look. She nudged him

and her smile took on another, deeper dimension. A conversation in gestures. He nodded and left with Benji.

Rohan and Cazzi were alone.

"Or we could just stay here," she said.

"Let's walk, I've been sitting all day."

She nodded, picked up her bag, and followed him out as he held the door for her. The air was biting cold outside and he pulled his hoodie around him, cursing his thin SoCal blood again.

Besides him, Cazzi hugged herself, her eyes hidden behind her sunglasses but a faint smile lingered on her lips and she turned her face to the breeze.

"Do you think I should make the album about her?" He asked her as they turned down a wide residential street. A few college-age kids were biking by, one of them filming. Rohan turned his face away as casually as possible.

"How would you feel if you did that?"

He bit down on his reflexively clever non-answer and thought. "I'm angry."

She nodded as if this was normal.

"If I make an album about my anger, I'll have to perform those songs for months, if not years."

"Are you afraid of hurting her or yourself?"

He shrugged. "I don't know. Both of us, I guess. I still care about her, you know? Just because it's over and I don't want it to start again doesn't mean I don't care."

"I get that," she murmured and the sadness in her voice said that she did.

"So how do I get her out of my head?"

She laughed and there was a bitter edge to it. "A lot of hard work."

"There isn't a shortcut?"

"Do you want one?"

He heaved an exaggerated sigh. "Is that a shrink thing?"

"What?"

"Answering questions with questions."

"I'm a student health counselor, not a therapist."

"What?" He stopped.

"Well, okay, I'm a counselor and assistant program coordinator of Wellness Education at Clementine College." She stopped too. "Did you think a therapist would just give her services away for free like this?"

"I..." He had. He felt like a dick.

She shrugged. "Not that I couldn't be. I have a Ph.D. but it's in human sexuality. My master's is in counseling psychology but I took a different path."

"So...should I call you Dr. Cazzi?" He joked.

She shot him a look over her sunglasses. "Does my advanced education intimidate you?"

He shook his head. "My mother's a doctor."

She nodded and they continued walking.

Silence stretched between them. "I never finished high school," he blurted. "I mean, I have a GED but after the band took off..."

She let the unfinished sentence hang in the air before asking, "Do you wish you had?"

He shrugged. "Angie never finished either. She's successful as hell."

"Why are you comparing yourself to her?" There was no heat to the question, just curiosity.

"I'm not."

"Is the album in reaction to her?"

Rohan opened his mouth to deny it. To lie, like he'd lied to himself for so long, telling himself he was just fine as he did everything he could think of not to cover up how distant Angie was becoming, how she was never home, how they weren't nearly as in love as they were supposed to be.

The lie tingled in his tongue. Letting it go felt like giving up but he'd already done that, hadn't he?

He realized he was gripping his amulet tightly, the rough edges of the carving bringing him down to earth. He noticed her looking so he released his grip. "I didn't mean it to be," he said finally. "I don't want my comeback to be based on her, not when it's launching our label. We didn't start Now or Never Records just to prove we still have talent. We're by artists, for artists, not a bunch of suits screwing us over for profit. So everyone who's thinking about signing is gonna be watching to see how my album succeeds."

"Patrick told me about it. That's a lot of pressure."

He shrugged. "That's business. So it can't be about her. Especially since she just kneecapped our production."

She nodded. "Understandable, but four years is a long time. The person you are is irrevocably influenced by her. I'm sure it's the same for her. You contain echoes of each other and those years, good and bad."

"We are echoes of each other. Reverberating forever." Though he doubted he echoed as much in Angie's brain as she did in hers.

"Another line for a song you'll never use?"

"I don't want to be just an echo of her. I'm more than that," he said, frustrated. "Is it hopeless to write about something that isn't this?"

She shrugged. "I'm not an artist but I suspect this will overshadow everything for a while. You have to process it or it will never leave you."

"Getting under someone to get over her won't work?" He gave her a sexy grin, just to see if it would even work. It was good to flirt without feeling guilty.

Her cheeks were pink but whether it was from the cold or him was up for debate. "I wish," she said. "It would've made my life a lot easier."

Something about the way she said that bothered him. "Who

broke your heart? Because I'm pretty sure Rick would happily kill them."

Her laugh was far too bitter for the question. "This isn't about me and you know it. I am not your muse and I am not your quick fix." She turned to him, stopping. "You seem nice enough and I'm happy to help in what little way I can, but don't become dependent on me. This is something you and only you can work through. And whether that's through song or therapy or both is up to you." She shrugged. "As is whether any of or how much of your processing is public. You can't control what she'll do. You can only control how you respond."

"That's the thing though." He scuffed his shoe on the concrete, feeling like a child. "Sometimes I feel like I can't control myself when it comes to her."

"Oh?"

"Not like that. I'd never hurt her," he said hurriedly. "I just— It's really hard to be without her approval, you know?"

"She's charismatic."

"You've met her, it's more than that. It's worse and better all at once. Star power to the hundredth degree. Loving her is like worship and man, she is vengeful."

"Sounds like more lyrics." She started walking again and he followed her.

"It's like purging, talking about her."

She raised her eyebrows.

"Oh come on, I'm a celebrity. I know how people stay thin."

"Is being with her like binging?"

He thought about it, his body hot and flushed remembering the heady good days. "In the best way when it's good. Overwhelming and just as sickening when it's bad."

"You're still using the present tense."

His lips twisted in an almost smile. "It doesn't feel real yet. But it will be. I'll get to past tense."

"You don't want to try and work it out?"

"You don't know how many times I've tried. I can't. Not anymore." He shook his head. "Anyway, I feel better. Lighter. Free, you know?"

She nodded and they rounded the last corner, the nondescript facade of 929 Studios came into view. He hadn't been lying about feeling better but the sudden looming end of their walk made him feel worse all over again.

Rick and Benji were crossing the street, take-out bags in hand. Rick watched them. Benji nodded at them but seemed more interested in getting back to the studio, head down, hood up. They must've been recognized at Chipotle. Benji hadn't been comfortable with fan interactions since they'd gone public as non-binary. Too many people either telling them how wrong they were or thanking them with their trauma stories.

Cazzi waved, smiling.

Rick waved back, a smile kicking up the corner of his mouth.

Her smile widened but she said, "What's up with Patrick?"

"What?"

"He's being distant and weird. Is he okay? Did he say anything to you?"

Rohan looked at her. "Um, honestly I couldn't tell. Want me to ask him for you?"

She laughed. "Thanks, but I'm an adult. I can ask him myself." She chewed her bottom lip as she said it. He realized he was staring at her lips and dragged his gaze away before she noticed.

Angie chewed her bottom lip when she was stressed. She always checked the habit, stopping before she took off her lipstick.

"What's going on with the two of you, really?"

Cazzi sighed. Her mask slipped and the way she looked at Rick reminded Rohan of the way he used to lose his breath every time Angie came into the room. That sheer, hopeful longing like the breathless raw burn of overworked lungs.

Then her mask returned. "Worry about your album. We can take care of ourselves."

She sped up and met Rick, smiling. Even where Rohan was, he could see Rick's smile stutter, just for a moment.

That too reminded him of Angie. And a whole different kind of hurt.

––––––––

CAZZI CAUGHT the flicker in Patrick's expression and honed in on it, all of her training going into overdrive in the exact way her professors had warned her not to allow. *Learn to turn it off,* they'd said, *don't analyze the people in your life. You won't like what you see. You'll overthink every little microexpression, every little lie.*

But with Patrick, she couldn't help it. She'd been watching him for too long with hope in her eyes. The training just helped her figure him out better. So why had he grimaced, just for a second, at seeing her coming towards him?

She filed the question away for later, drawing level with him. He handed her a burrito and she knew it'd be exactly the way she liked it. She put it in her bag with a smile.

Benji nodded to her and veered off to talk to Rohan.

Patrick cocked his head in Rohan's direction. "How is he?"

She exhaled. "Once he accepts that he can't wish the grieving process away, he'll be fine. Grieving but fine."

"You okay supplying free therapy?" His brow furrowed like he was remembering the times she'd drained herself dry doing volunteer therapy during her master's program.

She shrugged. "For now. I'm not going deep. I do wanna help, but I can't fix anything. I can only help the process along."

"Mm." But there was the faint impression of a frown around his lips.

"How about you?"

"Me?" He looked at her like he hadn't expected the question. Or maybe he hadn't expected her to ask.

"How are you doing? This seems stressful."

He shrugged. "You?"

Deflection.

She narrowed her eyes. "I'm fine."

"You seemed stressed."

"Long day." It was her turn to shrug like her stomach wasn't slowly snarling itself into knots.

"Well, you can go home now."

She frowned. "Do you want me to go home?"

"What do you want?"

"I want you to actually talk to me." They were in the studio lobby now, Benji and Rohan already off in the recording room but she still kept her voice down.

He blinked. "Huh?"

"You're avoiding me."

"I'm right here."

She took a deep breath. Held it. Exhaled. "You're deflecting my questions and you literally ran away and hid in my yard but still haven't told me why. Patrick Marcus Jones, you are avoiding me and you damn well know it."

He crossed his arms. "I'm at work right now."

"I'm doing a lot of emotional labor for your boss, and by extension, you. The least you can do is give me a straight answer."

"He's my business partner, *not* my boss and I didn't ask you to do anything. I'm not happy about this either." He fidgeted. She could almost see the shape of the truth as he danced around it.

"Why?"

"I'm worried about you."

He cares, she reminded herself and her twisting stomach, *it's not pity.* "Why?"

"I always do. Because," he lowered his voice. "Of what happened to Tanya."

She flinched, fingers going cold as her brain cycled through its escape options. *Flight. Fight. Freeze. Fawn. Fight. Flight. Freeze—* She squashed it. "Unless there is something you haven't told me about your friends, this has nothing to do with that."

"It's not them."

"Oh?" She breathed deliberately, as slowly as she could.

"It's—I'm worr...forget it. I'll tell you later."

She closed her eyes and pressed her first level calming sigil until the urge to scream died. When she opened them, Patrick was staring at her fingers. She pushed her sleeve up deliberately, showing him all the sigil tattoos marching up her arm.

"Those are new."

"No, Patrick. They are not," she ground out. "They're about a year and a half old."

It was his turn to flinch. "I thought you preferred to draw them on."

"I needed something more permanent."

"Caz, I—"

"Tell me about the kiss, Pat. What was that about?"

"I'm not talking about that here."

She nodded. It was reasonable. She was reasonable. So reasonable if she dealt with deities she'd be praying for patience.

The urge to run, to hide, to scream scrambled her thoughts.

She nodded again, her fingers playing up her arm and tracing the next sigil on her arm. *It is my will to quell my trauma response and see the situation with clear eyes.*

The scrambled thoughts retreated and she looked at Patrick again. There was agony in his expression. He said he was worried and she knew he still sometimes treated her feelings with kid gloves even after all these years. Her traitorous brain wondered if there was pity buried under all that.

No. Patrick would never stoop so low as to pity her.

"I'm going home," she said. Her voice was false, a deep-fake version of herself. There were three doors and a hallway, she'd clocked them the moment she'd entered. She counted them again, grounding herself. "Call me when you're ready to talk."

"Wait!" Rohan jogged down the hall. "Can you just stay for a moment? I need—"

"I just got her to leave," Patrick snapped, cutting him off. Then his words registered. Horror dawned on his face.

He was blocking the front door. If he touched her, she'd lose it completely. She moved towards it, trying to skirt him.

"Caz…" Patrick moved with her, blocking the exit. His eyes were full of worry, of fear, of pity.

No, no, noooo.

"What? Why?" Rohan demanded.

She glanced at the second door, the one to her left and the closest. It read "Studio 2" in small letters by the door. No exit. Her stomach tried to climb up her esophagus and she forced it down.

"Cazzi, is everything okay?" Rohan came closer, blocking her in.

Trapped. They were trapping her. Locking her in. With their pity and their words and what happened to Tanya.

No.

Cazzi hit the third door faster than she could think. Self-preservation won over sigils and she ran.

<hr>

Rohan had a second of clarity as Cazzi sprinted out the side door and it was this: He needed her or he was never going to finish this album. It wasn't a rational thought, but it was compelling. One look at Rick's frozen face and Rohan dashed after her.

The side door led out to a smoking patio just big enough for a table with an ashtray and surrounded by tall white stucco walls for privacy.

Cazzi stood in front of the far wall, breathing hard. Rohan skidded to a stop by her, purposefully in her eyeline so as not to startle her. Angie reacted badly to being startled.

She didn't look at him but her fingers flexed and he caught a glimpse of spidery line work tattooed on the inside of one arm.

"Hey," he said, trying to sound casual and not at all winded. "Wanna talk?"

She looked at him, her eyes wild. He knew that wildness, he'd seen it when Angie had one of her flashbacks. Except with Angie, he'd be already drowning in her remembered horror and grief before he'd even gotten this close. This was trauma, but it was trauma contained.

For how much longer remained to be seen.

"No." Her voice was brittle but calm. She looked at the wall again. It was half again as tall as her. Smooth as stucco could be.

"Alright. Can I help?"

"No." She hesitated. "Yes. Go away."

"I don't know if that's a good idea." He didn't like the way she eyed the wall. Angie was erratic when she was in her flashbacks. He'd come home to destruction, frantic cleaning, massive fights, and once a few suspiciously straight, even cuts on her arm she'd claimed came from a broken glass. Anything she needed to do to feel in control.

"I'm fine."

"You're about as fine as I am, if not worse."

"Don't make this about you."

"Cazzi." He reached out slowly.

She backed away, all the way to the door.

"Shit," he pulled back his hand. "I'm sorry."

Then he reeled out of the way as she came barreling towards him, only to hop onto the patio table and launch herself onto the top of the wall. She landed on her belly with an audible grunt.

"Jesus!" He stumbled towards her. "Caz, are you okay?"

She hooked a leg over the wall. Raised her fist in a thumbs-up and rolled off the top of the wall.

Rohan stared aghast until he heard the muffled thump and rustle from the other side. He dashed back through the studio. Rick caught his urgency and followed without a word, passing him in a desperate burst of speed.

They rounded the side of the studio and there was the wall and the flattened bushes. But no Cazzi.

Rohan stopped dead, Rick spinning in place, looking for her.

"What the hell is going on?" Benji pounded up, panting. "Goddammit, I barely smoke anymore, why do I still run like a smoker?"

"Rick freaked out Cazzi and she scaled the wall like a fucking action hero."

"She did a runner?" Benji whistled. "Over that? What did you *say* to her, Rick?"

"Does it matter? She might be hurt!" Rick snarled.

Rohan and Benji stared at him, shocked. In over a decade of friendship, Rohan had never heard him raise his voice in anything that wasn't song.

Rohan scanned the area. No sign of her.

"Is that her bike?" Benji pointed at the lone bike locked to the rack by the front door.

Rick groaned, phone to his ear. "She isn't picking up."

"Well, she probably went home," Rohan said, trying to be calm even though his mind spun off into much worse scenarios. He channeled his mother and thought as logically as he could. "We'll split up. Benji, you stay here in case she comes back. Rick, you go to her house and I'll loop around, see if I can find her in the neighborhood."

Rick shook his head. "If we chase her she'll just freak out more. Besides, she doesn't want to see me."

"So you suggest we wait to see if she turns up injured somewhere?" Rohan snapped. "I'm not going to stand by just because you had a spat and you're too up your own ass to apologize."

Rick took a step forward. "You know nothing about her. Nothing about us."

Rohan swore and turned away, walking fast. He'd had a song brewing in his head since the walk but it would have to wait.

"Where are you going?" Benji demanded.

"Exactly where I said I would," Rohan snapped, getting in his car. The engine purred to life.

But he didn't circle the neighborhood. He went straight to her house.

6

"*You run fast*
You run far
Run while the blood is still warm
Run from the coming storm
Alone and unwanted
Sing along with the rasp of the haunted

When Daddy's a corpse
And Mommy's the knife
You're raised by the radio man
Who's wrong when it's right

I love that man
Who would destroy me
I love that voice
That darkens my soul
Oh, I love him
I love him
I...
loved him"

—"Radio Man" by Angela Alice on *Murder Baby*

Cazzi hurt. All over. The adrenaline had burned off with all the running, and dragging herself home was agony. Every thump of her bag against her side, of her feet on the pavement was a dull flare of pain.

It wasn't like her to get this reactive this badly, this fast. Not in a long time.

But it's not like you and Patrick have spent much time together in a long time.

She shut the thought down, just like she'd shut down any thoughts about why she was so reactive. She was less than a block away from a bath and smoking a bowl of indica with high CBD levels. She could break down then.

There was a car parked in front of her house. Nice but not flashy. The last time she'd seen it, it'd been parked next to the gothest Tesla money could buy.

Which meant…

Yep, there he was. Sitting on her porch, alone.

Oh, that hurt more than the full-body bruise of her fall. Patrick hadn't come to check.

Rohan had. Because Rohan thought she was useful.

This is what she got for doing favors for friends of friends. *A friend would've come and found you. So would a significant other.*

Tears warmed her eyes.

She slapped her hand over her sigils, the magic and pain blending together until the urge to cry died. She said nothing as she climbed the porch, trying not to wince as her hips and legs and back complained.

He stood but matched her silence until she fumbled out her key and put it in the lock. "You scared me shitless."

She shrugged. "You can't come in."

"You're hurt. Bruised, if not worse."

She paused at the authority in his tone. Then remembered. "Doctor's kid, right."

"I have first aid training."

She narrowed her eyes. "You think I don't?"

"I think you do, so you know you need help."

"The 'help' of a strange man is the last thing I need."

He dropped his gaze. "How much do you know about Angie?"

She took stock, realizing she couldn't move fast enough to keep him out of her house if she made a break for it. If she sat down on her outside reading chair and waited him out she didn't think she'd be able to get up again. "I've heard her on the radio. She's a Satanist. Maybe a witch."

His eyebrows jumped at that last observation but said, "Her father was murdered and she was the one who found him."

Damn. "That seems private." But it explained a lot.

"Nothing about Angie is private." There was a bitter twist to his words. "Not if she can use it."

"Fine. So she has trauma. My condolences."

"Yeah. So I know an episode when I see one."

She went cold.

Oblivious, he continued. "I'm not gonna ask about it but please, let me help. We both know you might have a concussion and anyone can see bending down is going to hurt if it doesn't already."

She met his eyes. They were earnest. He meant his words but that wasn't what made her open the door. It was the helplessness and old guilt buried behind it. He would help her because he couldn't help his ex. That was enough insurance for her.

Cazzi opened the door and motioned for him to follow her in, barely containing her wince as her shoulders and arms protested the sudden movement.

He stood up slowly, not crowding her, the relief in his face almost painful to watch.

ROHAN FOLLOWED Cazzi into her house as closely as he could without panicking her again. He wouldn't put it past her to slam the door in his face.

He stood awkwardly as she closed the door and limped towards what looked like the bathroom. She moved gingerly like she'd aged half a century in the fall over the wall. It took all his years of media training to keep his face unchanged when he'd seen her. Blood was drying along her hairline, mingling with the leaves and dirt in her hair. One knee of her dressy jeans was ripped and her ankle boots were scuffed. She took her coat off, slowly but not slow enough, judging by the set of her jaw.

He grabbed it from her, hanging it over the six other coats hanging off the hook by the door. It barely stayed.

Under her coat, she wore a black top with a wide neck and drapey sleeves. Very witchy. *Hmm.*

She pushed her sleeves up, revealing lines of symbols climbing up her forearms.

He studied them, noting the bruises blooming and the cuts scabbing over the tattoos. "Sigils?" He asked, surprised and excited. He rarely saw sigils in the wild, especially ones he didn't recognize, and that made them more fascinating. She either created them herself or they were really obscure. He wanted to trace them until he could figure out exactly what they meant but he kept his hands to himself.

Her gaze jerked up to meet his, eyes narrowed.

"Did you use the Austin Osman-Spare method?" He asked. There were no recognizable pictorial shapes in the designs so he suspected they were built out of letters—phrases really if you got down to it. He didn't see it much and it was his favorite method.

She cocked her head like she was waiting for the other shoe to drop. "You know sigils?"

He hesitated, common sense catching up with his enthusiasm.

This wasn't a normal thing for a pop star to be into, the internet trolls would have his head if they found out. Not that anyone thought he was normal anymore, they were all certain Angie corrupted him.

Cazzi tugged her sleeves back down.

For some reason that really bothered him. He drew his pendant out from under his shirt before he could think too hard about what could happen if this landed in the media. "I have one too."

She grabbed the pendant, too fast and too hard, yanking him to her until his head hovered over hers. He could smell her hair, something citrusy and nice.

"You made this yourself?" She traced her finger over the sigil etched on the front. Given the way he'd scratched it into the gold, it wasn't a shocker she'd figured it out.

"Yeah." His voice came out hoarse. He hadn't expected it to be so distracting to be able to feel the warmth of her without actually touching.

"You used Osman-Spare too," she murmured, flipping the gold disk over, and inspecting the Seal of Solomon on the other side. That had been the original design but it didn't hold as much meaning as the sigil he'd created. Angie gave it to him because she knew he liked sigils and it looked cool.

His neck was not happy about this angle but he couldn't quite bring himself to step away. "Yeah."

"Hm."

"You're a chaos magician?"

"Sigil witch," she corrected him. "Worked at an occult store throughout undergrad. Know a little bit about a lot. You?"

"I like symbols." That was an understatement. He'd been obsessed with symbols since he was a kid. He'd even helped design the Beatboyz logo. Well, the base idea was his but they'd polished until he could barely see his fingerprints on it. Story of his life.

He wrapped his fingers around his sigil, touching her fingers in the process. They both went still. There was no spark, but an intense sharpening of awareness. The warmth of her fingers burned, the hitch in her breath echoed in his ears, the scent of her hair wrapping around him.

He let go abruptly. Her fingers spasmed on the disk then released. He straightened slowly. "First aid kit?"

"Bathroom, under the sink." She gestured down the hall but didn't move, looking suddenly drained.

The bathroom was small, with a blue sink and a short tub lined with essential oils.

"Green box, left side." She said, appearing behind him when he got there. "Thank you."

He nodded. The cabinet was a mess of bottles and bathroom stuff but the box was stashed on top for easy access. "Sit." He pointed at the closed toilet.

Sighing, she did so and winced. He grabbed some alcohol wipes and went about cleaning the abrasions he could see. She stiffened at his touch but relaxed as he kept his movements purely medicinal. She didn't complain either, even though they both knew it stung.

He checked her pupils and ran his fingers over her head, checking it for tender spots. Her hair was soft and fine but he didn't dwell on it. Her eyes were half-lidded when he was done but that was probably fatigue.

"Can I check your back?"

Her eyes snapped all the way open, her gaze inspecting his face like she could cut him open and dissect his motives with just her sight. "Understand that I will hurt you again if you make me feel threatened."

"Understood."

She searched his face again before nodding and turning her back to him, raising her shirt.

He sucked in a breath. Her left side was mottled with

blooming deep blue bruises extending over her back, hip, and ribs. He could make out another tattoo written in white ink along the back edge of one hip, but there was too much bruising to tell what it was.

She handed him a tube of arnica cream. "I know, I turn fun colors fast."

"What, this? Merely a flesh wound." He rubbed some cream in as gently as he could but she still hissed.

"Watch it, black knight or I'll bite your kneecaps off." She squeezed her eyes shut. "Just do my back. I'll get the rest."

"I'm going as lightly as I can. Also, I think that's my line." Not that getting a Monty Python reference perfect really mattered right now.

"Yeah, yeah." She took the tube back, dropping her shirt into place. "Run along now. You have an album to agonize over."

"I can't write it without you," he blurted.

Her expression was incredulous. "Yes, you can."

He shook his head. "I need you."

She sighed. "You need me as much as you need another four years with your ex."

"No. Unlike her, you're good for me."

She frowned. "You know this isn't romantic, right?"

"I'm not threatening the torch you're holding for Rick, don't worry."

"Just checking. This is getting real fixated, you know."

He held out a hand and helped her stand up. "Go sit somewhere comfy and tell me where your anti-inflammatories are."

"Thanks but I got a bowl and a bath calling my name. I don't need help for that."

"Wait, you're a stoner?"

She rolled her eyes. "Yes. If I give you a hit, will you leave?"

"I'm driving."

"Oh. Right. Offer rescinded." She headed to the kitchen.

"Look, will you come in tomorrow?"

"To the studio?" She looked at him like he was crazy. "Did you not see my back? Did you not just see me have a fucking breakdown?"

"Yes, but—"

"Go." But she pointed at the couch. "Sit there and write a fucking song. I am going to smoke my bowl on the patio. If you bother me, I will kick you out."

"But—"

"Rohan." Her anger was nothing compared to the firestorm of Angie's rage, but it was potent. Worse, it was cold and it was final.

He sat. She tossed him a pad of paper from some hotel and a pen. She pulled down a neatly labeled jar full of bud and a futuristic-looking black vape. She cleaned and refilled it with the ease of a habitual stoner.

He stood up. "What if I cook for you?"

"What?" She stared at him through the kitchen cutout.

"I'm good," he said. "I won a cooking show."

"Patrick made me watch it with him."

"Oh." For some reason, this was a shock. "Well, then you know."

"Uh-huh," she rolled her eyes.

He walked into the kitchen. "So what do you like? Any dietary restrictions?"

"You're serious?"

"Well, yeah." He filled a mug with water from the pitcher on the counter and handed it to her. If she was gonna smoke she might as well be hydrated.

"Look, man," she said, taking the glass. "All I want right now is sugar and chocolate. If I decide I want real food, there's a very crushed burrito in my bag. You don't have to keep trying to bribe me." She took a sip, paused, and downed the rest.

"Please," he said, "moving helps me think. Cooking will be good for both of us, trust me."

She shrugged, handing the mug back. "Knock yourself out."

Then she brushed past him, going out the glass patio door and lighting up. She closed her eyes with the first inhale, opening them as she exhaled, her pale eyes picking up the glow of the sunset. Her gaze gleamed like a dragon's as the faint smoke billowed out of her mouth.

Dammit, but he did always like his girls scary pretty.

She's not for you, you just got out of a relationship, remember?

He shut the thought down. He was fine and he definitely wasn't attracted to her.

"Don't stare." She stuck her head through the door. "Write, cook, whatever. Just don't stare."

She slammed the door. The sound cut through the room, clean and clear. The room had good acoustics. He hummed to himself, enjoying the way his voice sounded in the space. He poked around the kitchen, smiling at the well-stocked baking cabinet. He pulled out a pan and some non-stick spray.

He could feel the words forming so he put his recording app on and turned on the oven. Then he sang:

> *Eyes in sunset*
> *This is what you get*
> *Smoke on your tongue*
> *Words in my lungs*

He played with the rhythm and cadence before writing it down. Still humming, he pulled out stuff he'd need. He didn't know the recipe off the top of his head, but he remembered the ratios and brownies were forgiving.

> *Blank faced*
> *Full of thunder*
> *Ready to strike*
> *Fight or flight*

Never surrender

By the time he had those words down, his chocolate and butter mix was melted and cooling.

You're not my muse
You're not amused
I've got no excuse
And nothing to lose
When I say when I say
I need you

Bruised and battered
Hop the wall
Leave me scattered
Ready to fall

The other ingredients were almost done, he stirred in some cinnamon and cardamom and tested the temperature of the chocolate and butter. Still too warm. He opened the freezer and found a place for the little pan amongst her truly impressive ice cream collection.

Torch in hand
You'll fight for your man
Do what you will
Tell me I don't need you still

Run away with your
Words sliding like swords
Through my thoughts
Leave me lost

He mixed everything up and poured it into the pan. On a

whim, he sprinkled the top with shredded coconut and tossed the whole thing in the oven. Cazzi was still on the porch, the smoke she exhaled barely visible anymore.

Something about her tugged at him. There was such strength in the way she picked herself back up. Maybe he could learn that from her because right now he was crumbling at the edges. Now that the brownies were in and he had space to breathe, he could feel pieces of him trying to break down.

It twisted his stomach, making his hands shake. He wanted to go beg some pot off her, anything to make these feelings go away. The life he built was over. He left the person he assumed he'd stay with. He'd—he'd—

He went to Cazzi's bag and pulled the smashed burrito out, putting it in the fridge for something to do. It hadn't exploded, luckily. But now he had nothing else to do. So he cleaned up his baking mess, doing her dishes and his before wiping down the counters.

Cazzi was still out there. Did she think he would leave if she stayed out there long enough? The words were back and he sang them to her because she wasn't looking at him.

You're not my muse
I'm not amused
And I've got no excuse
And nothing to lose
Trust me when I say
I need you

Please Caz
Keep me sane
And I'll promise
To do the same.

He wrote the words down and slapped the page against the glass.

She got up. Came close enough to peer at the words in the dying light. Her eyes tracked over the lyrics and he felt self-conscious. This was the second song he'd shown someone raw without hours of picking and fixing it. The first was yesterday when he'd sung his heart out and ad-libbed the song that had been brewing in him since talking to Cazzi.

She finished and her eyes came up to meet his. There was something raw and startled in her gaze. She opened the door and crossed her arms, standing in the doorway.

"That was some gorgeous emotional manipulation."

"You bring it out of me."

"Save the lines."

"This is real." He tapped the page. "Can't you tell?"

"I'm a sex educator, not a lie detector." Though she watched him carefully, some of the tension left her shoulders.

Just because it's real doesn't mean you're not manipulating her, his conscience whispered.

"And dammit Jim, I'm a doctor, not a bricklayer, but that's not the point."

"The fact that you keep getting all my references is more worrying than attractive." But there was a bit of a smile around her mouth. "It just means I'll need to get more obscure."

He grinned. "Surely, you don't think I'm doing this on purpose."

"Frankly, I don't care if you are." She took a toke. Held it, exhaled away from him and the open door. "Just don't call me Shirley."

GODDAMN, that smile. It was compounded by the pot until it shone through Cazzi, curling through her belly like lust. She had known on some intellectual level he had dimples. Now those dimples carved into his cheeks, plumping his cheekbones and making him look like a young Shahid Kapoor in the Bollywood rom-coms she'd used to watch in high school. Those dimples were killing her.

But that was just the pot.

And it was the pot saying, "Sing it to me."

Rohan's smile slipped, knocked loose by surprise. "What?"

She nodded at the paper in his hand. "If you're going to manipulate me, do it properly."

"Oh." His smile reformed, shy and sweet and real.

Shy? The Beatboyz sold out stadium world tours. She had the DVD of their tour album *Tomorrow Morning—Live in Australia!* to prove it. Granted she'd only watched it once. It never got normal seeing Patrick slotted into the exaggerated persona they'd designed for him in the band. Sure, he was quiet but he wasn't some cutesy timid creature. But then again, Rohan wasn't the adorable baby brother type they'd made him out to be either.... Adorable was not the word she'd use for the way he looked with his hands tucked in the pocket of his faded, tight jeans, his curls tumbling over his dark-fringed hopeful eyes.

The thought of Patrick, of the things he'd said tugged at her but she pushed them aside. She'd look at them later when she broke down.

Rohan gestured to her to sit on the couch and she did. Her body was looser than expected and she almost flopped right off the damn cushions. Also, did it smell amazing in here or was she really really high? "Impress me."

The microwave timer beeped. "Hold that thought." He went to the oven and pulled out a pan. The intensifying aroma of chocolate made her nearly float off her seat like a cartoon character.

"Never mind, I'm already impressed," she said before she could think better of it. She sat up on her knees to see the cooling pan better. "Are those brownies? Can I have some?"

He ducked his head through the cutout to flash his dimples at her. "They have to cool."

"How dare they?" She leveled a mock-serious glare at the pan.

He laughed. "I guess I'll just have to entertain you while we wait." It was a good thing he was turning off the oven as he said that because she felt her entire face go hot as her brain went straight to the gutter.

Fuck, she definitely smoked too much. "I guess you'll do," she said as loftily as she could. "But I'll have you know I've hosted many Bad Movie Nights in this very living room and our last one was *Snakes On a Plane*."

Rohan laughed. "And now you expect me to compete with those motherfucking snakes on that motherfucking plane?"

No, he definitely wasn't adorable. Even when the band's brand evolved some edginess, he'd been the good one, the golden child. God, he wasn't golden now.

"Look, Sam Jackson and those snakes carried that movie."

He smiled distractedly as he studied his lyrics.

"Do you sing without music much?"

He shook his head, still looking at the lyrics. "Been a while."

"You don't even sing to yourself, like when you're doing stuff?"

He shrugged. "I spent so long protecting my voice that I fell out of the habit."

"You and Angela didn't break out into impromptu duets?"

The ease went out of his expression, tension drawing the lines of his shoulders sharp against his sweatshirt. "Not in a long time."

"Hmmm." She nodded. Hadn't they done a duet way back when? She seemed to remember hearing it on the radio.

"Do you and Rick sing?"

She shook her head. "That kind of thing doesn't happen a whole lot when you don't see each other in person for a while." But they used to before Patrick went professional and moved into the band house.

"Do you sing?"

She laughed. "Sure. Just for fun."

"What do you sing?"

She giggled. That was definitely the pot. "I think you're stalling."

"Maybe." He smiled.

"Come on, sing, pretty boy." Oops. Shit.

"Oh, I'm pretty, am I? Are you sure you didn't have one of my posters?"

She rolled her eyes. She owned all the Beatboyz albums and movies complete with foldout posters, bought to be a supportive friend, but he didn't need to know that. "You know what you are. Are you going to sing or not?"

"Eyes in sunset," he crooned, his voice clear and melancholy. Not at all like the glossy auto-tuned version from the band's records. It rose out of him and filled out the room until everything seemed brighter, dreamlike. He met her gaze, transfixing her, his voice a hook in her belly, begging her to lean closer. "This is what you get."

The melody was simple and he had to break her gaze to read the lyrics but, damn, it was potent. If he were trying to get her into bed, she'd be fucked and happy about it.

When he sang "Please Caz…" it was a moan and she dug her fingers into the couch cushions to keep from reaching for him.

When he finished, she clapped wildly, not even remembering to play it cool. "That was fucking great!"

"So you'll come back to the studio tomorrow?"

Oh hell. "Only if you either write about or journal about your breakup every day."

"Seriously?"

She frowned at him. "You need to get it out somehow."

"Can I just talk to you about it?"

"You know that's emotional labor, right?"

"I'll pay you."

She waved his words away but before she could respond, he said, "I'll help you with Rick."

She froze. "How?"

He shrugged. "If nothing else, I'll listen if you need me. Return the labor. Anything else, you just have to ask."

She thought of all the secrets that she carried, some hers, most other people's, heavy and acidic, slowly eating through her. She hadn't gotten a new therapist since she moved up here, an oversight of time, convenience, and a bit of denial. If she got a therapist, she'd have to talk about what happened to Tanya and about Patrick and how he'd shut her out of his life for over a year and a half, despite being her best friend.

She'd been doing a lot more pot lately.

"I also stress cook and I'd be happy to cook or bake for you." He handed her a brownie.

When had he gone into the kitchen? She'd zoned out more than she'd thought. That made her tense. She took a bite of still warm brownie. Her eyes slide closed of their own accord. Chocolate and spices bloomed in her mouth complimented by the crunch of toasted coconut. It was rich, complex, and fudgy as fuck. She stuffed another bite in her mouth to stifle her moan. "This is so good."

She opened her eyes to see him inspecting his brownie. He poked the middle and frowned. Then he took a bite, his eyes closing in thought. There was a smear of chocolate on his bottom lip. She couldn't stop looking at it.

Distance. She needed distance. She jerked her gaze away and said, "Tell me something about you and Angie."

He blew out a breath, opening his eyes. "Like what?"

"Whatever. Tell me something and I'll tell you something."

You're losing your objectivity, whispered her warning bells.

What objectivity? She thought back. She wasn't his therapist, she was...

"Are we becoming friends?" He asked. Then he licked the smear of chocolate away.

Oh *god*.

She was stronger than this. Surely, she was. "Do you want to be friends?"

He looked at her like he was weighing the answer. "I don't really know you."

"Yet you're in my house."

"You could be some kind of murderer."

She hid her wince with years of practice. "I am."

He laughed. "At least you're a murderer with a sense of humor."

She shrugged and half-smiled.

They looked at each other for a long moment.

"Angie is a force of nature," he said. "Literally. It's like she feels outside her body. Does that make sense?"

Cazzi cocked her head. The way people described things always fascinated her. It was a window into the way they thought.

Rohan tried again. "When Angie feels things, emotions, whatever, they... spill out of her. She's a fucking metaphor in action. Her anger makes you sweat, her disappointment makes you shiver. She can control the temperature of a room with just her mood. Her concerts are like worship. I didn't believe in magic before I met her."

"That's... a lot."

Rohan looked at her like no one had said that to him. "Exactly! It's too much."

"What made you stay?"

"I left, you know. Before. But there's a reason we're called stars. We have gravity, pull."

"Charisma." That must be what she was wrestling with right now. Nothing real, just star power. Maybe if she told herself that enough she'd believe it. It didn't matter. Momentary attraction had nothing on what she and Patrick had.

"More than that. People can't help but be drawn to Angie, they used to be the same way with me. With all of us in the band."

His words triggered memories of people pawing at Patrick, trying to drag him closer. On-screen, on tour, in public randomly. He'd been so relieved when the band fell apart.

"The good times were so good." Rohan didn't seem to be able to see her now, not with all those memories in his eyes. "I couldn't believe it was real. Everything had a sheen."

Cazzi hummed in agreement, thinking of before the banishment when she and Patrick would hang out and everything was glossy, hopeful.

"Is that love?" Rohan's question was half rhetorical, all vulnerable.

"I think so," she murmured.

"You're in love with him, huh?"

She choked on the answer, years of lies and denials damming off the truth.

He nodded. "For a long time?"

She covered her face for as long as she could stand, before scrubbing her hair out of her eyes. "Since I don't know when." Her voice was hoarse.

He sat down next to her. "Wow. That's commitment."

She laughed. "That implies I have a choice."

"Don't you?"

No. "There's always a choice." She smiled. "And I'm choosing to kick you out and go take a bath so I can walk tomorrow without crying."

He stood up, tucking the page of lyrics into his pocket. "So…?"

"So I'll see you in the studio after work."

He was smiling when he left. Her smile crumbled when the door closed and she relaxed the guards on her emotions.

Despite the cloud of pot and easing of the arnica, everything hurt, even her feelings. With her last ounce of willpower, she dragged herself to the bathtub with the pan of brownies. The tears started when she was naked and the water rose to engulf her.

They didn't stop for a long time.

"Oh tragic plastic, too many emotions
Life's easier when you don't feel
Here I've got just the thing
Take the edge off, make it numb
(Remember to breathe)
Ahh now, isn't that fun?

Look at me
I'm the perfect woman
Sleep like a baby
Never a bad day, never sad
PhenoBarbie Doll, the perfect bride
Take me home, just nine-ninety five"
—"PhenoBarbie Doll" by Angela Alice on *PhenoBarbie Doll*

Waking up the next morning was hell. She was achy, groggy from the high and the crying, and slightly nauseous from too many brownies. But the worst part was she dreaded seeing Patrick.

She never dreaded him before, but now the thought of seeing him was lead in her belly. If she had Rohan's number, she would've called and canceled.

The dread only intensified as she dragged herself through the day, holding on to normalcy as tightly as she dared. So far, nobody had noticed, because when she'd gone over the wall, she'd thought to shield her face and it had gotten by unscathed. Learning to fall in martial arts classes had paid off.

A finger tapped the back of her hand. "What the hell happened to you?" Eva asked, sidling up to her until they were pretty much breathing the same air.

Cazzi looked up from the copy machine. She had been making an absurd number of copies of handouts for a reason that seemed dire a minute ago and felt very distant now. "What?"

Eva tapped her hand again and Cazzi realized the bruise there had darkened to a very noticeable purple. Oh, and there was a scrape reaching halfway up her index finger. "Oh, that? You should've seen the other guy."

"Oh yeah? Who was that?"

"The first rule of Fight Club—"

Eva cut her off. "Spare me the lines. I swear to god, between you and my sister it's impossible to have a conversation without consulting IMDB."

"It just means we've got layers."

"*Monty Python* and rom-coms are not layers."

"That wasn't from *Monty Python* or a rom-com!"

"I know what it's from, I haven't been living under a fucking rock." She pushed up the sleeve of Cazzi's longest, drapiest top with a finger and sucked in a breath.

Cazzi pushed it back down as calmly as she could.

"Please tell me you had a particularly good night at that dungeon."

"I had a *great* night at the dungeon."

"Bullshit, you haven't been there since you dumped Craig. Don't lie to me."

"Well, you asked me—"

"Cazzi Muldoon," Eva's voice was low enough to qualify as a growl.

Cazzi sighed. "Let's take a walk." She checked the time. "I need to wake up before I talk to Gender Studies."

"YOU JUMPED A WALL?" Eva cried.

Cazzi grimaced. "More like fell off it."

"Are you okay? You could've died!"

"It was barely taller than me."

"Not the point and you know it." Eva shook her head. "Christ. And you met Benji Omega!"

"Who?" Cazzi asked.

Eva blinked at her. "Benji Nakamura. Benji Omega? User-Friendly Omega?" When Cazzi continued to look at her blankly, Eva said, "*Suicide King*? 'Fuck Me, I'm Beautiful?'"

Cazzi's eyes widened. "Oh. Ohhh!" *That* was who they were? She'd been into pop-punk as a teenager but User-Friendly Omega was too dark for her. That said, you had to be fully out of touch not to hear "Fuck me, I'm Beautiful" or know about *Suicide King*. The album was iconic like *Hybrid Theory* or *American Idiot* or *The Black Parade*.

"You're meeting all the celebs," Eva grinned. The expression slipped as quickly as it came through, her brow furrowing. "You never told me Patrick was a pop star."

"It never came up." She never told anyone.

Eva rolled her eyes. "Pop star or not, he sounds like an asshole."

Cazzi bristled. "Patrick is the best person I know."

"Yeah, well the best person you know sent you into a reactive state so bad you threw yourself over a wall to get away."

"It's not his fault, it's my trauma—"

Eva cut her off. "Which he knows all about, right?"

"I mean, yeah but…" Her stomach knotted. She couldn't find a way to finish that sentence.

Eva opened her mouth to say something then stopped herself. "I don't know, Caz."

"What? You don't know what?"

"You're going back to that studio again?"

She sighed. "Rohan asked me to."

"So you're enabling a codependent stranger and in the process putting yourself back into a potentially triggering situation. Voluntarily."

"No. I mean, it's not like that."

Eva shrugged. "You're an adult but I know what you'd say to a student who told you something like this."

"Fuck off."

Eva shook her head. "I'm not judging you. I'm here for you. You need to talk? I'm here. You need to hide in my basement because you're being chased by Angela fucking Alice and her posse from hell? It's yours."

"I don't think she has a posse from hell."

"I never know with you witchy types."

Cazzi laughed and it hurt. She'd bruised quite a few ribs.

Eva noticed. "Judit's got some bomb THC balm that kills pain like nobody's business."

"I'm not gonna take her pain balm, she needs that shit." Judit was something like the opposite of Eva's step-sister. Their parents had a son together, split up, and then had Judit and Eva with other people, all in less than a mile radius. They were raised halfway between cousins and sisters and coined the term "demi-sisters" to describe it. But most of the time they introduced themselves as sisters just to watch people squirm while they tried to figure out a polite way to ask if the two very different-looking women were related or not.

"Eh, she's got tons. She'd be happy to spare some."

"But she's moving in two weeks…"

"Sacramento is only twenty minutes away, it's not like she's moving across the country. Don't try to distract me." Eva's face was pinched. Judit had lived with her since she'd left home.

Cazzi smiled but the expression faltered. "Am I not seeing this clearly? Patrick's never been like this. I can't stop thinking about it, analyzing everything. I can't figure out where I fucked up."

Eva put her arm around Cazzi's shoulders and squeezed gently. "Honey, all I know about this guy is that he stopped talking to you for years because the first time you kissed him you had no idea he had a girlfriend."

"Eighteen months," Cazzi mumbled.

"Semantics." Eva waved it away. "Caz, you're punishing yourself for something that's clearly his problem. You might wanna think hard about that." She pulled a tube of concealer out of her pocket. "Marcia gave me this for your fingers. For your meeting with Gender Studies."

Cazzi bit back a groan. So much for nobody noticing. She slathered the concealer over the bruise on her finger and another one on the side of her hand she hadn't even noticed. The makeup was two shades too beige but it was better than nothing.

CAZZI THOUGHT hard about Patrick all the way to the Social Studies building. The minute she crossed the threshold she tapped her sigil for strength, chanting in her head. *It is my will to be strong and choose myself.* Patrick faded to the back of her mind and she recited her pitch silently as she searched for the office of Gretchen Mills, the Department Chair of Gender Studies.

Her research told her Gretchen was in her mid-fifties,

white, and a third-wave feminist who had been in a riot grrrl band in the 90s with a tiny cult following before becoming an academic. Cazzi wasn't sure that would help her, but the pictures from that time had been too tempting an internet rabbit hole. She'd lost a good thirty minutes to them and the article Gretchen wrote comparing the Olympia riot grrrl movement to the male-dominated NorCal punk scene of the same time. Besides that and the classes Gretchen taught (mostly graduate-level Gender Studies courses), Cazzi's tired brain hadn't retained much else.

She hoped it would be enough as she knocked on the doorway of Gretchen's open office. The woman herself sat at her desk, eyes on her laptop. She gestured Cazzi in without looking up.

Cazzi sat in the visitor's chair, taking the chance to study the other woman. Gretchen looked youngish for her age, her shoulder-length corkscrew blonde hair barely silvered and her crow's feet offset by her red glasses. Her office was decked out in old concert photos, posters, and overflowing bookshelves. Her desk was stacked with papers held down by a paperweight stamped with a pink female symbol with a fist in the circle.

Gretchen looked up from her computer and squinted at Cazzi. "You're not in my classes."

"I'm Cazzi Muldoon." She stuck out her hand. "Student Health Center, we had an appointment?"

Gretchen shook her hand absently. Her nails were blood red and chipped, her grip firm. "Right, right. The class proposal."

"That's me," Cazzi chirped and immediately felt ridiculous.

"Hmmm, let me find your email," Gretchen turned back to her computer. She hadn't read her proposal. Cazzi's stomach tightened, heat building.

"I have a printed copy if you'd like." Cazzi offered it.

Gretchen took it and adjusted her glasses, skimming. "Why do you want to teach this class, Ms. Muldoon?"

"The sexual assault, pregnancy, and STI statistics on page five—"

"I'm aware of the stats," Gretchen said. "But why you? Why not one of my teachers?"

Cazzi blinked. "I'm not averse to possibly teaming up with one of your professors but as far as I know, none of them have a PhD in Human Sexuality or a MA in Psychology."

Gretchen looked at Cazzi over the top of her glasses. "Very impressive but they all have something you don't: teaching credentials."

The heat in Cazzi's core threatened her cheeks. She smiled, breathing deliberately. The trauma patient in her wanted to cave, apologize for being difficult. "Is my lack of teaching credentials your only objection?"

"It's what first jumps to mind," Gretchen's gaze returned to the proposal. "I have enough trouble getting funding from the dean these days, not to mention the Academic Senate is gonna have a field day with how much this will rile up parents if we mandate it."

Cazzi recalibrated. She hoped the Gender Studies department would be an ally or at least not a roadblock. She had to keep this moving because if it stalled too long it might die. "If I get the dean and the Academic Senate to sign off on it, will you and the department sponsor my class?"

Gretchen sighed, taking her glasses off and rubbing the imprints they left on her nose. "I'm not trying to be your enemy here. I'm just seeing a lot of obstacles." She put the proposal down. "It's an important class. I would love to say 'Yes, teach it, mandate it!' But I learned a long time ago that academics is a lot more about politics than learning. And the Student Health Department? You're technically staff. Can't you just fold this into whatever you teach the kids during orientation?"

Cazzi tried not to be offended at the pity in the way she said 'staff.' "We already teach the basics of consent during orientation.

We get about forty-five minutes to cover that and all the sexual health topics we need to cram in. After five hours of orientation, do you think the students will retain enough to make informed decisions let alone counteract whatever harmful misinformation they've been taught in high school or at home?"

Gretchen grimaced. "Looking at your numbers and speaking from experience, no."

Cazzi nodded. "Would you be willing to sponsor my class if we got approval?"

Gretchen smiled tightly. "If you get the dean and the Academic Senate to sign off, Gender Studies will sponsor it." Her tone said she didn't expect Cazzi to be successful.

CAZZI FUMED on the way to the studio. Her mother was a researcher at UCLA so she should've known there would be politics like this. If she and her parents ever talked about anything real, she'd have picked her mother's brain. Hell, if she'd felt comfortable talking to Patrick's parents after he'd ghosted her, she'd have called them for advice. They were both tenured professors and it would've been invaluable to talk to them. His parents had practically been her second parents when they'd been growing up within a block from each other. Their moms had met during their Ph.D. program. She missed his parents, she realized. Them, Patrick's younger sister Sabrina, and his Nana.

Another thing you messed up with that fucking kiss.

She shook her head at the thought. The Jones family had no idea the kiss happened. Cazzi still got Christmas cards from them and Sabrina still texted her sometimes for sex advice. But Cazzi felt weird reaching out.

She had to drive today and she used the extra time that gave her to wrestle her bike into the trunk. She wished she'd had the piece of mind to ride it away yesterday. It made her feel more out of control that she hadn't.

When it was in her trunk and she couldn't stall anymore, she squared her shoulders, breathed deep, and tapped her lowest level calming sigil, chanting the mantra in her mind. *It is my will to be calm and collected.* A wave of ease spread over her, smoothing down the knots in her stomach and slowing her heart rate.

She hadn't decided if she wanted to talk to Patrick today but when she entered the studio, the decision was made for her. He looked up at her and his expression went flat, his shoulders going tight. "You're here to talk about yesterday." The dread in his voice was like swallowing crushed glass. A sure, slow, agonizing death.

"Actually, I'm not." She gave him her glossiest professional smile.

"Caz!" Rohan looked up, headphones half on, and gestured her over. "Thanks for coming!"

"We can talk later if you like," she murmured and left Patrick to whatever he was doing.

He nodded, but she knew it was only to appease her. The last thing Patrick ever wanted to talk about was feelings.

Rohan, meanwhile, gestured her over like an enthusiastic child. Even Benji, next to him, smiled. The minute she sat in the chair next to him, Rohan plopped a pair of giant noise-canceling headphones on her head.

He grinned, dimples flashing. They were just as killer as they'd been last night. *Damn.* "Ready?"

She could barely hear him but she nodded. He pressed play. A sparse, distorted guitar track started and Rohan's voice was crooning through the fog, singing about sunset eyes. She sat frozen as the track built in waves until Rohan's voice was exponential, soaring, and angelic.

It was rough but it was glorious.

It was about her.

The chorus was already hooked in her mind and her head

bobbed. But there was his voice, pleading with her name. The music curled around the line, bittersweet and aching.

She couldn't help it. She looked at Patrick. She'd listened to enough of his music to hear him in a voiceless phrase.

He watched her, gaze guarded. What had he thought about Rohan singing her name in the booth?

The petty part of her hoped he was jealous. The compassionate part hoped he'd understood nothing was going on. The petty part was louder.

She took the headphones off as the song ended and smiled up at Rohan. "That was awesome."

"You like it?" His joy was infectious and her smile became realer by the moment.

"Yeah. Do you have to use my name though?"

His smile dimmed. "Does it bother you?"

She shrugged, keeping her expression light. "I just try to keep a low profile is all." She doubted it would hurt her chances to teach the seminar but the idea of her name in any kind of media kicked up her anxiety.

"It fits nicely," Benji remarked. "Caz could be short for all kinds of names. Cassandra, Cassie, Casper, umm…"

"Castro?" Rohan supplied.

"Castro." Benji gave him a look with so much shade it could've qualified as an umbrella. "You're going to tell people you were singing to a Cuban dictator."

"I'm showing my political awareness," Rohan replied.

"Well," Benji said, putting down their headphones. "As long as you're showing depth. Now, will you be growing a beard for the music video, or will a cigar be enough?"

"Throw in a beret and one of those weird military jumpsuits, I wanna be subtle."

Cazzi laughed. "Okay, fine. You can use my name. Just don't dress up like Fidel, please."

"Why?" Rohan asked, "You don't think I can pull off a beard?"

"Someone's fishing," Benji muttered.

"I'm sure you can pull off whatever your little heart desires." She patted his shoulder. "But honey, tyranny doesn't look good on anybody."

Benji laughed. "Put that shit on a T-shirt."

"Thank you?"

"Hey, I'd wear it." They shrugged.

"Well, I'll call you when I need models for my line of pithy PC tees." She laughed. "Say that ten times fast."

Benji and Rohan looked at each other. "Pithy PC tees, pithy PC tees…" they intoned, in sync with perfect enunciation.

"Oh shut up." She rolled her eyes. "Show off later. You have an album to make."

"She's right," Benji stood up. "Me and Rick are going to mix this track. Do what you do, and get me some good shit. We need singles." They leaned down as they passed Cazzi and whispered loudly, "See if you can get him to show you that brilliant track he won't let me use."

Cazzi looked at Rohan, saw the way his shoulders tightened and his gaze slid away. "How are you doing today?" she asked when Benji was out of earshot.

He frowned. "I'm not thinking about it."

"Alright."

"How are you?" He touched her arm, fingers hovering over one of her worst bruises, hidden though it was by her shirt. But his eyes cut to Patrick, the real question unspoken.

She debated what to tell him. Now that she was here, sober and not reactive, the idea of their friendship felt murkier than ever. "Better. Though I ate far too many of your brownies."

He dipped his head until his gaze caught hers and held it as if he could see through the front she put up. She felt more seen by a man than she had in a long time. She shied away from the feeling. He was essentially a stranger. Someone who wanted her for what she could give him.

"I don't have to be okay," she said, bristling. "And you don't have to fix me."

"I wasn't trying to." His hand slid down to cover hers, the touch light, barely there. "But I promised I'd help, remember?"

She looked away. "I remember."

His other hand came up and pressed hers between his palms, still light, still gentle. "You fix me, I fix you."

"You can't save anyone, Rohan. Not me, not her."

"I wasn't trying to save either of you."

"Okay," she said. "Okay."

"And what was that about not being able to save people? Isn't that what you do every day?"

She shook her head. "You can't save people who don't want to be saved. You can only help them save themselves."

He scribbled something on the pad next to him. "So I supposed you're gonna want to hear that demo."

"The brilliant one you won't use?" She looked at him. "Do you want me to hear it?"

ROHAN WATCHED her as she listened to the song that had spilled out of him two days ago. Her eyes were closed, her brows knit tight in concentration. Her fingers moved unconsciously, flowing like a conductor's baton along to the music. He wondered idly if she'd had some dance training. There was something about the way her hands moved that was more than natural grace.

He could feel Rick's eyes boring a hole into him but Rohan couldn't stop watching her. She was so held together he had to pay close attention to catch her microexpressions and slips.

She took her headphones off, her lips pursed thoughtfully.

"What'd you think?"

"From a musical perspective or a psychological one?"

"Um, either?"

She paused, gathering her thoughts. Then she cocked her head and met his eyes. The compassion and empathy there made him both want to run away and melt into her arms. "It made me ache for you. It made me think about the people who have neglected me. But it also gave me hope. I want to have this song to listen to for my next heartbreak." Her eyes were distant and sad as she chewed her lip. "But I also see a lot of your relationship in it and I can tell it's very personal. If it were mine, it would never see the light of day."

"Because it's embarrassing?"

"Because of my own hang-ups. I hate people knowing my business. But I think, in your position, people would already know and I can see the benefit to controlling the narrative."

"So you think I should use the song."

She shook her head. "I won't make that decision for you."

A green metal to-go cup landed hard in front of the sound-board next to her.

They both looked up.

"Drink," Rick said, letting go of the cup and stepping back. "It'll help."

Rohan looked at Cazzi as Rick walked away. He expected her to be annoyed. He didn't expect her eyes to be sheened with tears.

CAZZI'S FINGERS closed around the cup. It was green, Patrick's favorite color if not his favorite shade. A little too neon, too metallic. The warmth of it soaked into her hands as she cradled it between her palms. She breathed in the complex aroma of herbs, too many to identify.

She took a sip. The temperature was perfect, not scalding but wonderfully drinkable. It was earthy but she tasted hints of turmeric, ginger, damiana, and lavender.

All the herbalism she knew, she'd learned from Patrick, and

she knew turmeric and ginger were for inflammation, damiana for the pain, and lavender was for relaxing tense muscles and nerves. In short, everything you needed to heal from falling off a wall.

Tears built behind her eyes. Her kitchen shelves were stocked with jars of teas specially blended just for her. They'd been the only thing that made her feel remotely close to him in their year and a half apart. Every cup reminded her of another time he'd brought her tea: new blends he'd come up with, old blends made from his grandmother's recipes, and in a pinch, chamomile from whatever coffee shop was closest.

She took another sip and gathered herself.

Rohan was looking at her again, wearing that expression that said he saw so much more than she wanted him to.

"Will it?" He asked. "Help, I mean?"

"If Patrick says it will, then it will," she said. "Now what are you going to write your single about?"

———

PATRICK WATCHED her as she drank the tea. Her shoulders relaxed. The stiffness eased its way out of her movements.

"Rick. Rick? Rick!" Benji snapped their fingers in front of his face until he looked at them. "Hi, yes. Stop staring at your long-lost lady love and pay attention to me, okay? I mean, for fuck's sake, am I the only one who wants to see this thing made under budget?"

Patrick let Benji bitch. He listened to the track again. Every time he heard Rohan sing her name, anger fizzed in his brain. Patrick wasn't a hothead. Even if he was, it would've been trained out of him long ago. His father wouldn't have tolerated so much emotion in his son.

No. He had Dad's ice-cold temper. That didn't make thinking through rage any easier. He couldn't slide into the track the way he usually did, immersing himself in the sonics and soundscape until he knew exactly how it should sound. No, with this damn song, he was forced to listen to it over and over again until the words were meaningless and he could almost ignore Cazzi's name.

He'd never been good at ignoring her. Even in those months when they hadn't spoken, her absence was a dull ache, a phantom limb.

But he'd gotten used to that distance, that ache. Now she was here. The ache sharpened, the distance disappeared and these feelings were like an open wound. He was bleeding out. He was losing his mind. The words he needed to say burned, stuck and intelligible.

I think I love you, I'm pretty sure but all I can think about is the first time when I let you kiss me even though I was taken. If this is love, that's okay right? It was a small mistake, it's over, I'm free... but if it's not... if it's not am I just a cheater like Grandpa Pat?

It was all his fault. He was hurting her though he was trying not to. But if he started answering her questions he'd unravel. He'd have to relive everything he'd kept from her for two years. He was so much more fucked in the head than she knew, and if he told her...

Where did he start? When his ex accused him of cheating before he'd even kissed Cazzi? When his family found out Grandpa Pat kept a mistress for twenty years and it tore them all apart? Or that when he'd kissed her back that night eighteen months ago he'd gone into an anxiety spiral for two days thinking he was going to turn out like the man he was named for, the man he'd looked up to?

His breath went shallow, tension clamping over his lungs. It was all he could think about, all he could feel. Nothing else punctured the gray. Not the anxiety of the deadline, hissing, and crackling in the background of his thoughts. Not the buzzing feedback of his rage as Rohan flirted his way closer to her. Not the reverb of her kiss.

An hour later, Rohan was busy scribbling more lyrics and Cazzi needed a break. She stood up, stretching. Her back popped like dry wood in a fire, but the pain faded.

Picking up the to-go mug, she crossed the room and placed it next to Patrick. He looked up at her, his locs bunched around the big noise-canceling headphones that were everywhere in this place.

She nodded at the door. He glanced at Benji then back at his computer. He took the headphones off and even as he followed her out into the lobby she knew they wouldn't have much time.

He frowned at her choice of venue and she knew he was remembering her freak-out yesterday. She shrugged. "The options were limited." She wasn't going out on that patio if she could help it.

He nodded, his expression guarded. "I'm not ready to talk."

She pushed down her first reaction, which was to scream "WHY?" And said in her most reasonable voice, "Okay." He'd see right through her but it was the thought that counted, right? "Fine. But are we okay?"

"Peachy keen." He gave her the least convincing thumbs-up in the history of thumbs-ups.

"Was it the kiss?" The question slipped out of her before she could stop it.

His expression shut down. "I told you, I'm not ready to talk."

"Give me something, Patrick." Her reply was hoarse, nearly a whisper. "I'm losing my damn mind here. Am I the only one? Am I misreading this?"

"No." He wasn't looking at her but his hand found hers all the same. Their fingers intertwined. She could scarcely breathe for the hope of it.

"But?"

"It's complicated."

She had the brief, violent urge to crush his fingers, twist them until he told her everything. Her stomach curdled at the thought, the acid eating its way up her spine, the familiar burn of self-hatred.

I am not my thoughts, she reminded herself. *I am not my capacity for violence.*

"Come back, Caz," Patrick murmured, squeezing her hand gently. "You're here. In the studio."

"I'm not having a flashback." Her words came out peevish.

He just smiled. "Where'd you go?"

"Just in my head a bit. I'm worried about you."

"Me?" Again, he seemed taken aback. Or panicked, maybe. When had she started having trouble reading him?

"Why do you always seem so surprised when I worry about you?"

He shrugged.

"I've worried about you before. We look after each other." She watched him as she said it, watched the way his smile became placating.

"Yeah, we do."

But she didn't believe him. The earth suddenly didn't feel so solid. They didn't lie to each other. They didn't always tell the whole truth, but they didn't lie. Or at least so she'd thought.

A lot can happen in eighteen months.

Rohan stuck his head out of the studio door. "Hey, Caz, I need you. Both of you, actually."

Patrick let go of her hand.

In the studio, Rohan and Benji stood, arms crossed like disappointed parents.

"What's up?" Patrick asked.

The two other musicians shared a glance. Benji said, "We don't think this," they gestured at Patrick and Cazzi, "Is going to work."

Her heart dropped into a pit of dread and rage. Who the hell did they—

"In the studio," Rohan rushed to add. "The two of you here at the same time, we mean."

"You," Benji pointed at her, "distract Rick. And you," they pointed at Rick, "Make her crazy."

Patrick's mouth dropped open but Benji preempted him.

"I'm sure you two have some cute story explaining everything, but we're trying to launch a record label and an album on a shoe-string budget. We're already down a backer." They glanced at Rohan. "But that's probably for the best. Anyway, you need to handle your shit outside of working hours so we can make this happen." They looked Patrick dead in the eye. "Or you need to get out of the way."

Patrick's eyebrows flew up and he crossed his arms.

Rohan sighed. "Look, Rick, you're our friend and you're a brilliant producer."

"And a financial stakeholder in Now or Never Records." Patrick pointed out.

"We couldn't make this label happen without you," Rohan said, "We're not asking you guys to stop seeing each other."

Cazzi found her posture mirroring Patrick's. "Then what are you asking?"

"That you don't see each other in the studio," Benji said. "I've put together a schedule…"

Cazzi thought about walking out right then. She was doing them a favor, dammit. Rohan *knew* half the reason she was doing this was to get time with Patrick.

Patrick picked up the sheet Benji held. She peered over his shoulder. They'd gotten a hold of her office hours somehow and extrapolated her schedule from there.

The invasion of privacy made her skin crawl. At least Benji wasn't so thorough that her meeting with the dean in two days was on there. Then she'd have to go yell at some student workers for violating the department's privacy policy and she was already precariously angry.

ROHAN WATCHED the two of them with a knot in his stomach. It was entirely possible he'd lose both of them with this stunt. But Benji had been adamant—and right. They needed to nip this in the bud.

Early in the day, Benji had been advocating to get rid of her completely. "First Angelica, now this?" They hissed when Rick had gone to the bathroom, "This Cazzi woman is derailing what's left of our momentum. I can't handle her fucking freak-outs on top of Rick's sulking, your blocks, and coordinating the business side of all this."

"I need her," Rohan insisted, handing them his phone full of lyrics.

Benji scrolled and sighed. "Dammit. Okay. I can figure this out."

The minute Cazzi and Rick stepped out, Benji had the schedule in hand. "You know it can't go on like this," they said. "I signed up to deal with you and Rick. I am not patient enough to add the dynamic she brings in."

It hadn't taken much convincing for Rohan to agree. So little, in fact, he felt guilty about it. But not guilty enough to put a stop to it.

Rick looked up at them. "Okay." He handed the schedule back.

"Okay?" Cazzi grabbed the paper before Benji could. "You're okay with this?"

Rick shrugged. "They're right."

Cazzi stilled, her expression smoothing. "Ah."

Rohan wished he could see the thoughts behind her mask, wished he knew her well enough to guess whether she would walk. Her eyes came up and met his.

It was like looking into the void. Like there was nothing there but if he leaned in any closer he'd be sucked in and never seen again.

She put the schedule down on Benji's laptop keyboard. "I think I'm done here," she paused just long enough for Rohan to panic. "For today."

Her expression was still smooth but her tone suggested they were all on thin ice. With that, she gathered her stuff carefully and left.

Rohan wasn't sure whether to be relieved or worried.

8

"She's all I ever wanted
Her body's got me haunted
So funny and cool
Hottest girl in school
I'm at arm's length
I wanna be face to face

There's a girl I know
Who pushes me as far as I'll go
She's that fantasy, you know the one
A hundred guys want her
She doesn't want one

Oh baby she told me maybe
Not yes or no
Means I'll never let you go
Oh baby you got me stuck
Neither here nor there
Makes me wanna
Push

> *My*
> *Luck"*
> —"Push My Luck" by Beatboyz on *Heatbeatz*

The next day Rick almost seemed relaxed when Rohan met him at the studio. Rohan hadn't realized how on edge his friend had been. But things went quickly downhill when Benji brought up co-writing *again*.

"Is it that you don't think I can help?" Benji asked. "You realize this is what I do, right?"

"I'm not questioning your songwriting skills, really, I'm not," Rohan rubbed his nose. "I just don't want help. Why is it bad that I want to do this by myself?" He felt like a child. Cazzi wouldn't be off work for hours and no one here seemed to understand why he couldn't accept writing help.

"Art isn't produced in a vacuum, especially not music," Rick pointed out. "You're chasing the sound and you do what you need to, bring in who you need to, to get it."

"That's why I'm working with you two. That's why I'm getting Cazzi to help. But the lyrics are *mine*."

Benji put their head in their hands. "We're going in fucking circles."

Rohan's phone vibrated, amplified by the hollow metal table it was on.

He didn't look at it.

"Oh just take it," Benji said, "Maybe it's your muse and you can take *her* help."

The phone vibrated again.

"Don't be bitter," Rick muttered, not looking up from his phone.

"Cast your shade elsewhere, you love sick puppy," Benji snapped. "I'm not here for this budding triangle."

"Triangle?" Rohan asked, confused.

The phone buzzed.

Benji rolled their eyes. "Ugh, this record label shit makes my DIY punk days look positively corporate."

"You were goth-pop, don't try to be cooler than you were," Rick shot back.

"I was talking about when I was in my mom's scene, jackass," Benji said. "If you wanna tell the Razor Bitches they weren't punk, I'd do it armed."

The phone vibrated again. Rohan picked it up, looking for any way out of this conversation. What he saw on the screen knocked the breath out of him. "Shit."

That got their attention. "What?"

"It's Angie." He stared at her picture on the screen. It was a selfie of the two of them when they'd first gotten together. A real one, not a publicity shot. He'd forgotten she'd ever looked so happy.

"*Fuck that*," Rick said. "Send her to voicemail."

Rohan glanced up in surprise. He hadn't realized Rick didn't like Angie. His former bandmate met his gaze without an ounce of apology.

The phone stopped ringing and immediately started up again, the picture flashing back on the screen. In it, Rohan grinned at her like she was the siren song of his universe.

"She's just going to keep calling," Benji said, their voice flat. "Isn't she."

"Yeah," Rohan said.

"Block her," Rick said, his attention turning back to his phone.

The phone buzzed.

"All my stuff's still there." There, being her house, the house that'd theoretically been his too. Except it was in her name, filled with her things, decorated to her taste, and he'd only ever felt he existed in two rooms.

"She probably burned it all," Benji said.

The phone vibrated angrily.

"Just cuz that's what you'd do…" Rohan started, trying to make it a joke.

"Don't compare me to her," Benji cut him off. They dead-eyed him. "Do you remember how many times you showed up at my house needing a friend because she was driving you out of your mind?"

"I—I," Their intensity caught him off-guard.

"There was blood, Ro."

The phone buzzed.

He remembered it dripping out of his palm, falling to the floor, mixing with the gold slivers. "It was mine."

"Does that make it better?"

"It wasn't— she didn't hurt me." It was surreal saying the words. He was a guy, this wasn't a conversation he'd ever imagined having. "She wasn't even home. I cut myself accidentally."

"She might not have hit you, but she fucking hurt you." Benji's expression was fierce.

Rick watched him solemnly.

"Like you haven't been self-destructive, Suicide King," Rohan snapped, but his words felt weak.

His phone stopped buzzing.

"You know that character, that album is not about me," Benji said, their voice determinedly even as they repeated the same thing they told every reporter, every fan. "Yes, I've been self-destructive and I've written tons of songs about it. But the songs never saved me. I damn well wish I'd had someone I'd been able to listen to who could've pointed it out to me. It would've saved me a lot of bullshit and pain."

The phone rang again.

Rohan picked it up.

"Ro," Angie sobbed. "Ro, I'm so sorry."

Even her voice over the phone was magnetic. He found himself leaning towards it. But his gaze caught Benji's and he straightened up. "I'm not."

He hung up, turning off his phone.

It should've felt like triumph but thirty minutes later he was creatively blocked and Benji was frustrated.

"Why are you protecting her? She's a fucking bitch," they snarled. Their snarl, honed over years of being on stage, rivaled Angie's.

Rohan slapped his hand on the table. "Just because she calls herself that does not give you the right to."

"Whatever." They looked away, crossing their arms.

"Look, we were shitty to each other. It's not just all her."

"Don't defend her to me," Benji said. "Just don't."

"Love doesn't disappear just because you break up," said Cazzi, out of literally nowhere.

Both Benji and Rohan looked around but it was just Rick holding his phone out. "I think you confused them both." He told his phone.

Cazzi's chuckle crackled through the speakerphone. "Ambush mediation does that, Pat."

Rick shrugged and looked at them. "I was tired of listening to you two."

Cazzi sighed. "I have ten minutes left on my lunch. Let's make this quick."

"Are you going to fix us now?" Benji narrowed their eyes at the phone like they could see her through it.

What was Rick thinking, bringing her in right now? Ambushed was exactly how Rohan felt, defensive and vulnerable.

"Benji," Cazzi sounded exasperated. "I don't fix anyone. That's not what we do. Now, Pat has been keeping me far too up-to-date about this so lemme lay this out the way I understand it: Benji, you want to help Rohan write his songs for professional and personal reasons. Rohan, you do not want Benji's help, but will not give them a clear reason why. Is that correct?"

"You're taking their side," Rohan said.

"I'm not taking anyone's side," Cazzi replied smoothly. "Is my summary correct?"

"Yeah," Benji and Rohan chorused, their voices two shades of sullen.

"Lovely. Rohan, can you please think about why you feel so strongly about accepting help from Benji? You don't have to tell us anything right now."

Rohan frowned and crossed his arms. He didn't want to think about it. His reasons were sound, why couldn't anyone trust that?

Rick started humming, the tune forming until he was nearly singing it. Rohan's fingers clenched the instant he recognized the song. His melody, what was left of it.

"Stop it," Rohan growled at him.

"Wait, wait," Benji stared hard at Rick. "Oh, baby you got me stuck," they sang, their voice a passable impression of Rohan's.

"Don't."

"Neither here nor there, And it makes me wanna push my luck..." Those lines were the only ones left from what he'd originally written. The hook would haunt him forever from a song that had been torn apart and would never again be his.

"Benji!" Rohan shouted. "Stop singing that shit."

Benji cocked their head. "You wrote 'Push My Luck'?"

"No," Rohan said as Rick said, "Yes."

"Patrick," Cazzi said quietly and Rick's mouth shut.

"You wrote the Beatboyz's biggest hit?" Benji asked. "Why the hell didn't you tell me?"

"It's not my song," Rohan glanced at the phone. "They... killed it."

"Killed it?" Cazzi asked but understanding dawned on Benji's face.

"The label," they said.

"Yeah," Rohan's fingers twisted around his talisman. The rough edges of the carving scraped his skin. "I gave it to my stepdad and... when I got it back..."

He remembered how excited he'd been, presenting his demo to James. He'd bragged to the rest of the band about it. How flattening it had been when he'd arrived to record it to find it a shell of the track he'd written. Catchier, sure but generic and almost stalkerish when you read between the lines. Even his smarmy fucking bandmate Martin had pitied him then. It all seemed so naive now.

"It was shittier," Rick murmured. "Rohan's stepdad was our talent scout, our manager," he told the phone.

"Ahhh," Cazzi breathed.

"Classic move," Benji said.

"He's not the bad guy here," Rohan said quickly. "The execs took it from him."

"You think I'd do that to you? Isn't the whole point of this label to not be like the shitty labels that own our masters?" Benji looked hurt. "You know why User-Friendly Omega lost its first manager?"

Rohan shook his head.

"Because I ran him out of the studio with a plastic fork for trying to get me to tone down *Suicide King*."

"A plastic fork?" Rohan repeated, feeling dazed.

Benji shrugged. "I was high, sleep-deprived, and it was that or a spoon."

"You are one of the few people that could make a plastic fork frightening," Rohan conceded. They were actually one of two. The other was Angie. She'd once made a grown man nearly cry with fear using only a toothpick and a smile.

"My time is up," Cazzi said, breaking through his memories. "But I think we're making good progress."

"Hold up, don't go yet."

"Talk it out, you two. I don't think you really need me, but if you do, I'll be there in a few hours."

"Can't you stay for a few more minutes?"

She paused for four agonizing seconds. "Three minutes, Rohan."

Rohan grabbed the phone from Rick and turned it off speakerphone. "I can't do this," he hissed, walking out into the lobby.

She exhaled audibly. "What, exactly, can you not do?"

"Write with someone else."

"Didn't you do it with Angie? 'Strange Bedfellows' is a great song."

"Yeah, but it stopped being mine when it dropped. Everyone thought I was the featured artist, just a voice. I wrote everything but her parts."

She made an understanding hum. "You think Benji will overshadow you?"

"I think if there's another name under the lyrics everyone will assume..."

"How is Benji helping you different from me helping you?"

"Well, you're not a writer."

"No, but you bounce ideas off of me, you borrow my phrases—"

"Only one or two."

"I'm not after a writing credit. I'm just trying to understand."

"I-I" Rohan thought about it. "You're not in the industry. Benji's a better writer than me."

"Why do you say that?"

"Have you listened to their stuff? They wrote amazing songs for User-Friendly Omega, and after they left they wrote more great shit for other people. The only real thing I've done since Beatboyz fucking imploded was duet with Angie and fail to write an album with my old bandmate."

"Pat?"

"Leo."

She hummed her acknowledgment. "Patrick and I watched him on that drag show. She should've won."

"I thought we were talking about me." Rohan meant it as a joke, but the words came out pissy.

"Rohan," she sighed his name. The sound was like the barest of touches, trailing over his skin. "You have my attention. Now listen. You have a confidence problem, one that I can't fix in less than a minute. But you have to understand that you are worth more than what people say about you."

"I know that! You think I could've survived being in a boy band if I didn't know that?" Rohan snapped. He wasn't insecure. He wasn't weak or lacking in confidence. He was fucking RK.

She thinks I'm some sad little fuck up. That I'm one of those tragic child stars.

"Right. I think our time is up." There was no warmth in her voice. It was as cold as Angie's at her worst.

"I'm sorry, did I offend you?" His tone was scathing, an echo of old fights with another woman.

She inhaled sharply and exhaled hard. "You don't get to treat me like you and Angela treated each other. I'm doing you a favor. Don't waste it."

The call disconnected.

9

"Overthinker, overdrinker,
Can't make up my mind
Said, I know your kind,
Cute but you'll never be fine
Let me make this simpler,
And she said,

Fuck me I'm beautiful
This tie ain't suitable
This dress is removable
And you're so doable
So fuck me,
Beautiful"

—"Fuck Me I'm Beautiful" by User-Friendly Omega on *Anhedonia*

Cazzi fumed. She fumed through the last of her meetings, under her composure as she counseled two students, and all through her bike ride, barely plastering a smile on her face when she was stopped at a red light by a student leaning out of a car window.

"Are you a condom pixie?" A girl in a car full of girls in matching sorority sweaters asked. The sweaters giggled nervously.

"Wings and all." Cazzi patted her bike, pretending she didn't want to just ride away. She smiled at each girl, reminding herself they were human beings with lives and stories and not just irritating obstacles to getting away as soon as possible.

They felt a lot like obstacles.

"Uh, yeah. Cool. Can we get some?" Asked the student hanging out of the window. She wasn't wearing a seatbelt.

"Put your seatbelt on," Cazzi said.

"I'm good."

"No seatbelt, no free condoms."

"Fine." The girl slid back into her seat and did up her belt.

Cazzi dug a generous handful out of her saddlebag, and handed them through the window. Then she sped off without her usual attempt to chat with the students about sexual health. Still fuming.

It wasn't all Rohan, though, boy, she was done with him right now. No, the thing was, Patrick hadn't asked her to mediate out of the blue. She'd texted to ask him how he was and instead of giving her anything about him, he'd narrated Benji and Rohan's conversation until she'd gotten so frustrated she'd offered to help. Which was deflection and manipulation and it pissed her off. She'd already texted him that she wasn't coming into the studio until Rohan wrote a song with Benji.

She wasn't sure she'd come back even when that happened. If that happened. Instead, she went to Judit and Eva's to help Judit pack.

But when she got there, User-Friendly Omega's "Fuck me, I'm Beautiful" was on and she had to explain why she immediately, vengefully skipped the song and then even more vengefully skipped Beatboyz's "Push My Luck."

Halfway through her rant Eva shoved a hard lemonade and a brownie in her hand.

Judit sat on the floor, packing, and shaking her head. She was soft and curvy like her demi-sister but that was where the resemblance ended. She was strikingly Eastern European looking, taking strongly after her Hungarian mother with high cheekbones, hazel eyes, and nearly black hair. Her hair was up in a messy bun and she still wore pjs but her movements were easy and relaxed. Not too much pain today, Cazzi guessed.

"Artists are the worst," Judit said. "So damn needy."

"I thought your favorite couple were artists," Eva said, failing to sound casual.

Judit's eyes narrowed. "They're graphic designers, it's different."

"So it's getting serious then if they're asking you to move in." Cazzi sipped her lemonade. Eva frowned at the box she was packing.

Judit shrugged. "I'm moving into their carriage house, not marrying them."

"Which is illegal," Eva muttered.

"And not on the table," Judit said. "Anyway," she looked up at Cazzi. "Do you want a reading before I go? It sounds like there's a lot going on with your love triangle there."

"Love triangle?" Cazzi laughed. "I should fucking hope not."

"It's a classic, two hot pop stars, one seemingly normal woman…"

"Sounds like a fanfic," Eva said. "Or a really hot three-way."

"Oh Christ, stop. Just stop," Cazzi said. "That brownie was delicious but I don't want to taste it a second time." The brownie also hadn't been as good as Rohan's but no way she was mentioning that.

"Oh, so you're not attracted to this hotness?" Eva pulled up a picture of Rohan from his Instagram. It was a publicity shot, a throwback from the edgier Beatboyz days. He was beautiful, a thirst trap, staring out of the screen with smoldering eyes and a hint of dimples.

He looked… she wanted to say young but he was still pretty young. Carefree, maybe. Like his shoulders were lighter and the world was a bit simpler even though he was deep in the jaws of the boy band machine.

"I'm getting the cards," Judit said, standing.

Cazzi blinked and looked up. "I don't want a Tarot reading. Not right now."

Eva shook her head and mouthed "Triangle." Then she said aloud, "Hun, you're in a weird position, you're acting like a therapist but you're not this guy's therapist. You're not even getting paid for this, you're doing a favor for your fucking crush. This is only gonna get even more tricky and stressful."

"I hear you, and you're probably right, but I need you to shut up and give me something to pack." Cazzi downed the last of her lemonade.

Eva handed her an empty box and thankfully let the subject drop.

10

"There's nothing I can say
I wish I could
Wish I could
But my lips are sewn shut
Can't pull these stitches out

Silence is gold
You're getting cold
I can't speak
Can't make it better"
— "Stitched Lips" by User-Friendly Omega on *Suicide King*

The phone rang, echoing in Patrick's ear. His stomach was in knots.

"Pat." Her voice was flat but he could hear the nuances: the bass sharpness of anger, the breathiness of hope, the fraying vibrato of pain.

Her pain called to his. He wanted to reach through the phone line and hold her. "I want to talk."

Her inhale was quiet and he heard a door closing. "I'm listening."

There were so many feelings, so many thoughts backed up in his throat. He'd once been told some people think in words. It still blew his mind that everyone else didn't have to sort through colors, riffs, sounds, and images to translate their thoughts into speech. It explained why other people couldn't read a song like a book, couldn't pull it apart and put it back together, better. But now, he wished he thought in words too because that's the way Cazzi thought.

She breathed. It was such a familiar sound. Years on tour, years spent apart, spent together, spent alone and he'd know the shape of her breath anywhere. He closed his eyes, leaning against the back of the studio wall, and counted the beats of her inhales until his breathing lined up with hers.

How could he tell her he'd been keeping secrets again? That he hadn't stopped?

Ten years ago, she'd have demanded he spit out whatever bothered him but all that schooling gave her patience. These days her silence matched his and she could wait him out.

"I," he stopped.

God, he was going to hurt her. He was already hurting her, and she'd been hurt so much. He still remembered her face when she'd tried to go back to school after what happened. She'd lasted half a day and called him for rescue. He'd gladly ditched his own classes to drive her away from that hellhole.

She'd looked so fragile, close to breaking completely. All he'd had to help her was a cup of Starbucks chamomile tea and a drive to the ocean.

Sometimes, he thought what happened to Tanya had started his anxiety.

Her breath in his ear was like waves. The beach had been deserted that cold Tuesday afternoon. "Remember the beach after what happened?" The question slipped out before he could stop it.

"Yeah. Always."

"It's like that."

Her breath hitched. "Did something happen?"

"Not like that. I-I feel like I'm back there." He felt just as broken up and helpless. Like he was going to hurt her any minute.

"I'm not that girl anymore." There was an edge to her voice, biting and sharp. This week must hold the record for the most times he'd made her mad, ever.

"No. You're not."

"Is this it?" she'd asked all those years ago. "Am I toxic now?" Now he understood what she meant.

"I feel toxic," he murmured.

"You're not."

"I'm hurting you."

She hesitated. "You are. But we can figure it out."

Her words were matter-of-fact. He tried to react accordingly, but they ripped a hole in his stomach and he spoke before he could sort it all out. "I shouldn't have kissed you."

She let out a ragged half-laugh. It reverberated with pain. But when she spoke, her voice held more compassion than he would've expected. "What makes you say that?"

For some reason, that made him angry. Why did she get to be composed in all this? He was collapsing in slow motion but she seemed to be keeping her head above water. "Don't shrink me."

She sighed but there was a sharpness to it that told him it was forced through her teeth. "Patrick, I'm done dancing around this."

"What?"

"I'm in love with you." She inhaled hard, the sound almost a sob. "I've been in love with you for god, I don't know, forever."

He was stunned. No words came. Everything was incandescent, every sound was a song. She loved him. Was in love with him. Had been in love with him. Then the light snuffed out and the anxiety spiraled in. She loved him, but the person she loved didn't have all the baggage he'd been hiding from her.

The person she loved didn't freak out every time he kissed her because the first time was all wrong and all he could think about was his fucking cheating grandfather making his Nana and mother cry, about his ex's suspicions, how she'd been right because of course she was right, he'd proved that, hadn't he? He let his guard down and accidentally cheated and ruined his best friendship in one fell swoop.

"I don't expect anything and I know unreturned love can be a burden but I need to be honest. I need to break this pattern. I'll always be your friend but…" she paused. "If that kiss wasn't some fluke… if that meant something to you…"

She waited and he couldn't feel anything, couldn't say anything. She waited and he slowly turned into a statue, the eternity of unspoken feelings freezing flesh into stone.

The words *I love you too* battered themselves against the inside of his stone lips. Because this would all be worth it if he loved her.

"Okay," she said, so quietly he barely heard it. "That's okay."

But she hung up.

11

"Bam bam thought it'd be loud
Bang bang I bet you're proud
It was so quiet
I nearly missed it
Not a single sound
When that knife slid between my ribs

Oh thought I was smart
Trusting you with my heart
But I was so dazzled
I couldn't see
You betraying
Betraying
Betraying me."

—- "Betraying me (Bang Bang)" by Beatboyz on *Heartbeatz*

Cazzi waited for the tears. They didn't come. She felt like a robot.

Disassociation. Shock.

She smiled at Eva and Judit, made her excuses, left. Biked home.

Sat on her bed. Deactivated the sigils she'd invoked today. Nothing much, just a bit of calm, a bit of strength, a bit of pain relief. Back when she used to draw the sigils, the ritual of drawing them put her in the mindset she wanted and washing them away let her mind relax. Now that they were tattoos she had devised a new ritual.

Ritual was good. Ritual was important. Familiar. Grounding.

She pressed the first sigil and whispered, "Thank you. You are released."

A little strength left her, her shoulders slumping.

"Thank you. You are released."

A little calm left her, her fingers shaking.

"Thank you. You are released."

A little pain returned, her healing aches intensifying.

Still no tears. She could feel them lurking, pressing up behind her eyes, closing her throat.

She went and got a cookie.

There was an edge of surrealness to everything as she stood, eating it over the sink. She'd told Patrick she loved him, opened her heart, torn out her biggest secret, and handed it to him and he'd said… nothing.

She ate another cookie and opened up her pot cabinet.

Indica, sativa, hybrids in various forms laid out with notes on the effects, dosage, and side effects with a container of CBD gummies for slowing her roll. She'd just pulled out her vape when there was a knock on the door.

In her distant state, she knew it wasn't Patrick. She didn't want to see anyone, not even him.

Choose yourself, she told herself.

She opened the door anyway.

"I'm having deja vu," she said.

"Well, you know what that means," Rohan said. His clothes

were rumpled, his hair stood on end, and his eyes were tired. His smile was mostly real. "There's been a glitch in the Matrix."

"Uh-huh." Cazzi crossed her arms, resolutely not amused.

"You're still mad at me." He grimaced. "Fair. I was an asshole."

"I'm getting really tired of this pattern," she said.

"Also fair. Look, can I come in? I know I'm hardly A-list anymore but…" he glanced out at the few cars going by and shrugged self-consciously.

Cazzi considered him, weighing how much she wanted to be alone against getting a healthy resolution and how hard it would be to get him out of the house once he was in it. "Five minutes," she said, letting him in.

He flashed her a real, if sheepish smile. It bounced off her disassociated feelings and she barely registered how gorgeous it made him.

She closed the door and went into the kitchen, setting the microwave timer for five minutes. Then she returned to selecting a strain for tonight.

"Wow." He followed her and stared at her pot cabinet. "Are you running a dispensary?" He picked up one of the Post-Its, reading through her notes. "Or are you experimenting on yourself?"

She said nothing. He could waste his five minutes if he wanted. She didn't care. She contemplated the strains in front of her.

Somewhere, in the back of her rational brain, all this apathy scared her.

He stopped, looking at her. "Are you okay?"

She considered the question. "No."

"You wanna talk about it?"

"No." She wanted her cathartic cry but not in front of him. Not in front of anyone.

He studied her, his frown so deep he was probably risking wrinkles. "Is this about our fight?"

"Not everything is about you." She selected a strain. "But I'm not real pleased with you either."

"It's about Rick."

"No means no, Rohan." She pulled a bud out, put it in her grinder.

"Okay, well I'm here if you change your mind."

"Only for another three minutes and thirty-three seconds."

He glanced at the microwave clock. "That's not helpful."

"I'm a human being, not a therapy robot." She ground the bit of nug up. It felt good to crush something, to make an impact. "I don't always have to be helpful."

"I don't think you're a therapy robot," he said, but he said it too quickly. "I worried about you, as a friend."

"*Are* we friends?"

"I thought so."

She nodded. It was nice to know where she stood, at least in his mind. "I hit a nerve today when I said you have a confidence problem."

His lips twisted and his eyes unfocused like he was seeing and hearing something else. "No shit."

"Wanna talk about it?"

"In," he glanced at the timer, "twenty-four seconds?"

She sighed. "Did you write a song with Benji yet?"

"You were serious about that condition huh?"

"Answer me."

The timer started beeping.

"We did." He grimaced.

Beep-beep beep...

"How was it?"

Beep beep-beep...

"Rough."

She turned off the beeping. He looked at her and she looked right back.

"Why are you here?"

"To apologize I—"

"Yet the word sorry hasn't come out of your mouth."

His brow furrowed. "I was getting to it."

"I told you that you had five minutes."

"I didn't think you were serious."

"Do you think I just say shit to say it?" Her face heated, her body responding to the anger she didn't quite feel.

He rubbed a hand over his face. "No, I think you're one of the smartest, wisest people I've ever met."

She crossed her arms and waited.

He crossed his arms and stared right back at her.

She waited.

He fidgeted.

She stared into his dark eyes. In the yellow kitchen light, they looked amber, and she picked out flecks of gold with topaz striations. When had she leaned closer?

He looked down at her like he maybe wouldn't mind if she got closer.

She pulled back and grabbed her dry vape off the counter, the familiar boxy shape reassuring in her hand. "Go home, Rohan."

"I am sorry," he said, softly. "I'm sorry I'm a mess and I'm leaning on you and being an asshole about it and that I didn't take your conditions seriously."

She nodded, looking down at the vape. She was tired, body and soul. "You want me to come back." She watched his face from under her lashes.

You want me?

"Yes." There was no hesitation. "No more drama, I promise."

"Don't make that promise. You can't keep it."

She thought he'd get mad again but he just laughed. "Okay, fair. How's this: I'll do my best to keep the drama to the minimum."

She found herself smiling, just a little. He was too damn

charming. If she wasn't careful, she'd be wrapped around his finger. She suspected she wouldn't be the first—or the last.

If he wasn't completely and utterly sincere he'd be a lot easier to resist.

She looked him over, cataloging the set of his shoulders, the hope in his face, the slight tilt of his smile, the way his fingers unconsciously tapped a rhythm on her counter. In her shitty kitchen light, he was in soft focus, beautiful without trying. Light and shadow conspired in chiaroscuro to pick out the lines of his muscles through his green long-sleeve shirt, the sharpness of his cheekbones, the length of his eyelashes, the gloss of his dark hair.

"Okay." She knew she'd regret it, knew she was choosing someone else over herself.

But it was nice to be wanted.

THE NEXT DAY at the studio, Cazzi listened to the song Benji and Rohan wrote. It was rough, even she could tell. But it was a step.

When she was done he handed Cazzi her own cookie tin with a fresh batch of snickerdoodles inside. She raised her eyebrows.

"Bribe?" Rohan asked hopefully. "Rick said you liked them."

Hearing that was only slightly like being punched in the heart. She bit into a cookie and used it as an excuse to close her eyes. It really was delicious though. His spicing was strong but complex, the cookie itself soft and just the right amount of sweet as it melted into her mouth.

"How is it?" he asked.

She opened her eyes. "Ten out of ten would be bribed again."

Benji laughed.

Rohan grinned, dimples on full display. "Noted."

"How did you feel working together?" She asked when she was done eating. They all sat on the giant leather couch against the back wall of the studio and she was crammed up in the opposite corner, turned so she could see them both.

Rohan and Benji exchanged a look and shrugged.

"Words please."

"We fought a lot," Rohan said.

"No, you fought me on every little change." Benji crossed their arms.

Cazzi nodded. "How did that make you feel, Benji?"

"I wasn't aware this was couples counseling now." They picked up a cookie and bit it in half like it had wronged them.

"I'm not a couples counselor but I think we can all agree you all need a little help right now. Why not accept it when it's offered?" She gave them her mildest smile.

They glared but broke eye contact quickly, shrugging and brushing a shock of black hair out of their face. "Okay, it sucked. It made me wonder why I was even trying to build a label with you," they turned to Rohan, "when you can't even write a song with me."

Rohan scrubbed his hand through his unruly curls. "I know. I know it's stupid and I need to get over it. I'm trying, okay?"

Benji let out a wordless grumble but they nodded. On the seat next to them, their phone buzzed. They glanced down at it and swore. "Goddammit, I have to take this." They grabbed the phone and dashed out.

"I am trying," Rohan said, looking at her.

"I believe you."

He smiled and there was a curling twist of feeling in her stomach. Most of her dissociation was gone, though she still hadn't cried, but now she was wishing for that distance back. Rohan was undeniably attractive, but fuck, she did not want to be attracted to him.

"Thank you for coming back." He reached over and squeezed her hand, a quick, surprisingly noninvasive gesture. "I don't know if I've said this, but I really appreciate you. I think I would be losing my mind if you hadn't turned up when you did."

"Because of Angela?"

He shrugged. "Her, the album, this whole hang-up about having a co-writer. Plus, now I have an excuse to bake." He paused. "How are you? Are you doing better?"

It was her turn to shrug. Her meeting with the dean had been anti-climatic, he'd refused to go over the collective heads of the Academic Senate. In the end, she'd been put on the docket for next month's meeting and that was that. But he wasn't asking about her consent seminar. He was asking about the thing she didn't want to talk about. That she wouldn't talk— "I don't think it's hit me yet," the words tumbled out without consulting her. *Dammit.* She was slipping.

"What hasn't hit you?"

She chewed her lip, debating. She hadn't even told Eva yet. But Eva didn't get love like that. She'd kill for her friends, die for her siblings no matter their blood relation status, but romantic love? Wasn't her thing. She couldn't understand why Patrick made Cazzi so irrational. Judit had already written him off because of the way he'd cut Cazzi out of his life.

"I told Patrick I love him." She nearly swallowed the words but Rohan heard them.

Rohan's eyes widened. "And?"

She shook her head. Those tears she'd been waiting for choked her. She breathed until they receded. Her fingers stole under her sleeve, finding her third-level calming sigil and tracing it from memory. *It is my will to restrain my emotions.*

The tears receded even further.

"He doesn't love you?" He looked shocked.

"He didn't say anything."

"At all?"

"At all."

"Holy fucking hell," he breathed. "I'm so sorry, Caz." His hand brushed her shoulder. "Can I… do you want a hug?"

She debated. If he hugged her she'd probably cry. But dammit, she hadn't had a hug in what felt like too long. She nodded.

He leaned forward and very slowly, pulled her into his arms. She let herself soften, her head resting on his shoulder, her arms going around him, and… oh.

He was a good hugger. Like really good. Like she wanted to melt completely into his embrace and stay there forever. He felt safe. Warm. Solid but not hard. And oh, he smelled amazing. Like peppermint chapstick mixed with a subtle sandalwood scent and healthy human.

The door banged open.

They jerked apart. And stared.

Angela Alice stood in the doorway, face contorted in rage.

Angela in full stage regalia was a silver-blonde ice queen, who, despite being draped in all white with white contacts and dead white makeup, still managed to be goth. The Bitch Queen was a terrifying ghost that scared parents all over the world. Despite having met her a few days before, that's how Cazzi remembered her.

Angela Alice out of regalia and with only a slash of dark blue lipstick, it turned out, looked like a white blonde Angela Alice fangirl who hadn't bothered to go full-on. She could've been any other slender white girl with a lot of black in her closet. It helped that her high-necked sweater covered that iconic neck-to-chest double-headed inverted cross tattoo. But there was no mistaking that rage.

It radiated from her like heat, suffocating and strong.

"So this was your plan." Her voice was like smokey honey, raspy and low, sweetened by the round hints of Southern twang. "Break us up and steal him for yourself."

Cazzi could barely breathe. She pressed her fingers to the protective sigil on her sternum. Strength she hadn't even realized she was missing leeched back into her bones and her breath came easy again.

"Witch," Angela Alice murmured, like she was reminding herself.

"Bitch." Cazzi nodded like it was a greeting.

The singer's dark blue lips quirked. Then she turned to Rohan, dismissing Cazzi as completely as if she had slammed a door in her face. "Did you leave me for her?"

12

"*You look at me*
Like I'm the sky
Full of stars
Ready to cry

You look at me
Like I'm the moon
Hanging heavy
Full of doom

I'm your heavy heart
Your problem child
Deep and dark
The hands that pull
Us apart"
—"Sky Song" by Angela Alice on *Bitch Queen Cometh*

Rohan crossed his arms and stood up, towering over his ex but still feeling like he was protecting himself. He'd really been hoping he'd be wearing something more grounding than his sigil when he met her next. "I left you for me."

"Cute," Angie sneered. She was as frighteningly beautiful as she had been the day he'd met and fallen for her but he no longer felt entranced.

"What the hell are you doing here?"

"In the neighborhood." Her sarcasm was so thick he could feel it against his skin. He glanced at Cazzi but she seemed fine, her fingers pressed between her breasts. He was willing to bet there was a hell of a protection sigil under there. The thought was distracting. He pushed it aside.

"What about me saying no on the phone did you not understand?" He demanded. The talisman scraped against his chest under his shirt.

"You're using some witch to get back at me and now you're taunting me on top of it? Have some decency, Rohan." Her voice was plaintive, heartrending, but her anger made the room feel five degrees colder.

I am my own person. His body was taut and he fisted his hand against the desire to reach out and comfort her. She'd won far too many fights that way. "Decency? Decency is being supportive of my solo efforts, decency is not constantly steamrolling my problems and emotions with your own. Don't fucking talk to me about decency."

"Oh you wanna talk about your flaws?" Angie pushed up her sleeves, revealing Baphomet on one arm and the Leviathan cross on the other. "You're needy and whiny and so sensitive you get mad at a compliment. Heaven forbid I don't pay enough attention to you or leave you alone too long or *go to a party by myself.*"

"You were gone for three fucking days and barely texted. If I hadn't checked your Instagram I'd have thought you were dead!"

Cazzi cleared her throat. When they ignored her, she said, "Okay, let's all take a deep breath and sit down."

Rohan didn't move. His fists were still knotted at his side. He would never hit Angie and she had never hit him but he'd seen her take down rowdy fans who'd fought their way on stage and tried to touch her. No matter how rich and famous she got, Angie would always be that teenaged girl with a pocket knife who'd hitchhiked from Florida to LA after her father was killed. It was something that took him far too long to learn: Angie was mean when she had to be.

He focused on the feeling of his talisman against his chest. Angie was mean but she would not throw the first punch, at least not physically.

"Don't make me do this," Angie hissed, taking an abrupt step towards him.

"SIT. DOWN." In the small, soundproof space, Cazzi's yell was stunning. Rohan found himself sitting. Angie sat on the far side of the couch, looking as surprised as he felt.

"That's better." Cazzi smiled her therapist smile. "Now why don't you both take three deep breaths?"

Rohan and Angie glanced at her, then each other.

"Don't make me yell again." Cazzi's smile held the same reasonable calm psychos on TV had before they tried to destroy the world.

Rohan inhaled loudly.

"Thank you." Cazzi's smile warmed. "In... and out... Angela holding your breath just makes you look childish. There you go, thank you. And again, in... and out... now—"

"Am I interrupting something?"

Rohan opened his eyes to see Benji standing in the doorway, freezing as they saw who was here. But what shocked Rohan was Angie's face. Angie was slack mouthed in shock and...blushing?

CAZZI TOOK one look at the combative expression on Benji's face and swallowed a sigh. There was no way this was going to end well. Benji stood, framed by the open door, eyes narrowed and fixed on Angela.

Who stood up like she'd sat on a pin, her cheeks bright red and her eyes huge.

Rohan stood too, "Benji…"

"Is this—are you—" Angela seemed… rattled as she stared at Benji. What about Benji could possibly rattle the woman who once faced down a mob of Westboro Baptist Church protesters alone and in person? "Benji Omega of User-Friendly Omega?"

Cazzi felt Angela's shock even through her sigils, her heart speeding up and her cheeks heating in response.

"Why are you here?" Benji's voice was low and cold.

"You *are* Benji Omega, right?"

"I was."

Angela frowned, seemingly noticing Benji's coolness for the first time. "What the hell happened?" She looked at Rohan. "Why didn't you tell me you were working with them?"

Rohan stared at her. "Seriously? We had a whole conversation—"

But she clearly wasn't listening as she turned back to Benji. "Why don't you perform anymore? You're amazing! I saw UFO when you guys played the Roxy in 2011. It was the best show I've ever seen. It fucking inspired me."

Benji's eyes narrowed. "If I wanted career advice, I'd ask. Now go away. We have more than enough shit to do without you hanging around."

Angela Alice tipped her chin up and Cazzi swore the temperature in the room dropped. "Are you dismissing me, Omega?"

Benji tipped their chin up too, staring down their nose at her. They were nearly the same height so that was a feat. "Yes."

"You disappoint me, Omega. You're just as pretty as you used to be but you're as fake as a wedding cake."

Benji blinked. Frowned. "And you, Coma White, are a copy of an imitation. Don't be proud of it."

Were they speaking in code? Was this some kind of reference Cazzi didn't get?

The Bitch Queen bared her teeth. "Fuck off you washed up hasbeen," she snarled and swept out of the room, slamming the door.

"I should go after her." Rohan started for the door but Cazzi blocked him.

"I'll do it."

"I don't think she'll listen to you." He pushed her shoulder gently like he was testing her resolve. The press of his body was more distracting than she'd like but she had bigger things on her mind.

"Trust me."

"Yes, do," Benji interjected, looking thoughtfully at the closed door.

"Huh?" Rohan turned towards them and Cazzi darted out.

It wasn't difficult to find his ex. She leaned against the back door of the studio, breathing hard. She drew herself up the minute she saw Cazzi. "What?" she snapped.

"I come in peace." Cazzi raised her hands to show they were empty.

"You're going to try and shrink me again." Angela crossed her arms, glaring down her nose at Cazzi. She looked ready for a parking lot throw-down. "Go ahead. Try."

Cazzi shrugged. "I'm just breaking a pattern."

"What pattern?"

"Tell me if this sounds familiar: you and Rohan fight. A lot. Lots of yelling and high tension. One of you stomps off, the other follows. More fighting ensues, someone backs down, and then it's all sweetness, apologies, and make-up sex."

"That's how all relationships work."

"The thing is, it's not."

"Maybe if they're fucking boring. A good passionate relationship is."

Cazzi hid a grimace. "What's passion to you?"

"What's passion? Are you fucking kidding me?" Angela stared at her. Then her expression turned to pity. "Oh, you poor thing, you don't *know*."

Cazzi buried her irritation, promising herself several rounds with the punching bag in her backyard for this. "Explain it to me."

"You can't explain passion."

"Then what do you write songs about?" Cazzi raised her eyebrows.

"That's different."

"Well, if you can't do it…"

"I can fucking do it, don't try that reverse psychology shit on me." Angela snapped. She leaned in. "Passion is the fire burning in you. It's great sex and crazy fights and that moment on stage when the entire stadium is crying and singing with you. It's love and hate and rage, pure fucking rage. It's the animal part of us that reminds us we're alive. It's the meaning of life."

"Sounds heady." It did. Cazzi had almost been swept up in Angela's words. Only holding the image of her protection sigil in her mind kept her grounded.

"It's amazing," Angela sounded wistful.

"And kinda stressful."

"Life is stress."

"But love isn't."

"Do I need to explain love to you too?"

"Sure." That punching bag was going to get a sound beating.

"Love is a whirlwind of good sex and fun. Yeah, sometimes there's fighting and it hurts and sometimes you go through his phone because you're damn certain he's leaving you for someone." She gave Cazzi a narrowed-eyed stare.

"You met me at the exact same moment Rohan did."

"Yeah, sure," Angela drawled. "And I'm the Queen of fucking England."

"Tell me more about love," Cazzi said, trying to derail her.

"No. You tell me about love."

"This isn't about me."

"Bull-fucking-shit. Tell me what love should be, little Miss Therapist."

Cazzi ignored the dig. "Love is supporting each other but in a balanced way. It's that warm feeling when you see them and can't help but smile. It's holding each other and feeling at peace. It's not always great, it's not always easy, but the trust should be there and everyone involved should be ready to work to restore it if it's gone." She thought of Patrick and felt a pang but pushed on. "Sexual romantic love is like friendship with sex and wooing. It shouldn't constantly make you stressed, it should be comforting."

"Boring." Angela yawned.

"You were in love with Rohan weren't you?"

"And?"

Cazzi exhaled quietly so she wouldn't sigh and pinch the bridge of her nose. She'd had worse sessions with students and in grad school when she used to volunteer at a local prison, but she wasn't at her best. She was tired and stressed, out of her wheelhouse and probably out of line. Why was she even doing this? Neither Rohan nor Angela would thank her. It wouldn't make Patrick love her. She felt fragile, about to snap. "Walk with me." She nodded at the empty field behind the studio.

"Hell no. I don't know you."

"You can see for miles out here, it's flat as fuck." Cazzi shook her head. "You know what? I don't care. I'm too stressed to help you anyway." She walked out past Angela, through the parking lot, and into the field, dead weeds bending under her feet.

Footsteps crunched behind her.

"You're right, you really can see for miles out here." Angela wasn't even winded as she jogged up to her side.

Cazzi shrugged. Social niceties were beyond her and she wasn't about to waste any sigils on trying.

There was only a moment of silence before Angela broke it. "So what's going on here?"

Cazzi looked around the dirt and the far-out trees. "I think there's a small teaching airport a couple of fields over. I heard they crash here sometimes."

"Sure, whatever. So you're Ro's rebound fuck?"

"None of your damn business."

Angela grabbed Cazzi's arm, fingers digging into the meat of her bicep until Cazzi stopped and faced her. "You're trying to hurt me," she observed mildly, not really caring. The dissociation was back, blunting everything, even Angela's rage.

Somewhere, far off, she considered punching Angela, hard. Breaking that pretty nose.

I am not my capacity for violence.

"He's mine. I protect him, so you take your white knight complex and ride off, you twat."

"Irrational jealousy."

"What?"

"Intensity, jealousy, manipulation, volatility, deflecting responsibility, belittling, and that's just what I've seen in the twenty minutes. And now you're trying to hurt me physically." Cazzi met her eyes. "All signs of an unhealthy relationship that could escalate to abuse, if it hasn't already."

Angela let go, stumbling back. "I am *not* abusive. I protect abuse victims, I know the signs."

"Deflecting responsibility."

"Don't twist this. We're in love."

"*This is not love, Angela!*" Cazzi exploded. "Rohan does not need your protection, he needs you to leave him alone."

"What do you know? You literally just met." Angela sneered.

"You think this is the first or even the tenth time I've seen this?" Cazzi snarled. "You think you're special? You think you're different? I've seen so many people like you, so many partners like Rohan. You use your trauma like a shield, your temper like a weapon, your love like a noose. You have an out before it gets bad before you're worse than a shitty girlfriend. Get your shit together, Angela. Get help. I don't know who told you this was love, but they did you a massive disservice."

Cazzi stalked away, further into the field, ignoring the voice in her head demanding she stay and protect Rohan. Rohan was a grown-ass man and it was disrespectful to treat him otherwise. Besides, if she talked to anyone else right now, she might just murder them. Memories roiled through her stomach and she walked faster, hurrying towards the trees.

"Do you think I should go out there?" Rohan asked, staring anxiously at the door.

"No."

"Okay, but what if—"

"No." Benji pinned him in place with a look. "If you go back to her, I'm fucking done."

"Go back to...Angie? No! No, I'm worried about Cazzi."

"Good." They turned back to the keyboard and played a major G scale.

"You thought I was going back to her after that?"

Benji shrugged. "I've seen you crawl back after she's said worse."

"Have some fucking faith, Benjiro. I like myself better than that."

"It's not about whether you like yourself or not." They switched to the minor key. "I didn't understand, not until just now. A woman like that? She's a black hole, a void. She's got nothing inside so she'll devour as much as she can but she'll never be happy."

"There's no one like Angie."

"There's millions of people like her. She's just the worst I've ever seen." They played an eerie tritone.

Rohan said nothing. Benji's words hung there for a while, fizzing in his head with the lingering echoes of the tritone until he wrote them down, rearranged them.

You're the black hole in my sky
The void that's always hungry
There's no one like you
Except everyone like you

Oh bleach white
Psychic vampire knight
Sucking out my soul
There's I can nothing to do
To make you happy

He tossed them over to Benji. They read the lines, made some notes, and slid the notebook back. Rohan looked at it. They were minor but noticeable improvements. "With that tritone?"

He looked up and nodded.

They smiled briefly, then a thought crossed their face. "They've been gone a long time."

Rohan frowned. "Shit, you're right. I hope Angie hasn't murdered her." He meant it as a joke but when they both lurched towards the door, neither of them were laughing.

When they got outside there was no one in the parking lot.

"Is that her?" Benji pointed at a figure in the field behind the lot.

Rohan ran.

Angie stood stock still in the middle of the dirt rows, her fists knotted, practically vibrating with rage.

"Where's Cazzi?" Rohan demanded, fighting the urge to shake her as he skidded to a stop in front of Angie.

"She's just like me, you know. Unstable, full of stupid emotions," Angie hissed through her teeth. Her rage was hot against his skin but he couldn't care less. She was magnificent and he didn't have time for it.

"Angelica," Rohan growled. "Cut the drama and tell me where the fuck she is."

"Drama?" Angie laughed. "Drama ran off that way after calling me abusive and a shitty girlfriend." She stabbed her finger towards the distant tree line. Dark purple clouds were brewing on the horizon. "You two enjoy each other," she called as he dashed for the trees. "You fucking deserve it after the nightmare that was me."

***

CAZZI KEPT HER PACE EVEN. She'd stopped hurrying when she'd gotten to the olive trees across the field. Now she tried to stay calm as she circled back towards the studio.

She couldn't keep rabbiting. Even if it was easier in the short term.

She rounded the end of the orchard, or whatever this was, and saw him: Rohan running towards her.

She picked up her pace, jogging up to meet him. "Hey, is everything alright?"

"I thought Angie had unhinged her jaw and devoured you whole or something." His tone was casual, mild. Like he hadn't just run clear across a field to find her. She appreciated the sentiment. She didn't want to think about what that implied or how his chest heaved and his shirt stuck to his body in a way she had no business appreciating.

"I do have a phone, you know. I'm pretty sure I could get reception in her stomach."

"I don't have your number."

That wasn't going to change, as far as she was concerned. "Bummer."

"Really is," he said, falling into step with her as they headed back to the studio. "You okay by the way?"

"Are you asking if I did another runner?"

He shrugged.

"I went for a walk. I don't always run away from things."

"Well, Angie could've been trying to eat you."

She laughed. "Is she really a cannibal? I thought that was an internet myth."

"No, she's a vegetarian. But you never know."

"Yeah, vegetarians are well known for their cannibalistic tendencies."

Rohan rolled his eyes. "Whatever."

She stopped. "Hey, are *you* okay? That was intense."

Rohan stopped too. "That was Angie."

"You mean she's always like that?"

"I mean, yeah. She's had a rough life, you know?"

Cazzi kept the worry out of her face and voice. "I've heard."

"Benji and everyone talk about her like she's some sort of crazy villain but she's not bad, just messed up."

"Mmhmm."

Rohan hunched his shoulders. "I'm not going back to her if that's what you're thinking."

"I'm not." She had been thinking exactly that.

"What *are* you thinking, Dr. Muldoon?"

She shook her head. "Angela said I have a white knight complex, but I think she was actually talking about you."

He shrugged. "Well, she'd know. She's got a big one."

"Her?" Cazzi peered across the field but she couldn't see Angela or her complex. Maybe Benji had chased her off.

"Yeah. It's buried deep and she doesn't like to talk about it but she loves saving people. Her touring company is full of her saved. It's the most terrifyingly loyal group I've ever seen." But he smiled.

"Sounds like a cult."

"It might be, someday." He laughed. "Between them and the foundation we started, there's probably a small army of people who adore her."

"Uh-huh." She didn't quite see the humor in that but he didn't seem to be alarmed so she figured she'd follow his lead. "Foundation?"

He pushed his hand through his hair and the shyness she'd seen in him before returned. "We bought a building in Downtown LA and turned it into a place to help unhomed people. You know, soup kitchen, clinic, job center, essential supplies, that kinda thing."

Cazzi blinked. "I had no idea."

He shrugged again. "Angie was homeless when she came to LA and so were my Nānī and Mom for a while after they ran away from Nānī's husband." His lips twisted and Cazzi noted he refused to call his grandmother's husband his grandfather. "I had free time after the band broke up and I kinda threw myself into it."

"That's really cool," Cazzi said, already wondering if she could maybe teach a class there the next time she had to drag herself back to LA. "But wait, now that you broke up…"

He shook his head. "My stepdad set it up so neither of us could dismantle it. Only the board can. We were mostly just the money bags."

Somehow Cazzi suspected Rohan did more than that. "That's still important."

He smiled. "It's a family effort. James and Nānī are on the board and Mom volunteers in the clinic. Angie and I drag everyone we can into it." The smile faltered. "I'm not sure how it'll work now but it will. Neither of us would give that up."

Meaning they'll always be connected somehow.

Rohan touched her hand, making her stop again. "Is there anything I need to know about what happened between you and Angie?"

You were in an unhealthy relationship and I just showed off one of the reasons why I didn't actually become a therapist. She shook her head. "She's fine. I dropped some hard truths on her and she will either absorb them or go into denial. I can't say I've made her go away or gotten through to her, but I tried."

"But you're okay, right? I know she can be a lot if you're not used to her."

She shrugged. "The walk helped." She started moving again. "It completed the stress cycle."

Rohan blinked. "Okay…"

"When you get stressed, your body floods with chemicals that are supposed to help you escape the threat. When that stress isn't a lion trying to eat you, you don't burn them off by running or fighting. So you just carry it around unless you burn it off or channel it."

"Is that why you jumped the wall the other day?"

"That and sheer bloody fucking panic." *Among other things.*

He laughed. "So you rabbit, good to know."

"Yeah, well, fighting and freezing just get me in trouble and I don't think I could fawn if I tried so sometimes rabbiting just seems smart. I'm trying to curb that instinct though."

Rohan was about to say something but they hit the studio parking lot and Benji came tearing out of the building.

They skidded to a halt in front of them. "We have a goddamn problem."

13

Rohan's heart dropped. What had Angie done now? Then he caught himself. She was probably on the way back to LA. There was no way even she would have time to—

"That—" Benji cut a glance to Rohan and visibly revised what they were going to say. "*Woman* tweeted that you two were over and dropped a surprise album *Lemonade* style all in the last five minutes!"

Rohan exhaled hard. "Is it about—?"

"Yes."

"Oh fuck," Cazzi breathed.

Rohan swore viciously in Hindi. He wasn't fluent but his grandmother swore like a sailor and he reverted whenever he was shook. And god, he was shook. Even for Angie, that was fast and vicious. "Did she say where we were?"

Benji shook their head. "We have that much of a head start—for now." They groaned. "I knew we should've leaked the break-up ourselves."

Fuck, now he and James would have to do damage control.

"It would've tainted the whole album, everyone would think it's just about her." Not to mention send the board of their foundation into a tizzy. He shot off a quick text to his stepdad, asking him to handle the press for now. He got a curt "On it," almost immediately. But he knew he would be getting a call from his family soon. Rohan stuck his hands in his hair, grabbing his curls like a lifeline.

"Too late for that now." Benji pointed out. "Now are you willing to write about her?"

"I don't think now is the time—" Cazzi started.

"Yeah," Rohan said. "Yeah, I fucking am." He could already feel his phone buzzing in his pocket. He turned it off.

Benji grinned, an expression so dark and twisted it looked straight out of an old User-Friendly Omega video.

"Dammit," Rohan growled, pacing. "I should've known. I should've fucking known. Angie shares fucking everything, why the hell would this be any different?"

"She didn't tweet about your break-up before though," Cazzi said.

"She didn't think it was real," Rohan said and stopped. "Fucking hell, she thought I was sitting here waiting for her to come back like some sad little puppy. Like I was some goddamn extension of her. Like I couldn't live without her." He kicked a nearby tree and immediately regretted it as pain shot up his toe. "Fuck!"

A hand touched his arm gently. He almost pulled away but the look in Cazzi's eyes stopped him. "I have a punching bag at home if you want to leave the trees alone. Might hurt less."

"Fuck that," Benji said. "Come write. Let's use this shit." They hooked their arm in Rohan's and dragged him into the studio. "I wrote some of my best stuff angry." There was a determined gleam in their eyes.

"I'm not writing metal," Rohan pointed out, but let them pull him along anyway.

"Like you've never heard an angry pop song."

"Don't you think having some time to process might give you a better, less shortsighted song?" Cazzi said, following them.

"What time?" Benji shot back. "We're on a deadline here."

Rohan thought about how much of this was coming out of his pocket and how much time they'd already lost to this bullshit and sped up.

But back in the studio, his bravado evaporated. He stared at the empty page and despair crested like a wave. It was over. It was over and she was going to crush him. The album would flop. The label would tank and he'd be just another broke former child star. He'd have to go on some humiliating celebrity reality show or attempt a memoir nobody would read just to keep from living in his parents' house. "I can't write about her. I can't do this."

Benji stopped bustling around the studio, and looked at him, crossing their arms. "I have limited patience for this narrow-minded shit."

"What the fuck are you talking about, narrow-minded?"

"You're sitting on a gold mine of emotions. Yeah, they're about her but they're also yours and they can also be generalized. And we both know specified generalization is the key to a good pop song."

"Benji," Cazzi warned. "I think this is a good time to listen, don't you?"

Benji glowered at her but nodded. "Sorry."

"People will only listen to my album to hear about her." Rohan grimaced. Even he could tell he was whining.

"Of course they will! It's the information they have about you so they'll try to draw whatever connections they can. No matter what you write about. So what if they only listen because of it?" Beji said.

"So it's hopeless. I'll always be in her shadow."

"Would you like to elaborate on tha—" Cazzi started.

Benji cut her off. "Bitch, she's using you and the emotions you generated in her. Why the fuck not return the favor? What people think doesn't matter as long as they respond to, talk about, and buy your shit."

Rohan frowned.

Cazzi sighed. "They're not wrong. Maybe that's why people will listen to it first, but if it's good they'll keep listening."

"It'll be good." Benji's expression brooked no disagreement. "Look, it's not about you. It's about art and it's about money. Might as well get some damn catharsis out of it." They sat down rather pointedly behind the drum set in the corner and tapped out a basic 4/4 beat on the snare with a finger.

Rohan thought about it. He'd thought he was taking the high road before but what if he wasn't? Had he thought Angie would respect his privacy?

Angie, the woman who'd made a hardened reporter curl into a fetal ball when she'd described walking in on her father's murder on national TV. Or who'd been known to tweet about being on her period. In detail. And here he was, being overly precious with feelings that kept coming out in song anyway.

He nodded and then a thought struck him. "Wait, you said *Lemonade*-style. She didn't do a full album movie did she?"

Benji's eyes widened and they checked their phone one-handed, scrolling until— "Fuuuuuck. It's coming out next week." The finger tapping the cymbal stuttered then sped up. "On her YouTube channel."

"How did she have time to do all of that?" Cazzi asked, bewildered.

"She didn't," Benji said grimly. "So either it's slapdash and terrible or —"

"She's been working on this for a long time," Rohan finished. "Shit. I've been blind."

Cazzi frowned.

"You think she's been setting you up for this?" Benji pulled their guitar out and tuned it, still sitting behind the drum kit.

"Are we sure this album is about your break-up?" Cazzi asked.

Benji held up their phone. Rohan leaned in to look and then wished he hadn't. The album cover was up. It was called *Romance Inverted* and featured Angie's distinctively tattooed fingers tearing a picture of Rohan and her in half.

It was like being punched in the face. In the photo she was tearing up, they were wrapped around each other, taking a silly selfie that hadn't been meant for anyone but themselves. It was framed and Angie always took it on tour, it was his picture for her contact. She'd never even posted it on her private feeds. God, they'd been so happy in that fucking picture.

She's mocking me. He tried to shake the thought away, to be compassionate about what might have been going through her head but somehow compassion wouldn't come. Instead acid climbed his gut.

"Subtle," Cazzi murmured, only the slight narrowing of her eyes betraying any emotion. "She doesn't half-ass anything does she?"

"Not unless it's a relationship," Rohan muttered.

"Ouch. Good line." Benji hummed to themself, strumming. The guitar wasn't plugged in so Rohan barely heard the notes, but what he heard felt right. "You can't half-ass anything/except you and me." They crooned, matching Rohan's range.

"Yes!" Rohan pointed at them, perhaps more exuberantly than was warranted. But fuck it. If Angie was going to air their dirty laundry then he was going to get his say. "I didn't even want to be/your everything/just your anything/anything to you," he sang back.

The words echoed in the small room, giving him goosebumps. He kept going, his voice rising. "But that was too much, wasn't it?/too much to ask that you'd give a shit."

Benji dragged him to the soundboard, jammed headphones on both of them and handed him a mike. They plugged the guitar in, strumming, the chords filling Rohan's ears. "Start from the top."

Rohan grabbed the mike. The chords thrummed in his pulse, dark and just as pissed as he was. He closed his eyes and put gravel in his voice:

> "You can't half-ass anything
> Except you and me"

He thought of every time she'd blow him off. He'd understood. They were both busy, but he'd tried, at least, to show up to her events, to her gigs when she asked, to the parties where she'd wanted him on her arm. But when he'd asked, she'd so rarely shown up. Until finally, he'd stopped asking. He lightened up the growl, letting the ache bleed through and make his voice soulful.

> "I didn't want to be
> Your everything
> Just your anything
> Anything to you."

Showing up here today was probably the most attention she'd paid him in a year.

"But that was too much
Wasn't it?
Too much to ask
that you'd give a shit."

His voice was still rough, his anger leaking out through grit teeth. He remembered when they'd been good. When seeing her was a shot of adrenaline to the chest and an instant hard-on. It just made him madder. He opened up and belted:

"You were an adrenaline shot,
A Viagra pop,
A thousand watts
Straight to my heart."

God this hurt, like tearing out his soul and waving it like a flag. He opened his eyes and saw Cazzi watching him. Her eyes were huge, her face pale, her mouth tight but she nodded as if he was reading her thoughts verbatim. He sang his rage to her, knowing she'd understand.

"You made me crazy,
Then took my meds away,
You maybe hate me
But you made me this way."

He belted the last line then hesitated, the pain surfacing under the rage

"Chorus," mouthed Benji. Behind them, Cazzi gave him an encouraging smile.

> "You never half-assed anything,
> Nothing but you and me,
> I wanted to be
> Anything,
> Anything to you…
> But I'm nothing.
> Nothing but…
> me."

He leaned back, panting. He felt lighter, exhilarated, and drained.

THE NEXT DAY, when Rick heard the tale of Angie's visit, he shook his head. "We're going to make this album a masterpiece."

"Better than hers," Benji added, putting their phone on silent. It'd been ringing off the hook lately and if it was anything like the calls Rohan was getting, he didn't blame them for not wanting to pick up.

"Please tell me it's terrible." Rohan couldn't bring himself to listen to it.

"It's fucking amazing." Benji's eye twitched. "It might be her best work yet."

"Ours will top it." Rick sounded more determined than Rohan had heard him in a long time.

The three of them worked for days, later and later until Benji fell asleep over the soundboard, Rick passed out on the couch with his laptop on his chest, and Rohan could only think in verse.

Cazzi came and went but didn't say much. She was like a reassuring ghost, her presence, her sympathetic smile, and the occasional word of advice kept him from falling apart completely. Sometimes she took out her computer and worked while he sang in the booth or sat with Benji experimenting at the soundboard.

He watched her frown as she typed and half of him wished he could smooth over whatever problem pinched that divot between her eyebrows, the other half was content to watch, fascinated to see unguarded, sober emotions on her face.

They hadn't touched since the Angiepocolypse, as Rick was calling it, but Rohan could feel her the moment she entered the room. He'd been the same way with Angie, but where her presence was looming and large, Cazzi's was the eye of the storm, still and thoughtful. In the few quiet moments between work and face-planting on the bed, he remembered the warmth of her in his arms.

In between everything, he itched to touch her again. To touch her more. He told himself it was nothing but he could barely look Rick in the eye sometimes. He could barely stop himself from looking at her sometimes.

Which was probably why he asked if he could drive her home on Thursday night. They had gone late, all of them eating takeout from across the street and Cazzi frowning at her screen harder than ever. For once he was leaving around the same time she was instead of stumbling out of the studio hours later. Benji had taken off a few minutes ago, leaving them alone.

The frown she'd worn while staring at her computer carved itself deeper into her face at his offer. "I think I'll be alright."

He shrugged, trying to sound more casual than he felt. "No worries, I figured since we're going in the same direction…"

Cazzi tipped her head, her gaze turning inward, considering. She looked at her phone quickly and sighed. "It's supposedly raining out there."

Since the studio had no windows and was soundproof, he'd have to take her word for it. "Is that a yes?"

She sighed again. "Yes, but only because I'm tired. But," she looked him in the eye. "I'm warning you now, I get cranky in cars."

Cazzi held her breath and then forced herself to let it out. She hadn't really disclosed anything, though it had felt like a gesture of trust to say even that.

His brow creased. "If you get carsick I can open the windows."

"Thank you." She didn't correct him. The sentiment was enough.

They walked out into the night, which was indeed rainy and she unlocked her bike as Rohan pulled the car around. He lifted it easily and stowed it on the folded-down back seat of his fancy car.

"So what are you doing after this?" Rohan asked once they were on the road.

"Gotta finish up my work." She answered on autopilot, most of her attention on her breathing. She felt okay but sometimes these things turned quickly.

"You're still working?" He looked aghast.

"Not officially, but I have a proposal to finish up."

"The answer is yes."

She was tired enough that it took her a moment to parse what he said and another, longer, shocked moment to realize it was a joke. She sputtered out a laugh but deliberately made it seem like she'd missed the double meaning. "I wish it were that easy, but even at a school this liberal I'm having a hard enough time trying to start this damn class."

He frowned. "Why?"

She sighed. "Politics. Internal and external."

"What does the class cover?"

"Oh well," she drew herself up against the seat. He glanced at her, watching curiously as she launched into her pitch. "These days kids learn about sex from porn and rumors. Sex education in high school is a crapshoot based on where you grow up that leaves graduates missing essential knowledge about things like how virginity is a construct, the hymen can't be popped, and how to ask for and give consent."

He stared at her before seeming to realize he'd been stopped in front of the stop sign for far too long, not that there was anyone around to care.

She soldiered on, talking fast. If she couldn't pitch this to Rohan how was she supposed to give a presentation to the Academic Senate? "By mandating that our students learn the basics of sex we can reduce the numbers of unwanted pregnancies and instances of sexual violence while taking the stigma and shame out of kink, sexuality, and gender variance. If that isn't a worthy cause, I don't know what is." She inhaled hard. "What do you think?"

"The hymen can't be popped?" He looked dazed.

"Nope, it keeps growing back until it withers at about twenty-five. But ninety-seven percent are open in the middle so it's not a problem and some vaginas are born without them." She shrugged. "Despite what everyone tells you, penetration shouldn't hurt the first time, with proper lubrication and foreplay."

"Ohhh, that makes sense, biologically. I feel like if more people knew that, the whole virginity thing would but well, less of a *thing*."

"Yes! It's such a heteronormative construct. I mean, what is virginity for someone who doesn't want P in V sex? Or do they lose their virginity if they try anal first? Or oral? What about the penis-haver? What if they are a gay man? Do they never lose their virginity because they never have P in V? Or are they a virgin if they only have oral sex or hand jobs?"

"Exactly!" Rohan laughed. "Man, I wish they'd taught that in high school."

"See, you get it! By the way, if you're interested I have some books…"

Rohan held up a hand in surrender. "After the album's done. I don't have time to read my social media feeds let alone a book."

"Alright." She looked out the windshield, not really seeing the road. It was so hard to find people who liked to read as much as she did. Judit was the only person she knew who could keep up with her. Patrick had been a fellow bookworm as a kid but had grown out of it at some point. Maybe she should find a book club. You know, in her copious free time.

"That's not to say I won't ask for a book recc in the future," Rohan said.

She shrugged. "It's okay if you don't."

He looked at her as they rolled to a stop in front of one of the few red lights in town, staring until she looked back. "I will and I'll read it."

"Okay," she mumbled, smiling. She could tell he was sincere and that meant more than it should.

14

"*I can't, I can't stop*
Talking you out
I can't, I can't start
Figuring you out.

Oh girl, you've got me twisted
Spun me around so fast I must've missed it
You make no sense
I've got no defense
But I need to know, know, know
How to let you go, go, go."
— "Let You Go" by Beatboyz on *Heartbeatz*

On Friday, Cazzi stepped into the studio lobby, bracing for another evening spent being an emotional crutch. She didn't mind, partially because Angela Alice was on her shit list, partially because she could tell she was needed, and partially because watching an album come together had a fascinatingly historic feel to it. Though it was tiring, she soaked up the creative energy Benji and Rohan put out as she watched something iconic being made.

The album was good, really good as far as she could tell. Yes, she went home drained without feeling like she'd done a thing, but she went with the most recent track stuck in her head. Which was both awesome and frustrating. There was nothing like having a song so new she couldn't even listen to it on constant revolution in her mental playlist.

But someday she'd be able to say she'd been there when RK's first solo album was made. Whatever it ended up being called. That was being debated, rather heatedly.

Her thoughts were full of the music as she headed towards the studio door. It opened and there was Patrick.

She froze.

He froze.

The breeze from the open courtyard door made his locs sway. The skin under his eyes was bruised from lack of sleep but his gaze was clear as he stared back at her.

They hadn't spoken since that fucking phone call.

"Hi," he said.

"Hey," she breathed.

"I'm late."

She shrugged. "I'm early."

He took a step forward. She didn't move. Let him come to her. Or not. She almost told herself she didn't care but the way her skin came alive, like it was responding to a magnetic field centered around him, gave lie to that.

"You doing alright?" His gaze skimmed her. It was a clinical look, assessing.

"It's hectic but exciting. I can see why you love it so much."

His face softened, a smile pulling at his lips. Then it disappeared again. "You're okay?"

She still hadn't cried. The tears were an ever-hardening knot growing against her lungs. "I'm fine." She tipped up her chin, looked him hard in the eye, daring him to be okay. "You?"

"No." He took another step closer. It would only take one more to put him in her space.

"No?" Her anger slipped away. It was her turn to look him over. Tired eyes, ashy knuckles, hollow cheeks. "What's wrong?"

"I miss you."

She took the final step, looking up at him. "You've lost weight, tell me you aren't starving yourself over me." She said the words lightly but worry clawed its way into her belly.

"Just too many energy drinks and not enough food." His smile was tired.

"You want some tea? I have those blends you've made me."

He shook his head.

"Or cookies? I just made a fresh batch."

"Maybe tomorrow."

She made a mental note to bring the rest of the batch.

"I'll take a hug right now if you'll give me one."

Like that was even a question. She lurched into him burying her face in his neck and squeezing him to her. He wrapped his arms around her, laying his head on top of hers, his locs curtaining them away from the world. He smelled like he had for years, of Old Spice and Shea Butter but there was another floral scent under all of it. Lavender. He must be really stressed.

"Tawny," he murmured. Just like that day on the beach after…

"I'm sorry," he said.

"For?" She murmured the question into his shirt, so close to his skin she could almost taste him.

"Everything. I've been a shitty friend lately."

"Yeah, you have."

"You still like me, right?" Those words. Her words, over a decade old and just as vulnerable as the minute they were spoken.

"Of course I still like you." There was no other answer. Half of her was back at the beach, listening to those very same words rumble through his chest.

"Okay," he murmured against her scalp.

She burrowed deeper into his chest. Her eyes remained dry.

CAZZI DRIFTED through the evening with the phantom of his embrace surrounding her. It held her as Benji and Rohan argued about whether the album needed a sexy song, a dance song, or both. She left early when it was clear they didn't need her.

Stepping out of the studio into the night made her more lonely than she'd felt in a long time. It was Friday and the chill in the air dissolved the remaining phantom feel of Patrick around her. She didn't want to be alone tonight.

Cazzi called Eva and was invited over immediately. She stopped home, put together a variety pack of cookies and pot, and headed over.

She arrived in the middle of bickering. It was like she hadn't left the studio at all, except Judit and Eva bickered about the couch.

"I bought it," Judit pointed out, her pretty face make-up free and her hair thrown up in a messy bun. She looked like she'd just rolled out of bed and from the shadows under her eyes and the lines around her lips, it hadn't been a good pain day. Cazzi felt like shit. She should be checking in on Judit more.

"We went half and half," Eva sat on the couch, her arms crossed.

"Actually we split it three ways," Cazzi said, kicking off her shoes.

Her ex-roommates stared at her, looked at the couch, then back to her. "Do *you* want it?" Judit asked, somewhat peevishly.

"My place is way too small for two couches." The one they were arguing over was an overstuffed monstrosity they'd gotten from a thrift store. It had taken a good half hour to maneuver into the house. Cazzi didn't want to even think about trying to get it out again. "Isn't your new place pretty small too, Judit?"

"It could fit a couch," Judit bristled.

"Uh-huh." Cazzi ambled to the toolbox, stashed exactly where it had been when she lived here, on the bottom shelf of the bookcase. The shelves were mostly empty now, only Eva's books leaning haphazardly in piles. The sight made her sad as she grabbed the measuring tape and tossed it to Judit.

Judit caught it with a grimace. "You're going to logic me, aren't you."

"Worse," Eva cackled. "I think she's going to use geometry."

"You say that like I remember anything from high school math." Cazzi put her bag down on the table. "I brought treats, by the way."

"Hell yes!" Eva said, abandoning the couch. "Cookies?"

"And pot."

"Oh hell yes." She grabbed a cookie in one hand and rummaged through the bag of pot. She picked a jar up and read the label. "God I love your scientific mind."

Judit drifted over and tossed the measuring tape on the table. "You're right, it wouldn't fit." She sighed. "I have the best naps on that thing."

Cazzi put a hand on her shoulder. "There are other couches in the sea."

Judit gave the couch a mournful look. "To me it was perfect."

"Are you going to love it with all your wasted heart until it looks like whatever the couch equivalent of a mummy is?" Cazzi asked.

"*Love Actually*," Eva muttered, rolling her eyes. "Hold on, I think I have a bunch of giant cue cards. You can stand out on the porch and be emo at it. That won't be creepy at all."

"You two just don't understand the pure agony of being in

love," Judit joked and then caught sight of Cazzi's face. "Okay, I take that back. Eva doesn't know."

"The joy of being aromantic," Eva said smugly. Then she looked at Cazzi and asked sympathetically, "How *is* that whole thing going?"

Cazzi gestured at the assortment of pot. "How do you think?" She sighed. "He's acting like I never told him I love him and today we had this kinda sweet moment and, fuck, I just don't know."

"What about the other one?" Eva handed her a jar full of an indica blend with high CBD content that Cazzi's notes said had given all three of them a silly, relaxing high with minimal achiness on Judit's part.

Cazzi picked up the jar and started packing the vape. "Other one?"

"Don't pretend. You know who I'm talking about."

"Yesss, spill the tea." Judit sat down and propped her chin on her fists, eyes gleaming.

"Okay fine." Cazzi sat down too. "But I'm invoking both of your client confidentiality codes."

"Client confidentiality activated," Eva said.

"Psychic's honor." Judit raised her hand in the Boy Scout's salute. "Now spill."

So Cazzi did. By the time she was done, they were good and stoned on the back porch, staring up at the stars.

"You need a reading," Judit said. It wasn't a question. "That's a big fucking tangle and it's not going to unravel easy."

Eva giggled. "The total agony of a hot guy sandwich."

"It is agony! Look at her. She's suffering from Patrick's emotional fuckwittage." Judit gestured angrily at Cazzi.

Cazzi peered at her, trying to focus. "You've been reading *Bridget Jones' Diary* again, haven't you?"

"She found the first two books on a shelf and lost a whole day of packing," Eva reported.

"Did not. It was more like half a day." Judit grinned. "They're definitely flawed but still funny." Then she smacked Eva's shoulder. "But for real, remember when your best friend in high school ditched you for that guy she was dating? You were devastated."

"You really don't have to explain emotional shit to me, I'm a fucking counselor." Eva wrapped her arm around Cazzi's shoulders. "Oh honey, I'm sorry you're surrounded by emotionally stunted men, but hey at least you got to meet Angela Alice and that singer from User-Friendly Omega. You're swimming in eye candy."

"And half of Beatboyz," Judit added. "I used to have a poster of your best friend on my wall when I was in high school."

"Yeah, well me too," Cazzi said, "But mostly to embarrass him."

"*Mostly*," Eva waggled her eyebrows.

Cazzi laughed.

"I had RK's poster too," Judit said. "Boy, he was pretty."

"Still is," Cazzi muttered.

"Oh!" Eva pointed at her. "Oh! I fucking knew it."

"What? I have eyes. Benji is attractive too."

Eva waved that away. "But which do you think is hotter?"

Cazzi's face got hot and she was glad it was dark. "Uh, I guess Rohan."

"Ah ha!" Eva was pointing again.

"You're reading too much into this," Cazzi protested.

"I don't know," Judit said, "Benji is a goddamn sexual icon, especially since they came out. That spread they did for *Paper*…"

"Oh!" Eva clutched her chest. "I nearly died looking at it."

"It would've been a good way to go," Judit said solemnly.

"Yeah, but that's after make-up, lighting, photoshop, and all that shit," Cazzi pointed out.

"Doesn't matter," Eva said decisively. "Benji Omega is empirically more panty-wetting than RK."

Cazzi snorted. "You make it sound like people pee themselves just looking at them."

Judit laughed so hard she nearly fell out of her chair.

Eva cackled. "Oh man, total agony of love aside, I'm super fucking jelly you get to hang out and watch RK, Ricky Rick, and Benji fucking Omega make an album."

"Honestly, all that aside, it's pretty great." She smiled, basking in the glow of a good mellow high.

"I'm still giving you that reading," Judit said.

"Please do," Cazzi said, feeling optimistic.

Judit brought her cards out from her room and laid the deck on the table. Her movements were sure, professional. People paid her good money for this nowadays.

"Should I pay you?" Cazzi asked.

Judit waved the question again. "You gave me all the no bullshit sex education no one bothered to, and I couldn't ask Eva about. I don't think you understand how much anxiety and self-loathing you saved me."

Eva frowned but said nothing.

"Kink and queerness are nothing to be ashamed of," Cazzi said.

"I know that *now*." Judit chuckled. "The point is, you're my sex expert and I'm your diviner. Don't think of it as a favor."

"Aw, thank you." Cazzi's cheeks were hot but she couldn't stop smiling.

"Good thing I'm still good at this high," Judit said. "Stop me if you're not ready."

"Stop."

"Seriously?" Judit looked at her.

"Yeah." Cazzie scrubbed her hands over her face.

"What's wrong, honey?" Eva rubbed her back.

"I'm scared? Is that stupid? Excuse the ableist language, but is it?"

"Of course not." Judit covered Cazzi's hand with hers. "The future is scary, especially these days. Do you want to wait? We could do this tomorrow."

Cazzi shook her head. "If I don't do this now, I'll keep pushing it back until we forget about it. I need to face this. I feel like I've been rabbiting non-stop since Patrick came into town."

"Okay." Judit squeezed Cazzi's hand then returned her hands and attention to her deck. She shuffled it, the multi-colored crosses of the Thoth deck flashing between her fingers. It was a beautiful deck, designed by Aleister Crowley and Judit's favorite. "Let's do it one card, one question at a time."

Cazzi nodded.

"Think about your first question."

Cazzi took three deep inhales, each exhale longer than the last until she felt light with oxygen. Eva rubbed her back.

How do I fix my relationship with Patrick?

Judit picked out a card and flipped it. A night-black skeleton appeared, cavorting with its scythe, limbs at unnatural angles. Eva gripped Cazzi's shoulder. *Death.*

Judit gave them both a reassuring look. "Don't panic. No one's dying. This is a really big change, more of a metaphorical death, like a shedding of skin and shit that doesn't serve you. It's a good thing, in the end. But it's not going to be fun."

"Fuck," Cazzi murmured. Her stomach knotted.

"It'll be okay," Eva said.

Cazzi focused on her breathing. In and out. In and out. It was just a card. Who cared if Judit's cards were rarely wrong? There was still a chance.

No one will ever love you like he does.

Judit nodded, sliding the card back into the deck. "We can stop here if you want."

No one will understand you the way he does.

Cazzi shook her head even though she was high enough the movement made her feel like her brain was wobbling in her skull. "Let's do another one." Anything to get out of her head, she could feel herself starting to spiral.

"Think of your question." Judit shuffled again.

Can anyone love me the way Patrick does?

Judit flipped a card on the table: The Lovers, with its gaudy interracial royal wedding. "Oh hey, that's better. I mean, pretty self-explanatory but it does come with a couple caveats: love yourself first, your partner can't fulfill you, and don't expect them to fix everything. As RuPaul says, if you can't love yourself, how the hell are you going to love anybody else? But shit, you got some true love coming!" Judit clapped her hands and grinned at her. The expression was over the top, forced.

Eva squeezed her shoulder.

Cazzi tried to feel good about that but couldn't. Sometimes it freaked her out how on the nose the damn cards could be. She gave Judit a weak smile anyway.

"You want to go again?"

Cazzi chewed her lip, considering. She could ask about her class, but she wasn't sure if she could take any more.

Judit shuffled her cards restlessly, her gaze distant, not demanding. She flipped a card up, answering some question for herself. She smiled at what she saw and placed it on the table.

The Star, fractal and ethereal, spilling her cups somewhere out in space stared up at Cazzi. "Everything will work out," Judit said softly. "It'll be good."

"What will be?"

"Your happily ever after."

"Life doesn't end on a happy epilogue," Cazzi replied, still staring at the card. "It ends with death."

Eva sighed. "Caz…"

Judit shrugged. "This chapter will end well if you're careful and choose yourself."

Cazzi met her eyes. "You're sure?"

"As sure as I ever am." Judit smiled. "It's not gonna be easy but you'll get there."

"And we'll be here, keeping you sane," Eva said, leaning down slowly to wrap her arms around Cazzi's shoulders for a brief squeeze. "Cuz we're cool like that."

Judit ignored her demi-sister and looked at Cazzi. "Okay?"

"Apparently I'm going to be." Cazzi hoped she sounded more convinced than she felt.

Eva patted her back. "Don't think about it."

"How exactly am I supposed to do that?"

"Let's do something fun!" Eva said.

Two images popped into her head. One, of Patrick staring at her from his pool lounger about half a second before she'd kissed him and killed their friendship. They'd been having such a good visit up until then, sitting out in the dark, smoking and laughing. She'd just finished grad school and he'd been between projects, so she'd crashed at his place for a week. Just the two of them and Scoot, who'd been an adorable kitten then. It had been perfect, her version of a picket fence, until Cazzi ruined it.

The second image was Rohan singing to her, about her, in her living room.

"Oh no," Judit muttered.

"Oh yes," Eva said. "She needs to blow off steam! She needs fun!"

"I thought this was fun," Cazzi said, distracted. Rohan wasn't fun, he was… complicated.

Eva wasn't listening. She was on a roll. "What if we went to the studio and met everyone?"

"Um, what?" Judit said. "Random much?"

"It's," Cazzi checked her phone. "Nearly midnight. They're done." She frowned, remembering the sheer number of Monster cans littering the coffee table in there. "I hope they're done." She mumbled.

"Field trip!" Eva crowed.

"Back to where the majority of my stress is coming from? How is this helpful?" But ridiculously, and maybe this was the pot talking, Cazzi wanted to go. Maybe she could hang out with

Patrick and just *be*. Maybe they could recapture something of what they used to have.

"You're way too stoned," Judit said.

"Come on Judy! It'll be like old times, the three amigas tearing it up." Eva's cheer sounded forced.

"I'm pretty sure the only thing we tore up was old mail we were too lazy to shred," Cazzi said, even though she could feel guilt creeping up on her.

"Drop it, Eva," Judit said.

"Come onnnn, give me this. You're moving away and Cazzi's already left us."

"Literally right here," Cazzi said but guilt clobbered her at the begging look on Eva's face. Her friend had never quite gotten over Cazzi moving out six months ago. Eva hadn't understood, but how could she? Cazzi's reasoning hadn't exactly been rational. But Cazzi never forgot when she'd finally broken down and told the sisters about what happened to Tanya there had been a flicker of fear, of doubt, a minute recoil. Cazzi had almost ended their friendship right there but years of therapy helped her let it go.

It had been momentary, it had been long ago in undergrad, but after Patrick's ghosting, every distrustful thought Cazzi had ever had about anyone bubbled up. And since Eva and Judit were the only people in her proximity who knew, well, Cazzi had to get away. The feeling only intensified the longer Patrick stayed away and the more her friends worried about her.

"It's not the same," Eva said with a shrug.

A glance at Judit showed Cazzi she wasn't alone in her guilt. The last of her resolve collapsed. She could fix this, at least a bit. She sighed. "Lemme make a call."

She went inside and called Patrick, even though her training and therapy told her firmly she wasn't choosing herself in this decision. As she suspected, he was still up.

"Caz?" There was a trace of alarm in his voice.

"Hey weird question but you all are out of the studio right?"

"Um, no, we're still working. Why?"

"I hate to ask you this, but would you mind if I brought some friends to meet you all? They're cool if stoned." She half-hoped he'd say no, the other half of her desperately needed him to say yes. To say *come over, I need you.*

"So are you."

She almost hated how easily he could tell. "Yep."

"Why are you asking?" It wasn't a no, but it was a test.

She glanced at her friends on the porch and drifted closer to the front door. "It's Eva. Her sister is moving out and I already moved out and…"

"You're feeling guilty."

"Yeah." She wondered if he'd point out the problem with that.

He was silent and she heard Rohan yelling in the distance, "Is that Cazzi? Hi Cazzzi!"

"Is *he* high?" She asked.

Patrick chuckled.

"Tell her to come back and party with us!" Rohan yelled.

"You're having a party?" And they hadn't invited her? She wasn't sure if she was offended or relieved.

"We ordered pizza and Benji decreed we were *allowed* to have some of those cupcakes Rohan's been thirstin' after all week." She could practically hear Patrick roll his eyes.

"So good time to swing by?" Cazzi asked. *Why didn't you invite me? Didn't you come here to see me? Are you afraid I'll kiss you again?*

"Umm well…"

"Come visit meeee," Rohan crowed.

"Are you sure he didn't get his hands on something stronger?" Cazzi asked. Patrick giggled and she straight-up knew. "Oh my god, are you guys stoned too?"

"Just me and Ro," Patrick said. "Benji is sober."

"Someone has to be!" Benji yelled from the background.

"This I gotta see," Cazzi said. "It's just pot, right?" She couldn't handle anyone flying higher than that.

"Just pot," Patrick promised. "Pinky swear."

———

THEY ARRIVED at the studio at a run. No one was sober enough to drive and the cops in Clementine were known to give biking under the influence tickets so they walked. Judit opted to stay home. Halfway there, Eva declared a race and it was on. Not very quickly, but it was on.

Cazzi won, just barely, slapping her hand on the outside door of the studio. She barely crowed her victory when the door swung open and Rohan threw his arms around her.

"You came!" He gave her a bear hug. It was over so quickly she couldn't even respond before he was on to Eva, introducing himself and shaking her hand as if he had a bat's chance in hell of convincing anyone he was sober.

He ushered them in and introduced Eva to everyone with jovial attentiveness. Eva soaked it up with a huge grin and a flirty look for Benji. The expression faded when she met Patrick and she shot Cazzi a glance before shaking his hand. Patrick shot a glance of his own at Cazzi over Eva's head.

There was a chuckle. Cazzi turned to see Rohan leaning on the wall beside her. "That will be interesting." His grin was light and free. It made him look like that picture from his Insta, taking years off his face.

"Having a good time?" She asked.

"I'm the host, that's supposed to be my question." His dark eyes sparkled. "But yes, I am. You?"

"I just got here." She glanced back at Patrick but he was fiddling with something on his computer.

"Never too early to be having fun." Rohan turned and yelled at Benji. "Play it again!"

Cazzi expected Benji to be their usual annoyed self but they grinned back. "You'll get sick of it."

"Never!" Rohan cried.

Patrick chuckled.

"Okay." Benji laughed and put on a song loud enough to make it feel like they were in a club. It had a driving beat, a melody that made her bounce in place, and Rohan's voice singing hooks so catchy she barely heard them and they were already stuck in her head.

Rohan grabbed her hands and suddenly they were dancing like dorks, no real moves, no real coordination, just moving in time and kind of together. He was a professional who could easily dance circles around her but he was laughing and she was laughing and suddenly she felt as light as his grin.

Eva danced around them, grabbing Benji and whirling them around. Benji played along with good humor, returning the favor and twirling Eva like a top. Even Patrick was jamming, shimmying his shoulders, and bobbing his head with a smile.

Then the song ended. The magic of the moment popped like a soap bubble, leaving them all breathing hard and smiling.

"What was that?" Eva asked.

"That," Rohan said, "Was an RK and Benji Nakamura original, with beats by the one and only Rick Jones."

Cazzi whooped. "You did it!"

"Yeah, we fucking did." Benji high-fived Rohan. "Now all we need is a sex song and a few more bangers before we can string this motherfucker together and start cutting."

"Oh come on, don't talk about that right now," Rohan said. "We're celebrating!"

Benji shrugged and put the song on again. They all danced to it and then Patrick took over the speakers, putting together a mix that defied the late hour until it was like they really were in a club. She danced with Eva, Benji, Rohan again, everyone but

Patrick, who set up shop behind his computer and refused to come out.

Cazzi found herself draped over the couch hours later, her body sore from dancing and her fading bruises. Rohan sprawled next to her, head almost on her shoulder, quietly singing along to whatever was playing. Eva and Benji were dancing but they leaned on each other, more out of exhaustion than affection. Patrick was still in DJ mode.

She closed her eyes, trying to focus on Rohan's voice in all the noise. It was clear and lovely if frayed around the edges.

An angel with battered wings, she thought, and then laughed at herself for being so maudlin. He was no angel. But then, who was?

But something about the way he sang, like he was singing for her alone, made her stomach flutter all the same.

"We should go," Rohan said during an instrumental section of the song.

Cazzi nodded. Her head landed on his shoulder and it felt so nice she left it there. Rohan shifted, moving closer and easing the angle of her neck. His arm came around slowly and tucked her against his side, warm and wanted. She relished the feeling, curling up and snuggling against him. It'd been so long since she'd been held like this.

The music died and she realized she'd closed her eyes.

"She's falling asleep," Rohan said. "I'll take her home." His voice resonated deep in his chest. She wanted to crawl into his lap, put her ear against his lungs, and listen to him talk forever.

"I'm beat too," Eva said. "I'll come with."

Cazzi opened her eyes with a sigh and stretched. Patrick watched her, his gaze burning and intense. "You coming, Pat?" she asked.

He shook his head. "Had an idea. I want to get it down while it's fresh."

She frowned. "You sure?"

He nodded and turned away.

Will this ever stop hurting? The thought rose like an unwanted memory, reminiscent of her conversation with Angela.

Tell me again what love should be, little Miss Therapist, whispered the singer's voice, smirking in her head.

Rohan's arm around her shoulders tightened in a brief, reassuring squeeze. The pressure grounded her to the present, banishing her thoughts. When had she become so comfortable with him touching her?

Eva glared at Patrick.

Rohan looked at Benji. "What about you?"

They shrugged. "I'm gonna crash on the couch, my place is too far."

"You're not with them at the Air BnB?" Cazzi asked, grasping at the subject change.

They shook their head. "I wasn't about to stay under the same roof as *her.* Besides, I own a place in Sac."

"Which part?" Eva asked. "My sister is moving there next weekend."

Benji gave her an assessing look. "Midtown."

"Judit's gonna be in Midtown too!" Eva said.

"Good for her," Benji said, their gaze darting away like they were looking for a way out of the conversation.

"Which part of Midtown?" Eva asked, seemingly oblivious.

"Let's head back," Cazzi said, "I need some sleep." She stood up, away from Rohan's embrace. But she held out a hand.

He took it and pulled himself upright behind her. Right behind her, the edges of his side brushing up against the edges of hers.

He was too close. He'd been too close for hours but she'd been too stoned to care. Now she was sober and he was too close and… she didn't mind actually.

Somehow he'd slipped under her defenses, under her trauma responses, and settled in close against her skin without even a kiss. If she didn't already know he wasn't a practitioner, she'd call him a witch. As it was, none of the magic workers she'd been around or dated had ever gotten this close so comfortably.

He was something else entirely, something else to her, and she wasn't sure what that was.

They said their goodbyes and left, Patrick still distant. She wasn't too lost in thought to notice that. *Explain love to me,* Angela taunted her again from her memory.

When had Patrick gone from being the only person who could always comfort her to being the only person who could always hurt her?

15

"You in my room
Lit by the moon
You're my 3 AM mistake
The chance I'll always take

Oh girl, can you keep a secret?
Can you keep this between us?
I want you tonight
You know this ain't right.
Let's keep this secret
Secret
Secret
So we'll never
Regret
Regret
This love."
— "Secret Love" by Beatboyz on *Not Sweet Not Simple*

It was significantly chillier than it had been the last time Rohan had been outside. Had that really been hours ago? It was also dark as hell, lit only by few and far between streetlights. The city boy in him, the one who'd heard horror stories about small town nights this dark, went on alert.

He drew himself up to his full height and surveyed the street.

"It's okay," Cazzi said, looking up at him. "Eva grew up here. It's safe."

Eva gave him a thumbs up. "The police chief is my uncle, which I have mixed feelings about, and Cazzi is always armed."

Cazzi rolled her eyes. "She means I have pepper spray."

"Reassuring," he said, zipping up his jacket. He was mostly sober now and not looking forward to his empty bed back at the rental. Angie hadn't been home enough in months for him to miss the habit of sleeping next to her anymore, but lying there by himself reminded him of all the nights he'd lain awake and thought about leaving only to talk himself out of it by morning. He wished he hadn't been so damn convincing. Who knows where he'd be now if he'd just fucking left?

Not here, he thought, looking out at the empty road.

There was a tug on his sleeve.

"You coming?" Cazzi asked.

He looked at her and she looked back, waiting for his answer like she'd wait forever. If she was anyone else, he'd kiss her. But if she was anyone else, he wouldn't want to.

This too shall pass, he told himself.

But he didn't think so because when he said yes and she smiled it hit him right under the ribs. The last smile that hit him so hard belonged to Angie, but this was different.

He pushed the thought down. Cazzi and Rick would work their shit out and live happily ever after or whatever. He wouldn't get in the way of that.

But when they dropped Eva off at her house and ambled

together, alone in the dark, all he wanted was for her to invite him inside just for another minute to spend with her.

Maybe he would've ended up here, no matter what, by her side, hoping for just a little more time with her.

Or maybe he was just sleep deprived and sappy. Either way the sight of her house filled him with a sickening mixture of hope and dread.

She sighed. "I haven't been up this late in a long time."

"More of an early bird, huh?"

She shook her head. "Only because I have to get up for work. I kinda miss being up late like this. It feels… more vibrant, almost, you know?" She grimaced. "Does that make sense?"

He nodded. "Some of my best memories happen after midnight." Some of his worst too, but why ruin the mood?

She smiled. "How am I both exhausted and wired?"

"Welcome to 4 AM," he said.

"Four!" Her eyes widened but she was still smiling. "Oh my god, how were we dancing for that long?"

He shrugged. "Drugs and music and good company."

She laughed. "You make it sound like we were in Studio 54 doing coke and dancing with movie stars."

"I suppose you're right, we were only multi-platinum recording artists and a couple of highly educated sex educators dancing to an unreleased soon-to-be-hit. Hardly glamorous."

"Hardly." She chuckled as she reached for her keys. "Oh, I'm not going to sleep tonight am I?"

His head filled with a thousand lovely ways he could keep her from sleeping. He ignored them. "Why sleep? Let's stay up and go get a massive breakfast instead."

"Nothing's open…" She paused, her key hovering over the lock.

He shrugged. "We'll just have to hang out until then." *Among other things.*

"But… don't you have to record tomorrow?"

"I can take a nap after breakfast. Come on, it'll be fun."

"Well…" She considered. "Oh fuck it, I can nap too. You wanna come in?"

His heart soared. "Yes, please."

There was something in her answering smile that made him feel like she'd had the same thousand lovely images running through her head.

THIS IS *one hundred percent a mistake*, Cazzi thought as she unlocked the door. The way he looked at her… The curls of desire in her stomach…

She was sober but less than four hours of sleep was the same to the body as being legally intoxicated. He'd had just as little sleep as her. She bit her lip and his eyes zeroed in on her mouth.

Oh.

Now she was looking at *his* mouth. God, what a mouth. She leaned against the wall dividing the entryway from the kitchen and contemplated it. Those lips, that dark stubble…

He smiled one of those real, sincere smiles he'd been wearing all night and those curls of lust spiraled out until she clenched her fists against the wall. Dammit, what was she doing? And why was he so far away?

She met his eyes and crooked a finger.

He stepped closer until he filled her vision and she had to look up at him. She loved a tall man. Societal programming, probably, but she embraced it. He was so close, as close as you could get without touching. She could feel the heat of him. Everything in her wanted more.

Everything except the sensible parts, the parts that whispered terrible things like *Patrick* and *rebound* and *consequences*.

Fuck 'em. Fuck 'em all.

"What do you want, Cazzi?" His voice hummed between them, smooth and seductive.

"Do you want to kiss me?" She asked. She needed to be sure.

He cupped her jaw gently and slowly, so damn slowly, leaned down, and brushed the world's lightest kiss on her lips. The barest touch and her nerve endings lit up like lightning.

She found herself clinging to him as he drew back. "Tease," she gasped.

"Oh, I'm sorry." His grin was as dazed as she felt. "Did you want more?"

In reply, she grabbed him by the collar and dragged his mouth down to hers. This time he didn't hold back, pressing her against the wall. She wrapped her arms around his neck, tangling her fingers in his lovely thick hair. He kissed her like he'd die if he didn't and oh god, she kissed him just the same.

The press of him against her. His hands roamed over her sides, her hips. She was on her tiptoes, his erection grinding between them, she shifted until it ground in just the right place and...

This is escalating fast.

She pulled back. He stopped. They stood there, breathing hard, looking at each other.

Her body begged her to keep going. But the sensible parts of her brain just got louder.

Consequences.

Rebound.

Patrick.

Fuck.

"You okay?" Rohan's voice brought her back to the present.

She refocused on him and smiled, far too politely given their hips were still pressed together.

"Uh-oh." He stepped back just enough so they weren't touching anymore.

"Uh-oh?"

"You went all blank."

She looked at him incredulously. "Blank?"

"Yeah, your face gets, I don't know, all smooth and fake. A polite mask."

"Blank faced/Full of thunder," she murmured. Well, that lyric made more sense now.

"You remember that line?"

"That song's been stuck in my head." She glared at him. "I'm not the only one with the polite mask. Don't think I don't know when you give me those fake smiles or when you're flirting just because you think it'll get you somewhere."

"Is that what you think this was?" He looked ready to prove his sincerity until she couldn't think straight.

She shook her head hard because the promise in his eyes was too damn good. "No, this was real. That doesn't mean it was a good idea."

His face shut down, just a little. She wanted to take her words back, bring back the way he'd looked at her before, but she told herself it was better this way.

"I get it if you wanna leave now."

His eyebrows jumped. "It's not even dawn yet."

"Nothing else sexual is happening between us."

He shrugged. "I can't say I'm not disappointed but that's cool. I'm a grown-ass man and I like hanging out with you." He looked down. "Just give me a minute and we'll be fully platonic."

"Is that what you call getting soft?"

He laughed. "It is now."

She laughed too. "You want tea or a snack or something? I'm hungry."

"Well, if you're eating…" He followed her to the kitchen and rummaged through the pantry and fridge like he lived there.

She raised an eyebrow. "The Spanish Inquisition is back in my kitchen."

"Yep," he said cheerfully. "Our chief weapon is surprise—surprise and snacks."

She gestured at her munchies cabinet and freezer. "At risk of being threatened with a comfy chair and a dish rack, I surrender."

He laughed. "Did Rick make you watch those obsessively too?"

She turned on the electric kettle with a snort. "No, I got hooked on them through my Dad and sent Pat on tour with the complete series—much to my Dad's dismay."

"Oh, so you're the reason I know way too much about Monty Python." He grabbed a tin of her cookies and turned the kettle off. "Trust me," he said when she opened her mouth to protest.

He pulled out a saucepan, some black tea, sugar, a stick of cinnamon, her bottle of cardamom, and her milk. "No cloves?" He grumbled.

She opened a different cabinet and handed a jar to him. "I don't cook with it, just put it in tea or chew 'em when I get a toothache." Patrick taught her that trick.

He nodded and set the herbs with some water on the stove to simmer.

"Chai?" she hazarded a guess.

"Masala chai," he said. "I used to make it with my Nānī all the time when I was a kid."

"Were you two close?"

He nodded. "She used to send me on tour with care packages of snacks and Bollywood movies. My personal trainers hated those snacks," he chuckled. "They always made me work those calories off."

Something clicked in Cazzi's head. "Are you the reason I've seen every Shah Rukh Khan action film of the 2000s?"

Rohan grinned. "Rick and I used to crash in each other's hotel rooms and do movie nights. Leo too until…" he frowned.

"You weren't friends with…" she searched her memory for the name of the fourth Beatboy. "Mark?"

For some reason that made him laugh. "You mean Martin? Have you met him?"

She shook her head. "You're the only other one I've ever met."

"Huh," he checked the tea and stirred some milk and sugar in before covering it again. "It's so weird we never met. I thought Rick and I were tight, at least while we were in the band."

Cazzi shrugged, playing casual. "He was really protective of me when we were younger."

Rohan looked about to say something but changed his mind. The chai was simmering so he tossed in some loose-leaf black tea and turned it off, covering it again.

"It was so weird seeing him famous," Cazzi said without thinking. "It was like seeing a doppelgänger, you know? I mean, I knew him, we were best friends but there was this guy with his face and his body who millions of people thought they knew. I'd see these fan sites speculating about him or someone who didn't know we were friends would tell me some rumor about him and… it was like I lived in an alternate reality." She petered out, embarrassed. She'd never said that to anyone. She didn't tell people she knew Ricky Rick of the Beatboyz, why would she?

Rohan strained the tea into a big jar she had forgotten she had and poured it into each mug. "I get that. I feel like there were two of me: Beatboy RK and actual Rohan." He blew on his tea. "Honestly, I get them mixed up sometimes. They used so much of our private lives to shape our public persona. Everything on tour was fodder, every thought could be a tweet if vetted, hell, my stepdad was our manager." He shook his head, leaning against the counter.

"That must've been hard," Cazzi said. "And hard to be away from your Nānī and mom for so much of the year. I know it was a lot for Patrick." *And for me.*

"I was used to not seeing my mom much, but yeah I think I missed her more than I admitted. But I really missed my Nānī, she practically raised me. My mom was an ER doctor when my father died so Nānī came to live with us and take care of me."

"I'm sorry about your dad."

He shrugged, his shoulders stiff. "I don't really remember him. Nānī and James told me so many stories about him I feel like I do but it's like... I dunno. I'm sad I never got to know him but also James and my mom are really good together so being sad doesn't feel exactly right."

She nodded. "There's no right way to grieve or miss someone. Especially if you never knew them."

He sipped his tea and smiled. "We all have tea together every Saturday now that James and I don't tour anymore and Mom went into private practice. It makes my Nānī so happy."

She couldn't imagine her family being that close, but she smiled back, realizing as she sipped her tea her body language mirrored his.

Which turned out badly for her as the tea was so hot she barely tasted it and definitely burned her tongue. "Holy hell, do you have an asbestos tongue?"

He poured cold milk into her cup. "Better?"

She took another sip and hummed in pleasure. The tea was sweet and milky but full of lovely spice. "Delicious."

He smiled. "We've gotten to the part of the night where we talk about our deep dark secrets haven't we?"

It was her turn to shrug. It would take a lot more than some pot, no sleep, and a great kiss to make her spill her secrets. She grabbed an armful of snacks from the munchies cabinet and walked to the couch. She dumped the snacks on the coffee table, pulling her phone out of her tight work slacks pocket so she could sit without it jabbing her. She'd been wearing them for far longer than was comfortable but, oh well. He followed, ferrying their mugs and the tea jar over. The still-hot jar went on a Halloween pot holder she'd gotten from the Dollar Store years ago. He put his phone next to hers, both face down and already sinking under the tide of snacks.

"Can I ask you a question?" He sat down on the cushion next to her, just out of reach. She told herself she was glad he wasn't closer.

"Maybe." She opened the tin of cookies and shoved one in her mouth. It was one of his snickerdoodle bribes and she chewed slowly, savoring.

"How many tattoos do you have?" He opened a bag of chips, taking a handful.

She thought for a moment, counting. "Ten. You?"

"Two. Are all yours sigils?"

"No. Yours?" Dammit. She knew where this was going and she should've said nine.

"This," he pushed up his sleeve to show the Beatboyz double B logo on his bicep. He grinned with amused embarrassment. "I was eighteen."

"And the other one?"

"That's something I'm going to have to get destroyed or changed or something." He grimaced.

"Oh?" Now she was intrigued. "Please tell me you got 'No Ragerts' across your chest."

In answer, he raised his shirt. She was momentarily stunned by all that lean muscle and smooth brown skin. Then she saw it, right over his heart:

RK

AA

"You got a tattoo of your guys' initials?" She tried not to sound judgmental but it was something she'd never consider even if she spent decades with someone let alone only four years.

He smiled ruefully. "We both did."

"Let me guess, it seemed like a good idea at the time?"

He shrugged. "We're both romantics. Or at least we used to be." His smile faded and he dropped his shirt. She told herself she was more relieved than disappointed.

"I'm sure you can find an artist to do a really good cover-up of that. You'll never know it was there."

"I'm not sure I want it turned into something else. I might just get it blacked out."

She winced. "That's gonna hurt."

"Says the woman with ten tattoos. Are they all on your arms?"

"If you're going to ask to see them, just ask."

"Okay, can I see your tatts, Caz?"

Her cheeks heated at hearing her nickname on his lips. It hadn't mattered before but now that she knew what those lips felt like... She realized she was staring at his mouth again. He absolutely saw her staring. But he didn't move.

"Well? I showed you mine, show me yours." The twinkle in his eyes told her he knew exactly what he was implying.

She rolled her eyes to tell him she wasn't buying it and rolled up both her sleeves. Four sigils marched up each forearm. Her three calming sigils and one for strength on the left. On the right were her pain, confidence, health, and don't-see-me sigils.

"Did you design these all yourself?"

"Yep." They were coping mechanisms built out of mantras that helped ground her when her trauma kicked up. A stop-gap measure she leaned on perhaps too much lately. Her past therapists had been mostly cool with her methods but it was something she had to tackle with each new person, hoping they wouldn't get weird about her magical thinking.

He didn't ask what they meant, which was good because she wasn't sure she'd answer him. Instead, he said, "Where are the other two?"

She debated telling him to fuck off. With a mental shrug, she said, "Don't get excited." And unbuttoned her now very wrinkled blouse.

"Don't get excited" was one of those phrases that ranked somewhere around "don't think about pink elephants" in terms of futility. Especially when it was coupled with Cazzi unbuttoning her blouse. Rohan tried very hard to think about pink elephants and not the soft round curves and shadows of her breasts. The sigil disappearing into her black bra almost distracted him. Stark black ink traced inverted and upright pentacles slashing their way through a figure eight. This wasn't an Osman-Spare sigil, built out of words. He wondered what had inspired her to make something more pictorial when she clearly gravitated to the other method.

"Protection?" He guessed, his voice embarrassingly hoarse. Goddamn. The tattoo was positioned so the bottom upright pentacle curved along the rise of her breast and it was far too fascinating.

She nodded, rebuttoning her blouse. "So," she said and a phone started vibrating.

Rohan glanced at the coffee table where their phones were somewhere under all those snacks. "Who the fuck is calling this late?"

"Or this early?" She pushed aside the lid of the cookie tin. "I hope everything's okay."

Another phone went off, the dueling vibrations ratcheting up Rohan's pulse. Nothing good made someone call you at this time of night. What if Mom or Nānī or James were hurt? What if Angie had done something really drastic? He grabbed for the nearest phone and answered it.

"Hello?" He said as Cazzi grabbed the other phone and did the same.

"Rohan?" Rick sounded surprised.

"Is everything okay?"

"Why are you answering Cazzi's phone?"

"I'm—what?" Rohan looked over at Cazzi, who stood by the sliding glass door, holding what was now obviously his phone. "Is this an emergency?" He asked Rick.

"No, but—"

"I'll call you back." He hung up and handed the phone to Cazzi. "That was Rick. No emergency. Who called me?"

"Angela." She looked troubled as she exchanged her phone for his.

"What'd she want?"

"She just said 'I knew it' and sobbed. She hung up before I could say anything."

Rohan tamped down the impulse to immediately call Angie back. "You okay?"

"This is going to be a shitshow."

"What is?"

She turned and looked him full in the eye. "We answered each other's phones at five a.m., Rohan. They're going to think we're fucking."

"You don't think Rick is going to take that well." He really shouldn't feel a kernel of infernal glee crackling in his stomach. Rick was his friend, after all. Probably one of his oldest friends. God, he was an asshole.

"Neither of them will," Cazzi paced.

"Call Rick, tell him we were just hanging out."

"You want me to lie to him?"

He shrugged. "Tell him what you like. Just lemme know if I need to duck when I see him."

Her eyes narrowed. "He doesn't have any claim on me. Neither of you do."

He put his hands up. "Wasn't implying anything, I swear."

"Hm." She called Rick, watching Rohan as the tinny dial tone trilled in the quiet. "Hey," she said into the phone. "No, I'm still up. We were just having some tea and killing time before breakfast... I dunno, thought it would be fun. It's been a minute since I did that, you know? Yeah, you can come if you like. …Oh, okay, yeah, no, I get it, you're busy. Okay, well if you change your mind… hey, what'd you call me about anyway? Oh, okay. Yeah, I get that. Well, call me if you—" She lifted the phone from her ear and glared at it. "Dammit, he hung up on me."

"I'm sorry."

She shrugged. "He's been pissing me off a lot lately. Let him be mad for a change." She checked the time. "I know a place that should be open soon. Wanna walk down?"

16

**THE END OF AN ERA: SCREAM QUEEN DUMPS HER HEART
THROB**
*...Sources close to the couple insist Angela broke his heart,
however, according to a statement put out by RK's team, "the
break-up between RK and Ms. Alice was regrettable but mutual."
When asked to comment, Angela would only say, "Watch the
special. I'll show you mutual." We can't wait for that tea to be
spilled.*
—Celebrity Watcher Magazine

By the time Cazzi and Rohan got to Downtown Clementine, it was still dark and they were just unlocking the doors of Badlands Diner. Badlands was decorated in B-horror movie memorabilia and was about as campy as a diner could get. It was one of Cazzi's favorite places in town.

This early it had a few scattered customers, mostly students who hadn't yet gone to bed and the early morning freaks who actually wanted to be up and doing things at six a.m. Though the clientele was sparse, Rohan and Cazzi headed straight for the booth off to the side mostly hidden behind a large and possibly real potted plant.

Rohan sat with his back to the door and took his hood off. He toyed with a pair of sunglasses.

Cazzi nodded at them. "The sun isn't even up yet and it's too bright for you?"

"Hm?" He looked down at his hands. "Oh, old habit."

"The celebrity 'wearing sunglasses inside' trick?"

He laughed. "Only if I'm really hoping for some attention."

She smiled and studied her menu. "What's making you nervous right now?"

Out of the corner of her eye, she saw his hands still. "That obvious, huh?"

"Not especially."

"Are you sure one of those sigils isn't for mind reading?"

She laughed. "You don't have to tell me if you don't want to."

His smile slipped. "I'm worried the gloves are going to come off with Angie."

Her shoulders got tight. "The gloves were still on?"

He shook his head. "The press is going to find me soon."

"You think she'll tell them?" Her stomach dropped.

Rohan shrugged. "Depends how mad she is. But it's really only a matter of time either way." His shoulders hunched as if paparazzi were arriving at any moment.

"Know what you want?" A sleepy college kid in an apron asked, yawning as he came up to their table. Then his eyes landed on her. "Oh hi, Dr. Muldoon!"

"Hi, Levi." Cazzi smiled as if being seen by students wasn't what she'd been trying to avoid by sitting behind a goddamn fern. She traced her don't-see-me sigil reflexively. *It is my will to be only seen by those who I want to see me.*

"Fun night?" He looked slyly at Rohan. "Hey, you look familiar. Do you teach at Clemmy?"

"You know, I get that a lot." Rohan turned on his fake smile.

"Really?" Levi asked, incredulous.

"No." Rohan hung his head in mock shame. "But a boy can dream."

"Can I get the Revenge of the Son of French Toast, Levi?" Cazzi cut in.

"Oh, sure." Levi whipped out his notebook. "And what'll you have, tall, dark, and non-teacherly?"

Rohan ordered and Levi gathered up their menus. Then he paused. Cazzi could almost feel Rohan holding his breath with her. "Hey, Dr. Muldoon?"

"Yes?"

"Um." Levi shuffled the menus. "Do you have—I mean, is the pixie…?"

"Oh! Yes. But I need you to say the word before I give them to you."

Levi sighed. "Condoms," he mumbled.

"Well done. Latex or non-latex?" Cazzi matched his volume as she rummaged around in the inside pocket of her jacket. She'd stashed condoms in every single jacket and bag she owned the minute the program had gotten approved.

"Non-latex please," he practically whispered.

"Here you are." She handed him three. "But remember, with great pleasure comes great responsibility."

He smiled at her, shyly. "Thanks, Dr. M."

"Of course, Levi. That's why the Condom Pixies exist." She smiled back.

Levi left and she turned back to find Rohan staring at her. "What?"

"So many questions," he said, leaning forward. "First off, Condom Pixies?"

"It's a program Eva and I put together to help make the Student Health department more approachable as well as make sure the kids could have access to condoms outside of more daunting traditional routes. It's Eva's baby. I'm just a minion." She grinned and flapped her hands like they were pixie wings.

"By traditional methods, you mean buying them, like the rest of us?"

"It reduces the financial barrier to entry for low-income kids. Also, the pharmacy here is run by some pretty old-fashioned… types." She censored herself at the last minute when she saw one of said pharmacy employees walk by, leveling a judgmental gaze at the clothes Cazzi'd been obviously wearing since yesterday. She met her gaze square on and stared until the other woman looked away.

Rohan raised his eyebrows when she returned her gaze to his. "Long-standing rivalry there?"

"I've only been here a year, but yeah, ever since the college started embracing sex ed and counseling they've had issues with some of the old-school locals."

"Really?"

She nodded. "Nor Cal is surprisingly conservative once you leave the Bay. It's alright here, Davis, Sac, and Humboldt County but it can get weird elsewhere. We're a newish college though. The town was here before we were, so they aren't all tied to the campus like in some college towns."

Rohan shook his head. "This is why I still live in LA."

She made a face. "I'm never living there again. Eighteen years was enough."

"Holy shit! Holy shit!" Levi skidded up to their table. "Dr. Muldoon! Is this you?" He thrust his phone into her face.

Her stomach dropped again and she forced her face to remain calm. "Levi. Please respect my personal space."

"Sorry! Sorry! But is it you?"

She leaned back and assessed the grainy picture. Rohan and her were walking together but the quality was so bad she couldn't tell where. She could barely tell it was them, actually. It looked like a zoom of a zoom of a zoom of a much bigger picture. The caption said, "Is that guy who I think he is???" The comments suggested Rohan was anyone from himself to various Bollywood stars to a certain very popular telenovela star. She squinted more than she needed to. "Um, I don't think so. Where was this taken?"

"Somewhere in town I think," Levi said excitedly. "Do you think Marco Ramirez was really here? He's about 70% of my spank bank."

Cazzi let that last piece of information slide right out of her head. It was too damn early to be this chipper and oversharing. "Can I?" She motioned for the phone. When Levi handed it to her, she showed the picture to Rohan. "What do you think, does that look like Marco Ramirez?"

He peered at it and frowned. "Hmmm. Could be." He handed the phone back, the screen locked.

"Well, then that's definitely not me. I've never met him," she said with a regretful look. "Too bad. I love *Mi Casa, Mi Amour*."

Levi chattered about the show and how hot Marco was until the kitchen dinged the bell repeatedly.

The second he was out of earshot, Rohan said, "Dammit."

She exhaled. "That wasn't a press shot though. I think it was cut from someone's personal photo."

He shook his head. "It's enough."

"Well, we best not be seen together anymore in public then."

Levi arrived with the food and rushed off.

"Agreed," Rohan said after the student left. She felt a brief flare of disappointment. "I don't want to give Angie any more ammo."

She frowned, her disappointment retreating. "Are you worried she might do something to harm you?"

He started shaking his head but hesitated. "Honestly, I don't know. She's extremely driven, sometimes to the point of obsession. I thought I knew what she was capable of but now I'm not sure. I don't think she'll lash out physically but I wouldn't be surprised if some ugly rumors pop up."

"Are you sure she won't try anything physically harmful?" Cazzi kept her tone neutral as she buttered her French toast. "She grabbed me pretty hard when she came by the other day. The impulse is there."

Like recognizes like. Whispered a nasty voice in the back of her head.

I am not my capacity for violence, she replied.

"She grabbed you?" Rohan's knuckles went pale around his silverware.

She shrugged. "I handled it."

He sighed, his knuckles remaining tight. "I'd like to say after four years I know what she's capable of but the truth is, I don't. She shares more TMI shit than our friend Levi does but there are certain things she does not talk about. Like what happened between the ages of sixteen to nineteen when somehow she got from the ass-end of Florida to LA with barely any money, a switchblade, and no car. Or why her mother killed her father."

He pushed his eggs around. "She used to have a roadie that she found out was essentially imprisoned by her husband. Angie didn't call the cops. She went in herself. I don't know what she did to the guy, but he wouldn't even be in the same room as his wife, even when the woman begged him to be. He ran off somewhere and the roadie quit for a while. Now she refuses to work for anyone else but Angie."

"Damn," Cazzi breathed, both worried as hell and impressed.

"Yeah." Rohan shoved a bite of eggs in his mouth though he didn't look particularly hungry anymore.

"Hey," Cazzi reached across the table and laid her hand over his. Her whole palm tingled with sudden awareness. "You're not alone. You've got friends. We'll figure this out."

His hand turned over and grasped hers, interlacing their fingers. The awareness doubled. "Thank you."

They finished their food in silence, no longer holding hands but under the table, his knee pressed against hers and she pressed back.

Nothing, she told herself, could come of this.

17

Reporter: "How did you feel when you found out that you'd been chosen to be part of Beatboyz?"
Patrick: "Surprised."
Reporter: "Why?"
Patrick: "I didn't audition."
Reporter: "How did you get in?"
Patrick: "RK's stepdad saw me. I did our school talent show on a dare." [shrugs]
Reporter: "And then?"
Patrick: "I got in."
Reporter: "That's some dare. I bet you're glad you did it."
Patrick: "Uh-huh."
Reporter: "Who dared you?"
Patrick: "My best friend."
Reporter: "Whose name is…?"
Patrick: "Private."
—Transcript of interview with Rick Jones from the documentary *Beatboyz: The Beat Never Stops.*

R ohan's brain was cotton, his muscles sluggish and the heavy diner food begged his body to nap. Why had he thought skipping a night of sleep was a good idea? He glanced at Cazzi.

Oh, yeah.

She walked next to him, hands in her pockets and face tipped towards the morning sun. Though she looked passably like she might not have stayed up all night, he could tell by the way she walked she was tired. Her pace was slow despite the empty streets but he wasn't in a hurry.

Rohan yawned behind his hand. "This was so much easier when I was nineteen."

She squinted at him, the rising sun hitting her sunglasses at the right angle to let him see her eyes through them. "What?"

He gestured at the sky so he didn't put his arm around her shoulder and tuck her against him. "Staying up all night."

She groaned. "Tell me about it. I gotta work on my class proposal."

He grimaced. "How's that going?"

She shook her head. "I need an ace in the hole. Something to cut through all the objections they're gonna throw at me."

"What are the objections?"

"Does it have academic value? Is there a need for it? Why should you teach it?" She reeled the questions off without a breath in between, her face tight and frustrated. "I need a department to sponsor it, possibly a co-teacher, the university is going to be resistant to something that seems in loco parentis, and there are going to be at least a few parents objecting to me corrupting their precious virginal babies with carnal knowledge that could save them from a lifetime of bad sex, regret, shame, and trauma."

Rohan blew out a breath, resisting the urge to reach over and touch her. "Damn."

Cazzi shook her head. "I've got enough horrifying statistics to cover the need, the academic value kinda gets covered under that and teaching the kids ethics, the gender studies department will back me if I get the Academic Senate to sign off. The parents already complain. As it is, this is probably going to end up being a Jan term course instead of the graduation requirement I want it to be."

She sighed. "So it just comes down to blowing them out of the water at my presentation for the Academic Senate and making them forget I'm not a professor and thus could not possibly know how to teach." She rolled her eyes.

Rohan mulled this over. He didn't know what a Jan term was or who the Academic Senate was but he could guess and the picture she painted sounded frustrating. He thought back to when his bandmate Martin went through a period of watching C-SPAN on the tour bus. "Can you bring in some experts to testify?"

"The Academic Senate isn't court," Cazzi said but she looked thoughtful. "Maybe I could have some of my colleagues give case studies."

"Yeah," Rohan said. "Eva would do it."

Cazzi nodded.

"You should get some doctors to come in and tell some horror stories," Rohan said, stifling another yawn. Maybe he would take a nap after all. "When my mom worked in the ER she'd bring home with the most effective cautionary tales."

Cazzi grimaced. "I bet."

"She used to come home from the night shift while I was having breakfast. I once was late to school because she wouldn't let my stepdad drive me until she made absolutely certain I would never consider mixing ecstasy and prescription painkillers. Apparently, some EDM kids thought it would be double the fun." He paused. Night shifts always put his mother in a strange place. "I've never had my stomach pumped but I have a real vivid mental picture."

"Jesus," Cazzi said. "That sounds intense."

He nodded, remembering his mother's eyes pinning him to his seat. "It didn't happen that much. She's much more laid back now."

Cazzi's shoulder bumped against his. "It's okay if that still bothers you."

Did it still bother him? He certainly didn't miss the lectures or how stressed his mother would get or how she'd sleep at weird hours of the day and night but he knew she'd loved helping people in the ER. Sometimes he wished she'd left the ER before he joined the Beatboyz and essentially moved out at fourteen. He shrugged. What happened happened. He'd had James and Nānī to take care of him when Mom couldn't and she'd been there when she could. He knew she loved him.

"The trick," Cazzi said, her tone musing. "Would be to get some doctors who didn't believe some of the antiquated bullshit still going around. You know I once almost slept with a doctor who tried to convince me to use conditioner as lube?"

"Really?" Rohan squashed the swell of jealousy strangling his lungs.

"Oh yeah," she said. "He did not like it when I gave him the rundown on exactly how wrong he was. Especially when I whipped out my peer-reviewed sources in response to him getting all 'I'm a doctor and you're just a lowly grad student.'"

"You would get along with my mom," Rohan said. "When I was in middle school she saw my health class homework was teaching anatomy wrong. So she called my teacher to correct him. He refused to back down and told her she was welcome to teach the class herself."

"Did she?"

He covered his face at the memory, laughing at his preteen

embarrassment. His mother had shown up in full doctor mode, stethoscope and all. "Yes! And it was on genital anatomy."

"Oh *no*," Cazzi groaned. "How mortified were you?"

"I would've hidden in the bathroom for the rest of the day but she took me out of school after class and we got kulfi." He smiled. "It was actually pretty awesome. I mean, I got made fun of for months after but hey, ice cream."

"Ice cream makes everything better," Cazzi said with a smile.

"Is that your professional opinion?"

"Oh yes," she said. "I keep a freezer full of ice cream in my office."

"You do?"

She laughed, the sound warming him. "I wish!"

"You should!"

"If there was a budget for it, I would," she sighed, the moment deflating around them. "Sometimes I feel like a band-aid on a bullet wound. Like I can only help so much, you know? I can't fix our education system or stop the people who tell girls they're used gum the moment they get touched sexually or make people ashamed for being queer or kinky or ace. Our country elected a president with a shit ton of rape cases against him and there are grown men in politics who think vaginas won't let in sperm if they're getting raped. Hell, I can't even hand an adult college student a goddamn condom without getting the side-eye from some nosy busybody."

She looked so sad he gave in to his instinct and put his arm slowly around her shoulders. She rocked into him and he tucked her against him, brushing his lips against her hair. "Everything counts," he said. "The world is shit right now and every good thing is precious. You help people and those people will take that help and pass it on. These things build up."

"You think?" She looked up at him. There was something terribly lost in her eyes.

"Yes," he said. "When I was still in Beatboyz I thought we were making fluff. Popular fluff but fluff. But when fans talked to me they'd tell me how our music got them through break-ups, grief, high school, the worst times of their lives. So yeah, if 'Betraying me (Bang Bang)' can get someone through a rough patch I think your work can help people."

She wrapped her arms around his ribs, laying her head against his pec, awkwardly side-hugging him. She was a few inches shorter than Angie. It was jarring to realize Cazzi wasn't larger than life, but short enough that she couldn't lay her head on his shoulder. He stopped and wrapped his arms fully around her. They stood in the middle of the sidewalk on a residential street but there was no one around to mind. Hell, he would've done it even if there was.

CAZZI SPLIT OFF from Rohan near his rental and meandered home, enjoying the early morning air. She could still feel his arms around her. Something about the way he held her made tension leave her body. Yet casually touching him made her nerves light up and come to attention. That plus the kiss—well, he could be trouble. But she'd enjoy the glow now, while it was too early to feel real.

She rounded the corner and her stride stuttered.

Someone was on her porch, she could just see them through the gap in the hedge. They sat in her chair, facing away and looking at their phone. She couldn't see any defining features except a large back covered by an even larger gray sweatshirt with the hood up.

Cortisone and adrenaline hit her system like twin grenades. She stilled her hand as it reached for her pepper spray, and kept herself walking normally.

Evaluate then react, she reminded herself.

Then he moved and she knew exactly who was under that

hood. Everything relaxed and then tensed up again as she remembered she was mad at him.

"I thought you were busy," she said as she opened her gate.

He unfolded from the chair. He no longer danced much, as far as she knew, but he still moved like he did. Rohan did too, but Patrick had been dancing since before she'd met him and it showed. She remembered the shows they'd put on for their parents and the neighbors in the shared apartment complex courtyard. If social media had been a thing back then, they'd have been viral.

"I couldn't concentrate," he said.

"Oh?" Hope and irritation clashed in her.

"Where's Rohan?"

She shrugged. "Probably home by now. We just had a close encounter with possible exposure but luckily you guys are a little before my students' time."

"Mmm, that demographic was at the tail end of our era."

"God, that makes me feel old." She laughed.

"I don't think you're allowed to say that before you're thirty."

"Oh yes, tell me how the great three-oh is, old man. Those ten extra months you have on me really make a difference."

He stared into the distance, squinting in a way she knew for a fact he thought made him look wise. "You'll see when you get there."

"Uh-huh. Well, luckily the internet thinks Rohan looks more like Marco Ramirez than RK these days."

"Someone got a picture of him?"

"Both of us. I'm not sure when but we were in the background of someone's photo."

Patrick made a low, growly thoughtful sound in his throat. It set off sparks in her stomach, but they were muted by everything unsaid between them.

She unlocked the door. "Come in."

He followed her inside.

"Want anything?" She nodded at the kitchen.

He shook his head and made a beeline for the couch.

She trailed after him. "Just so you know, I may fall asleep if we sit here too long."

He looked at the cups and assorted snacks on the table. "Did you have the munchies?"

"Nah, but staying up late is hungry work."

He shot her a speculative, suspicious look.

"What? What was that?" She demanded.

"So you just talked, then?" His tone said he thought they did everything but.

Guilt shot through her. She crossed her arms, narrowing her eyes. "Did you just come by to pick a fight?"

"No," he said but there was a hard edge to his voice.

"You're jealous," she realized.

"Of course I am!"

She blinked. "What are we, Patrick?"

"We're friends. You're my best friend."

She shook her head. "You're my best friend too but this, this isn't friend behavior."

"Friends can get jealous." He was doing that stubborn thing with his jaw that meant she was fighting a losing battle.

"I've had so many partners you've never been jealous of. So many friends. Why the hell is Rohan, of all people, making you all green-eyed? I thought he was your friend."

"So did I," Patrick muttered.

"If this is something between the two of you, don't put me in the middle of it."

He shook his head. "It's not about him."

"So what's it about then?"

"You're trying to shrink me again."

"You're deflecting again!" She cried and stood up. "And neither of us have had enough sleep for this. You can stay here but I'm going to bed."

"Alone?"

She stopped, halfway down the hall to her bedroom, and turned. "Don't you fucking tease me. You know I'm in love with you."

"What if I wasn't teasing?" He stood too, watching her with a look she couldn't decipher.

"What do you want, Patrick?"

"I don't know." He sounded miserable.

"Then figure it out." She left.

CAZZI DRIFTED in and out of sleep, dreams blending with memories.

"I know what you're going to say, but what the fuck Patrick, am I unlovable?" She lies back against her bedroom wall, propping the computer on her knees.

From the screen, he gives her an incredulous look. "Unlovable? That was six months, try two years."

"Yeah, but there's like, a shit ton of photographic evidence that people love you all over the internet."

He shakes his head. "Not the same and you know it."

"Okay, fine. I was fishing for compliments or reassurance or whatever."

Patrick snorts but doesn't oblige. "Did you love him?"

"No." She shrugs. "But all the chemicals were there. Among other things."

"What was it you told me? 'Dopamine does not a romance make.'"

"Damn your memory." But it warms her that he remembers.

He grins. "You like it."

She groans but can't help grinning back. She loves making him smile. "Damn your perceptiveness too."

He laughs. "So what happened to yours?"

"I told him about what happened to Tanya and he started treating me like glass."

"Mmm." She knows what he's thinking: Better than the last one.

"I'm not delicate. I am a capable, independent woman, dammit."

"I never said otherwise."

She sighs. "How are you doing, by the way?"

His relationship imploded a week ago and he's already gone through the worst of the grieving. She's done her best to support him, hoping he doesn't notice she's rejoicing under her sympathy. Her sudden break-up isn't a coincidence. She ran out of patience, knowing Patrick was free and she had a chance for the first time in two years.

Call her mercenary, but she knows what she wants. She's known since she hit puberty and looked at him with hormones in her eyes. She could never tell if he reciprocated, he certainly hadn't been happy when she kissed him, but how was she supposed to know he had a girlfriend if he never talked about her? Especially when he'd kissed her back before telling her.

He didn't talk to her for over a year and a half. Until he called last week and needed a friend. It was all she could do not to say fuck you to her bank account and hop on the next plane.

All that higher education in sex and psychology didn't prepare her for how much she still needs him. Still wants him. Still loves him. How seeing his name on her screen makes her light and airy, too overwhelmed to stand. How hearing his voice makes her ache so hard she invokes her calming sigil just to keep from crying hysterically happy tears.

The intensity scares her rational self but even it knows she'll always pick up the phone when he calls. It's still surreal to hear him actually speaking to her after all this time, to see him on her screen in real-time, not in an old music video or news clip.

"I'm okay," he's saying. "But I shouldn't be, right?"

"Everyone grieves for a break-up differently."

He considers this, a frown creasing the skin between his eyebrows. "I don't know if I loved her."

"That's okay." Her voice is hoarse. She clears her throat. "That's okay. Your feelings are valid, whatever they are."

"You're shrinking me." His eyes crinkle.

"Sorry." She shrugs. "It's just what I do now."

"It's cool. I like it."

"Then I won't stop."

"Can you even turn it off?"

She opens her mouth to say something breezy but stops and thinks about it. This is Patrick. She can say anything. "Sometimes. But I dunno, sometimes I'm just analyzing everything, you know? But I like that. I like breaking interactions down and figuring out what goes on beneath the surface."

He nods. "Makes sense."

"Yeah?"

He smiles.

"You're not going to elaborate, are you?"

"Nope. It's a puzzle for you."

"Well, clearly you're being an asshole."

He laughs.

"And you want me to analyze you."

"Uh-huh."

She leans closer to the screen. "But what do you want me to see?"

He gives her an enigmatic look, but there's a tightness to his expression that hadn't been there a second before. A slight, unconscious slide backward from emotional openness.

She pulls back. "You know that's not how counseling works."

"It's not?" His smile is out of a PR picture, too playful, too knowing to be real.

"How are you, really?"

He blows out a breath, the falseness falling from his face. "You know me too well."

"You say that like it's a bad thing."

"Only when I'm trying to hide shit."

Like serious girlfriends? She thinks. Or how you feel about me?

"Don't bother. You know I'm too nosy for you to have secrets." *She tries to make it sound like a joke but it rings too true to be funny.*

He cracks a smile anyway, a real one. "Me too, for you."

"I might have secrets." She plays casual, overdoing it to make it seem absurd.

"You call me after every session you have with your therapist to dissect it."

Not for the last nineteen months. She shrugs. "What about you?"

"I'm a vault."

"A vault who used to call me every day."

The past tense hangs in the air between them.

"A lot can happen in a year and a half," he says finally.

"Yes," she says, "It can." The things he missed spool out in her mind. Her first real job in the field, moving to a new town, making new friends, new lovers, new tattoos, how much of a stoner she's become. Every little thing she wanted to tell him, every GIF she would've sent him, every minute she missed him. The incessant ache of him in the back of her head, a nerve ending she deliberately blunts, a torch, a hope she never stopped nursing.

"Tell me everything I missed."

She does. Almost. It's like old times, he smiles and laughs and frowns in all the right places, slotting back into her heart, her life just the way he used to.

He tells her about those nineteen months in broad strokes, filling in the details with his gestures and his microexpressions. She knows there are things he's talking around, shit that'll come out of the woodwork later when he's processed enough to put them into words. It's just like it used to be. She's content to wait, and take what she can get until he's willing to give her everything. She knows the vault will open eventually...

The memory dissolved, so completely that it felt closer to a dream.

Where did that hope go? She wondered. *Also what the hell is that noise?*

The vibrating started up again and she snatched the phone, unlocking it without opening her eyes.

"Cazzi Muldoon," Angela Alice said, her voice thoughtful.

Cazzi sat bolt upright, opening her eyes. "How did you get this number?"

"I needed to talk to you," Angela said as if that explained everything.

"About?" Her stomach was somewhere six feet under her house.

Angela took a shaky breath. "Was I a bad girlfriend? Was I abusive?" She sounded on the edge of crying.

Even over the phone, Cazzi's throat closed and her eyes burned. She pressed her fingers against her protection sigil and the sympathetic reaction faded. "Are you asking me to absolve you?" Like hell, she would. She could still see Rohan's face as he considered whether his ex might try to destroy his life. Unbidden, she remembered him kissing her. She pushed the memory away.

"I need to know."

"I can't help you." It was all she could do not to scream. Who knew if Angela was recording? How far would she dig into Cazzi's life to satisfy her obsession? *Fuck.*

"Oh god. Oh, Lucifer. Oh, Baphomet," Angela sobbed, the sound of her tears as sharp as broken glass.

Cazzi pressed her sigil harder until her breastbone ached with the pressure and she was closer to anger than angst. "Emotional manipulation."

"What?" Angela gasped the word out like she'd forgotten she had an audience.

"You're trying to get me to tell you what you want to hear by manipulating me with your tears." *White girl tears,* she thought disdainfully.

Angela let out a shaky exhale. "Oh."

Cazzi said nothing, just waited. If she hung up she had a feeling Angela would just call her back.

"My mother does that too." She paused. "That's an excuse, isn't it?"

She's adapting. Trying to find an angle she can use.

Cazzi kept silent.

"I'm not a good person," Angela said, defiant. Like it was a badge of honor to admit it. "But I never wanted to be a bad partner. I loved him, you know. Still do."

"Is that what you call that album? That special?" Cazzi fought to keep her voice even. "Love?"

"Have you ever been in a bad relationship? The kind that slowly chokes you from the heart out until you scream so you can breathe?"

Cazzi started to say no, then stopped herself. There was a horrible, creeping familiarity to her words. Suddenly it was hard to find air, like Angela had reached through the phone and grabbed her by the throat, clamping her in place. She couldn't think, she could only listen as the other women kept talking.

"Oh, it starts out good, fuck that, it's great. It's the best thing ever. And then you commit and commit and commit and suddenly you've loved yourself into a trap. And he's needy, Cazzi. So needy. He wants so much from you. Love. Support. Attention. Reassurance. He was lost until he found you. You pour yourself into him, you drop everything at the chance to see him, you cheer him on, you hold his hand and you're happy to do it. You can barely hold yourself together as it is but you'll hold him together as you crumble because how can you not? It's so much. It's too much. But you can't leave."

Cazzi felt sick, her stomach twisted and full of Angela's words.

Angela sighed. "You can't leave. Because everyone expects you to. They expect you to fail because you're *evil* and he's too good for you. Because you're a self-destructive mess and he's a fucking golden child. Because he makes you want to be better, the best, the dream living on the pedestal he put you on. Because you love each other... and that's the worst trap of all." She went quiet. "You'll fall off that pedestal, you know. It's so fucking far down, he'll never hold you up that high again. You'll disappoint him over and over. It'll hurt you both. So so much."

Cazzi was choking. She forced herself to speak. "What do you expect me to say?"

"Nothing," Angela said, decisively. "Nothing. Ro and I were shitty to each other. We yelled, we fought, we hid from each other. We made a goddamn toxic mess and now it's over. It's over and I'm going to make a shit ton of money off of it."

Cazzi focused on the one thing that didn't make her feel like she was drowning. "If you're going to make a shit ton of money off of your and Rohan's pain, the least you can do is leave him alone, don't you think?"

"You'd like that, wouldn't you?"

"Yes," Cazzi said. "Consider it payment for all this unpaid emotional labor I just did for you."

Angela choked out a laugh. "Right. And maybe someday we could be friends." She sounded wistful.

Cazzi was getting emotional whiplash from this conversation. "Seek help, Angela. Find a therapist."

"It's Angelica," she said. "My real name is Angelica. And by the way, you and Ro look cute in that picture. I used to love holding his hand."

Angelica hung up.

Cazzi sat in bed, forcing air into her lungs until she felt like she was breathing instead of drowning.

She walked out into the living room where Patrick was curled on his side on her couch. She sat next to him and lay her head on his shoulder, hating herself when touching him just made her feel sicker, more tense.

He frowned at her, sleepy but awake. "Who was that?"

"We have a problem," she said. The words hummed in her mind, echoing with all their double meanings. Her hand inched up under her sleeve, stroking over her calming sigils. She wanted to drag her nails along them, use the pain as a distraction. She settled for tracing them from memory.

We have a problem, Patrick. Because when Angelica was describing her shitty relationship, she reminded me too much of you and me.

ROHAN PACED. No one could make him angry like Angie could. He used to think that was a mark of passion. Now he wasn't so sure.

Cazzi watched him with tired eyes. Besides her, Rick drummed his fingers in angry 5/4 time against the arm of the rental's gingham couch and tried to out-glare the chicken figurine closest to him. Benji leaned on the wall by the window, staring out like they expected the press to come down the slight hill of the backyard like a horde of invading barbarians.

They turned to meet his gaze. "You look like you want to set something on fire."

He raised an eyebrow. "You say that like it's a bad thing."

"Get me some gasoline. I've got a lighter in my purse." Their grin was psychotic.

"As exciting as arson sounds, do we have a fucking plan for dealing with this—" Rick leveled a glare at Rohan. "Goddamn woman?"

Cazzi sighed. "You act like calling me for free therapy isn't something everyone does."

"Not me," Benji said.

"Congrats," Cazzi said drily. "You're clearly problem-free."

"It's because I'm perfect." Benji leaned in like they were telling her a secret.

"My goodness." She leaned forward, playing along. "A perfect human. How do you feel about being studied? Only minimal anal probing, I promise."

Benji pretended to consider it. "Only minimal anal? I'm not sure."

"Well for a perfect specimen, I'm sure we could up the anal." Cazzi pretended to take a note. "What size probe do you prefer?"

Rohan's face went hot, startling him. He couldn't remember the last time he'd blushed over sexual innuendo.

Benji smiled their pin-up smile. "How big—"

"Can we focus?" Rick snapped.

"Sorry," Cazzi bumped his shoulder with hers. "Coping through humor."

Rick huffed. "It's you I'm worried about."

She seemed taken aback. "She just wanted validation. She didn't get it."

"And she called me needy," Rohan grumbled. The accusation stung, even second-hand.

"She's obsessive. She'll be back," Rick insisted.

Cazzi looked at Rohan. "You know her best. Will she try to hurt me?"

He thought about it, trying to put himself in the tornado of Angie's mind. She'd rarely been jealous, she'd never had reason to be. He tried looking at Cazzi through Angie's eyes, both at the woman in front of him and the woman smiling at him and holding his hand at Badlands in the picture some fucking early morning amateur pap took. If there was anyone for Angie to be jealous of, it was Cazzi.

He'd never seen Angie attack anyone physically. She even captured spiders and put them outside. When someone—her fans, protesters, the press tried to grab or manhandle her—that was when she'd lash out. But she tended to grab them and force them to look her straight in the eye or push them away. Nothing excessive, everything controlled to look reasonable on camera. It was the way she looked when she was angry that scared people. The deadness in her gaze said she could cause harm and had before. He'd never quite figured out how much of that was an act.

He looked at Cazzi, trying to imagine Angie lashing out at her.

She probably respected her. Angie was known for surrounding herself with the most interesting femmes she could find. But Cazzi said she'd grabbed her and now Angie'd tracked down her number and called her.

"I… don't know," he said at last, "But if you didn't give her what she wanted, I'm sure she'll try another angle."

Cazzi nodded. "I talked to my department head. We think she called our receptionist and somehow wheedled my number out of him even though all our student workers are under strict instructions not to give our information out to anyone."

Rohan wasn't even surprised. Angie could talk anyone out of anything, given enough time. He wondered what else she tried to get from Cazzi besides validation.

"You don't know for sure?" Rick asked.

"I'm going to talk to him in person tomorrow." She yawned. "Look I gotta go get some sleep. I'm gonna head out—"

Benji's hand landed on her shoulder and pushed her back onto the couch. "We need to talk about the picture."

Cazzi's eyes widened, her cheeks going pink. The expression was gone in an instant, the color fading almost as quickly. "Sure. I squeezed his hand because I was comforting him about Angelica."

Rohan raised his eyebrows at Angie's full legal first name. There was a swoop of disappointment in there too but he ignored it.

Rick frowned.

Benji shot both men a look. "I couldn't give a fuck about what you two were doing. I care about the optics of what you two were doing."

Rick's frown deepened.

"Mmm," Cazzi said. "They're jumping to the obvious conclusions, aren't they?"

"Haven't you been on social media?"

"I don't have any accounts."

Benji drew back, shocked. "Not even a lurker account?"

Cazzi shook her head. "The mental health stats for social media show that—"

"Stop." Benji waved her words away. "I think we should give them a showmance."

Rick went rigid.

Benji patted his shoulder. "No one said it was going to be real."

"No." Cazzi's voice snapped like a whip.

It hurt like one too. Rohan kept his expression as neutral as possible.

"Come now," Benji cajoled. "All you have to do is spend time in public with a beautiful man. How hard is that?"

"Benji, let it go," Rohan said. The day he let his business partners badger girls into fake-dating him was the day he stopped dating altogether.

"It's not about that," Cazzi said.

"What is it about?" Benji asked.

"None of your damn business," Rick practically snarled.

Cazzi put a hand on his arm and told Benji, "Just trust me when I say being in the public eye like that will be very damaging to my mental health."

"You think being with this one will be any different?" Benji nodded at Rick.

"Benji," Rohan snapped. "If she doesn't want to do it, don't push it."

"Fine," Benji crossed their arms. "But we have to come up with something or *she* is going to make it seem like you were cheating."

Rohan went cold. "She wouldn't."

"You said you thought she'd spread rumors," Cazzi reminded him.

"I know, but I figured they'd be close to the truth. I *cannot* be seen as the asshole who cheated on Angela Alice."

"The fans would tear you apart," Rick murmured.

Rohan sat down on the coffee table. If Angie told the world he'd cheated, they'd believe her. Of course, they would, whatever her sins, she was white. What was left of his golden reputation would dissolve.

There was a tap on his kneecap. He knew without looking it was Cazzi. Ever since that kiss, every touch, every inadvertent bump buzzed his nerves like a tattoo gun. He turned his gaze up at her.

"Then you have to tell your story."

"What about the picture?" Rick asked.

She shrugged. "It barely shows my face, you can't see my tattoos. Tell them I'm an old friend, a handsy fan, your therapist, I don't care, just don't use my name."

"She'll out you," Benji said.

"She might," Cazzi allowed.

"We'll protect you as best we can," Rohan said, fiercely. No one was going to hurt her because of him.

A possessive voice in the back of his head whispered *Because she's mine.*

Rohan pushed the thought away. He wasn't that guy, wouldn't be that guy, even if Cazzi wanted him.

Cazzi smiled sadly. "That's sweet, thank you. I can handle it."

"I've got it covered," Rick said. There was definitely a territorial edge to his glare.

Rohan narrowed his eyes.

Cazzi frowned at Rick. "You've got what covered, exactly?"

"Protecting you," he said. "I've done it before, I'll do it again."

Rohan didn't even need to see Cazzi draw herself up to know Rick fucked up.

"Of all the paternalistic, overprotective bullshit—"

"It's true." Rick's words weren't loud but they had a finality to them.

"Oh really?" Cazzi crossed her arms. Her eyebrows went up and there was a frightening gleam in her eyes.

Rick took a deep breath. "After what happened to Tanya—"

"No." She snapped the word out. "This isn't about that. Is protecting me why you disappeared for nineteen months? Why you won't tell me what the hell is going on with you now? Why you won't ask for the help you so clearly need?" She stood up. "I don't need protection, Patrick. You damn well know I can defend myself."

Rick stood too. "You can't win this the same way you won back then."

Cazzi went so white Rohan stood up, worried.

"I didn't win a damn thing," she said, her voice harsh. "I thought you, of all people, understood that."

"Tawny—" Rick said like he'd been punched in the stomach then snapped his mouth shut like he'd said something infinitely worse.

Cazzi made a hurt sound in her throat that felt like a raw wound blooming in Rohan's chest. She turned to leave and Benji moved to block her. "Don't," she told them, her voice hoarse.

"Just—" Benji raised their hands placatingly.

"Benjiro Nakamura," she snapped out their name. "You can't control this the way you seek to control everything around you."

Benji froze.

She swept by them and looked at Rohan. "I'm not running away," she said. "You know where I live but I can't be your therapy Barbie right now."

He reached out but hesitated before touching her. "If you need anything…"

She nodded but didn't touch him.

The minute the door slammed in her wake, Rick collapsed onto the couch, covering his eyes with a wrist. "God, I fucked up."

"You're fucking up pretty consistently in that department," Benji said, but they seemed unfocused. "Did she just call me a control freak? I'm not a control freak, you know. I'm very chill. Everyone says so."

Rohan patted their shoulder and sat down next to Rick. "Hey, you okay?"

"What the fuck do you think?"

Rohan grimaced. "Wanna talk about it?"

Rick uncovered his eyes just enough to glare at him. "Oh, now you care? Did she reject you?"

"What?" Rohan drew back, startled.

"I know you're after her. You're on the rebound, I'm driving her crazy, I bet you two are *just comforting each other* left and right."

"I—" Guilt cascaded through him like a viscous wave, making his lungs squeeze.

"I thought you were my friend, man."

"I am but I honestly don't know what's going on here. Are you in love with her? She's in love with you." Rohan felt lost and guilty and like he'd rather be anywhere but here.

"Oh god, I hate love triangles," Benji groaned. "Why don't you just share her? Isn't that what polyamory was invented for? So no one has to choose?"

Rohan rolled his eyes. "I doubt it."

"Look, you guys could work out a sharing schedule…" Benji stopped, eyes going wide. "Oh my god, am I a control freak?"

"Yeah, but it's a good thing," Rohan said distractedly.

"I love her," Rick told the floor. "But I don't know that I'm in love with her. I don't know if I'm capable of loving anyone or anything right now."

"Of course, you can," Rohan said, automatically.

"Shut up, Ro," Benji knelt in front of Rick. "Look at me."

Rick grudgingly looked up at them. "I'm not a child. Besides, it's nothing, I'm just—"

"Shut up. Shut up and tell me everything." Their tone was sharper than Rohan had ever heard it.

"That's contradictory—"

"Yeah, I fucking know that," Benji cut him off. "And I also know depression. Intimately. So talk to me."

Rick shook his head. "I'm just down, it happens. It's fine."

"Oh hell, stop being such a *man* and deal with the fact you have emotions."

"Benji," Rohan interjected. "How can he talk to you when you're being such a jackass?"

"It's tough love," Benji snapped back. "Clearly being sweet and gentle and waiting for him to open up like a delicate flower has not been working."

"You're not going to solve my depression with a fucking intervention," Rick said.

"Ha! See, you admit you're depressed."

"What is this, gotcha therapy?" Rohan said. "Benji, you're too fucking much right now."

Rick stood up. "You are hands down the worst, most unprofessional people I've ever worked with."

"Dude, we're just trying to help," Rohan said. "Cut us some slack here, you ran off the person with the most therapist training."

"Help? You're trying to help by getting in her pants?"

Benji groaned from the floor. "What is so fucking fascinating about this girl?"

"Just cuz you're not into girls—" Rick started.

Benji thumped their head against the couch arm. "Just because I'm not into your fucking dream girl doesn't mean I'm not into girls, period."

"Look," Rohan said, trying to derail the conversation before it got even less productive. "I'm not trying to get into Cazzi's pants." His conscience twinged but he ignored it.

"Then why did you pick up her phone at five a.m.?" Rick demanded.

"Because we were still hanging out and we mixed up our phones, it happens."

Benji raised an eyebrow. "Mm-hmm."

"What's that supposed to mean?"

"Means I've seen your phones. They aren't exactly identical."

"Who's side are you on?"

"No one's. I just want the album done and everyone on speaking terms by the end of it."

"Well, then read someone else, RuPaul. This library's closed."

Benji stared at him.

"What? Leo was on, I watched his season." And every season after the one his ex-bandmate was on, but that wasn't relevant right now.

"That was a good season," Rick acknowledged.

Benji gaped at him now.

Rick shrugged. "Leo is my friend." He glared at Rohan. "A real friend."

Rohan rolled his eyes. "Cazzi and I have not slept together! How many times do I have to say it?"

"And you promise to never have sex with her?"

Rohan went cold. He wished he could make that promise but absolutely didn't want to.

"Ultimatums. Great, that'll end well." Benji threw up their hands and walked a few steps away.

"Well?" Rick said.

Rohan had restraint, dammit. He was a grown-ass man who could control his own dick, as many disappointed groupies could attest. He could do this. He barely knew her, his history with Rick was so much longer.

He opened his mouth to promise.

"Okay, I'm gonna put a stop to this," Benji said. "It's a disaster waiting to happen."

"This is between us, Benji," Rick said. "Fuck off."

"Look bitch, I don't have to be Ask Amy over there," they gestured vaguely in the direction of Cazzi's house. "To tell you that this shit is a bad idea."

"They're right, Rick," Rohan said, relieved at the possibility of an out.

"God, you really can't man up and do something yourself, can you?" Rick spat.

"What the fuck do you think this album is?" Rohan shot back.

Rick ignored him. "You can't make a promise without Benji protecting you, you can't break-up with Angela without Cazzi, you can't get over her without Cazzi, you can't do this album without us—"

"*Rick*," Benji snarled. "We just got him to accept help—"

"At least I accept help!" Rohan shouted. "How is going it alone working out for you Ricky Rick? You're bitter, depressed, you won't talk about it, and you can't be in a room with the woman you claim to love without hurting her. Is that what manning up is?" He stopped, breathing hard. "Does it feel good?"

Rick took a deep breath, then another. His face shut down, went blank, just the way Cazzi's would. Then he turned and walked out the door. Exactly the way Cazzi had.

18

"*To my fans:*
The last few weeks have been hard for Angie and me as we
ended our relationship. We each have our own ways of dealing
with this new chapter in our lives. Angie has turned to her work
and I have turned to my friends.
Many of you have seen the photo of one of my friends listening
to me as I processed my grief. She and all the many people who
have stepped up and reached out during this have been my rocks,
keeping me grounded in this tough time. They have my eternal
gratitude. I appreciate all the fans who have granted me their
patience, loyalty, and respected my privacy.
All my love,
RK"
—Statement from RK's Instagram.

CURSE OF THE EVIL EX?
According to a source close to RK, Angela Alice has been
terrorizing him and his friends as they try to make his upcoming
solo album. 'She's been calling non-stop, randomly appearing,

*and threatening people,' the source said, 'Honestly, we're afraid
of what she'll do next.'*
—*Celebrity Watcher Magazine*

Cazzi woke up the next morning with an emotional hangover. She pulled herself out of bed and Googled Rohan. She read the statement on his Instagram, scrolling through the comments of support, speculation, and outright accusations.

Damn, she was glad she wasn't a celebrity.

But if she and Patrick ever dated would she have become one by association? The thought seemed moot now but she mulled it over as she got ready for work. Would she have braved the public stage even a little if she had been with him? Even then it wouldn't have been as big as pretending to date RK. Dating Angelica ensured he'd appear in the tabloids every few months while Patrick had managed to fade back from that kind of attention.

She puffed out a breath at the idea of *wanting* that much attention. But maybe it was better if you were famous instead of infamous.

It didn't matter. She didn't want to date Rohan and frankly, she was seriously questioning her desire to date Patrick. Yes, she loved him. Yes, he cared about her. But as it stood now, their relationship was crazy-making and she knew Eva was right. If a student told her about a relationship like this, she'd be thinking about how best to get them out. Oh, she'd help them try to fix it, but she wouldn't have much hope and she'd be prepping them for the inevitable end.

Oh fuck, was this really the end?

God that hurt. Tears prick her eyes even though she thought she'd cried herself dry last night. She couldn't even be relieved her disassociation had broken, she'd felt too broken herself. Though she knew it could be a healthy thing, she was ready to stop crying so much.

She parked her bike at work and activated pretty much every sigil on her arms, grounding herself in the present, not the what-could-be or what-might've-been. She felt nearly human when she walked through the door.

And stopped.

Benji leaned over the reception desk, laughing with the obviously enamored student staffing it. They wore a loose, cowl-necked black sweater, tight black jeans, and silver Converse. She couldn't tell if they thought they were dressing down but they looked like they'd just stepped off the set of a music video.

Cazzi grit her teeth, took a deep breath, and tapped her protection sigil just for the extra boost. She strode forward.

"Benjiro," she said, her voice cold and polite.

Benji straightened and smiled at her, showing off subtle but gorgeous eye makeup and perfectly styled hair. It was dazzling.

She crossed her arms and waited.

Benji dropped the wattage of their smile. "Do you have a moment, Ms. Muldoon?"

Cazzi considered. She wasn't overly pissed at them. She actually felt a little sorry for them, caught up in the drama when all they wanted to do was finish the album and help their friends. But she didn't like them showing up at her work.

She nodded. "My office." She led them in and closed the door. "What's up?"

Benji dropped into the comfy client chair and sighed.

Cazzi set her bag on her desk and powered up her computer. In all likelihood, Benji had come for one of two reasons: they either wanted to vent or they wanted something from her.

"I have a staff meeting in," she checked her calendar. "Thirty minutes. Lots to do before then."

"Angelica's shitshow is streaming tonight," they said.

"I'm aware." It had totally slipped her mind.

"Are you coming over to watch it?"

"I hadn't decided." God, she didn't want to. She desperately wanted to remove herself from the constant onslaught of emotions.

Benji straightened a few knick-knacks on her desk then paused when they came upon the anatomical models of genitalia. "Is this required decor for sexologists or something?"

She tamped down the knee-jerk desire to roll her eyes and felt instantly bad when she realized there might be a quite reasonable explanation for why they were being an ass. "I'm sorry, are these dysphoric for you? I can put them away."

They shook their head. "I'm perfectly happy with my dick. I'm just not attached to the gender it comes with."

"We try to teach our students that genitals are not inherently gendered."

Benji waved this away. "Yes, yes. Thanks. I'm not here for therapy."

Cazzi sat down across from them and folded her hands. "What *are* you here for?"

"You look so composed when you aren't jumping walls and crying."

She contained her flinch. "Negging me and my trauma reactions don't help your case, whatever it is."

Benji blinked. "That was shitty, wasn't it? Guess it's just my way of trying to control the situation," they smirked.

Cazzi checked her watch. "If you're pissed because I called out an issue you hadn't admitted to yourself, then say so. I really don't enjoy trading barbs. It's pointless, painful ego masturbation."

Benji's eyes narrowed at her name, then they sighed again. "You're causing me a lot of problems. Not your fault, I know, but you're not a problem I can easily fix. And yes, I know, I'm a fixer, same as you."

"Benji," Cazzi said. "Get to the damn point."

"I know feelings and love and lust and shit are complicated.

I've been there." A haunted look crossed their face. "But I'm worried about my boys. Both of them."

"I am too."

"Good." Benji stood up. "Please don't come tonight. I think we all need a break."

It was Cazzi's turn to blink, the words hitting her like a sucker punch, thumping the air from her lungs. When she got her breath back, she asked, "Are you relaying their wishes or your own?"

"Does it matter?" They had the gall to look remorseful. "You and I both know it would be better for all of us. Besides," they leaned down and gazed at her with sincere sympathy. "Wouldn't you like a break?"

ROHAN PACED. The chickens on the mantle stared balefully at him. The one Cazzi had almost brained him with looked especially judgmental. He couldn't sit still or he'd lose it. Angie's horrid movie thing was in forty-eight minutes and he hadn't done anything productive all day unless you counted ignoring all the calls, texts, DMs, and social media commentary that erupted since his statement. Something flashed up on his phone screen, catching his eye from across the room.

It was James's face requesting a video call. Dammit. His family's messages were the only ones he answered but his tepid assurances apparently hadn't done the trick.

Oh well, what else was he going to do?

He picked up the phone and took it outside, answering the call as he did.

James' face appeared on his screen. "Hey kid," he said with a sympathetic smile. Rohan's stepfather still looked like a short Lando Calrissian after all these years, though his collared shirt and loose tie told him James had called him the minute he'd gotten home from work.

Rohan sighed. "Hey, Dad."

"You holding up?" James shifted the phone and Rohan could see the familiar couch and walls of the living room. Homesickness socked him. He missed Sunday tea time with his family.

Rohan shrugged. "I'm keeping myself offline."

He nodded. "Good, good. Your Mama and Nānī are worried. Can I bring them on the call?"

"Yeah," Rohan said though he knew he didn't have the bandwidth to reassure them too. But he wanted to see them.

"Shobi! Mina!" James yelled, leaning out of the frame. "The boy is on the phone!"

His mom and grandmother showed up so fast he knew they must've been hovering close by. They jammed themselves on either side of James and waved at the camera.

"Hi beta," his mother said. Dr. Shobi Kapoor had gone into private practice years ago and now had stable 9 to 5 hours but it still was strange for Rohan to see her relaxed and awake in the daytime.

"Are you okay?" His Nānī asked at the same time. "I hear that girl left you."

"*I* dumped her, Nānī."

"Good." Nānī bobbed her head approvingly. "She wasn't marriage material."

James cast his gaze to the ceiling behind his mother-in-law's head but even through the screen, Rohan could tell he was trying not to laugh.

"Mum!" Shobi cried.

Rohan found himself rubbing the tattoo over his heart through his shirt. They'd gotten inked but never once talked about marriage. Somehow he doubted Angie wanted much to do with it after what happened with her parents. "I'm not getting married any time soon." If ever.

"Not if you keep dating women like that," Nānī said, her voice sharp and her accent getting crisper with annoyance. It was odd to hear her so intent on marriage. Her own hadn't worked out, she'd gotten divorced at a time when women rarely did and Indian women in a new country didn't at all. She'd never remarried and raised his mother by herself working as a midwife and a nurse. But ever since he'd started getting close to thirty with no ring in sight she'd gotten antsy.

"Don't pressure him, Mina," James said, his voice gentle but firm.

Nānī sighed. "I just want to see you happy, beta."

"I know, Nānī," he said. "If I find someone to marry you'll be the first to know."

"I hope not," she laughed. "The girl should know first."

"She'll know," Rohan said and for some reason, Cazzi's face flickered across his mind's eye. She'd probably have strong feelings about marriage, something thought-out and academic. Though he couldn't guess if she'd be for or against it.

"Do you need us to come up?" Shobi asked.

The thought of his small but very vocal family underfoot while he tried to record made panic light up his insides. If nothing else they'd drive everyone up the wall, except maybe Cazzi. She'd probably get along just fine with Ma and Nānī. "No, no, I gotta finish recording."

"But—" Shobi started and then glanced at James as if gauging how much bullshit Rohan was slinging. James shook his head. "Okay." But she didn't look happy about it.

"Not okay," Nānī said. "You recorded all your other albums in LA, why can't you do that with this one?"

"Money," Rohan said. "It's cheaper, Nānī."

"Oh," Nānī frowned.

Rohan couldn't stand to see her sad. "But I'll be back down soon and I'll come stay with you, I promise."

Nānī beamed. "Good."

"She kicked you out, hm?" Shobi said, eyes narrowing. Good

thing Angie wasn't anywhere near Ma right now or she'd be in trouble.

Rohan grimaced. "We haven't had that talk yet."

"You want me to send someone over to pick up your stuff?" James asked. Knowing him, he'd show up in a full suit with movers and an NDA. Unless he let Ma and Nānī take over and then it would be all the cousins they could round up. The idea freaked Rohan out. Angie liked her privacy. She wouldn't let in half his family tree. His dismay must've shown because James said, "I'll make it as smooth and discreet as we can make it. Do you think she'll make a scene?"

"Yes," Nānī said.

"It's possible," Rohan said.

"We'll handle it," James promised. "I'll talk to her label if I have to. I'm sure they're already in damage control mode."

Rohan's stomach dropped. "Is the coverage that bad?"

"Not as bad for you," James said, slipping into manager mode. "A lot of people do not like Angela Alice on principle. Her reputation and that album are not painting her in the best light. We'll see how the album movie is."

"Yeah, I'm not looking forward to that."

"Oh beta, you're not watching that, are you?" Ma asked. "You don't need to watch that. Right, James? He doesn't need that in his head."

James frowned. "Ro, I'll watch it. You don't have to."

"No!" Rohan cried. "Don't watch it, please. Any of you. I-I don't want you to."

Ma sighed. "Beta…"

"*Please.*"

"Of course, we won't watch that trash," Nānī said. "No views from us."

Ma nodded. "We don't need to give her any more of our brain space."

James nodded too but the look in his eye told Rohan he'd watch her movie later no matter what his stepson said.

"*Breathe*, beta. Breathe," Ma said and Rohan smoothed his expression so he didn't worry her more. "You'll get through this. We'll help you."

After catching up on some family news, Rohan finally got off the call and went back into the house. Where he resumed pacing.

Angie's thing started in five minutes and Cazzi wasn't here. Not that she'd said she would be but he'd hoped... no he'd assumed. Dammit. He opened the back door and headed for her house.

"Where are you going?" Benji called from the kitchen table, slipping off their headphones. Rohan hadn't even noticed them there.

"I'm going to get Cazzi."

"Ohhh."

Rohan turned to see them looking vaguely embarrassed. "What? Did you do something?"

Benji shrugged. "I went to see her this morning. I asked her not to come."

His brain started screaming. Rohan's fists knotted at his sides. His mother's voice murmured under the noise in his brain. *Breathe, beta. Breathe.*

He breathed. One deep breath, then another.

"Care to explain why?" He had his grandmother's temper and it came with the shades of her upper-crust British boarding school Indian accent. He used to have the accent more, but it'd been trained out of him when he'd joined Beatboyz.

Benji crossed their arms. "You two are running that poor woman into the ground. I think she deserves a day off, don't you?"

"Don't spin this like it's about her."

"Spin or not, it's true. You didn't see her this morning. She looked wrecked."

Rohan opened his mouth to argue but stopped himself. Fuck, he was the asshole here, wasn't he? "I should've made sure she was okay."

Benji's expression softened and they walked closer until they could talk without yelling. "Do you care about her? Like really care?"

"She's my friend."

Benji studied his face. "Just between us girls, are you in love with her already?"

Rohan stuttered, shocked. "I—why do you ask?"

Benji shook their head. "Trying to gauge the situation."

"Do you think Rick is in love with her?"

"I think he thinks he should be. I'm not sure he's in a place to be able to." Benji frowned, looking concerned. "He needs to get help."

"Do you think this is like your friend—"

Benji shook their head. "Sly was and always will be a class unto himself."

"A king, maybe?"

They looked at him sharply. "Figured that out, did you?"

Rohan shrugged. "The internet did. I just stumbled on it."

"Well, the timing was always suspicious. I always told people I wasn't the Suicide King. But the media never wanted to connect him leaving the band and the album coming out. Then again, he was a bassist, they're practically wallpaper as far as most people are concerned. Singers are better stories."

"Makes for a great conspiracy theory."

"What's a band without a good conspiracy theory? Speaking of, we'd better go in."

Rohan grimaced, dread filling him. He looked in the direction of Cazzi's house. "Is it selfish that I really want her here?"

"Yes," Benji said. "But I get it."

CAZZI BRACED herself as the not-HBO special or visual album or whatever it was started. She liked Angela Alice's music in a sort of shallow, *sure I know the hits* sort of way. She wasn't prepared for her visual aesthetic. Yeah, she'd seen a few pictures of the theatrics of her concerts on a newsfeed or two, seen her dimly lit album covers in stores with Angelica in full Bitch Queen regalia, her pure white eyes tracking you down the aisle. Even meeting and arguing with her was nothing compared to seeing her darkness cross-sectioned across the screen.

Maybe she should've gone over and watched with Rohan.

The album opened in silence with the singer in a dark room dressed in all white, her hair streamers of silver-blonde, and her pupil-less eyes rolled up to the ceiling. She rolled her head down until her eyes met the camera and they filled with hissing static, the shot zooming in until the audience fell into her gaze. Then the screaming started. And the blood. Pouring out of Angela's chest as she pulled out her own heart and a man who looked suspiciously like Rohan as he tore out his heart for her. It was sticky red B-movie blood that seemed somehow just as visceral as the real stuff.

Holy fucking hell.

Cazzi had to hand it to the woman: she could sing and she had range. Angelica's ability to project her emotions translated well to the screen as she swayed and cried and bled and flew and screamed. Her voice went from creepy whispers to operatic grief to full-throated heavy metal roar and Cazzi was hooked on every note, horrified.

It was a car crash of emotions, impossible to look away from. She literally laid her heart out on-screen, dissecting it and twisting it into something horribly beautiful. There was a story in there somewhere but mostly it was just emotions and murder. A lot of murder. As far Cazzi could tell, Angelica played an alien from…somewhere who killed everyone she touched because…reasons.

Cazzi's training ticked along under her deep fascination, parsing the tropes and reading between the lines. The implications made her want to reach for her phone so she could text Patrick and verify some of her hunches or ask Rohan...

Oh god, Rohan.

He must be dying inside. This was so personal, even as it was allegorized into fantasy. The metaphor was thin, the truth obvious but distorted beneath the surface. It made neither of them look good.

Shit, she should've been there. But fuck, the thought of trying to hold his hand through this while Patrick glowered at them made her stomach twisty and sick. Not having to worry about that was a weight off her shoulders, except she felt bad for feeling relieved.

It was going to be a long night.

ROHAN WANTED to sink through the couch and die. He'd known it would be bad but not like this. There were so many of his words twisted up with hooks and barbs and thrown at him that he should be getting co-writing credit. It was like she'd recorded every fight they'd ever had and reworked them into this horror show where they were both monsters.

Oh yes, she hadn't skimped on her own flaws but her flaws had always been something she could exploit. Everyone expected the heavy metal Satanic ice queen to be fucked up. That's what people paid to see. They'd expected him to be the good one. But that sure as hell wasn't the way she saw him. And god, she'd seen him.

From the minute his doppelgänger ripped his prosthetic heart out, it was like looking into a funhouse mirror of his feelings. While Angie went around killing everything, he followed behind her, resurrecting himself and shambling at her heels like a zombie puppy. His doppelgänger dragged her down, pulled her away from her kills, put her on a literal pedestal, and knocked her off, fighting with her at every turn. Is that how she saw him? A supporting character at best, a burdensome, infuriating obstacle the rest of the time? How long had she felt this way? Why the hell had she stayed if he was so useless? Why had he been fighting for her for so long?

"This bitch," Benji hissed next to him.

"This fucking bitch," Rick agreed from the armchair.

Rohan realized his body was knotted up and taut but couldn't remember how to relax it. There was no way this had been choreographed, cast, filmed, and edited in a week.

Benji held their hand out. "Not as good, I know, but…"

Rohan clasped their hand. It was awkward. He'd never held hands with anyone who wasn't female. But it helped.

THE MINUTE the damn thing was done, Rohan was out of the house, gulping down the cold night air and wishing it was something stronger. He stumbled off the deck and hit the wet grass of the backyard, the dew making his bare feet numb. His stomach tried to push itself up out of his throat and the screaming in his head was back. This time it sounded like Angie's distinctive roar. He was too warm. How was he still so warm when it was fucking cold out here?

His phone was on silent and when he pulled it out, his notifications were in the triple digits.

James, his friends, the press, everyone had called, texted, mentioned, or DM'd him. Even as he stared, Leo called.

He didn't want to talk to any of them.

"You okay?" Rick stood on the deck, Benji hovering behind him.

Rohan grasped for words. "She must've been planning this for months." His voice sounded too low, too quiet. He should be screaming.

"We're going to make her pay." Benji's face was terrifying: backlit, and shadowed until they looked nearly demonic. Their knuckles were white around their phone.

Rohan bared his teeth at their words.

"It's shitty," Rick agreed, his voice hard. "But it's also free publicity. I think we should release a single."

"The dance song? Now?" Benji shook their head and looked down at their phone, brow furrowed in the blue light.

"No, one of the angry ones." Rick cleared his throat and sang, "You can't half-ass anything/anything but you and me."

Rohan's own words slapped him in the face. They were so right, so pissed. "Do it."

"Yasss," Benji hissed the word out, glancing up. "Let's mix that shit tonight."

Rohan grinned. It didn't feel nice.

"I'll get my computer." Rick headed back inside.

Benji turned to follow then looked back at Rohan. "You're going to see her, aren't you?"

He narrowed his eyes, sizing Benji up. "You gonna try and stop me?"

They shook their head. "Better with her than going down to a bar."

"Ringing endorsement."

Benji's lips thinned. "She's a problem, Ro. It's too soon for you to break yourself over another girl."

"Fuck off," Rohan growled. He felt like he was made of rage.

Benji raised their eyebrows. "I hope you don't take that anger out on her too."

Rohan lost his breath at the thought. "I'd never hurt her."

"I never said you would. Just… remember who's at fault here."

"I don't harm people, Benji. I'm not Angie."

"We all harm people, Ro." Benji smiled slowly. "The trick is only doing it when you mean to."

Rohan went cold. "You're planning something."

"Nothing terrible," they said. And winked.

"Promise?"

"You're far too good for her. After that fucking special… if that had been about me…" They looked down, composing themself. "I'd find a way to make sure she never worked again."

"Don't think that hasn't occurred to me. I'm… look, just promise me you're not going to do something we're all going to regret."

They tsked. "You have the worst expectations."

He shrugged. "Hazard of living with Angie for so long."

Their nostrils flared. "I told you not to compare me to her."

Rohan rubbed his arms, suddenly cold. "Just… promise, okay?"

Benji sighed. "Fine. I will keep my revenge sane and safe."

"That's the best I'm going to get, isn't it?"

"Yep. Have a good night with your shrink." Benji stepped inside. Then turned and tossed some flip-flops at him. "Try not to freeze your ass off." They closed the door.

The flip-flops were pretty much useless in the chill but Rohan put them on anyway. Then he trudged up the small hill and out the back gate towards Cazzi's house.

19

"The Romance Inverted 'movie' is a jilted white girl having a big-budget tantrum over being dumped. Would be adorably stupid if she wasn't shitting all over my best friend and one of the nicest guys in the industry."
—@BenjiNakamuraOmega

"Aww your condescension is just too cute @BenjiNakamuraOmega! Such an unbiased review! Don't forget to buy the album, in stores now ;]"
—@thatbitchangela

"@thatbitchangela don't worry. We're going to tell the real story in RK's upcoming solo album. Single drops tomorrow, hunny. How's that for shameless self-promo?"
—@BenjiNakamuraOmega

Cazzi sat on her porch, breathing in the night air and waiting. If no one showed up, she'd be shocked. And maybe a little disappointed.

Then she saw him and something that had felt off-kilter all day settled. She sighed, resigned.

She had feelings about Rohan. She had feelings for Rohan.

Great, just fucking great. That wouldn't be confusing at all.

He pushed open the front gate she'd left unlatched and carefully closed it behind him. She'd been watching him the whole walk over here but now his eyes met hers.

She stood up and opened her arms. He walked right into them. They held each other wordlessly. He shook. She held him tighter.

"You okay?" He asked. "Benji said you looked wrecked this morning." He studied her face.

"What a compliment," she said drily, then shrugged. "I'm as good as I can be. You?"

He inhaled hard. "You said you had a punching bag?"

"Already used it tonight." She slid her hand down and took his. "Come on."

She led him to the standing punching bag she'd left up on the back patio.

He put his fists up, toed off his flip-flops into a neat pile, and proceeded to batter the heavy bag until the entire thing nearly toppled. Cazzi watched him from a patio chair, noting the technique she could see under the flurry of his anger. He'd been trained at some point but not for a long time. On technique alone, she could probably take him in a fight.

She hated that she would probably always measure people, especially men, this way.

He stopped, panting. Sweat dripped off his curls.

"Feel better?" She asked.

"She made me into a monster." His voice was growly. Angry. Sexy in a dangerous sort of way. "A fucking burr who wouldn't leave her be a person." His eyes blazed as he looked at Cazzi. "She'd been planning this for *months*. There's no way she wasn't. I'm a fucking *idiot*."

Cazzi grimaced sympathetically. "You can't know things she didn't tell you."

"And—and—she had the fucking *nerve* to try to get me back, *knowing*, fucking knowing, she had that locked and loaded. Dangling over my head like that sword of whatever-the-fuck." He kicked the punching bag. "I can't stop overanalyzing everything she's said and done and shit! I'm so over this. I wasted so much time fighting for that woman. I should've listened when literally everyone warned me away from her."

He dropped his head against the punching bag. Silence descended, only his harsh breathing filling the air. Cazzi let it extend until she was sure he had spoken his fill. She wanted to give him space. This was not entirely out of her experience but she knew there were aspects of this she'd never fully get.

"I think," Cazzi said slowly, in case he still wanted to vent. "We are dealing here with someone who has no idea how to leave a relationship."

"What? No, that's—" Rohan stopped and thought. There had been other boyfriends, Cazzi knew. She'd done some deep Googling. The rockstar that went to rehab, the businesswoman who'd gone to jail, the drummer who'd cheated on her and married the other woman. A pattern. "But—but why did she try to get me back?"

Cazzi shrugged. "We all play out weird scripts given to us by the people around us and the stories we are told. That's how we learn how to love, whether we recognize that or not."

"So, what?" He pushed his bangs back, the gesture rough and angry. "I'm supposed to feel sorry for her?"

"Oh no, fuck her. I just like taking apart people's behaviors to see what makes them tick."

"Do you do that with me?"

She gave him a look. "What do you think our sessions are? Me spouting bullshit until something sounds good?"

He took a step towards her. "So what's your assessment then? What do you know about me?"

"Well, your knuckle is bleeding." She pointed at his hand. "But I probably could've figured that out with only a Master's."

Rohan glanced at his knuckles and back at her. He took another step closer. "Deflection," he said.

Cazzi raised an eyebrow and stood up. "What, pray tell, am I supposed to be deflecting away from?"

"Did I ever tell you how hot it is when you say smart shit?" He was barely six inches from her now.

Her stomach dipped and curled. "Say that to me when you're not trying to come down from an intense amount of anger."

"Why?"

"Sex might break the stress cycle, but that doesn't mean it's the right choice. If I'm even going to think about diving into the hot mess fucking you would bring, I'm gonna do it when you're emotionally here, not trying to get revenge on the Angelica in your head." She turned to go inside. She needed this conversation to be over. Her bravado would only last so long.

His fingers caught in her sweatshirt, not pulling but not letting go either. She turned back. "Rip that and you can leave right now."

"I'd like to clarify a few things," he said. But he let go of her sweatshirt, holding up a finger. "One, this isn't about stress or vengeance or Angie. I like you. A lot. I would still like you even if we never had sex at all. Though, I'd be a bit sad about that." He held up another finger and his eyes darkened as he met her gaze. *Pupil dilation*, she thought vaguely. *Attraction.*

That didn't mean the feeling was real though. She batted the thought away. She was worth liking, she reminded herself. Many people liked her.

It's not like he was talking about love.

"Two," he paused, smiling slowly. It made her breath hitch and her clit ache. "Does this mean you want to fuck me?"

She shrugged, trying to play it cool. Probably failing. "The thought had occurred."

"Oh, had it?" His eyebrows rose. "Do tell. When did it occur? How frequently?"

Far too much.

She laughed, her cheeks hot. "Now you're just fishing." She opened the sliding glass door and stepped inside.

"Just trying to gather all the facts." He closed the door behind him.

"I'm not stroking your ego just because I refused to stroke other things."

"Hey, I didn't even offer you other things to stroke. You jumped to conclusions."

She rolled her eyes. "It was more like a short hop."

His arms came around her from behind, slowly, brushing her sides. He was telegraphing his movements, she realized, moving so she could get away if she wanted. She didn't move. He wrapped himself around her and buried his face in her hair. "Did I mention I like you?" His lips moved against the barest edge of the shell of her ear.

She went still, startled, overloaded. Her body hyper-focused on every place he was touching her and the way he had molded himself to her, he was touching her a lot. "Yes." *I like you too, maybe more,* she thought but couldn't bring herself to say.

It was... nice. Like, really nice. She relaxed her muscles, leaning into his embrace.

"And that I appreciate you?" He rubbed his cheek against her hair.

"Yep." She smiled though he couldn't see her. She couldn't remember the last time she'd actually felt appreciated by a man.

"Okay, cool." He let her go. "Just checking." He collapsed on the couch. "Let's watch something."

"Are you asking me to Netflix and Chill?" She wanted to kick herself the minute the words left her lips.

That slow, sexy smile was back in full force. "Wasn't my intention, but…"

She slapped her hands over her very warm cheeks. "Joke. It was a joke."

"You should get one of those signs they have in *Monty Python's Flying Circus*. You know, 'A Joke.'" He mimed holding up a placard with a Vanna White flourish.

"Smartass." She leaned over the back of the sofa and poked his shoulder. God, his nerdy jokes only made him hotter.

"That's lower. This is my smart shoulder."

She laughed. "You think you're funny, don't you?"

"I'll have you know, I've been told I'm very funny on several occasions."

She snorted. "How many times was it by people trying to sleep with you?"

"Not all of them, I hope. One of them was my mother."

That startled another laugh out of her.

"See?" He said triumphantly. "Told you I was funny."

"You're a dork, that's what you are."

Rohan gasped in mock offense. "Not true! My Ma says I'm the coolest person in the world."

"Dork."

"Nerd."

"Actually, I self-identify as a know-it-all," she said with as much pretentiousness as she could manage.

He laughed. "I should've known. Clearly, you are too bougie to be anything so common as a nerd."

"Clearly."

They spent the rest of the evening bantering about nothing and half-watching mindless YouTube videos until she fell asleep.

SHE WOKE up at two a.m. with a start. She wasn't in bed. She wasn't alone. There was a body around hers.

Body.

The word echoed the way it always would. The clinical breath of her worst nightmare revisited.

These things were always worse at night.

She scrambled upright. The figure next to her grumbled and tried to snuggle closer but she almost vibrated off the sofa at the pressure of his arm against her shoulders.

Better than fingers on thighs but not much.

Ten fingertip bruises. Dark blue on white, white, white.

She stood up and forced herself to breathe, cataloging the room around her. She knew her house, even in the dark. In front of her: the TV, off. The coffee table, in shin-barking distance. The bookshelves, organized by subject then author. To the left: the kitchen, visible through the cut-out of the breakfast bar. To her right: the glass doors to the patio, moonlight streaming over the table and chairs she got for twenty bucks at a local thrift store, and the garden she kept promising herself she'd start.

Behind her: Rohan on the sofa. The present. Not the past.

She pressed her hand to the back of her hip, to the last tattoo. The one she hadn't shown him. The lost name written in a looping script, burning into her palm.

"You okay, Caz?"

She turned.

He was sitting up, watching her. "You wanna talk about it?"

No. Never again. Even if she should. She shook her head. She wanted to go back to sleep, hopefully not to dream. But she'd probably lie awake telling herself all the things she'd done to defeat her trauma, reminding herself how much better she was now.

And she was better. She just wasn't cured.

"You want a hug?"

She thought about it. Sometimes the idea of being touched

made her want to set herself on fire so no one'd ever touch her again. But when she considered the idea of Rohan holding her right now, her shoulders relaxed just a bit.

He opened his arms and she walked in. He pulled her into his lap, burying his face in her hair. "I got you," he said. "Anything you need."

She hugged him back, melting into his embrace. "Same," she said. "Same."

It's too soon, she told herself. *Too soon to risk telling.*

He kissed her forehead. The lightest, sweetest touch.

She melted against him as he stroked her hair.

Too soon. Too soon to tell. Don't ruin this yet.

ROHAN WOKE up in her bed, alone. It was a weird rush of familiar angst and unfamiliar surroundings.

You're weak, hissed a shitty little voice in his head. *Needy, just like she said.*

Shut up. He shunted the voice away and sat up, studying the room. Who knew when the next time he'd been in here would be? Well, the banter last night had been promising, but they hadn't done *anything*, not that they *should*, but well, what if after four years he'd lost his touch?

He concentrated on the room. It wasn't even low-key witchy, it was fully screaming "WITCH!" with its star and moon wallpaper, framed prints of sigils and goddesses, a shelf full of books on magic, and an altar in the corner. Even the bed had a purple comforter adorned with golden eyes.

And there she was, watching him from the doorway, her eyes calm. Inspecting him as he inspected her.

"Nice bed," he said.

She looked at it and then let her gaze meander up his body as if he was wearing much less than all his clothes. As if to say *it looks good with you in it.*

He smiled and licked his lips. Her gaze zeroed in on the movement, her own lips parting as she bit the bottom one.

Oh no, he definitely hadn't lost his touch.

"Good morning to you too." Her voice was rusty, so opposite her normal smooth tones. There wasn't much polished about her this morning. Her clothes were wrinkled and there were dark hollows under her eyes. It felt intimate to see after years of being surrounded by people who could be Insta-ready in ten seconds or less.

In the few moments before she smiled and he lost his train of thought, he remembered her standing in the middle of the living room last night before they'd moved to the bed, still and brittle. One hand fisted, the other covering her hip, her breathing shallow. Her whole being gray in the moonlight. The way she'd curled into his embrace like she might just burrow into him and never leave. That thought hadn't scared him then and it didn't scare him now. Which, ironically, scared him.

Her hip. He remembered, suddenly, the tattoo emerging from the bruises on the back of her hip. The one she hadn't shown him. It was white ink so he could barely make it out but after some puzzling, he thought it said: Tanya.

She smiled.

Fuck, to wake up to that smile every morning. He'd forgotten what it'd looked like when a woman smiled at him like it made her happy to see him in her bed.

"Tea?" She raised a steaming mug he hadn't noticed.

"I'm not angry anymore," he said.

"What?" She looked caught off-guard. Her cheeks turned pink and he almost cheered.

"Just letting you know." He shrugged as if this was a casual thing and he wasn't desperately hoping she felt this too.

She blinked and seemed to compose herself. "That's what you're leading with? You're not angry so we can have sex now?"

He grimaced. "Too early?"

"Oh god." She bit her lip again. "Yes, in far too many ways." But she sat down on the bed within reach.

It was all he could do not to reach. "Tell me about them. The ways it's too early."

She shrugged. "I'm falling out of love with Patrick." She covered her mouth, looking suddenly stricken. "That's not what I meant to say."

"But is it true?" His whole body was one held breath, light, airless, burning.

She considered, looking very serious. "This doesn't mean I don't have feelings for him. I'm just... just losing them." She took a sip of tea, her hand shaking. "It's horrible. I feel like parts of me are crumbling away. I'm... dissipating around the edges."

Rohan held out his hand. It was strange to hear her put words to the sand-trap feelings he'd been having under all his anger at Angie. His exhilaration quieted. "Like quicksand," he said.

She touched her fingers to his, not quite holding his hand. "Yes. Like I'm giving up. Failing at love or something."

"I think you need more than one person to make love work." He hooked his fingers to hers. "It's like a rowboat. Sure, you can get there by yourself but it would be so much better if both of you were rowing."

She nodded. "I like that analogy. It's versatile."

"Yeah, it's how my mom explained an orgasm to me."

"Very nice." Cazzi looked impressed.

"It sure scarred teenaged me," he laughed. "She has no filter when it comes to body stuff."

"I can relate." Cazzi smiled into her tea.

She'd like you. His mother never said it, but he suspected she'd never been a fan of Angie.

"What else?" He said.

"Hmm?"

"You said it was too early in far too many ways. What else?"

"Are you trying to seduce me through therapy?" She raised her eyebrow, her smile turning wicked. "Because that's highly unethical."

"And how does that make you feel?" He traced the lines of her palm.

She burst out laughing. "Conflicted."

"How so?"

"Well, on one hand, I like to think I'm very ethical."

"But?"

She turned very pink again and he found he liked it. "But on the other hand…" She looked up and met his eyes. "On the other hand, I really want to fuck you."

He grinned. "I like that hand."

"Yeah, well, you're clearly biased." But she put her mug on the floor.

"Clearly." He tugged at her arm, leaning her towards him. She slid closer. When she was a breath away, the thought he'd been suppressing popped out of his mouth. "You're not going to regret this, are you?"

Again, she considered. "I don't think so. You've been tested recently, right?"

"Yeah, they were all negative. Look, we don't have to—"

"Good. Me too." She grabbed his face and kissed him. "I think I'd regret it more if we didn't," she murmured against his lips.

"Well, when you put it that way…" He pulled her into his lap and kissed her, his hand skimming down her side.

OH, his hands. They were so hot she could feel them through her shirt. She arched towards him, positioning herself until she ground down... right... there. He groaned and she groaned because, damn, it was good.

He nipped her throat and she lost her breath in the best way. But she stopped him when he went to kiss her again. Only just, but she knew herself and she couldn't have a good time before: "Rules," she forced out, "Ground rules, quick: any hard nos or maybes I should know about?"

He paused and she watched him restart the blood in his brain. "Um, no feet, no fingers in my ass, maybe stuff with food?" He shrugged against her. "You?"

"No cutting or burning, period. No bruising in visible places; no rape play, no food with even a hint of sugar anywhere near my vulva, no shrimping, and no pushing my face into your dick to make me deep throat, I'll do that if I feel like it."

He blinked. "Shrimping?"

"Toe sucking."

His mouth opened, closed, opened again. "I had no idea there was a name for that."

"What can I say? I'm educational *and* fun."

"Yeah, you are." He grinned, winding his fingers in her hair and giving it an experimental tug. "Good?"

"Yeah." Especially when his other hand wandered down to slip under her shirt and cup her breast.

"Tell me what you like." She liked the demand but not the insecurity buried under it. He scraped his teeth against her throat and leaned into the sensation.

"Well, I have this yes/no/maybe app..."

"Later. I want to finger you. Can I finger you?" He sounded so urgent. She loved it.

"Hell yes." She reached down and paused, hand hovering over his dick. "May I?"

"Please." His free hand trailed up her thigh, fingertips dipping under the waistband of her pj pants, pulling them down until they met the band of her underwear. She grabbed his dick and forgot how to think, let alone move as his fingers dipped down and down until they traced over her clit. It was electric. She gasped, her head dropping onto his shoulder.

"Good?" He repeated and she heard that insecurity again.

"Yesss," she hissed, nodding against his shoulder in case that wasn't enough. She popped the top button of his pants. His fingers pressed against her clit. She had just enough mind left to unzip him and snake her hand through the flap of his briefs. Her fingers closed over his thick warmth and it was his turn to gasp. The angle was awkward but seemed to work for him. His head fell back and she bit his throat, leaning in and running her thumb over the head of his dick.

"Good?"

He nodded, his breathing rough. His fingers slipped down further through her slick folds to curl into her. His palm ground into her clit as he pumped in and out. Her eyes squeezed shut, reveling in the blooming, rising sensation. Her hand moved over his dick automatically but her back was arching as she rode his hand.

She was so, so close…

She pressed against him hard, shifting the angle just a bit, and… the top blew off her head, the orgasm whiting out her vision.

He caught her as she slumped back, boneless, letting her float in the sensation. And oh, what a sensation. She knew the names of the chemicals flooding her body, knew exactly what they did, but she couldn't say what they were to save her life right now. Her brain was only working in short bursts and mostly it was saying *Fuck. Yes.* over and over again. It'd been so long since she'd had an orgasm this good.

"Did you…?" He asked as her vision cleared, his smile telling her he probably knew the answer.

"Oh yeah." She grinned. "And now it's your turn." She leaned in and whispered, "How do you want to come?"

"In you," he growled.

She shivered as his chest vibrated against her aching nipples. "Where?"

His breath hitched. "Where do you want me?"

"Let's start here." She ground her very sensitive clit against his erection. They lost a moment, grinding against each other with only the thin, damp layers of her pants and undies dividing them. The friction alone was getting her closer and closer again...

"I think that can be arranged." His grin faltered. "Do you have...?"

She rolled off of him and opened her bedside drawer, pulling out a shiny plastic square. "Condom Pixie, remember?"

"Oh, so what you're saying is we're not in any danger of running out?"

Her face got hot. "Slow your roll. I still have to go to work this afternoon."

"How long do we have?"

She glanced at the clock. "Three hours before I have to get ready."

"I can do a lot in three hours."

"Oh really?"

He leaned over, covering her body with his, kissing her deep and slow until she nearly forgot her name. "Really."

"Prove it."

He plucked the condom from her hand and she took the opportunity to shed her pants and undies.

"The shirt too," he said. "Please."

She complied, watching him as he stripped down, exposing all that beautiful brown skin, ink, and lean muscle. He didn't have the six-pack from his posters anymore but somehow that was better, realer. He put his clothes in a semi-neat pile, coiling his amulet on top. Then he rolled the condom on with the ease of long practice, which was almost as sexy as the strip show.

He pulled her back to him, settling her on top.

"Ready?" She asked.

"For you? Always."

"Flatterer."

"Did it work?"

She eased the tip in and he abruptly stopped talking. "What do you think?" She slid him in as slow as she could stand, enjoying the glorious fullness. "Oh god, you feel so good."

He groaned, thrusting up into her and she forgot what words were. All that mattered was the feeling of him in her.

Every nerve was still echoing with her last orgasm but she was cresting that wave again. By the look on his face, Rohan was too. She leaned down, deepening the angle, and licked her way up his neck, enjoying the salt taste of his skin. "I'm close."

"Me too." His hands clamped onto her ass, pushing deeper and deeper and, oh god, oh god, *there*!

She froze, reveling in the sudden wondrous cacophony of sensation. Below her, he pumped into her a few more times before she felt him stiffen too, pressing her closer as they fell into the rush of feeling together.

Cazzi woke up two and a half hours later, sore and exhausted and... happy. She turned over, facing Rohan. He was curled up next to her in a near-fetal position that couldn't be comfortable, sound asleep. She took a moment, watching him. His face was relaxed but his fists were clenched, the sheets twisted around him, his hair fluffed up and haloing on the pillow. Something raw and tender ached in her chest.

I want to do this forever.

She sat up.

Nothing can come of this.

These feelings were deeper than they had been. Was she falling just from a bit of oxytocin and endorphins? Okay, it was more like a lot of oxytocin and endorphins, but still. She wasn't dickmatized, right?

Of course, she was. She wasn't naive. She might not see everything but she liked to think she knew her own mind pretty well.

She just hadn't thought she'd be this shallow.

What about her undying love for Patrick? The thought hurt. Yes, she knew there was no real undying love and nothing ever was as rosy as it looked, especially not relationships, but dammit here was her biggest blind spot. She'd been in love with him so long it had become part of her self-image. Sex educator. Sigil witch. Functional stoner. In love with Patrick. Hopelessly.

But how hopeless could it be when she was so effortlessly wrapped around Rohan in a matter of days?

Sure, she'd had other relationships. She'd even fooled herself a few times into thinking she was over Patrick, but deep down, she'd always known: if he'd called, she'd have come running. As fucked up as it was, that had always been a relief. Like the feeling of the ground under her feet when she thought she was too far into the deep end.

If she still loved Patrick, she knew who she was.

If he called right now, what would she say? Would she lie? Would she apologize and justify herself?

She wasn't sure.

"I can hear you thinking." Rohan's voice was rough and sex-hoarse as he looked at her.

It made her want to climb back on him. "You're a mind reader now?"

He laughed. "You just think loud."

"I'll have you know I've been commended for my quiet thinking."

"Really?" He untucked an arm and draped it over her. "By who?"

She pretended to think. "Ummm, the Quiet Thinkers of America?"

"Now I know you're making shit up."

She laughed.

His smile faded. "You're thinking about Rick, aren't you?"

"Now, yes. During, no. Are you thinking about Angelica?"

"It's weird you call her that."

"She asked me to. I always respect preferred names, even if I don't care for the person carrying them."

He shook his head, curls fluffing against the pillow. Her whole bed smelled like him. She wondered how long it would linger. "I wasn't thinking about her. Not until you brought it up."

She shrugged. "It's okay if you did. It'd make sense if you associated her strongly with sex."

He mirrored her shrug. "There wasn't much sex by the end and what there was wasn't good."

"It happens. Especially when a couple isn't connecting on an emotional level. Though," she paused. "That's not always the reason why."

"You think she was cheating?"

Cazzi shook her head. "I can't speak to that. There are lots of reasons: past history, trauma, different stress levels and responses, changing desires, boredom, hormonal changes, communication issues... I'm lecturing again."

He sat up and kissed her. "I told you, it's sexy when you say smart shit."

Her face got hot. "Careful. I have to go to work soon and I suspect you need to record."

Rohan swore, grabbing for his clothes. "You're right."

"I'm surprised Benji isn't blowing up your phone." She pulled a fresh pair of underwear from her drawer.

"They know where I am."

Cazzi froze. "Does...?"

"I don't think they would've told him." The cheer in his voice flattened.

Maybe he was as deep in this as she was.

It won't work. You have to tell him why he shouldn't be associated with you.

Maybe she wouldn't.

You'd live a lie? Hypocrite. The sneering voice in her head sounded more and more like Angelica and Cazzi didn't care for it. She tapped her strength sigil, reminding herself. *I am as strong as I need to be.*

"What's up?" Rohan noticed the movement.

"Just talking to myself. You know, like a normal person."

"Oh yeah, we're normal." He put on his amulet. "I definitely don't talk to myself at all."

Cazzi wanted to ask if that's how he wrote his songs, but she caught sight of the time and swore instead. She rushed through the rest of getting ready, stuffing herself into clothes and food into her mouth. Rohan handed her a glass of water and she drained it in one long gulp.

Rohan sped up too and they were out the door in ten minutes flat, pausing only for an almost awkward, almost domestic kiss at the door.

"Listen," she forced the words out. "We're friends, right? You know this is a one-time thing? I just want to be clear."

"Sure," he said. "Are you coming to the studio?"

She shook her head.

"Okay," he said and kissed her quickly again, again, again. "Last one, I swear." A longer kiss, then he was done.

That should've bothered her, but it didn't. What bothered her was he was probably right.

ROHAN ARRIVED at the studio after a quick shower and change, trying very hard to not look like he'd just had sex. Fantastic sex. Multiple times. With the woman he was teetering on the edge of being in love with.

Even as he thought it, he knew he was lying to himself.

Fine. He was pretty much in love with.

Right, buddy, keep telling yourself that.

He ignored it. She said it was a one-time thing, that they were just friends. He had to respect that. Even if it stung. Even if he already had fifty-two half-assed plans to try to change her mind.

Benji looked up from their computer and clapped when he came in. "There's my boy!"

"Hey, what'd I miss?"

Rick looked up and dead-eyed him.

"Good news and bad news," Benji said.

"You wasted half a day of recording," Rick said. "Where were you?"

"He was dealing with the bullshit of last night," Benji said, smoothly.

"I was asking him."

It took all of Rohan's resolve not to snap back. "I needed a break. Now I'm back and ready to work."

"What was her name?" Rick asked.

"The single is doing great!" Benji burst out. "Our streaming numbers are huge and we're getting radio play already. There's talk that it's gonna hit the Billboard charts."

"That's great!" Rohan's anger dissolved.

"It's not all good news," Rick said. "This is our last day in the studio—and the rental."

"What?" Rohan's stomach dropped. "I thought we had another week."

"Yeah, that was the week *she* paid for." Benji's eyes narrowed. "She pulled some strings and somehow got around the norefunds rule. It took all my negotiating skills to get us today after what she put both places through."

"*Goddammit!*" Rohan's shout made his own ears ring. "And the royalties…"

"Aren't coming until next quarter," Rick confirmed.

"Fuck. Are we out of money completely?" Rohan fisted his hands in his curls. James called him half an hour ago to tell him he'd gotten Rohan's stuff out of Angie's house. No doubt this was retaliation. Maybe there was something he could sell? There were probably assets he could liquify but he'd been living off of residuals for years —good residuals but nothing like the contracts kept him and his family flush during the Beatboyz years. He'd diverted a big chunk of it to the Foundation though and he'd taken Nānī on several big international trips recently. Dammit, he didn't even know the state of his own finances let alone his company's. He should've taken that damn business class James kept nagging him about.

"The recording budget, yes," Benji said. "We have enough to pay the cover designer, barely. If I didn't have the distribution deal in place we'd be fucked."

"Can we do an all-digital release, just to start?" Rohan asked.

"Could, but it'd be risky. People still buy CDs and vinyl is having a resurgence," said Rick, who'd actually gotten a music engineering degree after Beatboyz. With a minor in business. James was very proud. "Not much money in digital once the tech companies get their cut."

"We need another place to record. We still need three more songs." Rohan felt hopeless.

"We could do a shorter album," Rick suggested.

Rohan shook his head. "It doesn't feel complete yet."

"Dammit, I knew I should've built a studio in my Sacramento place. Or fucking renovated the bathroom. It's too damn echoey," Benji grumbled. Rohan remembered that bathroom—it had Benji's unframed Associate's Degree in business staked crookedly to the wall with a railroad spike through the middle hanging over the toilet. When asked about it Benji just said, "School didn't agree with me."

"The bathroom?" Rick looked thoughtful. If only Rick's home studio hadn't been flooded by a burst pipe a few days before they were set to start.

"The vocals for 'Hold on I'm Coming' were recorded in a bathroom. Stax Records had some special Italian tiles or something," Benji said. "Though to be fair, My Chemical Romance recorded *I Brought You My Bullets, You Brought Me Your Love* in a basement but it fucking sounded like it. But lots of big artists have recorded in bathrooms and garages and shit."

"So you're saying we could record at someone's house," Rohan said, slowly, an idea dawning on him. But no, he'd asked too much of her already.

"Not mine," Benji said, "Either of them. The house is a mess and the apartment is tinny as hell, trust me. I've tried."

"I—currently don't have a home right now," Rohan said, the realization hitting him hard. Where was he going to go after this? Back to his parents' house? Move into the vacation house he'd bought years ago and rented out to a cousin almost immediately? Maybe he could rent something on his credit card, given that most of his money was tied up in this damn album.

Benji looked at Rick. "The studio is the only soundproof place and my sister told me the carpet has to all come up cuz of the flooding. Apparently, it molded." He shrugged. "She and my grandmother are there right now. Cat sitting." He paused, his expression taking on the conflicting mixture of tension and affection that could only mean his mind was on one person. "But I do know a place…"

Rohan was already shaking his head. "We can't ask Cazzi. I've asked her too much." He looked at Benji. "Come on, you or your mom have to know someone in Sacramento."

Benji looked thoughtful. "I haven't stayed in touch with many people up here. I'll talk to my mom." They sent a quick text.

"She has a spare bedroom," Rick said.

"My mom? No, she turned that into an art room. It's a fucking health hazard, full of knives," Benji said.

Rick and Rohan paused to digest this.

"No," Rick said after a moment, "Cazzi has a spare room."

"Where? That place is tiny," Rohan said distractedly.

Rick shot him a suspicious look. "It's next to the bathroom. Looks like a closet if you don't know what it is. That's where her library is. Sounded good, far as I could tell."

"There are more books?" Rohan pushed down the barbed reminder that of course, Rick would know more about Cazzi's life, about her house, than he would.

"Ask her," Benji said. "Mom said she'd ask around. At the very least we should be able to borrow some equipment." They looked thoughtful. "But a library will do until I can get something lined up. If we miss our deadline for getting the masters to distribution we may lose the deal."

"No," Rohan said. "I told you—"

"I'm not asking you." Benji nodded at Rick. "Ask her. She won't say no to you."

This doesn't hurt, Rohan told himself. *This is only pain. This is only a battle. The war is not yet over.*

He stopped that train of thought. *It's not a war.*

In the corner of his mind, the possessive voice hissed, *Not yet.*

CAZZI WALKED out of her office with Yanni, Josie, and the sniffling student worker feeling like a complete asshole. Even though she and Yanni had been as gentle and forgiving as they could be, policy said receptionists could not give out staff information without approval. Josie, as the admin supervisor, wanted to fire the student but Cazzi, who knew he was barely scraping by on what little the work-study position paid, managed to talk her down and convince Yanni. The kid was on probation and banned from phone duties for a while. His hours would be cut because of that. Josie would make sure of it, judging by the way she'd stomped off.

Cazzi hoped he could still make rent.

She was about to head to her office and bury herself in some paperwork when Yanni said, "Can you come to my office for a minute? I think we need to talk."

Her blood went cold, but she followed her boss into her office and sat down as the older woman closed the door. Cazzi fought the feeling she'd been called into the principal's office.

The last time she'd been in a principal's office was when she returned to school after what happened to Tanya. It had been a cursory meeting, the sympathy too pat to be real. It should've warned her the administrative staff wouldn't be much help with what happened afterward.

"Cazzi?"

She shook off the memories and smiled at Yanni. "Sorry, just processing."

"There does seem to be a lot going on right now." Yanni smiled sympathetically.

"What do you mean?"

Yanni clasped her fingers loosely and put on her counselor face. "That woman getting your phone number is worrisome. I thought we had trained our students better than that."

Cazzi allowed herself to grimace. "I don't think you can train for someone like her."

Yanni cocked her head. "Who, Cazzi? You haven't yet told me who she is and she didn't even have to tell Matt who she was to get him to give her your number."

Cazzi schooled herself to stillness though she desperately

wanted to trace her sigils. "My friend recently left an unhealthy relationship. His ex is not letting go well."

Yanni frowned. "Are you in danger? Is your friend?"

She shook her head. "I don't think so."

Yanni narrowed her eyes. "But you're not sure."

"I don't think she'll come visit the department if that's what you're asking."

"Good," her boss said. "But do be careful, physically and emotionally. These situations can be draining, even if you're not directly involved."

"I know."

Yanni's gaze softened. "I know you do."

Cazzi nodded and stood. "Did you need anything else? I have to do some orders for the Condom Pixies…"

"You're sure you're okay?" Yanni looked genuinely concerned.

No. I'm falling out of love with my best friend. I'm in some ridiculous fucking love triangle. I'm losing my mind to old memories, stress, sex, and pot. Angelica is maybe stalking me and I'm maybe catching feelings for her ex. Matt may not make rent because Angelica talked him into giving her my number. And on top of all that, one of the only two people in this town who really knows me is moving away in less than a week. I need therapy, a vacation alone, and my course to be approved as a graduation requirement without having to fight for it.

Cazzi smiled carefully, in case her mask was as brittle as it felt. "I will be. In time."

"Of course." Yanni stood up and opened the door for her. "Needless to say, my door is always open if you need something. Even if it's just to talk."

Cazzi's eyes abruptly burned, tears pressing up against their backs. The urge to spill everything from Angela Alice all the way back to what happened to Tanya right here on the faded throw rug under her feet was almost nauseating. It was blue and yellow, almost the same color as the stars on her skirt that night—

She pressed her third-level calming sigil through her sleeve. *It is my will to restrain my emotions.*

"Thank you," she said. "I appreciate it." She wanted to say more. She needed to talk to Yanni about getting some of the department to help bolster her presentation with their testimony but if she tried she knew she'd lose it.

She walked like a calm and normal person to her office and closed the door. She sat down in her chair. Looked at her computer screen. It was off and she saw her reflection faintly. A pale ghost. She'd been so pale in those pictures, the ones from that night. She hadn't wanted to look at them but it'd be an accident. A file folder left on the dining room table from a meeting with a lawyer.

And there she'd been, all wild hair, wild eyes, white skin, wrapped in blue and yellow stars and adorned with fingertip bruises. Small and in shock. Stuck in an evidence file forever.

Those bruises, that white skin, her size. They'd all saved her, legally anyway. That and the rather damning video evidence.

Her phone rang.

She checked the caller ID and her stomach dropped. It was Patrick. Did he know about Rohan and her?

No. He wouldn't be calling. He'd just cut her out of his life again.

The thought made her nausea rise up again, the jagged urge to cry punching her in the face. She took a breath. Another. A third.

The phone kept ringing. She considered not answering. But she did.

"Hey," he said.

"Hey, I'm at work." Her voice was so normal it surprised her.

"I know, sorry. How are you doing?"

The old hope welling up in her was dull, more habit than true feeling. She mourned its sheen as she said, "I'm functional. You didn't break me."

"I'm sorry, I know I fucked up I—"

"Is this why you called me? To have an emotionally volatile conversation during my work hours?" She covered her face, glad the door to her office was closed.

"No, fuck, I just—just need to ask you a favor."

"Dammit, Patrick. What is it?"

Patrick took a deep breath and the hope fractured into worry. "Angela fucked us. We're being kicked out of the studio and the rental today."

Oh no no no no... Worry burrowed into her skin and metastasized into prescient dread.

"So I was wondering..." Another deep breath told her he was fighting the same dread. "Could we crash at your place and record in that spare bedroom?"

No no no no no. "I don't have a spare bedroom."

"That library—"

"Is a walk-in closet. I don't think it could fit two people with all the shelves I put in."

Benji's voice came out of nowhere on the call. "That could still work."

"Am I on speaker?"

"No, Benji just has freakishly good hearing."

"In-Ears and earplugs, baby," Benji said, their voice brittle-bright.

"It's okay if you don't want to, Caz," Rohan called in the background.

"Shut up!" Benji snapped.

"Please," Patrick said, his quiet voice cutting through. "We need this. Just a few days, until we figure something else out."

Cazzi rolled the idea around in her head. It was suffocating, the thought of having all that drama staying in her house. But... but she couldn't let Angelica win. She couldn't let that album fail. Couldn't let Rohan down or Patrick or even Benji, who frankly was getting on her nerves.

She'd just really throw herself into work and helping Judit

move. They'd be gone in no time and she could find another therapist and work on undoing all the damage this fucking visit had done.

"Just a few days," she forced out through numb lips. "I don't want to regret this, Pat."

"Me neither."

"Then try not to hurt me. I'll be home at five." She hung up, placing her phone carefully down to keep herself from throwing it. When this was over, she wasn't going to talk to any of them for a month.

You can't cut him out. He's the only one who understands. Who knows and still loves you without pity.

But she wasn't so sure of that anymore.

21

"Anything to You is out now from Now or Never Records and trending on Spotify! Come listen and get the other side of the story."
—*@BenjiNakamuraOmega*

"@BenjiNakamuraOmega Oh yes, this truly is so much better than the album I spent months on. How long did this song take you guys? Ten minutes?"
—*@thatbitchangela*

"@thatbitchangela Nice to know you were working on a break-up album for months before being dumped. Didn't have the ovaries to do it yourself? Is that why you keep harassing us? Or are you just a sore loser?"
—*@BenjiNakamuraOmega*

"@BenjiNakamuraOmega, considering I'm sitting in that number one spot you're begging for, I don't think I've lost anything."
—*@thatbitchangela*

Five o'clock found Rohan, Rick, and Benji crowded in Cazzi's front yard, trying to look as inconspicuous as three B- to C-list musicians could with a bunch of gear and suitcases. Rick sat casually in the chair, whistling something classical. Rohan leaned on the porch railing, fiddling with lyrics on his phone. Benji was next to him, sitting on the railing, smiling and waving at the few neighbors passing by.

"How is that helpful?" Rohan asked.

"It's disarming." Benji waved at a little girl on a bike. She gave him a confused wave.

"They're going to recognize you," Rohan said.

Benji snorted. "If I wanted them to recognize them I'd glower, or stare soulfully into the distance."

"Point," Rick said. "I don't think I've ever seen a picture of you smiling."

"Thus why no one recognizes me."

Rohan rolled his eyes at his phone, trying to keep from staring at the road, looking for her.

"My god, could you all be any more conspicuous?" Cazzi rode up and got off her bike. "I've had three people stop me to tell me there's a bunch of strangers on my porch."

Rohan looked her over as inconspicuously as he could. She looked tired but nothing about her said *I had a lot of great sex this morning with Rohan Kapoor*. Which was mostly a relief.

"Were they congratulating you for having such hot visitors?" Benji asked.

"One did, one implied that I was an immoral slut who shouldn't be allowed around children." Cazzi didn't seem phased by this.

"Someone's jealous," Benji scoffed.

She shrugged, wheeling her bike around the side of the house. "At least no one seemed to recognize you or call the cops. I'll be right back."

A few minutes later, she unlocked the front door from the inside, ushering them inside. Benji then Rick, then finally Rohan was face to face with her. He paused, looking down at her, almost overcome by the urge to kiss her as if he was coming home. As if he did this every day.

Her lips parted slightly like she was imagining the same thing. Then she looked away and he kept moving and the moment passed.

But the urge didn't.

———

HE TRIED to cook dinner but Cazzi's fridge was bare. Instead, they ordered pizza and he rode with her to pick it up. She wouldn't let him drive.

"So why can't they deliver?" He asked on the ride over.

"Because I live in the Bermuda Triangle of pizza delivery. Too close to the edge of town, I guess." She'd been distant since she arrived and it grated.

"You okay?"

"Yep." She lied without a single tell.

"Sore?"

That made her blink, emotion surfacing under her calm for an instant. "I did my dissertation on kink and consent in the BDSM community."

"So?"

"So I was very hands-on. Until you fuck me so long and hard I literally cannot walk, I won't be sore," she said with clinical calm but he could almost see a bit of smirk around her mouth.

"Don't tempt me." He was hard just thinking about it.

In the yellow street light flickering by, he could just make out her cheeks go pink. He suppressed a smile. The flush reminded him of this morning, when she was pink and ready, gasping for him.

"So," he said, as casually as he could manage. "You're a sub?"

Her cheeks were definitely pink now. "Switch, actually. But don't get any ideas."

"One-time thing. I know, I know."

She nodded. "It's not happening again."

"Too bad. It was really good."

"Yep," she said, parking. "It was." She turned the car off and sighed. She looked at him. "You're not going to make this difficult, are you?"

He shook his head.

"No, you wouldn't," she said, almost to herself. "You need me." But as she opened the door and stepped out, he thought he heard her say, "For now."

He grabbed her hand, stopping her. "More than just now." He pressed the kiss he'd wanted to give her earlier to her knuckles.

"We can't—"

He let her fingers go slowly, savoring the sensation of her skin against his. "I'm not pressing anything but please, don't think I only care about you because of this album. We're in this together, right?"

"Are we?" She studied him.

"If you want to be."

She held his gaze for a long moment then nodded. "Come on, cold pizza is a crime against nature." She speed-walked towards the pizza joint.

He grimaced at the thought of sad, congealed, greasy cheese and hurried after her.

***

CAZZI LEFT after dinner to help Judit pack. Eva handed her a hard lemonade the minute she walked in. Cazzi nursed it the whole time, drinking slowly so she didn't feel the buzz. Rohan was sleeping on her couch and the last thing she needed was anything that lowered her inhibitions. Her knuckles still tingled where he'd kissed her.

It made her feel guilty. Who fell this fast when she'd just been in love with the same person forever?

Someone who wasn't really in love.

Yeah, but which love was the illusion?

"You're a fucking saint," Eva said when she told her about all the musicians crashing on her couch. "I'd have told them to fuck off."

They were all in Judit's room, packing up her shelves.

"I thought these guys were all super successful and rich," Judit said, "Why can't they get a hotel?"

Cazzi shrugged. "From what I understand, they're sinking their money in this album and the record label they're hoping to launch with it. Plus Rohan has a charity."

"I thought Benji lived in Midtown." Eva unloaded a shelf and stacked the books next to her sister.

"Trust me, I've exhausted every other possibility," Cazzi said, putting together yet another box. "It's only until they find something else. We'll probably all survive."

"You know you can just crash here," Eva offered.

"Or at my place, once I move in," Judit added, readjusting the heat pack around her middle and pulling another stack of books closer to the box she was packing.

Cazzi hoped her gaze didn't show her worry as she cataloged the heat pack, wrist braces, and stiffness in Judit's movements. Stress tended to make Judit's pain worse and moving was a bitch. It only made sense she was hurting, but that didn't make it any easier to see. But Judit was putting a brave face on it, complete with makeup and a bra so Cazzi knew she didn't want to talk about it.

So she didn't. Instead, she asked Eva if she'd help her out by presenting on STI and pregnancy rates in the school since she'd done something similar for the Condom Pixies project.

"Hell yes!" Eva said. "Have Marcia bring her husband. He's a doctor."

Cazzi thanked her and made a note to talk to Marcia the next day.

"Is he hot?" Judit asked as Cazzi typed the note in her phone. "Cuz that would really sell it."

"Somehow I doubt sex appeal would sway the decision," Cazzi said, "Or I'd show up in one of my old grad school kink outfits."

"All I'm saying is that if he showed up shirtless with a lab coat and a stethoscope—oh and some sexy glasses and low-slung scrubs—you'd be a shoo-in for sure," Judit said.

"Have you been reading those doctor romances again?" Eva asked.

"Yeah," Judit said dreamily.

"I'm offended you think I'd be upstaged by some headless Dr. Nips Man Chest book cover when I have a stack of logical, dry arguments lined up," Cazzi said, deadpan.

"No, even better, your arguments would give him a giant hard-on and after your win, he'd sweep you off your feet for celebratory, mind-boggling sex," Judit said. "Better than all that mind-fuckery you've got going on."

"Sure," Eva said, "Except Dr. Nips is *our coworker's husband.*"

"Details, details." Judit waved that away.

"He's also like sixty and still grossly in love with his wife."

"Damn," Cazzi said, "There goes my Dr. Nips. He was so… shirtless and devoid of personality too."

Eva put a hand on her arm. "There are more nips in the sea."

They all paused, digesting the image. Judit screwed up her face in disgust.

"You know," Cazzi said. "I really hope not."

She helped until late and then walked home alone in the night. She reveled in the aloneness, even as her pepper spray dangled from her wrist. She knew she wouldn't get much time to herself in the next few days.

Patrick was waiting for her on the porch. "They're recording."

"You couldn't have sent me a text?" If she'd have known, she'd have stopped somewhere. "I gotta get to sleep soon."

"It won't take long," he said but his voice was stiff.

She shrugged. "Let's wait around back."

He followed her, sitting down at her patio table. She didn't sit. Despite what she'd told Rohan, she was sore from packing and... other things. She stretched instead.

"I'll make you some tea when we get back in," Patrick said, watching her.

She shook her head. "I'll just take some CBD before bed."

He sighed but said nothing.

"What?" She straightened, facing him.

"You have quite the selection in there." His tone was carefully neutral.

She crossed her arms. "Going through my cabinets already?"

"I wanted tea. I stumbled on your pot," he said. "It was surprising."

She snorted. "I don't know why. You're the one that taught me about its medicinal uses."

"Is that what you're using it for? Medicine?"

"Didn't you read my notes? Or was that too much snooping for you?"

"Don't get defensive." He sounded so reasonable.

It made her grit her teeth. "Don't judge me and I won't get defensive." She forced her jaw to loosen. The last thing she needed was a headache from this conversation.

"I'm just worried."

"About?" It was all she could do not to snap. His worries hadn't gotten them anywhere lately. She took a breath. He was going through something. She was going through the fallout of it.

This must be what he felt like after what happened to Tanya.

But no. Because she'd told him everything. She hadn't made him wait and guess and worry. He'd been the first person she'd called after she'd called 911 and her parents. Maybe that hadn't been fair to a sixteen-year-old. But she'd been fifteen and she'd needed someone to tell her it wasn't her fault.

In the dark, she felt that alley pressing closer, the memory welling to the surface like poison. The narrow space she had wedged herself, between the car and the wall, the grimy bricks staining her blue and yellow stars. The wait had almost been the worst part.

"Are you smoking a lot?" He asked, pulling her attention to the present.

"No."

"It's not good for your lungs—"

"I know. Health educator, remember? Besides, it's a dry vape."

He sighed. "I'm just trying to take care of you."

She barely kept from snapping. "You don't have to."

"I want to."

She lost her grip on her temper and snapped. "Why?"

"Because," he faltered. "You need it."

"Because you're feeling guilty?"

"Guilty?"

She raised her eyebrows.

"Cuz you ghosted me?"

"I didn't—" he stopped himself. Squeezed his eyes shut. "I was trying to do the right thing."

"And I was the wrong thing." Cazzi tipped her face up to look at the stars. This far out in this small a town, there were more than she'd ever seen in the cities she'd lived in. She liked that about living here, though the quiet that had taken some getting used to. It was weird having him in this space, this town she'd become a part of without him. "You must have really liked her."

Or maybe you never liked me as much as I thought, as much as I hoped, you did.

"It was stupid. I was afraid."

"Of me?"

He took a big breath, letting it out slow.

Finally, she leaned towards him, willing him to let her in, to open the vault.

"We're done if you want to come in," Benji said, staring at their phone even as they stuck their head out of the sliding glass door.

Cazzi looked at Patrick, wondering if the moment was shattered. If she'd lose her chance to have an honest conversation with him tonight.

He walked inside. She sighed.

Apparently, she had.

22

"I am your desire
Farther than the moon
Nothing behind my eyes
Not even my smile
Walked in the light for you
And burned like a bible

You loved my tragic
You loved my magic
My warm body
My cold soul
You thought I was a real girl
But

My heart is a dirty bomb
Forever going boom
The world hollowed me out
Tried to eat me whole
So I wrapped myself in barbed wire
But you still set me on fire"

—"Barbed Wire Girl" by Angela Alice on *Romance Inverted*

Cazzi stared up at the glow-in-the-dark stars on her ceiling. She'd stuck them up in a whimsical moment and now they seemed to mock her. There were people in her house and it felt strange. She wasn't used to the creaks and squeaks and mumbles they made as they slept on her blow-up bed, her couch, her sleeping bag.

She should've been asleep hours ago, but it was hard when pretty much all her problems were literally camped out in her living room. She felt trapped. If she could hear them move, they could hear her move. And she needed to move. Maybe they were all asleep but dammit, she didn't want any questions if they weren't.

She stood up, pacing on soft feet. It made her feel worse, caged. Her stomach coiled, the feeling wrapping around it and climbing up her throat until she felt suffocated.

Shoving her phone in her pj pocket, she went to her window and popped the screen out as quietly as she could. It scraped the wall as she set it down and she froze, listening.

The squeak of springs as someone on the couch turned over. She'd retreated to her room long before they'd decided who got what to sleep on.

Then there was blessed silence. And a serious chill in the air.

She put on hard-soled slippers and a sweater, pressing her don't-see-me sigil through the sleeve. *It is my will to only be seen by those I wish to see me.*

She stood there a moment, letting the invocation sink in, her ears pricked. Then she opened the window and climbed out into the back porch.

Her house was one story and had come with a step ladder left by the landlord for repairs. It leaned against the wall where she'd left it when she'd taken down her holiday lights. It was probably already full of spiders but she tried very hard not to think of that as she picked it up with as few fingers as possible and placed it under the eave by her bedroom window.

Opening it as quietly as she could, she climbed to the top and reached. She could just get to the roof, enough to pull the rest of her up.

This was dangerous, she knew, going up without telling anyone. It'd been a long time since she'd been on a roof, even longer since she *needed* to, but then, these were strange times.

She hauled herself up, her arms and shoulders screaming in a way that told her she'd regret this in the morning. Well, they could damn well get in line. She kept going, the tarpaper tiles catching and scraping against her fingers, her nails. She crouched on the shallow slant of the roof, listening again but all she could hear was the dopplering swish of cars in the distance.

Cazzi crawled away from the edge, slowly coming to sit on the spine of her roof with a sigh. The town spread before her: streetlights, house lights, fields, and the distant behemoth of the university.

It was all so small. Surreal, like a snow globe without the glitter.

That made her feel better somehow. A perspective shift, if she wanted to diagnose herself.

She hugged her knees. She didn't want to self-analyze but she couldn't go on like this.

Deep breath.

What do I want?

A successful career that changed people's ideas about sex and sexuality and helped end sexual assault and shame. A partner who loves me for who I am, even knowing my past. Not to lose Patrick.

Maybe a cat or two.

What do I need?

Therapy. Real love. A calm period where I can work out my shit and get back on solid footing. To feel safe.

Why don't I feel safe now?

Because I'm sitting on a goddamn roof in the middle of the night. I know, I know, deflection.

Try again.

Why don't I feel safe right now? Because I'm losing my mind to my trauma memories. Because Patrick keeps pulling the rug out from under me. Because Angelica is unpredictable. Because I might not love Patrick anymore. Not the way I did.

I thought I was better than that. There's been pretty faces and I've let them distract me but that's because I thought my feelings were one-sided but he's kissed me and I'm still...

Still what?

Not there. Not a hundred percent. He won't let me.

You think that's an excuse? You're blaming him for your weakness?

I'm not. I just can't—

Can't what? Love him? Because it's too hard?

The voice in her head was jeering, morphing from her own to Angelica's. Cazzi closed her eyes and put her head in her hands. She visualized her sigil for strength, holding it in her mind, large and burning until it blotted everything out.

She let it go and memory washed over her.

The silence scares her. The eeriness of being watched. Hundreds of eyes in hundreds of faces staring at her like she's on stage instead of in the hallway, in high school. People who can't even tell you her name know why she's been gone for almost a month.

It's like in one of those movies when the monster exits the castle before the villagers. The breath before the mob.

She stands, frozen.

Her mother warned her. "They won't see a victim. Teenagers are assholes."

But she hopes anyway. Maybe people will see past the rumors.

The faint bruises on her thighs are cold under her jeans. Her eyes burn. Her stomach rebels.

Under their breath, someone hisses, "Bitch."

Someone snickers. "Slut."

"Asked for it."

"Liar."

"Murderer."

Her vision blurs. She inhales hard, keeping her spine desperately straight. "Don't let them see your pain," Patrick whispers in her memory. She wishes he was here. No one would fuck with her then. They wouldn't dare. Not that he'd ever hurt anyone, not the way she had. But he's a man and he's big and she's neither.

She digs her nails into her palm and starts walking, keeping her face as blank as she can.

She keeps it blank when people bump into her, too often and too hard to be accidental. When the teachers won't meet her eyes and her friends won't even look at her. She's so numb that if there'd been a friendly face around when she finds her locker with the words "Killer Slut" scrawled across it, she'd joke that it was a good band name.

It's when she finds the note inside that she breaks. It says, "He got me too."

She sprints to the bathroom and locks herself in, sobbing and puking until she has nothing left. She thinks about calling home and remembers the pained hope on her parents' faces. They want so badly to put this behind them.

She calls Patrick.

He picks up even though he's in school in the performing arts magnet across town. "Tawny?"

"I can't do it," her voice is a hoarse quaver. "I can't be here."

"I'm coming. Meet me at the corner."

He picks her up sometimes because they live close and she's on his way home but she's never played hooky before and as far as she knows, neither has he. "You don't have to—"

"Don't worry about it. Be there soon." He hangs up.

She can't decide if it's flattering or not that he doesn't think she'll have a problem getting out of there. Or if it's worse she knows exactly how to do it.

School security measures may be resembling a prison more and more each day but like they say, if you walk like you're supposed to be there, most people don't question it. It helps if you're a small white girl who no one expected to last the day anyway. She walks out with the seniors on their free period and right into Patrick's waiting front seat.

There's a Starbucks to-go cup in the holder, waiting for her.

"Chamomile," he says. "All I could get on short notice."

He speeds away before anyone can ask questions. There'll be questions later when the schools call their parents with attendance reports. She doesn't care. She's trying not to panic about being in the front seat. She hasn't ridden in the front seat since... she bites her knuckle, letting the pain steady her.

Without asking, Patrick hops on the freeway and they are at the beach in no time. It's too cold and too middle of the week for most people so only the most persistent tourists are out. But he knows she loves the beach. They shuck their shoes and walk in the cold sand before either of them speaks.

"Is this it?" She asks. "Am I toxic now?"

"No."

"Nobody would talk to me, Clarry, Joanna, Dane, none of them would even look at me. The teachers practically ignored me. Now, I'm skipping school and dragging you down with me."

He shrugs. "I don't need school."

"Don't say that. Even pop stars need education."

"I'm not a pop star."

"Not yet." He's only just signed the contract but she knows once he moves into the band house after the school year ends he'll be famous. He's too good not to be.

He waves her words away. "They're shitheads."

"Who?"

"Your friends, your school. Bunch of fucking idiots. You did what

you needed to. You won." He looks at her, his expression fierce as if he's willing her to believe it.

She looks away. "There's no winning in accidentally killing someone."

"He tried to—" Out of the corner of her eyes, she sees his fists tighten.

"I don't think that matters." She hugs her coat tighter. "My dad's lawyers and that security camera were the only things that saved me from juvie." She's seen the legal bills and feels like absolute shit. There's no way her parents paid them without refinancing the cars and going deeper into debt. Which they had. She begged them to use her college fund but they refused.

"The justice system has nothing to do with right or wrong," Patrick says bitterly. He'd been stopped by a cop for no good reason just last week. They're all glad he'd come back with nothing more than a ticket.

"I know," she murmurs. They walk in silence, words building and falling apart in her head as she struggles with what she wants to say. Finally, something bursts out. "You still like me right? You're not just pitying me right now?"

He looks at her as if gauging how much she means the words. She wishes she could erase them from his memory. It's too raw, too vulnerable, too close to what she actually wants to ask.

He opens his arms and comes towards her.

To her absolute horror, she flinches. She flinches away from Patrick. Her stomach twists. She's broken. That fucking night broke her and she can't even be hugged.

He stops. "Can I... can I hug you? Is it okay?"

She nods and reaches for him. It has to be okay.

He wraps her in a hug slowly, tucking her head under his chin, telegraphing each movement. Like she's delicate. She feels delicate. Horribly fragile, until his big sheepskin coat, the one his dad handed down to him, envelopes her. She's cocooned, shrouded, protected. She burrows into his chest, listening to his heartbeat against the sound of the waves behind her. His arms tighten around her and the pressure makes her feel like she can breathe.

Is his heart beating faster? She can't tell. Doesn't want to know. She can't handle it if it is. But this, this is okay.

"Tawny," he says, the nickname rumbling in his chest. When did his voice stop cracking? When did it get so deep? "Of course, I still like you and you know I don't do pity."

"I know," she tells his shirt. He smells like Old Spice and Shea Butter.

"I can make an exception for you if you like..."

She snorts. "I'm good."

"Yeah." She can hear the smile in his voice. "You are."

And for the length of that hug, she is.

Cazzi surfaced from the memory like she was surfacing from a wave, salt water, and all. She wiped her cheeks. That was the Patrick she clung to so hard she couldn't see past him to the man who existed now.

The one who didn't want her as much as she, and maybe he, thought he should. The man who couldn't talk to her.

I need to let him go.

It was just a thought but it unknotted something taut in her belly. She exhaled hard. It wouldn't be that easy, but it was a start.

But what about the girl? The girl she had been. The scarred thing with the dead name who reached up from Cazzi's memory and tried to drown her in the worst night of their lives.

It didn't matter she'd tattooed that name on the back of her hip, the memorial to the last thing she'd lost that night. She didn't know if she ever really got over her the way she thought she had.

And what about Rohan? Her feelings there were just as jumbled, just as confusing. She liked him. She more than liked him. She was terrified. She could never be what he wanted. Could never be on his arm because eventually someone, somewhere would recognize her under the paltry changes of age, clothes, ink, and purple hair.

He's no stranger to controversy.

Neither was she, but she didn't know if she could survive it a second time. If her career could survive it.

Did she even want to be with him? Angelica was right, he was needy. But so was Cazzi and he always showed up for her. He was sweet and kind and funny and sexy as hell... But it was too soon, too close to his break-up and whatever was going on with Patrick was far from resolved.

We'll go slow.

But she didn't even know if he wanted a relationship. If she wanted one.

She turned to stare out over the patio. That was when she realized she wasn't alone. He stared up at her from the back edge of the patio and what little she could see in the dark made her breathless with hope and fear.

23

"I'm waiting out at the end of time
Where there's no reason, no rhyme
Watching everything explode
Again and again and again

Come meet me out there
To be bougie and free
At the end of the galaxy
Where it all ends
When we hold hands"
—"At the End of the Galaxy" by User-Friendly Omega on *And Down We Go*

Rohan woke up to the scrap of something metal against the wall. He lay on the deflating blow-up bed and listened. A window opened. It sounded like it was in Cazzi's room.

Okay fine, that was a normal sound, right? She probably wanted a bit of air. He started fading back into sleep.

Footsteps. Footsteps, above him. In his dozing mind, Cazzi

climbed the stairway to heaven to the half-remembered lyrics of Led Zeppelin.

There was a creak from the house, a footstep, and a groan of the roof above him.

Wait, the roof? The fuck?

He sat up, listening. Yep. He looked outside and saw just the edge of a white step ladder over by Cazzi's room.

That couldn't be good.

He snuck out of bed, stepping over Benji in their sleeping bag, and to the glass door, easing it open.

Rick grunted and turned over. Rohan froze, but Rick didn't seem to wake up. Benji was huddled up, completely buried in the sleeping bag and still, except for the rise of their breath. Rohan slipped out the door, closing it behind him gently.

He backed up to the far edge of the patio, scanning the roof. It was chilly out, the concrete numbing his bare feet, the breeze cutting through his thin shirt and flannel pants. He almost didn't see her, scrunched up as she was with her chin on her knees as she stared out into the night. Her black hoodie and pj pants engulfed her until all he could see was the side of her face. She looked like a sad ghost.

The image made his chest ache. No, it wasn't the image, it was that the image was her.

It's your fault she's sad.

No, he told the shitty voice in his head. *Not entirely.*

Don't think that makes you innocent.

She didn't seem to see him. It felt strange, intimate, to see her like this when she thought she was alone. When she wore no mask and was no one but herself.

He knew it was stalkerish, standing here like this when she obviously wanted to be alone. But while he'd like to think he was just trying to keep her safe, the truth was he liked watching her.

Another thing you're taking from her.

She put her head in her hands. The ache in his chest intensified. Would it be better or worse if he climbed up and held her?

Because he really wanted to hold her.

You know what this is.

Here, almost alone in the dark, it was much easier to admit he did know. He knew and it scared him because it was too fast, too soon, too right.

Rohan was in love with Cazzi.

And what good has it done her?

You're my brain, shouldn't you be on my side? He felt petulant just thinking the words.

You're the one talking to yourself, shouldn't you be the one in control?

Yeah, I am. So shut the fuck up. Rohan closed his eyes, trying to convince himself he could actually banish the things he said to himself.

There was a quiet sob. He looked up to see Cazzi wipe her eyes. She sighed, her shoulders dropping. Then she turned and saw him.

He froze, staring back at her.

She frowned and crossed her arms.

He sighed and came closer until he stood next to the white stepladder. "I wasn't stalking you," he called up, projecting his voice as quietly as possible.

She put a finger to her lips and gestured him closer.

He gave the ladder a dubious look but decided it seemed sound enough. Benji would probably kill him for risking his neck like this but he climbed up anyway. It was easy enough, though he didn't enjoy being this high or on a slant. Standing up made him feel like he was about to slip at any moment.

"You good?" she asked.

He nodded, sitting down next to her. Sitting was so much better than standing. "Nice view," he tried and failed to sound nonchalant.

"Afraid of heights?"

"Not fond of them sober, more like." He remembered a particularly drunk night involving a rooftop pool and a diving board. At nineteen, riding on the high of a show, going platinum, and being in a country where he could legally drink, it was the best thing ever. Ten years later, he was surprised no one got hurt.

"This is about as high as I'll go," she said. "But I love a good roof."

"I take it you couldn't sleep."

"Did I wake you?"

He shrugged.

"I should go to bed," she sighed. "It's going to suck when I have to get up in five hours." But she didn't move.

"Do you always climb the roof when you can't sleep?"

She shook her head. "Not for a long time. I thought it was a compulsion that was behind me." She worried her bottom lip with her teeth. "I thought a lot of things were behind me."

"I don't think things ever go away as much as we think they do."

She sighed. "I'm trying so hard to be okay with that."

"Do you have to be okay with it?"

She nodded. "I'm not always like this. I haven't been like this, for…" she paused, thinking. "I don't know, years. I went through so much therapy in grad school and college, that I thought it was… not fixed but manageable. Livable."

"Was it me?" The words tumbled out before he could swallow them back.

But she just shook her head. "It was everything. It… might be Patrick."

"Because he knew you when whatever happened, happened?"

"What do you know about it?"

"Nothing. Just that it happened to someone named…" A memory clicked in his head. "Tanya. Tanya, like the tattoo you didn't show me."

She hugged her knees closer. "Patrick was the only one who understood. The only one who... didn't change after what happened or after I told them."

Rohan's stomach knotted with worry. What the hell happened? Had Cazzi done something terrible? He didn't want to imagine she could do anything unforgivable but this conversation felt like something out of a *Lifetime* movie where it turns out she let Tanya get murdered by her evil stepfather who was also molesting her or something. Nānī used to love watching that shit along with *Ellen* and Bollywood movies when she babysat him. Rohan's childhood nightmares were all *Lifetime*-themed. He blocked the channel on every TV in every house he'd ever lived in, including Angie's. She'd never noticed.

"Is she okay? Tanya, I mean."

Cazzi looked at him with an expression he couldn't decipher. "Patrick really never told you?"

"Rick doesn't exactly gossip. He never told us anything that we didn't pry out of him."

"I can relate." Her mouth twisted. She sighed and scrubbed her hands over her face. "God, I don't wanna do this."

"Do what?"

"Tell you."

"About Tanya?"

She gave a bitter half-laugh. "Yeah, Tanya."

"You don't have to."

She nodded. "Tell me, Rohan, do you like me?"

The abrupt change of subject left him stuttering. "Um, yeah. I thought that was pretty obvious."

"I didn't ask if you were attracted to me. I asked if you liked me."

Don't tell her, lover boy. Not yet.

"I do like you. A lot. I did mean that when I said it before."

She smiled, but it was sad. "Good. I like you a lot too. So I think... you need to know this. Just in case."

"Just in case what?"

"In case there's a more identifiable picture of me and you. And someone who knew Tanya figures it out."

"Figures what out?" Rohan felt his frustration rising and leashed it tight. This wasn't one of Angie's games. This was Cazzi working up to telling him something big.

She took a deep breath and covered the spot on her arm where all her calming sigils were hiding under her sleeve. "Rohan... what happened to Tanya happened to me."

Rohan blinked. "Um." Did she mean...?

"Sorry." She cleared her throat. "That was cryptic. I was born Tanya Cazzi Muldoon. Because of what happened, I dropped my first name legally on my eighteenth birthday. If you ever Google Tanya Muldoon, you'll see why."

Understanding dawned. "That's why Rick called you Tawny."

She nodded. "He slips sometimes. But he was the first one to actually call me Cazzi when I asked. My parents didn't understand. They never quite got that I wasn't overreacting."

"They knew about what happened?"

"They knew." She inhaled hard. "Okay, this is gonna suck. But I want you to know what you're getting into."

He offered her his hand. "Caz, I'm here, whatever you tell me."

She smiled that sad smile again but she didn't take his hand. "They all say that." Then she told him.

24

What Happened to Tanya

Imagine me at fifteen. I have been in love with Patrick for three years and two months. But I know it's hopeless even before it starts. So when Frankie asks me out, I say yes. I think why not? I think this might make Patrick jealous. This will be the guy who makes Patrick notice.

So I say yes. Admittedly, I'm also attracted to him. Frankie is gorgeous, a baseball player with dark hair, honey-brown eyes, and cheekbones to die for. He's one of those guys that can get away with anything and still be cool. Even the name Frankie, he imbues it with some sort of mobster charm. So much so that sometimes the younger kids would catch themselves greeting him with an "Eh Fraaankie," in a New York accent ripped straight from *The Godfather*. And he'd give them a look that'd say, "Are you talkin' ta me?" and they'd bite their tongues in embarrassment.

He's two and half years, ten inches, and thirty pounds bigger than me. He's popular at school, but I've known him since before he got popular because he goes to the same dojo I do.

I know him, you know. I get him. We're friends.

When he asks me out, I think this is safe. My mother loves him, my father respects him, and we've been to each other's birthday parties. He picks me up in his dad's SUV. I buy a cute skirt and blouse for the date, my mother gushing as I pick them out. They match, sky blue and with yellow stars.

He takes me to a movie. I'm too nervous to pay attention to it at all. Wondering why he wasn't touching me, holding my hand at least. Afterwards, he drives us to an alley, downtown, saying we can be alone, his voice all rumbly and deep.

I'm thrilled, ready for my first kiss. He gives it to me, but his hands go places I don't like. He takes the skirt as a green light. I tell him stop. He says no.

I push him away. He grabs me back, his fingers prying at my thighs, telling me this is what I want. His fingers are so strong.

I panic, remembering rape stories in health ed., in the books they make us read, every cautionary tale about every girl who should've known better, every boy who apparently didn't. I slam my fist into his groin. He lets go and I've got the lock open and I'm out of the car and he's following me but I'm small and quick and running around the back and I get back in and lock him out, the keys in with me.

But I don't know how to drive, the keys fell somewhere, and he's pounding on the door and I'm scared, panic squeezing the air out of me.

Open the damn door, Tanya.

You're pissing me off, Tanya

Stop fucking around, Tanya

I can't find my purse. I can't find my phone. They're under the seat somewhere and I can't look away from him.

He cracks the glass. I don't know how but he does. His breath fogs the cracks.

Look what you made me do, Tanya.

The fuck is wrong with you.

Stop being crazy.

He's yelling and yelling. I want to curl into myself and die. I can barely breathe.

His elbow breaks through the window.

I do the only thing my panicked body can think of: I unlock the door, and kick it open with both feet and everything I have.

The door snaps open, the frame whacks into him, knocks him back.

He stumbles.

He falls.

It seems to take forever, the blood from his broken nose tracing his path until the back of his head hits the hinge of the dumpster.

He slides. Limp.

Then he's on the ground, not moving, that cracking, crunching sound of bone losing to metal hanging in the air between us.

I can barely walk, my legs shake so bad. I call his name but he doesn't answer and I look at his eyes and I know he won't ever answer and I feel sick. I check his pulse the way they do in movies: wrist, throat. Hold my hand over his nose, his mouth.

Nothing.

Fuck, I say, trying not to cry. I find my purse. I wedge myself between the car and the wall, trying to hide from the body that will never move again. I pull my phone out of that too tiny purse and dial the three numbers I hoped I'd never have to dial, and I tell the lady *Frankie's dead and it was an accident and no I don't know where I am, please help me.*

The operator wants to stay on the line, wants the number for my parents because I sound like I'm twelve right now. I promise her I'll tell them myself and hang up because she's already told me cops are on the way.

I don't want to call my parents, didn't want to make them

worry, but I do, telling them the streets I can see from my hidey-hole and finally crying.

My mom cries with me and doesn't want to get off the line. I don't either, afraid that someone will come and I won't get so lucky this time.

The wait is an eternity, rehashing and rehashing until I've told them everything a thousand times over and all they tell me is how far away they are.

Ten minutes.

Eight minutes.

Five minutes.

The cops are bright and loud, they coax me out of my safe place and ask me questions. They take pictures of Frankie, the alley, the car. My parents arrive. My father has already called his lawyer friends. The lawyer friends tell me through my father to shut up.

A tarp goes over Frankie and an ambulance arrives with a body bag. The paramedics declare me shaken but fine. They offer me a kit I don't need.

We migrate to the station which is brighter and grayer but smells better than the alley. There are questions. They take pictures that feel like mugshots and I'm too in shock to look anything but hurt. The bruises are already blooming. With the scrapes and the cuts and the grime I look like the victim they're not sure I am.

The lawyers show up and force the police to let me go or charge me. They don't charge me but they tell me not to leave town. My parents take me home, my mother crying the entire way, holding on to me and rocking back and forth until I feel carsick. Every time she sees the bruises she starts again.

I call Patrick. He tells me I did nothing wrong, that I won because I didn't let him rape me. I stare down at the bruises deepening to blue on my thighs: ten imprints of his fingers trying to pry me open. I keep hearing that crunch, keep seeing his face go wide and empty.

I stay home for a month. No charges are pressed. We have very good lawyers, I am small for my age, and as it turns out, Frankie was eighteen. There was a security camera that saw the whole thing, that's what keeps his parents from pressing charges. They don't want the publicity.

The cops say they won't release my name but somehow it will get out. I will have to shut down all my social media accounts because of the shit they say about me. I will have to get a new number because people keep calling and telling me I'm a murderer, that I deserved it. Some of these people are full-grown adults, strangers. There will be articles in the paper, small briefs that say nothing about any of this. They will never make up their mind about whether I am guilty or not. They will call me the "alleged victim." I will be afraid of going back to school, but when my dad offers to homeschool me, I will refuse. I will think I am brave, doing this.

I won't last a day back. I will finish the rest of high school online and change my name before I apply to college, out of state. By the time I'm done with grad school, Tanya is forgotten online and I am able to manage my trauma. I try to move on.

25

"Every day
I bloody myself fighting
I am teeth and claws
Can't ever back down

There must be a way out
There must be a way to be heard
To be louder than this silent shout

All these years later
You'd think I'd have an answer
Something better than
Blood between my teeth
Sharp even in a sheath
All grown up now
My life's a show
My trauma makes money
That's all you can ask for honey"
—- "Everything I Ever Wanted" by Angela Alice on *Romance*
Inverted

Cazzi took a huge, shaking breath. She'd never told anyone who wasn't a therapist all of it, all of the details that haunted her. She hadn't told it in a long time and she felt drained, light. Like she'd given blood and had that blood loss high. Floaty and slightly nauseous.

She didn't dare look at Rohan. She savored this, the moment before he showed pity or revulsion and she'd recoil. The same way everyone she'd ever told did. Everyone but Patrick.

A hand entered her vision, palm up.

She gathered her courage and looked at him.

"Thank you for telling me," he said, his eyes searching her face. Making sure she was okay.

"It's okay," she said. "You don't have to be nice to me." It would hurt less if he rejected her now. She suppressed her old instincts, the ones telling her to provoke him into leaving her. Those instincts had almost ruined her friendship with Judit and Eva.

He shook his head. "Is it okay if I touch you right now?"

She hesitated, assessing her feelings. "I think so."

He wrapped her in his arms slowly, pulling her into his lap. "I don't know what the right thing to say is here. But I want to say it, whatever it is," he said into her hair.

"I don't think there is a right thing. You can't make this better."

"Then I'm just going to hold you for a while, okay?"

"Okay." She let herself relax a little into his arms. It wasn't comfortable, but it was comforting.

"Is that why you became a sex educator? Because you didn't want that to happen to someone else?"

"I wasn't being noble," she snapped. Her third most hated reaction was being called an inspiration. She wasn't inspiring, she was lucky she wasn't in jail like all the women she'd spent her volunteer hours with in college and grad school.

"I didn't say you were." His voice was calm, unruffled.

She settled down. "Then yeah, that's part of it. Mostly, I was afraid of being one of those broken girls in books who were forever ruined by what happened to them. So I researched everything I could about sex, about psychology, and... it was interesting. So much of what I'd been taught, by teachers, by the media, by those damn books, was wrong. It didn't fix me, but it helped me understand myself and everyone else. People started making sense for the first time. It was like looking behind the curtain and seeing the scaffolding of how people's minds worked."

"Honestly, I'm very jealous of your ability to do that."

"Thanks, it took a lot of work. And admittedly, I don't know everything. Nobody does, the mind is so complex, and new discoveries are being made all the time. But that's part of the fun, I think."

"You're already doing amazing things with it."

She blushed, glad he couldn't see it. "Thanks," she mumbled.

She felt... almost... (she hated herself for shying away from the word but it scared her).

She restarted the thought.

She felt loved.

"You're welcome," Rohan said. He hoped he was saying the right things because it was all he could do to keep the words he desperately wanted to say off his tongue. If he said them, she'd run off and he'd just gotten to hold her.

And he needed to hold her all the more after what she'd told him. The story would haunt him, he knew, more than any *Lifetime* movie Nānī had watched or the ER stories his mother would bring home. Because it was real, it was hers.

And he fucking loved her.

He wanted to hold her forever while also wanting to kill

Frankie all over again along with every single person who'd told her it was her fault, who'd bullied and terrorized her.

But he didn't think that's what Cazzi wanted. So he held her and half-hoped she understood he was trying to tell her he loved her with his embrace alone.

26

"Amazing how a change in scenery can make an album really come together. #musiclife #recording #FromtheAshes"
—*@benjiomeganakamura*

"I'm forever impressed by how people can spin failure into a hard-luck success story. And by spin, I mean lie. #thetruthwillout"
—*@thatbitchangela*

"I'm forever impressed by how miserable people try to bring down the rest of us. Guess misery really does love company. #beadecenthuman"
—*@benjiomeganakamura*

"@benjiomeganakamura, darling, don't try to pretend you aren't just as miserable as the rest of us. #embracethemisery"
—*@thatbitchangela*

"@thatbitchangela, do us all a favor and get therapy. #mentalhealthisnotajoke."

—@benjiomeganakamura

Rohan heaved a deep breath in as he left the library closet they'd turned into a vocal booth. The room was claustrophobic, full of books and a bean bag shoved in a corner. When he stood in the middle, his shoulders almost brushed books on both sides. It made it hard to breathe and the dust didn't help, but the sound was good and the options were limited. And it smelled like Cazzi.

The woman herself had been coming home later and later since that night on the roof. Rohan tried not to take it personally. He also tried not to take Rick's looks and snide comments personally, but he was quite sure they were meant for him.

It was probably better Cazzi wasn't home much. The urge to greet her at the door with a kiss, to sneak into her bed at night, to touch her and touch her and touch her got harder to resist every day. Especially when he kept stumbling into little moments alone with her.

Like this morning when they'd run into each other as she'd been leaving and he'd been coming back from his run.

She'd stopped, about to hop on her bike and asked if he'd had a good run. He'd said yes. They'd said some small, forgettable things and the whole while he'd been trying so hard not to kiss her. Then she'd gotten on her bike and her fingers brushed his.

Her breath caught. His breath caught. She met his gaze, licked her lips, and he lost a small infinity of time staring at her mouth.

Then she'd cleared her throat and had to leave but when she told him that, her eyes were regretful. He'd held onto those small details all day. It made him feel like he was an awkward fourteen-year-old all over again.

Which was exactly what he'd just sung about.

You feel like my first crush

> *Girl, it's all too much*
> *What you do to me*
> *With just one touch*
> *You're gonna leave me*
> *Crushed!*

He'd catch all sorts of passive-aggressive hell from Rick for this one but it was a sugar-sweet pop love song and Benji already had it on the shortlist for album singles.

Benji pulled their headphones off when Rohan walked into the living room. "We need more layers on that chorus. Just for that last 'crushed.' It's falling flat."

"It'll sound like a Beatboyz song if we do that," Rohan said.

"It already sounds like one," Rick said.

"What if we went angstier with it? Closer to Twenty-One Pilots or Conan Gray?" Rohan suggested.

"So you want to make a cute song about having a crush, but you want it to be depressing," Rick said.

"No, I just wanna add a spike of angst to the end of the chorus." Rohan looked at Benji. "What do you think?"

Benji looked up from their phone hurriedly. "Um. I'm always a fan of angst. Try it."

"Try ungluing yourself from your phone down for a sec," Rick grumbled.

"Hey, I'm trying to secure us some more last-minute funding here," Benji snapped. "Or were you happy recording in a fucking bookcase and sleeping on a couch?"

"That's not all you're doing," Rick said.

"Excuse me?" Benji turned completely to face him.

Rohan sighed. He was so sick of this shit. "Guys, come on."

"Not a guy," Benji snarled, still looking at Rick.

"Yes, sorry." Rohan took another breath. "You all, come on. We're so close and we can do this. We're making good progress!

We have a name for the album now and we only have a few more songs left." He was excited about the album too. *From the Ashes* was turning into everything he had hoped it would be, if not exactly how he thought it would come together.

"Was that supposed to be inspiring?" Rick looked anything but inspired.

"Jesus Christ, can you cut the Eeyore act and fucking be a professional? Just for a bit?" Benji demanded.

"Can you stop baiting the Bitch Queen on socials?" Rick shot back.

Rohan held up a hand. "Wait, what?"

Rick shrugged. "Check Twitter."

Benji swore softly under their breath and stood up. But they didn't deny it.

Rohan pulled it up and scrolled. And scrolled. There Benji was, fighting Angie and baiting her in plain view of the entire fucking internet. The comments were off the chart, people picking sides. Both Benji and Angie ignored them but every time one of them tweeted about anything though… "What the actual hell, Benji?"

Benji sighed and rubbed their arms as if they were cold. "She's very easy to fight with."

Rohan closed his eyes. Counted to ten. "*Of course* she is. What do you think I've been doing for the last four years? But, come on. Benji, this makes you look bad. It makes all of us look bad. For fuck's sake, you used the album hashtag!"

"That wasn't aimed at her! That was just a promo tweet."

"You were baiting her. Talking about how we had to record somewhere else."

"She's making sly comments about everything I say. What am I supposed to do? Not promote the album?"

"That's probably what she wants," Rohan admitted.

"Hell hath no fury like a woman scorned," Rick murmured. "And she hath no fury like Angela Alice."

"Exactly," Rohan said. "Don't provoke her."

"So what, you're just gonna tiptoe around her feelings for the rest of your life?" Benji said.

"No, I'm playing nice until I have enough clout to actually handle her without destroying my career."

"You dated her. *Her.* A Satanist in God's America. People still love you. They'll love you even more now that you're not putting up with her shit." Benji said.

"Yes, but industry people *love* working with her. I know it sounds unbelievable, but every time I went with her to some industry event, people practically lined up to tell me how surprised they were that working with her was so great. She's charming, charismatic, professional, and funny. I was the same way, but I haven't worked much in the last four years and frankly, I don't think I'll be given that benefit of the doubt that she is."

"White girls," Rick shook his head. "It's amazing what they can get away with." He sounded tired.

Rohan nodded. Would Angie cry hard enough to get him canceled?

Patrick clapped him on the back, shooting him a subdued but reassuring smile. It felt like, for a second, they were as close as they'd been back in their Beatboyz days.

Well, he thought they'd been close. Since then Rick had been hard to pin down and Rohan had been wrapped up in Angie. He'd hoped working on the album would be like old times, but better because they had creative control.

How shitty was it that he'd let whatever vestiges of friendship they had go in an instant if Cazzi decided she wanted to be with him more than she wanted to pine after Rick? The realization didn't surprise him but it made him feel like a terrible friend. But it wasn't like Rick would choose any differently.

Rick turned back to the mixing software on his screen.

Rohan returned his gaze to Benji. "You want to piss off Angie? Ignore her. She'll lose her damn mind."

Benji narrowed their eyes. "This sounds suspiciously like taking the high road."

"It's not. Trust me."

"Isn't that what you did to Martin Mejia? Give him the silent treatment?" Benji seemed to be mulling the idea over.

Rohan shook his head. "Martin killed our band and never looked back."

Rick snorted. "Hard to ignore someone who doesn't care if you exist."

"Been there," Benji grimaced. "Fine. I won't engage. But promise me it'll make her suffer. I'm trying to avenge you, here."

Rohan raised his eyebrow. "I don't need a champion, Benji."

"Don't be such a man. Everyone needs someone to stand up for us when we need to sit down and take a breather."

Rick shook his head again.

Benji rolled their eyes at him. "Don't pretend you don't have one. You've done everything but throw her away and that woman still fights for you."

Rohan felt the green twist of jealousy in his chest.

It only intensified when Rick looked up at him. "I'm not so sure of that."

Benji followed his gaze. "Oh for chrissakes. You two need to learn to share."

Rick stood up abruptly. "Don't talk about what you don't know shit about."

"They're not wrong," Rohan said. "She fucking loves you and you treat her like shit."

"Is this supposed to be the bit where you tell me you'd treat her better?" Rick took a step towards him.

Rohan stood his ground. "You've already admitted you don't love her. Why do you care?"

Rick took another step forward. The living room was small. A few more steps and they'd be breathing each other's air. "You don't know shit either."

"Guys…" Benji started.

"Shut up Benji," Rohan snapped. Rage boiled in his veins. "You started this. You and your damn baiting."

"Yes, okay, that was a mistake. Why don't you two just go back to passive-aggressively glaring and finish this album before you get into a pop star catfight."

Rick ignored them. He crossed the rest of the room and stopped in front of Rohan. "You're trying to get her. You have been since she rescued your pathetic ass from your evil ex."

"Rick, you kissed her and then you fucking cold-shouldered her."

"What do you know?"

"Everything. I know everything."

Rick snorted. "I doubt that. You can't see anything past the cartoon hearts in your eyes."

"Maybe. But I can still listen to her. I can be her friend." Rohan shrugged as Rick mouthed the word 'friend' mockingly. "You aren't even being that."

"I'm working my shit out!"

"You're hurting her!"

"You can't function without a woman to shore you up!" Rick pointed at his face.

"Says the man who is barely functioning as it is."

"Fuck you. I'm fine!" Rick pushed him. Just a slight shove.

Hit him, Rohan's rage hissed. *Show him what he's dealing with.*

Rohan pushed Rick back, making his producer stumble. "Don't touch me."

"Guys!" Benji inserted themselves between the two men. "We are not breaking up over a girl. It's too fucking cliche."

"Move, Benji," Rohan ground out, his eyes on Rick. The other man looked ready to hit him.

Benji grabbed their collars and knocked them both back onto the couch. Rohan landed hard enough the impact on the soft cushions made him lose his breath. He stared at Benji, shocked.

Out of the corner of his eye, he could see Rick looking equally stunned.

"Children." Benji crossed their arms and straight-up tapped their toe like some pissed-off nanny. "If you think that growing up in the punk scene, spending over a decade touring in a goth band, and the last few years defying the gender binary doesn't mean I can kick your boy band asses to the Bay and back, you're fucking idiots."

"You caught us by surprise," Rick pointed out.

"You want a brawl?" Benji shrugged their cashmere sweater off and reached to undo their earrings. "I'll give you a fucking brawl."

Cazzi opened the glass sliding door and stopped, taking in the scene.

"How much can you hear through that?" Benji asked, their voice high and overly curious. Their hands froze by their earrings. It'd be funny if Rohan wasn't certain all of them were about to get torn a brand new asshole.

She held up the earbuds dangling from her fingers. "Depends." But she sized up the room like she knew exactly what was going on and it exhausted her. She wore a faded black hoodie and black jeans with a hole in the knee. Her hair frizzed around her face and there was a streak of dust on her neck. Rohan remembered she'd been out helping Eva's sister move all day. With a sigh, she stepped into the house.

"How was moving?" He asked.

She looked surprised and he felt like shit. When was the last time he'd asked her about her day? He'd been so busy with the album and trying to give her space after her confession that he couldn't even remember.

"It was good," she sounded guarded like she wasn't at all sure anyone cared.

"That was Judit's move?" Rick asked.

Cazzi's expression got even more guarded. "Yep."

"Was that whatshername's sister who was moving to Midtown?" Benji chimed in.

Cazzi's eyes full-on narrowed. "Don't fucking fight in my house and then try to cover it up." She looked at Rick. "You especially should know better." Her gaze turned to Rohan but she said nothing. He thought he saw something like disappointment in her expression and his anger withered.

She stalked to the kitchen, and pulled out a pint of ice cream and a spoon, before stalking back out towards the porch. "If you're going to settle your shit with your fists, don't you dare do it here." She slammed the door shut behind her.

Rohan let out the breath he'd been holding since she looked at him. "Fuck."

"Way to go assholes." Benji refastened their earrings. "Which one of you is gonna apologize?"

"You," Rick said.

"Uh, no," Benji said. "I'm the last person she cares about in this house. It's got to be one of you."

"Why are we fighting about this? We should all apologize." Rohan pointed out.

"Go ahead," Rick said. "You first."

"This," Rohan pointed at him, "This is why you keep pissing her off." But he stood up and headed for the back door.

"If you think you're going to take my place because we're going through a rough patch, you're fucking wrong," Rick called.

Rohan stopped and turned around, pitching his voice low so it wouldn't carry through the back door. "I'm not trying to replace you. I'm trying to be better than you. It's not hard."

Rick lunged up from the couch, only to be shoved back down by Benji.

"Put your dicks away, kids." Benji held Rick down with apparently no effort. "You can go back to measuring them later."

"You're such an asshole, Benji," Rick snarled.

"Oh Ricky Rick, you ain't seen nothing yet," Rohan heard Benji say as he stepped out onto the patio.

He put them out of his mind as he walked up to the patio chair Cazzi was in. "You okay?"

27

*"I'm no blank hearted darling
Lines to fill
With words and your voice
As I lay still*

*My heart is full!
It needs no one
Not me, not you!
I'm not your blank hearted darling!
My words can kill*

*I bite the hand that feeds
I bite the hand that needs
I'm all teeth
Angela dentata
Better watching your... [giggle]
fingers"*
— "Blank Hearted Darling" by Angela Alice on *PhenoBarbie Doll*

azzi looked up and of course, it was Rohan asking. She'd known him from the voice, from the cadence of his steps, but old memories told her it had to be Patrick because Patrick would always come for her.

She wanted so badly to believe the lie, but mostly, she was glad he hadn't come. The thought of talking to Patrick right now exhausted her. Rohan wasn't exactly low-maintenance but they could have a conversation without fighting and it felt like it'd been so long since she'd had one of those with Patrick.

Rohan stood in front of her, waiting for an answer. He probably wanted the truth too, not having the common courtesy to be so oblivious she could placate him with a polite lie.

Well, he wasn't getting the complete truth. She wasn't in the mood to give it.

"I'm tired," she said. Tired because she hadn't been sleeping because she'd been too wound up, too anxious, too sober because she didn't even want to smoke.

"Eating my feelings," she waved her spoon at him. Eating her feelings because if she got high she might get out of her own way and do what she'd been longing to do since that night on the roof. There was no way Patrick wouldn't notice if she dragged Rohan into her room in the middle of the night.

He sat down on the lounger across from her. "Isn't it too cold to eat ice cream out here?"

"Aren't you the one elected to apologize to me? Because I really don't appreciate you criticizing my dining habits." She hugged herself because he was right, damn him. "Besides, you're the only reason I'm out here."

"I know and I'm sorry. Sometimes things get heated when an album gets down to the wire. Martin once locked Leo in a closet because he ate the last cookie during a marathon recording session."

Her shock must've shown on her face because he hurried to

say, "Leo was fine. He broke the door down and dumped a box of Oreo crumbs on Martin's head." He chuckled at the memory. "Martin looked like he'd been down a coal mine when Leo was done with him."

"Cute," Cazzi said. "And only mildly psychotic."

"That's Martin and Leo in a nutshell." He grimaced like he shouldn't have said that.

She waved that away. "Fine. Whatever. But I already barely feel comfortable being home with all of you here. Coming home to a fight does not help."

He grimaced. "I'm so sorry. Is—is it me? Am I doing something that makes you uncomfortable?"

She sighed. "It's not you. It's the situation."

"Which I've camped out in your living room."

"Yeah."

They sat in silence. He reached out, offering her his hand. She wanted to take it, she really did. She could feel Patrick's gaze on the back of her neck. It'd be a fuck you to take it.

It would also be comforting.

She met Rohan's eyes and let her expression loosen, showing all the feelings twisting her into paralysis.

"Caz," he breathed. He looked as twisted up as she felt.

Kiss me. The thought startled her, igniting a full-body ache that made her lean towards him before she caught herself.

He leaned forward too but stopped when she did.

It was like this morning or last night or any of the dozens of small moments they'd shared over the last few days. Moments alone. Moments where she could've given in and kissed him.

God, she wanted to.

The back door slid open and familiar footsteps stalked across the patio. All the hairs stood up on the back of Cazzi's neck. The familiar magnetic pull tugged at her bones but it felt more like a warning than desire.

Rohan's face went grim, his eyes on Patrick as he approached. The footsteps didn't slow.

She inhaled, traced her strength sigil, and stood up at the same time as Rohan, sliding neatly between the two men.

Patrick stopped short in surprise and Rohan nearly ran into her, but she stood firm. If Eva could only see her now, inches away from both of them. Her prediction of a hot guy sandwich, fulfilled and twisted. She could feel the rage radiating from both of them. Patrick practically vibrated with it.

She took a fortifying bite of chocolate chocolate chip with fudge swirls ice cream. "Hello, Patrick." Her voice felt colder than the ice cream.

"You fucked him." It wasn't a question.

She raised her eyes and met his gaze. There was pain under that rage and it was a rusty knife in her gut. "I did."

Behind her, Rohan stiffened.

"So that's it then," Patrick's eyes went over her head to Rohan. "You've won."

"Rick—" Rohan started.

Cazzi's hand knotted into a fist around her spoon. "You're talking about winning me, Patrick?" Her voice scraped its way out of her throat. "I thought you knew better. I damn well know you know better than to literally *talk to a man over my head like I'm stupid.*"

"You're protecting him," Patrick's gaze came back to hers but it was narrowed, and she knew he wasn't really hearing her.

"No. I'm done with this."

Patrick's mouth snapped shut.

"Done with what, Caz?" Rohan asked quietly.

"This," she gestured at the three of them.

"So you're making your choice then," Patrick said quietly like he was already sure he wasn't it.

"Caz, you don't have to decide anything right now," Rohan

sounded worried. Was he worried she would choose him or that she wouldn't?

She shook her head. Tried to imagine letting this go on. Her stomach twisted with anxiety. She imagined cutting Patrick out of her life. She imagined cutting Rohan out. And she had her answer.

"I want you out," she forced the words out. God, was she really doing this? "All of you by tomorrow night."

"But the album—"

"Fuck the fucking album," she snarled, facing Rohan. "My mental health is more important. Finish it somewhere else."

His face shut down. There it was. She was no longer useful to him. That would kill the infatuation real fast.

"Tawny," Patrick murmured.

"No." She stepped away from both of them. "No, you don't get to play that fucking card. I am not Tanya. I haven't been Tanya for over a decade. I am not what happened to her, what happened to me. I was doing good, Patrick. I was doing so much better..."

"Until I came back into your life," Patrick finished for her. He looked like he might fall apart.

"It's not your fault," she whispered, regretting everything, especially the truth.

"Yes, it is," he touched her cheek. "I'm sorry, Caz."

"You need help, Patrick. Help I can't give." She caught his hand, holding it lightly.

"I'm working on it."

"Work on it with a therapist. See someone, please. You're scaring me."

"If I do, will you give me another chance?"

She shook her head. "You can't do it for me. You have to do it for yourself."

He pulled his hand back. "But I *want* to do it for you."

"No." She shook her head again. "You want me to wait. I've been waiting since I was thirteen, Pat."

"So what's a little more time?" He looked at Rohan. "Or are you already replacing me?"

Words jammed in her throat, wanting to reassure him but not wanting to hurt Rohan. "I-I—"

There was hope in Rohan's face and it shredded her.

"I knew it." Patrick turned to leave.

"No, listen to me." She grabbed his hand again and made him face her. "Both of you." She looked at them and summoned all the strength she had. "I'm not choosing either of you. I need to take time for myself. I need to heal."

"What does that mean?" Rohan asked, his expression guarded.

"It means I'm not talking to either of you for at least a month. You can't contact me, can't see me, can't send me anything. If you violate these boundaries, I will cut you out of my life completely."

Rohan's expression shuttered further. Patrick looked like she'd kicked him in the stomach.

"And after that?" Rohan asked.

"I don't know," she said. "We'll play it by ear. Try to work our shit out together. See what we want to be to each other."

"An eye for an eye," Patrick said.

"Sure," she said. "Except I'm actually giving you the courtesy of a warning instead of straight-up ghosting you."

He winced.

She walked away, heading back inside. She needed to pack and call Eva. Hopefully, she'd be still up and the couch was free.

"And what if we don't agree to all that? The month of silence?" Rohan asked. There was a hard, angry edge to his question.

She turned back. "Agree or don't. Just know I meant exactly what I said. If I don't contact you when the month is up, don't bother waiting for me."

HER FACE, god, her face. Dead white and final. It haunted Patrick as they packed up the gear, preparing to leave her house. No one would look at him, which was fine because he didn't want to look at them either.

She'd slept with Rohan. It hit Patrick again, a blow to the solar plexus. He kept moving through it. If he stopped now, he'd cave. Somehow Rohan'd wormed his way into her heart and she'd… fallen.

No. She still loved him, Patrick told himself. She had to or she wouldn't be this mad. The total opposite of love was indifference and she wasn't. So he still had a chance.

But did he want it?

Of course, he did. He loved her. Right?

But what if he didn't?

The static in his mind laughed at him, a coughing, pixelated wheeze and he felt his anger slipping away. He grabbed for it, like grabbing for a live coal, because the burn made him feel alive in a way he hadn't in far too long.

He had to find her.

The last of the gear was in the car. He stared at the full trunk for a minute then turned away. She was going to Eva's house. Eva's house was Cazzi's old house and he'd never been there but he knew it wasn't far so if he just started looking maybe…

"Where are you going?" Rohan's normally warm voice was cold behind him.

The rage flared hot, searing. The pain was bright, practically blinding. High-pitched like screaming. Rohan slept with her. He'd known they were working shit out and he'd slid in between the cracks because Rohan couldn't stand being alone. Patrick's hands closed into fists.

Calm. Be calm, son, his father's voice murmured.

"Away." Patrick didn't stop.

"No, you're not," Benji's voice split through the air the way it would cut through the noise of a crowd. "We need you."

Their voice asked for silence and Patrick gave it silence. But he stopped, turning to face them.

"Go," Rohan sounded dismissive, not looking at him. "You've done enough already."

"No." Benji crossed their arms.

"I'm leaving," Patrick said but didn't move. Why wasn't he moving?

"You certainly think you are." The words were condescending, the tone dead, factual. Benji gave him the shadiest up-down look he'd ever gotten.

Rohan narrowed his eyes at Benji. He still wasn't looking at him, like Patrick was the one who was wrong here, like Patrick was the betrayer.

Fuck them. Fuck them both.

"I am. The label, the album, everything," he ground out. Patrick needed to get away, it was all closing in.

"No," Benji repeated. "You're not."

"You can't keep me." He forced his feet to move, walk away from everything he'd built here. He was done with this shit. This town wasn't big but how much time did he have to search before someone called the cops?

"Bitch, you signed a contract. You wanna leave? Fine, but you'll be in breach of said contract. Don't think you haven't pissed me off enough to get litigious." Benji smiled, evil and dissonant.

The shrill of rage rang in Patrick's ears. "You're taking his damn side again. You always take his side."

Benji's glance at Rohan sliced like a knife and he seemed to feel it, shoulders hunching. He was hiding behind Benji, again. Couldn't fight his own damn battles, never could.

A man should always fight his own battles, the father in his head reminded him.

"I'm protecting my interests," Benji said finally, "You think I'm easy to employ?" They spread their arms, the flourish encompassing all the layers of identity they didn't bother to lay out. "This is my soapbox too, my platform, my risk. I don't know how you guys keep forgetting that with your stupid fucking dramafest."

Guilt cracked like ice beneath his feet. Cazzi was so bright, so blinding, it was hard for Patrick to see anything but her. Always had. It was too easy to lose his place in the world to wrap himself around her.

Even now he could feel her getting farther and farther away, the yawning silence of absence running under everything.

"Shit," Rohan said, "Let's just get this album done." He looked stricken, even more guilty than Patrick.

Good. He fucking should be.

"Rick?" He turned to Patrick. "Truce?" He reached out a hand, his face strained behind his good guy mask. He'd always played the nice boy in the band, the model minority in the pop equivalent of a "tokenism buffet" as his sister liked to call Beatboyz. Patrick wondered what the public would make of the talisman under his shirt or that he'd already moved on from the supposed love of his life. Only he could date Angela Alice and come out unstained.

He looked at Patrick like he expected him to get in line the way the fans used to when they stepped out of a venue.

"You fucking slept with her," the words tumbled out of Patrick's mouth like spiders or snakes or something equally horrifying. "You knew... and you did it anyway."

His hand faltered and fell. "I was thinking with my dick." He licked his lips and his fingers pressed against the pendant under his shirt. Then he straightened and looked Patrick in the eye. "And my heart. I'm sorry about the timing, but I'm not sorry I did it." His shoulders went back and Patrick remembered how fucking big he was all of a sudden. Not Leo big, but bigger than him with those shoulders and a few extra inches of leg.

He didn't care.

"She loves me!" Patrick slapped his own chest, the hollow echo grounding him.

Something like sympathy flickered through Rohan's eyes.

She doesn't love you. You've finally done it. You lost her. The words echoed and echoed until he wanted to scream. Hatred hummed in an octave so low he could feel it in his bones.

Rohan took her.

But did you want her?

"Go away," Benji pushed Rohan aside.

"But—"

"You're not fucking helping. Go sit in your car." They pushed him again, so hard he stumbled. It didn't look physically possible, given how willowy Benji was, but Patrick would never underestimate how hellishly strong they were again.

"Benji, you're not—"

"I know exactly what I'm not, and it's not fucking around when I say, you're making this a hundred times worse. Go. Sit. In. Your. Car."

Rohan stared them down a moment, towering and thinking. If Patrick knocked him off his feet he wouldn't be so damn tall. He tried to remember that leg sweep Cazzi had taught him years ago, the one he used to use on Leo when the other man got rowdy, but the thought of her was a dark wave and he lost time.

"Rick. Rick!" Fingers snapped in front of his face. In 4/4 time, but Patrick doubted Benji meant it to be. "Look at me."

Patrick looked. Had everything moved fast or was he slow? Rohan was gone, Benji stood in the streetlight, eyes darker than the night.

"I know this fucking sucks but we need you. You're the best. Will you work remotely? If you go home will you collapse or can you finish this out first?" Benji asked, their expression concerned.

"Don't pretend to be sympathetic."

Their lips thinned, concern slipping away.

"And don't fucking tell me about your tortured past." Patrick was being cruel. He didn't care.

"Just answer the damn question. Will you fall apart or will you be okay?"

Patrick was about to snap again when he caught the fear in their eyes and remembered the Suicide King had been a person before he became Benji's masterpiece. "My Nana is staying with me. I'll be okay."

"Okay," they whispered and he remembered they were human too. And his friend. Ice

"Don't leave me stranded," they said, eyes big and voice quiet. "Please. I'll help with Sabrina's album. We'll make it gold. Hell, we'll make it platinum."

Sabrina. How had he forgotten his baby sister's album was next on his label's docket? A docket that would only happen if Rohan's album paid off. His life felt like a trap yawning at his feet.

Fuck. It would be her big break if they could get her in on his coattails. Patrick looked at Benji's face and tried to figure out if they were being real or manipulating him masterfully. They stared back, tired and sincere. The trap snapped shut and swallowed him, holding him under until he drowned.

His chest was lead, the silence was deafening, solidifying into the ache of a phantom limb. He was losing, he was losing, he was lost.

Cazzi's light was out and he was painfully, painfully sighted again. The static filled the silence. The rage died, taking the pain and everything else with it. All that was left was cold. Cold so deep he could barely breathe.

"Okay," he said. "I'll finish it."

28

"I used to pine for you
Bleed for you
Wait up late
Go to bed empty
But hoping

I used to hang on your words
I know it sounds absurd
But life made sense when you told it
You spun the truth out of me
And I loved it

Oh, I set myself on fire
Calling it desire
Telling myself I wanted it
Telling myself it made me alive

But today baby, I'm rising from the ashes
Rebuilding from the ground up
I'm done playing with matches

I'm rising from the ashes"
— "From the Ashes" by RK on *From the Ashes*

One week later...
    Rohan sat on a folding chair in Benji's under-construction Sacramento living room and listened to the title track of his album, mixed and perfected by Rick from his house in LA. It was a banger, an anthem, it was everything he wanted to say. So why did he still feel so hollow inside?

Was it him? Was it good enough? He felt the uncertainty that sometimes crept in now that all his actions weren't mapped out and approved by marketing, management, and various stylists.

He played with his amulet, feeling the rough edge of his carving contrasting against the original design. Why was he still attaching himself to this thing Angie gave him? Why had he carved himself into a gift he never cared about?

He took the headphones off and threw his amulet across the room. It skittered across the half-finished floor and into a pile of building supplies that hadn't moved the entire week he'd been there.

"That bad?" Benji looked up from positioning a sawhorse as a footstool.

"Angie gave it to me," Rohan grumbled. "Should never have done magic with it."

"Oh right." Benji glanced to the corner of the room where the amulet gleamed. "I forgot you were a magician or whatever."

"Not a magician. I just sometimes play with sigils."

"Totally different, my bad." Benji sat, putting their feet up on the sawhorse.

"Hey, I don't make fun of you for thinking chairs and shit are alive." Rohan felt like a dick the minute the words left his mouth. He didn't actually have a problem with animism.

Benji frowned. "I believe animate and inanimate things contain spirits and need to be respected, there's a difference."

"Exactly," Rohan said, like he'd proven some point.

Benji gave him a look that said they were not buying his bull-shit but they were letting it slide—again. "Were you able to listen to the mix or were you too busy playing with your necklace?"

"I heard it."

"And...?"

Rohan kicked a stray nail. "I like it."

"But?"

"I don't know," Rohan dropped the headphones in his lap. "It feels like a lie. I'm not triumphant. I'm not even fucking okay. I feel like it's just another persona, fake like I was in Beatboyz."

Benji made a sympathetic sound. "I feel that but think of it as a postcard from the future. What you will be feeling."

"Will I though? Will I ever feel that good?"

Benji sighed. "You just got your heart trampled on by two women in quick succession. Nothing I say is going to make you believe things will be better. Just trust me, kid. They will."

"Voice of experience?"

"Yeah." Benji looked down at their hands, twisting in their lap. "Something like that."

Rohan sighed. "Is it bad that I still want her?"

"Which her?" Benji's voice was suspiciously neutral.

"Cazzi. I only met her like three weeks ago but... I can't stop thinking about her."

"It's only been a week. Give it time."

"You think my feelings will fade?" Rohan barely stopped himself from snarling.

Benji shrugged. "If you want them to."

"Did yours? About your Suicide King?"

Benji's laugh was rusty. "It wasn't quite like that. But no."

"Why? If you don't mind me asking."

They shook their head. "No closure. He won't talk to me."

"Well, I'm not allowed to talk to her."

They didn't seem to hear him. "I get it though." They fiddled with a loose thread in their sweater, seeming almost insecure. It was enough to make Rohan watch them closely. "I represent the best and worst time of his life. I was there for every relapse, every attempt. For the peak of his fame." Benji shrugged. "I don't know I'd want to be around him either if it was me."

"Do you think I'm that to Cazzi?" Rohan asked, the thought dawning on him like an apocalyptic sunrise. If nothing else, he'd consistently put his album first and her mental health second. Just like the label had with him and the guys in Beatboyz and Angie had done with him and her career. *Fuck.*

"Not everything is about you, heartbreak boy," Benji snapped. They walked out of the room.

He winced but murmured, "Heartbreak boy." His fingers fumbled for his notebook and rhymes bloomed in his head, mocking and sharp. He'd apologize to Benji as soon as he wrote this down.

Then he'd figure out how to make up for his shitty behavior with Cazzi.

29

*"The world revolves
Around the problems you can't solve
The dreams you choke on
The love you cry on*

*Hold me I'm needy
Give me I'm greedy
Can't stand on my feet
In your shadow I will creep*

*Heartbreak boy
Apocalypse sunrise shining
In the want want want of your heart
Heartbreak boy
Just waiting for an excuse
To break apart part part"*
— "Heartbreak Boy" by RK on *From the Ashes*

Two weeks had passed since Cazzi cut herself off from Rohan and Patrick. The phantom ache of not being able to talk to someone you loved… it felt like grief. It was grief. But she told herself it would pass. Once it did, clarity would set in and she would figure her way out of this emotional clusterfuck.

"Stop thinking about them." Judit looked up from her menu.

"That obvious, huh?" Cazzi refocused on her own menu. *Real food*, she reminded herself. She had to force herself to eat anything that wasn't chocolate these days.

She shouldn't have suggested Badlands. Now all she could think about was sitting there holding Rohan's hand. He already haunted every inch of her house, but apparently she liked her punishment out of the dungeon too.

Maybe she should make a trip out to the dungeon. But then she'd have to see her ex and be vulnerable and she didn't even want to have sex with herself right now, let alone get creative with someone else. Ugh.

"Yep," Judit said. "Okay, I'm dying to know. Which one are you missing more?"

Cazzi shut her eyes, hating her friend for just the briefest instance for even asking.

"Jesus, Judit," Eva said from next to Cazzi. Her arm wrapped around Cazzi's shoulders.

"Shit, I'm sorry," Judit sounded mortified. "It just popped out."

Cazzi opened her eyes. "It's okay. It just hurts."

Judit nodded, hands over her mouth, her eyes sympathetic.

Eva hugged Cazzi against her. "You did the right thing. You have a right to your boundaries, to choose yourself."

"Have either of them tried to contact you?" Judit asked.

Cazzi shook her head.

"Good," Eva said.

"I think I may have lost Patrick," Cazzi whispered. If she spoke any louder, she'd cry.

"I take it you're leaning towards him," Judit said. Disapproval was written in her eyes.

"Why do you keep telling her to choose?" Eva said. "I thought you'd be the poster child for keeping both."

Judit glared at her. "Because I don't think both of them deserve her."

"You haven't even met them, Judge Judy," Eva said. "If anyone should be picking ships it's me." She cut a glance at Cazzi. "But I won't."

Cazzi sighed. "Can we not talk about this? My presentation is tomorrow and I'm nervous enough as it is."

She was lying. She was too disassociated and numb to feel nervous.

Judit and Eva fell all over themselves to tell her she'd do fine —*better than fine, great!* She'd kill it, they'd love her. Cazzi nodded and smiled and pretended to believe them. She was having trouble caring. She made a note, adding it to the list she'd tell her new therapist.

The next day, she stood in front of the Academic Senate, four sigils deep, and gave them a smile Rohan would no doubt call her blank face. The five members of the Undergraduate Education Committee sat on the dais as she set up her presentation at the podium. She'd already been here for over an hour as the committee dissected various proposals with the kind of nitpicky precision that made Josie look sloppy. It was like going to a city council meeting but everyone was that one guy who cared *wayyy* too much about the placement of speed bumps and nobody agreed on anything.

She started her spiel, very similar to the one she'd given to Rohan not so long ago.

"These days kids learn about sex from porn and rumors. Only twenty-four states require sex education taught in schools and of those, only twenty require it to be medically, technically, or factually correct..." She watched the faces of the seven people in front of her, noting the nods, the frowns, the stone faces.

Eva came up and gave her part of the presentation as did Yanni, Marcia, and Marcia's doctor husband who gave Cazzi a wink when he was done. She wasn't sure how she felt about that but she was grateful he'd helped build her case.

"Do you know how many angry emails we're going to get from parents?" Grumbled a pinch-faced woman when Cazzi finished her concluding remarks. "We could lose prospective students over this."

"Ellen, this is the future. We need to be ahead of the curve, not behind it," Yanni said with a smile at Cazzi.

Her boss stood next to her and Eva stood on her other side. Marcia, her husband, Josie, and some of the student workers sat in the row behind them. It made Cazzi feel both grounded and doubly pressured. All these people were here for her.

"It's not our place to mandate this. An elective, sure, but a mandatory class?" The dean shook his head. "We are not in loco parentis."

Yanni counseled Cazzi to pitch it as mandatory first so they could negotiate down to the more likely Jan term option. It was a game she hated to have to play but Cazzi knew it was the most likely way to get a foot in the door.

"We already do a sexual harassment seminar during freshman orientation. Consider this an extension of it," Cazzi said. "We also have an elective evolution of human sexuality course in the psych department."

"Then why do we need another one?" Ellen asked.

"What if we made it just a general health class and made the sex stuff a unit?" Someone else from the far end of the dais suggested.

There was an agreeable murmur and bobbing of heads.

"You want to bury it," Cazzi said, her voice flat. She wanted to scream.

Yanni shot her a warning look. "We did include the option of a Jan term version in the proposal."

"Jan term could work," said a woman to the right of the pinch-faced Ellen.

"She's not a teacher," pointed out a man in an aggressively argyle sweater. "She's not even an adjunct."

"If you approve the class the Gender Studies Department will sponsor the class," Gretchen Mills said, standing up from the crowd.

"Thank you, Dr. Mills," the dean said in a tone that said *sit back down.*

Gretchen crossed her arms and stayed standing. "Yanni's right. We want to be ahead of the curve on this one. The kids want to learn about sex, might as well teach them how to do it without harming each other."

"This is a new school," the dean said, pushing his glasses up his nose. "We're not even fifty years old. We can't jeopardize our funding like this."

"We're a new school," Cazzi said, "I thought that meant we were supposed to be innovative, not trapped in someone else's broken traditions." She could almost feel Josie's eyes boring into her shoulder blades. The woman went to all the Senate meetings even though she wasn't on a single committee. "As a society, the way we're handling sex and relationships is broken and toxic. Do we really want to replicate that here? Or do we want to show our students how to break that cycle?"

"It's unrealistic."

"Higher education exists in an ivory tower. We study what's real but we strive for a world better than the one we live in," Cazzi pointed out. "Why should our sex lives and interpersonal relationships be any different?"

"This is a great idea." The dean gave her a kind smile. "But the parents are the ones that pay tuition. We can't afford to alienate them with a freshman seminar that teaches their precious babies how to do the exact thing parents don't want to think about their kids doing." He chuckled.

"I see," Cazzi forced the words to be civil.

"But maybe in a few years…"

"We don't have a few years," Cazzi protested. "The statistics I included on page five of my proposal prove that. STIs, sexual assault, unwanted pregnancy, our students are right in the most likely time of their lives to experience these things. We fail our students every day by not doing the one thing we are supposed to do: educate them."

There was a rustle as the board paged through her proposal. Eyebrows jumped.

"These seem rather high," the dean said. Some of the board nodded, looking stunned but many of the women, including pinch-faced Ellen, just looked tired.

Where the hell were you during #MeToo? Did you have your head in the sand or did that interfere with having your lips firmly planted against the collective ass of the tuition-payers?

"These are probably a fraction of the truth, given the statistics on underreporting which you can see on the page before that." Cazzi tried not to take it personally that they hadn't read her proposal. Yanni warned her it would happen. "And the page before that has the stats for sexual assaults reported on this campus."

"And you think a class would help this?" the dean asked, not sounding convinced.

"Why don't you let me teach the class and find out?" Cazzi challenged him. "Dean Kinney, this class would've meant everything to me when I was in college. When I was a freshman I barely knew anything real about sex and I had no idea where I could learn more or that there was so much more to learn. If there hadn't been a human sexuality unit in my Psych 101 class I probably would still be scared and ashamed of my own body. We can help our students avoid the things we went through. Isn't that the point of education? To give them the knowledge we wish we'd had at their age?"

The committee shifted restlessly, on the edge. How could she push them over to her side?

"I have a question," called someone from the crowd.

Cazzi turned to find the voice, her heart beating hard at the sudden interruption. She couldn't pinpoint the voice until the dean gestured a student worker over with a mike and she saw them. Benji lounged in an aisle seat halfway up the auditorium. They caught her eye and winked. But it wasn't them who took the mike. A tall woman in a white lab coat stood up and tapped the mike before saying. "Hello. I am Dr. Shobi Kapoor."

Cazzi went light-headed. Dr. Kapoor was too far away and badly lit for Cazzi to make out much of her features. She scanned the rows around Dr. Kapoor but he wasn't there. But Kapoor was a common name, right? Maybe it was a coincidence. Then her gaze caught on Benji. They smiled.

It wasn't a coincidence.

Dr. Kapoor was still talking. "As a mother and a medical professional, I must say I am very concerned with the school's handling of this matter. I spent twenty years working in the ER and I have seen firsthand many of the consequences Dr. Muldoon is trying to save your students from. What I don't understand is your response. Please explain to me how you justify placing your tuition over the well-being of your students." She crossed her arms and waited, pinning the dean with a look Cazzi was very happy not to be on the receiving end of.

Dean Kinney shifted uncomfortably but none of the other committee members volunteered to answer the doctor's question. "Well," he said. "It's not so much of putting tuition before students as strategizing to put the students' best interests first. We can't teach them without any money to pay our teachers."

"So you mean you are beholden to whoever pays you?" An older Indian woman in a sari stood with the aid of the chair in front of her. Dr. Kapoor handed her the mike and she repeated the question.

Benji booed, their voice echoing throughout the auditorium. Cazzi could tell they were enjoying themself despite the distance. A couple other students copied them.

"We pay you!" Yelled one.

"Yeah!"

"I want sex ed!"

"Woo sex!"

There were phones out, filming. Cazzi turned away from the lenses, facing the dean like that was the reason she was giving her back to the cameras. Unease curled and bled under her sigils.

The dean pounded his gavel on the table until everyone quieted down. "We are a private college, yes. But we were set up with a charter to educate and do the best we can for the students we teach. If the committee agrees, I suggest implementing Dr. Muldoon's idea on a trial basis starting with a Jan term class with the option to expand into a graduation requirement should it show promise or need in the next two years. All in favor?"

Three members raised their hands, including the dean. Argyle sweater and pinch-faced Ellen voted against her. But it was enough, just enough.

Cazzi had her class.

She walked out of the room, beaming the S&S Department congratulating her. The joy of winning was a punch of sunlight to the chest. She couldn't wait to tell Eva and Judit and... Rohan. Her smile dimmed and she looked around for Dr. Kapoor and the woman with her. But they were gone.

She'd never even told Patrick about her class. But Rohan, Rohan had been so excited, so supportive of her class. He'd be so happy for her. Had he sent them?

Even after you tossed him out on his ear?

It was necessary. She told herself.

Sure, but will he see it that way?

She didn't know. She liked to think he would.

She split off from the department to "go to the bathroom" but really just to decompress.

"Congratulations," said a familiar voice the minute she was away from the crowd.

She looked up at Benji. "Thanks." She'd spotted them lurking. They were hard to miss even when they seemed to be trying to be inconspicuous.

"He's not here." They smiled but their eyes were assessing.

"Dr. Kapoor...?"

"His mom, yeah," they said. "And his grandma."

"Did he send them?"

"Sort of," they said, "Ask them yourself." They stepped aside and there was Dr. Kapoor and Rohan's grandmother.

"Dr. Muldoon," Rohan's mom stuck out her hand. "This is my mother Mrs. Pandit." Mrs. Pandit nodded.

Cazzi shook Rohan's mom's hand like she hadn't slept with the woman's son and dipped her head respectfully to his grandmother. She was sure there was something more she should do to show her respect but she didn't think now was the time to Google it. "Dr. Kapoor, Mrs. Pandit, thank you for attending. I think your questions helped tip the committee in my favor. I can't thank you enough."

"Yes, well, I approved of your class plan. I would love to see a copy of your proposal," Dr. Kapoor said.

"Sure," Cazzi said, somewhat bewildered, and handed her an extra copy.

"Hm," the doctor put her glasses on and began to read.

"Who are your people, Dr. Muldoon?" Asked Mrs. Pandit, her lightly accented voice politely curious.

"My people—do you mean my family?"

Mrs. Pandit inclined her head and Cazzi realized she was being tested.

"My parents live in LA, my mother is a researcher at UCLA and my father is a law librarian."

"And where are they from?"

"My father's side is Irish and my mother's is Eastern European. I'm third generation American," she said.

Mrs. Pandit nodded. "So is our Rohan."

"I know," Cazzi blurted. "He told me a bit about you. Do you still practice as a midwife?"

Mrs. Pandit looked surprised. "I mostly teach and volunteer at the Foundation. I'm too old to be called out at all hours."

Cazzi nodded. "Understandable."

Mrs. Pandit kept quizzing her as Dr. Kapoor read her proposal cover to cover. Cazzi fielded questions about why she didn't go into medicine or become a therapist, her finances, and her thoughts on marriage which she managed to turn into a discussion on the institution rather than her personal beliefs. She wasn't even in a relationship with Rohan, they didn't need to know that about her. Benji spent the time on their phone, seemingly ignoring the conversation.

After she rebuffed yet another veiled question about whether she'd like children, Mrs. Pandit said, "You understand we just want the best for our Rohan. He likes you and his last choice wasn't so good."

"I respect that," Cazzi said. "But I haven't decided whether I want to date him much less anything further. My boundaries are my own and I ask you to respect them."

Mrs. Pandit drew back. "You do not compromise?"

"I compromise when I need to, but I will not compromise just to show you I am not Angela Alice." She probably just alienated his family but dammit she was not about to be walked all over just on the off-chance she might want to marry Rohan.

From behind her class proposal, Dr. Kapoor smiled. "Stop interrogating her, Mum. She writes a good proposal."

Mrs. Pandit sighed. "Another gora."

"Yes," Dr. Kapoor closed the proposal. "But I like this one." She looked at Cazzi, "May I keep this?"

Bewildered, Cazzi nodded. Her phone went off, reminding her she had a meeting and she politely made her escape.

30

"I scrimped and saved and planned
Building the perfect man
Ken to my Barbie
He'd never harm me

I built him strong and sweet
So I'd have a chance to be weak
I molded him to fit in my hand
So I could hold him
Pretty boy Ken
Would always love me

Oh I built perfection
I put him in action
And reader, he left me
He left me and I let him
They say let love go, it'll come back
But I stacked the deck
My Ken's never coming back."
— "FranKenstein" by Angela Alice on *PhenoBarbie Doll*

Rohan paced Benji's half finished living room. He hadn't meant to unleash his Ma and Nānī on Cazzi but they had surprised him and Benji with a flying visit. He'd been having a moment of madness, trying to convince Benji he could go watch the Academic Senate meeting as moral support. They'd been trying to talk him out of it and unfortunately they'd thought appealing to his family would help. Which then necessitated giving them a very sanitized version of how he knew Cazzi and why he couldn't attend. Before he knew it, they were off to Clementine without him, Benji offering to drive and promising Rohan they'd keep him posted.

What a fucking mess.

What is done is done. No amount of fretting will undo it, he reminded himself.

He grabbed his talisman in his pocket. His family knew he wasn't a practicing Hindu but he didn't think they'd understand his sigils or why he'd kept a gift from Angie. He hadn't worn the amulet since he'd chucked it across the living room, but he couldn't quite bear to part with it.

Maybe if he just called Benji he could get them to put her on. They'd been keeping him up to date but they'd stopped texting when the committee ruled. Rohan had whooped loud enough to make the living room echo when he saw she'd gotten her class, even though it wasn't exactly what she wanted. But that was a while ago, surely if they were still there they were talking to her. If he called Benji, he wouldn't technically be reaching out to her and then he could explain—

The front door opened. He froze, half-expecting to see Cazzi coming in with his family and Benji.

"How was it?" He asked. *Did you see her? Did you scare her off?*

"She won, but only a partial victory," Ma said. She shook her head as she moved to slip off her shoes then checked herself. Benji's floor was still unfinished. "Shameful, the way these institutions drag their feet. It's a good thing I had a lab coat in the car." She shrugged it off and hung it on the piece of rebar hanging out of the wall Benji used as a temporary coat rack.

"She's strong-headed," Nānī said. "But she is well-spoken and apparently writes a good proposal." She side-eyed Ma.

Ma shrugged. "Her data is sound."

"I don't think she hates you," Benji murmured as they passed him, "If that's what you're asking."

Rohan felt suddenly lighter. Maybe he could send her flowers? Would that be reaching out? Would it be too cliche? Did Cazzi even like flowers? He still hadn't figured out how to salvage things with her, if he even could.

Nānī patted his cheek. "Such a romantic. How did you survive Los Angeles for so long?"

He put his arm around her and smiled at his Ma. "I was raised well."

Benji rolled their eyes, but he could tell they were suppressing a smile.

CAZZI SAT on her patio that weekend, relaxing with a book and an edible. She was taking time for herself and trying not to think about the time ticking away towards her damn deadline. She should be celebrating. She should be working on her class. She should be actually reading instead of zoning out at the page.

She should be doing a lot of things.

She put the book down and took three deep breaths. Her new therapist had congratulated her for getting out of an unhealthy situation but reminded her that ultimatums weren't the best method for resolving an issue.

She'd sent her home to journal and reflect on whether she even wanted to be in a relationship right now. "And if you do," Dr. Kim had said, "What would that look like?"

Cazzi fiddled with her bookmark. Did she want a partner?

She looked through the glass doors to her living room. There was the couch where Patrick had slept. Where she and Rohan had fallen asleep, him holding her. Where she'd found the two of them fighting.

She missed being held. It had barely been two weeks, but the feeling haunted her. She wanted to be wanted, to be loved, to be supported, to come home to someone.

She closed her eyes and built herself a man.

He would be kind, she decided. Funny. Sweet. Compassionate. Empathetic. Understand trauma and respect her mental health. She'd be attracted to him. The sex would be good and he'd be good enough at communication that they'd be able to work it out if it wasn't.

What a fantasy, sneered a voice that sounded suspiciously like Angelica's.

She ignored it.

He'd get her sigil work, wouldn't scoff at her witchiness or be scared of her. He wouldn't try to shame her for her past or her sexual explorations. He'd be a proponent of her work.

Oh, you think you can find that? Trying to build yourself a new Patrick? Demanded the Angelica in her head.

He wouldn't pity her. Ever.

The Angelica laughed. *I see where this is going.*

He'd be able to talk to her about his problems.

Honey, the Angelica voice said, *he's certainly good at that.*

Cazzi opened her eyes.

You think just because you picked him, he'll want anything to do with you?

Shut up, she told the voice. Then she wrote the name in her journal and stared at it. Maybe she was high (she was) but it felt right. It felt even more right the next morning when she looked at the name sober.

That scared the shit out of her.

TWO AND HALF weeks after the Academic Senate debacle, Rohan did something mildly unhealthy. He set a Google alert for Cazzi's name. It wasn't like she had social media to obsess over and he'd been desperate one dark, lonely night.

After that, he was caught up in the whirlwind of putting the finishing touches on the album and promotion work. So much promotion work. He now had so much more respect for the PR people for Beatboyz. He, Benji, and Rick tapped into their networks, sent out promos, and scheduled themselves within an inch of their lives with interviews, live streams, and appearances. Rohan spent a week straight in photoshoots. Benji negotiated show dates. In what spare time either of them had they tried to scrape together funds for a music video.

Rick was... well, Rohan didn't know what Rick was doing because he only talked to Benji right now and only because Benji pulled up the contract they'd made them all sign when they started the label and shoved it in his face. Rohan was pretty sure Rick was fulfilling his contractual obligation to the letter and nothing more.

Frankly, he didn't care and he didn't blame him. He'd be pissed too. Well, he *was* pissed. Pissed at Rick, pissed for Cazzi. But mostly he just missed her, more than he had any right.

Was she thinking about him? Did she miss him too?

Maybe she did. A small kernel of hope formed in his chest but he pushed it aside. He couldn't bear it if he allowed himself to hope and he was wrong.

His phone pinged, making the custom sound he'd set for her. The Google alert notified him she'd surfaced in the blur of images and information that was the internet.

"Pining, beta?" His mother asked before he could look at it. She sat down next to him at the table.

Oh yeah, and he was crashing at his parents' place like a broke nineteen-year-old. He could've afforded to rent somewhere but the thought of sitting in an impersonally furnished place alone made him depressed, so here he was.

"Just thinking," he said.

"Mmhm." She sipped her chai and gave him a look that said she didn't believe him for a minute but would let it go. For now.

"The child is brooding." Nānī came out of the kitchen with her own cup of tea.

"The child is right here," Rohan reminded her.

"The child still has his spirit," his grandmother said approvingly. She sipped her tea. "I never liked that Angela girl anyway. She was too tragic."

"Mum!" Shobi cried. "Please."

Rohan stared at Nānī incredulously. "You've seen every single *Lifetime* movie ever. I thought you loved tragic."

Nānī waved this away. "Real life is different. You don't want someone who is all tragedy. You want someone you can laugh with."

Rohan thought about Cazzi and kept his face as neutral as possible. He was dying to check the alert but there was a strict no phones during family time rule and Nānī would absolutely take his phone away no matter how old he was.

"I see you started the tea party without me," James said from the top of the stairs to his basement office. He wore the Lando shirt Shobi had gotten him for the last Star Wars movie premiere as a joke. Every Halloween, without fail, Shobi, a die-hard Star Wars fan, made him go full Lando to match her Leia, Han, or one memorable year, Chewie costume.

"Your cup is waiting on the counter," Nānī said, her accent going boarding school crisp with false annoyance. "Best get it before it gets cold."

James saluted her. "Yes ma'am." He grabbed his cup with a smile. He sat down next to Shobi and squeezed her hand. "What'd I miss?" His eyes tracked over Rohan, checking in on him.

Rohan gave him the slightest nod, an old sign from their days as talent and manager.

Shobi smiled at him. "Mum is giving Ro a hard time."

James faked a shocked look. "Our Mina? Giving someone a hard time?" He winked at her. "I can't imagine her doing that to our poor grieving Ro."

Rohan shook his head with a chuckle. "Alright, get it out. I know you didn't like Angie either."

"On the contrary, she set you up on the publicity front. Kept your names in the papers for all those years. The break-up is unfortunate, but the buzz is through the roof."

He certainly wasn't wrong. Every other question in every interview Rohan did seemed to be about Angie.

"James!" Nānī wapped his shoulder with a cloth napkin. "No work at the table."

"It's not work!" James protested. "The boy asked me a question and I answered it."

"Fine," Nānī grumbled. "I'll allow it."

"Thank you, Judge Mina," James said, "Now as I was saying, Angela, while I may not agree with her on a personal level, has done your career a service. Not as much as going solo right after the band like Martin did would have—"

"Anyway," Rohan said, cutting him off before his step-father could launch into the well-worn and very not needed lecture. "It doesn't matter. I'm not pining over her."

"How is Dr. Muldoon doing?" Ma asked with a sly smile.

"Is it that girl in that picture?" James asked. "Or the one with the sex class?"

"What picture?" Rohan asked as if he didn't know his parents shared everything. "What sex class?"

He got three nearly identical "don't try that bullshit" faces for his effort.

He cleared his throat. "Um. Yes."

"You want to marry this one?" Nānī asked. "I'm not sure she wants to marry you."

The thought of coming home to her every day, of growing old with her brain and her laugh and her smile...*Yes.* "I don't know. I kinda messed up with her. I gotta fix that first."

"How do you know this girl?" James raised an eyebrow. "I was under the impression you only met her recently."

He gave them the barebones answer again but Nānī and his mother weren't having it this time. Eventually, he gave up and spilled his guts in broad strokes, omitting Cazzi's secrets and that they'd had sex already. That stuff was none of their business.

When he finished, Nānī sat back and kissed her fingers like an Italian chef. "*That* would make a great Bollywood film." She elbowed James. "You should tell some of your producer friends."

James frowned. "You stole her from Rick?" He'd discovered Rick and was protective of him.

"I didn't steal her from anyone. She's not an object, Pop."

"That's right!" Shobi said, approvingly. "But, beta, this love triangle business is messy. I had too many men admitted after fighting over a woman." She frowned. "Too many women too."

"I don't think he's in any danger of that. Rick's not like that," James said, firmly.

Rohan also left out the brawl Rick and he almost had.

"I say go get her!" Nānī said. "How much longer until the month is up?"

"A week and a half."

"Do you have a plan?" She leaned forward eagerly.

"I don't know that she's going to want to hear from me, Nānī," Rohan said.

"Of course, she is, beta," Shobi said. "She wouldn't have answered so many of your Nānī's questions if she didn't."

"What questions?" Rohan hadn't gotten a straight answer from anyone about what happened after Cazzi's presentation. It kept creeping up and worrying him randomly when he had too much free brain space. Or when said brain space wasn't taken up by all the things he could've done better in his time with her. He could've broken up with Angie sooner. He could've leaned on Cazzi less. He could've put not put his album above her mental health—

"Exactly!" Nānī said. "And you'd better have a plan to sweep her off her feet when she does."

Rohan mumbled something agreeable but shared a dubious look with James.

She'll pick Rick, he thought. *Won't she?*

Keep battling yourself and you'll have nothing left to fight for her, murmured a calm voice in his head.

"She lives up near Sacramento, doesn't she?" James asked like he didn't know exactly where Clementine was.

"So?" Rohan asked.

"Four hundred miles is far," he said mildly.

It's worth it. She's worth it—if she wants me.

Nānī waved his stepdad's words away. "Our boy will be famous again soon. Four hundred miles is nothing."

Rohan couldn't help but smile at her faith in him, even though he worried no one would ever love the album as much as he did.

An hour later he checked the Google alert. Clementine College's consideration of mandatory sex education had been picked up by an opinion columnist from a big paper and she argued for mandating it. Cazzi was only mentioned in passing and her department head did all the talking, but he knew that was exactly how she wanted it.

His chest ached with bittersweet pride but he couldn't keep the smile off his face. He copied the link into a post to send out across his platforms and hesitated. Would she want more attention called to this? Did he want to risk the inevitable blowback of comments?

Who was he kidding? This was important, of course, she'd want it highlighted and of course, he'd deal with the assholes in the comments. It wasn't like there weren't at least a dozen lurking in the comments of every post he'd ever made. As a pop star, former boy band member, and brown man, it was inevitable. Throw in Angie and he barely read his comments anymore anyway.

Before he could agonize too long about the perfect thing to say to make her love him in a single post, he wrote "Amazing work, here's hoping it starts a trend," tossed in a couple hashtags, and posted it.

But the tiny kernel of hope in his chest sprouted, putting out a tentative stalk.

31

ANGELA VS BENJI: THE FEUD WE NEVER KNEW WE NEEDED
Metal queen Angela Alice can't keep her name out of the
headlines. Between her contentious break-up with former
Beatboy RK, her chart-topping new album about said break-up,
her upcoming sold-out tour, there's been plenty to talk about.
But it's her ongoing Twitter feud with Benji Nakamura (AKA
Benji Omega, the delicious singer of User-Friendly Omega)
that's got us hooked.
"It's been a fun month," she said, speaking to us over the phone.
"I love a good feud. I still troll the Westboro Baptist Church
when I'm bored. But Benji is twice as fun as those idiots."
"I'm over it," Nakamura told us at the Songwriters Gala in Los
Angeles. "I'm more focused on the amazing album RK is about to
drop. It's been an honor working on it."
Angela laughed when we told her about Nakamura's comments.
"It's not over. Just wait."
Is she right? All we know is we'll be watching their Twitter feeds
closely.
—-Celebrity Watcher Magazine

"RK posted about us! We're viral!" The student worker cried, shoving her phone into Cazzi's face the minute she walked into the office. She was new and a sophomore and Cazzi couldn't remember her name for the life of her.

Cazzi grabbed the phone on instinct, bringing it to a distance that she could actually read without going cross-eyed. The tiny picture of Rohan in the corner of the post riveted her gaze, her stomach going fluttery in a way it had never done when she'd seen him in person. She forced herself to look at the actual post, noting he'd shared the nicest article that had run about the program, the only one that pinged the Google alert she had on her own name. He'd even made up a hashtag for it: #Clementine-SexEdRevolution.

Did he...? No, he was pissed at her, wasn't he? His expression after she kicked them all out made her wonder if he even cared if she ever talked to him again. That he'd tested her ultimatum immediately after she'd made it seemed more out of anger than wanting to stay in touch. His mother and grandmother attending her presentation with Benji was a puzzle piece she couldn't quite place.

But still it warmed her that he'd publicly supported her work. The likes on the post were in the hundreds of thousands too, which was nice. And impressive, given he'd posted it last night. She resisted the urge to look at the comments. If her inbox was anything to go by, she was better off.

She handed the phone back. "Exciting."

"I can't believe my school is going viral for a *good* thing!" the student worker said, bouncing in her seat. "I can't wait to take your class next year."

She couldn't help but smile at that. "I'm looking forward to having you."

In the privacy of her office, her smile dimmed. What did this mean? He hadn't violated her ultimatum but... she kind of wished he would. The urge to reach out to him herself made her fingers twitch. Instead she looked up the hashtag he'd made and sat back in shock at the number of celebrity endorsements his post spawned, including, somewhat disturbingly, Angelica's. She'd reposted his post and commented: "Don't worry. I still hate him. But he's right about this one. Good sex ed would've saved me a lot of grief."

Patrick reposted it too but without comment beyond the hashtag. That hurt more than she thought it would. She wondered if he'd even read the article and seen her name. Did he even realize it was the college she worked at? Or that she'd been nursing that project and never told him? Did he get how much it had meant to her?

How long had their relationship been dead before she killed it?

The grief that question brought was sharp but short, like a punch in the throat. But she was ready for it and barely choked.

He would hate her for this, for not picking him. Or maybe he'd be relieved, she couldn't even tell anymore. She'd once been able to tell exactly how he felt by the way he stood and now… she had no idea if he even liked her anymore or if he was playing out some kind of fucked up script in his head that she couldn't even begin to understand.

She missed him so damn much, but what she missed was a memory.

Everything ends, she reminded herself. *It's okay to walk away from someone that's hurting you.*

It was something she'd told far too many students but saying the words to herself loosened something in her chest.

Maybe, just maybe, she was going to be okay.

WHEN SHE GOT HOME, there was a small package on her porch. She hadn't ordered anything, had she? There was no return address. She picked it up and felt around. It felt... like a CD?

Frowning, she brought it inside. She set it on the table and stared at it. Who the fuck had sent her a CD?

It didn't start ticking or anything so she figured it was safe enough to open it.

The case wasn't one of those professional ones CDs usually came in, instead an album booklet had been stuck in one of those thin jewel cases people used to exchange mix CDs in. It reminded her of the long-ass MP3 playlists she used to jam into CDs to send with Patrick on tour.

It wasn't him right? God, would this hope ever go away? Her heart twisted with muddled emotions: curiosity, kind of hoping it was from him, mostly hoping it was from Rohan, a little annoyed one of them had reached out despite her boundary...

She flipped over the case, taking in the album art. Well, she would've but a Post-it fluttered off the front of the plastic case. She picked it up.

Congratulations on your class! This isn't me reaching out. I just thought you'd appreciate this. —R

"Not reaching out, my ass," she mumbled but still pulled out the liner notes to study them. It was Rohan's album, of course, the art featuring his profile, face smudged with grey and looking serious. "DRAFT" was watermarked across the front. She flipped open the booklet.

Every song had a note, either a behind-the-scenes snippet or a note on themes. She found herself sitting on the floor like she was a teenager again, reading all of them. The art was pretty minimal, just a few more pictures of him (she didn't linger on those at all, not at all) but the notes were exactly what she loved to read. Though short, they felt real, not like a caption on a social media post, polished within an inch of its life.

The note on the song with her nickname in it just said, "Thank you for everything."

When she turned to the thank yous, she skimmed through Benji's, her gaze catching on the same line Patrick had put in his as long as he'd been recording: *To my family, you know who you are.*

Was that still her? Did she want it to be? She wasn't sure. She forced herself to read on to Rohan's. He thanked his family, his Foundation, his co-artists on the album, Now or Never, and...

This album is dedicated to my not-muse, my truth serum. I put you through hell for this album but I hope you enjoy the liner notes. I wrote them just for you, the half of my heart I didn't know I was missing. May they live in your collection forever.

All my love,

Rohan

She reread his dedication three times. Her whole body was warm, airy, like she might float away. All these years she'd waited for a sign of love, a declaration and here it was. From exactly the right person.

THE DAY before the month was up, Cazzi realized she had a problem. She didn't have any way to contact Rohan without creating a social media account and being one of the probably millions of random accounts sliding into his DMs to be ignored. And she damn well couldn't ask Patrick.

Goddammit. Why hadn't she gotten his number?

She dived into research mode. She looked up Now or Never Records, Benji, the Beatboyz, anything she could remember. She collected phone numbers and email addresses and used them all. When she reached a real person they treated her like a fan and politely turned her away, promising (lying) that they'd forward the message on to Rohan.

By the time she was done exhausting everything she could think to do, she was anxious, knotted up, and shaky.

Feeling on the verge of panic, she called Judit and Eva. They met for an emergency milkshake conference at Badlands.

Judit didn't even bother to be discreet when she heard Cazzi wanted to maybe have a relationship with Rohan. She high-fived Eva.

"It's not for sure," Cazzi said. "He's a celebrity. I can't even stand to be interviewed by the fucking *Clementine Universibee*."

Eva cringed. "Have I mentioned how much I hate that pun?"

Judit smacked her shoulder. "Focus." She turned to Cazzi. "Do you love him?"

The question stole her breath. She thought of the name in her journal. The man she'd conjured. The way she'd missed his touch, missed seeing him appear randomly on her porch, how she hadn't been lonely until he left.

She swallowed and forced the truth out. "Yes."

"Then it'll work out." Judit smiled, her eyes distant.

Eva rolled her eyes. "Love doesn't magically make all the problems go away. Do you want to be a part of his life? Do you want him to be a part of yours? One of your biggest fears is being found by the people who," she lowered her voice, "know what you did. Are you okay with the possibility that might happen?"

Cazzi sighed. "I've been thinking about that."

"And?"

She grit her teeth and forced the words out. "I'll own it and try to use my past as a teaching moment."

"Is that what you want to do?" Eva asked, incredulous.

"No, it's not what I wanna do!" Cazzi snapped. "But there are plenty of people in jail for doing exactly the same thing but without a good set of lawyers or the privilege that I did. Maybe I can do some good there." She wrapped her hand around her milkshake glass, grounding herself in the smooth coldness.

"You don't owe anyone your trauma story," Judit reminded her.

"I know, I know," Cazzi took a sip of her chocolate milkshake. "But if it looks like it's going to get out, I'll need to get ahead of it."

"Alright, so you have a plan," Eva said. "So you're going to call him tomorrow and what, date long distance?"

She shrugged. "We'll work it out. Assuming he even wants me."

"Did you see the way he looked at you? If you telling him to fuck off for a month dims that spark, he's a hell of a lot shallower than I thought," Eva said. "Those puppy dog eyes were sappy as fuck."

"Well, there's a problem," Cazzi took another fortifying sip. "I don't have his number or email or anything."

Her friends gaped at her.

Eva spoke first. "You fucked Rohan fucking Kapoor and you did not get his digits?"

Cazzi shushed her. "It didn't seem important and I was trying to keep a distance."

"Was that before or after he put his dick in you?"

"Jesus Eva!" Judit said.

"It's a legit question," Eva said.

"He's gonna think I don't want to talk to him ever again," Cazzi moaned. Panic welled up in her belly.

"I'm sure he'll wait. He knows you need time." Judit said.

"Yeah, so, well, I might've said if I don't reach out after the month is up it means I don't wanna see him again," Cazzi grimaced. "I was mad."

Eva whistled. "I'll say," she said. "So what are you going to do about it?"

"I called and emailed and messaged everything I could find but..."

"He's a celebrity," Judit finished for her.

Cazzi put her head in her hands. "I don't know what I'm going to do."

The three of them sat in silence for a minute. Then Judit said, "I have an idea but you're going to absolutely hate it."

————

ROHAN TOOK a deep breath and opened up his mentions, wading through hate and fan love and people asking him to listen to their music and sob stories. He liked a few here and there, commented on the fan art and the posts by people he actually knew. Then he saw it.

@JuditReadsTheFuture posted a picture and tagged him in it. Except the picture wasn't of him or of the woman who owned the account. It was of a pair of pale forearms lined with familiar sigils. No caption.

He DM'd her immediately. "Who is this?"

"Cazzi's friend Judit (Eva's sister)."

She sent him a phone number. "Call this tomorrow. She wants to talk to you."

Rohan's stomach dropped and burst into sparks. Was this real? His finger hovered over the number, shaking. He pulled back.

No. He couldn't be sure the number was hers... and no. It wasn't time yet.

He closed the app and put his phone down.

32

"I'm waiting, waiting
Just call me baby,
Yes, no, maybe,
I gotta know
Which way you're gonna go

The clock's not my friend
I'm stuck waiting til the end
Baby, put me out of my misery
Say you wanna be with me
Tell me you love, love, love me."
— "Waiting (Love, Love, Love) by Beatboyz on *Heartbeatz*

The next day, Cazzi was a mess. She phoned in her work as much as she could stand, thankful she only had a few students come in for counseling and their issues were fairly simple. After every student walked out of their session she immediately checked her phone with the intensity of an addict but her dopamine hit didn't arrive.

Maybe he was waiting until the afternoon.

At lunch, she called Patrick. He didn't pick up. She hung up and breathed, eyes closed. The worst voices in her head said he'd ignored her call. She tried to accept that. He had every right to be mad.

She called him again. Her call went straight to voicemail. So she left a message. "Pat. I love you but I can't be in love with you. I would love to be your best friend again, or just friends again, someday. I'm not waiting, but I'm here if you need me. Always."

Then, because she couldn't help herself, she texted him a list of the names and numbers of a few psychologists she knew down in LA. She wanted to be sure even if he didn't want to talk to her, he had those numbers if he needed them.

He didn't respond.

It was almost a relief.

There was still no call, no text, no nothing from Rohan.

Maybe he was waiting until after work.

She stared at the outline of her class and could barely think. After half an hour wasted, she gave her phone to the student worker she trusted the most at the front desk and told her to bring it to her immediately if it rang. All she got was very excited for what turned out to be a robocall.

Maybe he didn't get the DM, she reasoned as she biked home. These things can get lost in cyberspace right? Goddammit, why didn't she know more about social media?

She was so lost in her thoughts she almost didn't see the figure on her porch. When she did, she almost fell off her bike.

Rohan. Rohan was on her porch.

So were about six of her neighbors and he was signing autographs, but still.

She skidded to a stop. He looked up, over the heads of fans around him. His gaze met hers and for the first time in her life, she lost track of the world around her. A bus could've hit her and she'd still be there, cradled by the way he looked at her.

She started walking, barely remembering to wheel her bike along beside her.

He said something. Her neighbors dispersed, their curious looks trailing along behind them.

She didn't care because he came off the porch to meet her. He was in front of her, grabbing her handlebars and she grabbed his face, pulling him towards her.

"We have an audience," he murmured.

"Fuck 'em," she said. "I don't care."

He put his hand on her shoulder, staying her. "I have to say something first."

She froze. Oh god, she'd misread this. She let go of his face, drawing back.

He caught her wrists in one hand, holding them lightly. "I want to apologize. Wait, um, here, this first."

She blinked, noticing for the first time the tin in his hand. She took it, popping open the lid, seeing him run his fingers through his hair as she did.

Cookies. The tin was full of cookies. Snickerdoodles, chocolate chip coconut, sugar cookies, decadent fudgy brownies, and something with pistachios she didn't have a name for.

She looked up at him, blinking fast against the sudden urge to cry.

"I didn't know which one you'd want, so I, um, made a lot," he shrugged, smiling uncertainly through the unruly curls he'd knocked loose over his eyes. Did he know how fucking gorgeous he looked undone and uncertain like that? Surely, he must.

"This is literally the sweetest thing anyone's ever done for me," she said.

"Yeah, well, I put my album over your mental health repeatedly and that was shitty of me." His hand skimmed through his hair again and settled against his neck, his lips pressed together.

She sighed, reality puncturing the moment. "Yes, it was."

He grimaced. "I shouldn't have. I know firsthand what it's like to be prioritized after someone's career. I'm really sorry I did it to you. I swear I will do my best to never do it again."

She nodded, picking up a coconut chocolate chip cookie. Unsure about what to say, she bit into it. Chocolate, brown sugar, and coconut exploded in her mouth, carried by a fluffy, wonderfully chewy cookie. Damn him, it was better than her version by a mile. She smiled as she took another bite.

"I know it's fast but… but I want to… would you be interested in, um, being my girlfriend?"

She paused, taking the words in, feeling her body react to them beyond the sudden lightheaded soar of her heart. Was she choosing herself in starting something with him? The light, airy happiness spread, loosening the taut muscles of her neck, the twist of nerves in her stomach, sensations she barely noticed until they were gone. She closed the cookie tin and looked up at him. "Okay."

"Okay?"

"Yeah," she grinned. "Can you just fucking kiss me now?"

He grinned and reached for her, his hands coming up to cradle her face. The touch of his lips was achingly sweet, safe and familiar, heady and new. He threaded his fingers in her hair, deepening the kiss until she felt full of light and ready to climb him like a tree. His smell surrounded her, peppermint, sandalwood, and warm skin.

Oh how she'd missed this, missed him.

"Why didn't you call?" she asked when he finally pulled away.

"I wasn't sure it was you and not some friend playing matchmaker." He searched her face. "Maybe I was being paranoid."

"Well, you're here, so I'm not complaining."

His relieved smile was so lovely she couldn't help but smile back.

"So you really want to do this? Even though I'm a public figure?" He smoothed her hair back, tucking it into her bun again.

She nodded. "I'd like to keep it as private as possible but I'm ready if someone recognizes me."

He hugged her awkwardly over her bike frame. "You got it. I'll back you up however you want to play it when it comes to publicity and all that."

She kissed him again. "Is it too early to tell you that I love you?"

"Only if it's not too early for me to say it back." When she nodded, he leaned down and whispered in her ear. "I love you, Caz."

She grinned and tugged his hand, leading him towards the back porch and her bike lock. "Come inside. I'll show you exactly how okay it is."

EPILOGUE

"This is the year that never ends
The year we hold tight to our friends
Everything changed
We'll never be the same

Trapped together
Orbiting each other
Don't talk for hours
But I can't complain
When I immerse myself
In

The way you grin, the way you laugh
Everything you do is a small pleasure
The way you toke, the way you talk
Everything you do is a small pleasure

I know this is a fragile thing
But I'm a bubble of hope
Giving myself just enough rope

> *But my heart, my only*
> *Being here, there, wherever*
> *It's all better with you"*
> —"Small Pleasures" by RK on *Home With You*

Cazzi stepped out into the living room, mildly nervous. She and Rohan had been quarantining together for months now but this was the first time she'd shown him this side of her. And boy, was it well displayed in this outfit.

The black catsuit hugged her tight, pushing her breasts up high and displaying her pentacle tattoo prominently. It seemed plain until the strategic mesh cutouts hit the light and that was without the even more strategic velcro bits open. The matching boots had solid, tall as fuck as heels and her hair was slicked back out of her face. She'd even put on some eyeliner to complete the look.

The only thing seemingly out of place was the beat-up duffle bag in her hand.

"Can I look now?" Rohan asked from the couch, hand over his eyes.

Cazzi inhaled as deeply as the corseting would allow. "You may," she said, pitching her voice low and sultry. She was no professional vocalist but she'd done some pretty hands-on research for her dissertation on kink life.

"Oh damn," he said, eyes wide as he took her in. "You look— wow, Caz." He swallowed. "I can't um, words. Wow."

She warmed, smiling. Rendering him speechless was one of her favorite things.

He stood up and came towards her, running his fingers lightly along her arms, her sides. Nowhere sexual but she shivered all the same.

"What's in the bag?" He asked as he draped his arms around her waist. "Do I get a matching outfit?"

"That can be arranged," she murmured, savoring the image of

Rohan in something this skin tight. "But that's not what's in here."

"Oh?" His fingers slipped down her wrist and he plucked the bag from her fingers.

She grabbed the bag, using the gesture to drag him against him. "Did I say you could look?"

His breath caught and he grinned. "We're playing like this? Alright." He let go of the bag. "Can I look, please?"

She paused, searching his gaze. "Green so far?"

"Green all the way, Caz," he replied. "I'll let you know if that changes."

It wasn't like Rohan was a stranger to kink, he knew the stoplight safe word method and they'd talked extensively about their respective experiences and fantasies but Cazzi had never brought kink into what started as a pretty vanilla relationship. She'd heard horror stories though.

But this is Rohan.

True. All these months sheltering in place together had taught her a lot about him. They'd spent so much time talking, planning, propping each other up, trying to make sense of the uncertain future. He was sweet, kind, thoughtful—unless he was consumed by creating music—funny as fuck, smart, and an amazing cook. Sure, he basically owned her kitchen, left his socks everywhere, and sometimes needed more attention than she had energy for but he was never a judgmental asshole like the people in those horror stories. She trusted him.

Her shoulders relaxed and she smiled. "Come on, you'll like this."

He kissed her cheek. "Oh, I definitely will."

And boy, did he.

PATRICK SAT FROZEN in front of the waiting room screen. If he moved an inch he'd bolt. God, what was he doing? Nobody knew, not even his sister Sabrina in her room downstairs. Not that she'd mind, she'd encouraged him to do this but he couldn't admit he was feeling so low he'd taken her up on her suggestion.

His Nana, in her room across the hall, especially didn't know, he wasn't sure what she'd say. He and his mother tried to get her to go to therapy or a support group after Grandpa Patrick's mistress crashed the Memorial Day cookout two years ago and effectively caused a rift in the family. Instead, she'd left her husband and pretended everything was fine.

He glanced at his phone. The screen was locked but in it lurked Cazzi's words, the list of names he'd ignored for so long. He wanted to be her friend—but he couldn't stand to even text her. He couldn't stand the thought of watching her being happy with someone else and how fucked up was that? He didn't want her shrinks, her concern, her pity.

He'd listened to her voicemail more times than he'd care to admit.

He spent eight months telling himself he'd get over it. He'd spent over a year and a half without her, why couldn't he do it again? He was functioning, he was fine.

Then last month the review for his sister's new album came out: *"Doc Conjure's debut from Now or Never Records is heart-wrenching without being maudlin, a feat achieved almost entirely by the brilliant composing and mixing by producer Rick Jones aka former Beatboy Ricky Rick."*

He'd waited for the glow of pleasure, the swell of satisfaction, a fucking kewpie doll, anything. Nothing. He'd felt the same way when the reviews for Rohan's album praised him but he'd figured that was because the victory was bittersweet.

Every time he thought about her the static in his head went hollow and he lost his breath to the void. She was his phantom limb, the part he kept reaching for even though he'd cut it off.

He tried not to think about her. He read all of Doc Conjure's reviews, trying to soak in the praise. He celebrated with Sabrina and Nana. Then he went up to his room and stared at the wall.

He'd achieved what he wanted. He'd transcended his boy band roots and gotten respect for his work. So why wasn't he happy?

He'd opened her text like he had more nights than he'd care to admit. Stared at it until he was light-headed. Then he'd called every single doctor on the list. Static hissed and curled around the memory of that night. He reminded himself it wasn't normal, this wasn't okay and that's why he was sitting here now, staring at this impersonal waiting screen.

A real man fixes his problems himself, his father intoned in the back of his head.

Except nothing he'd done fixed it. He ran every morning, ate like a nutritionist's wet dream, tried every herb he could think of, barely went on social media, journaled, meditated… and it all took the edge off. He could function. Nobody worried. He seemed fine. But the feelings always came back. Humming under his thoughts during the day, whirling and buzzing at night until exhaustion claimed him or he could bear it no more and paced the house.

It wasn't normal. Wasn't okay.

So he was fixing it.

The screen flickered and a Black woman appeared, smiling at him. "Patrick? I'm Dr. Ashley. It's nice to meet you."

Patrick pasted on a smile. "It's nice to meet you too."

"Let's talk about what's going on with you."

He told Dr. Ashley everything, slowly at first, stumbling over his words until he couldn't seem to stop talking.

She listened patiently, her eyes kind. Talking hurt, but in a good way. It was cleansing. By the end of the session, he was drained but hopeful. Whether or not Cazzi was in his life, he'd make it through and someday, he'd thrive again.

Ready for Patrick's book? *Love at the Rock Show is out now!*

Loved this book? Leaving a review helps others who
might enjoy it find it (and it helps indie authors
keep writing).
Thank you!
<3
Katla

ACKNOWLEDGMENTS

Oh damn, here we are. Thank you so much for reading my first ever published book! Like most (all?) books, *Love in the Liner Notes* was written and polished with the help of a small village of people. If I leave anyone out, please know it was out of brain fog and not malice.

Much appreciation to my parents for encouraging my creative endeavors and to my teachers, especially my creative writing teachers Mr. Ronkin and JM Huscher.

I have been writing this book on and off since college so it's gone through a wild number of drafts (and titles). To that end, I deeply appreciate all the help from my various rounds of beta readers. The first brave round who read the shittiest draft (or at least tried to): Dad, Toni Hawks Floyd, Laura T. Emery, and Scarlet Kay. The amazing second round who got me to the querying stage: Florian K. Hart, Livian Yeh, Isabelle, and Scarlet Kay (again). And the final wonderful round who got me ready to publish included: Vendela Engblom, ShanShan Guo, C.A. Vargas, and Keri Anne.

In addition, I was lucky enough to be able to talk to some great experts who helped me figure out the whole self-publishing whirlwind including Liza Street, Karen A. Parker, Markus Ironwood, Brendle Wells, and the super knowledgeable indie authors in the Let's Get Published discord server.

I would've been adrift and frankly, really down without my wonderful writing friends. I stayed afloat because of my communities over the years: Let's Get Published, the Writer's Group, and the To Be Named writing group. Thank you to Alyssa Cole for that last group, which was founded in her fantastic romance writing course. Also, thanks to the Minneapolis pagan community and Magus Books & Herbs where I learned so much.

Thank you to the people who gave me advice about life experiences outside my own: Georgina Kamsika, A, and Mom. I did a lot of research to make sure I did my best to portray the characters outside my experience of being a white woman but please note no one character is meant to represent the whole range of experiences for any one group. All mistakes are mine and mine alone. To learn more about people like my characters, please read and consume media by people in those identity groups.

Last but not least, thank you to my partner, the better half of half my life for all your support over the years. I love you.

READY FOR BOOK 2?

Broke pansexual psychic Judit is scraping by. She's got chronic pain, no insurance, and survives (barely) on Tarot reading gigs. Fresh off a nasty breakup and a sudden rent increase, she jumps at the opportunity to work a merch booth for Rohan's festival tour. Unfortunately, it comes with an unexpected bunkmate.

Patrick didn't intend to join the Endfest tour, especially not with Rohan. In fact, he fully intended to quit the label they started together. Just his luck when the bassist in his sister's band breaks his wrist and Patrick is the only one who can fill in. Oh, and the woman who helped him when he was having a panic attack, who he'd kind of liked but never gotten her name? Turns out she's Cazzi's friend and bunking in his bus.

Judit and Patrick are forced to share a bus while navigating the drama of a mismanaged festival, other people's exs, and drunk drag queens. The more time they spend in adjoining bunks the less they find to hate about each other. But can this summer fling last or does what happens on tour stay on tour?

Love at the Rock Show out now!

ABOUT THE AUTHOR

Katta Kis' first job was playing a vampire baby in a student film, sealing her fate as a goth child for life. After a variety pack of jobs and apartments, she is currently settled in Northern California. She cohabitates with her two adorable demon babies masquerading as cats and her high school romance which never ended. When not writing, she can usually be found reading.

Keep up with her through her newsletter!